I MARRIED KAYOG

Prime Mating Agency

REGINE ABEL

COVER DESIGN BY
Regine Abel

ILLUSTRATIONS BY
Hojolabor
Invidious
Tommy
Vvevelur
Lau Isa San
Niklas Cloister
AriesRedLo

Copyright © 2025

CONTENTS

I MARRIED KAYOG

She was his peace and his salvation.

His whole life, Kayog has made it his mission to project the image of the male who has it all. But deep down, he's broken by the endless torment that plagues him. Until Linsea. His impossible dream. His peaceful dove. The mesmerizing song of her soul enthralls him and makes him covet a future he knows he can't have. He shouldn't pursue her, but how can he not when she's his soulmate?

The moment Linsea lays eyes on Kayog, she's enthralled by him. Smart, charismatic, talented, and handsome, he's a literal rockstar whose attention everyone vies for. And yet, he only has eyes for her. Discovering the dark secret he desperately tries to keep hidden behind his mask of perfection should make her run. Instead, it makes her want to fight for him... for them.

With the odds stacked against them, can they overcome the insurmountable obstacles thrown their way, or will their relentless efforts to save his life seal his doom instead?

DEDICATION

To those who perceive and experience the world differently. The narrow-minded will label it a defect or an anomaly. The wise will see it as an opportunity and a blessing. You are not a freak, you are a gift. And the world needs the beauty that only you can see and offer.

To those who will stand by you through the storm, who will pick you up when you fall, and who will fight for you when you can't. No matter how dark the times, true friends and family will always shine a light on your path, however subtle it may be.

To soulmates.

TRIGGER WARNING

This book makes some references to—or has scenes involving—
a few sensitive topics, including mental illness, substance abuse,
high-risk pregnancies, suicidal ideation, and infant mortality.

Please approach this book carefully if these topics can be
triggering for you.

CHAPTER 1
LINSEA

The gleaming domes of Acadia Galactic University beckoned me as I sauntered down the path to the main entrance. My eyes flicked this way and that as I took in the diverse crowd of off-worlders milling about, engaged in animated conversations, or trying to locate a friend or acquaintance. I recognized many faces, some of them merely for being part of a famous family, others for having interacted with them in the upper circles of galactic politics or peacekeeping.

It had been a long time coming for me to finally attend this prestigious establishment. And knowing my dearest friend would also be in attendance made it all the more exciting.

Long before I reached the first steps at the bottom of the ten-meter-wide staircase leading up to the large terrace in front of the entrance, I spotted my beloved Tala. Her bright-colored outfits always made her easy to find among large crowds. Her long, flowy, bright-orange skirt gave a teasing glimpse of her endless legs through a slit that stopped just above her right knee. A light-yellow, sleeveless, fitted top hugged the gentle curves of her narrow waist. A beaded tribal necklace hung around her long and slender neck down to her navel with matching earrings. The same colorful beads adorned the tight curls of her black hair. The ensemble made her dark skin glow and screamed of her joyful personality and pride in her heritage.

She beamed, her obsidian eyes lighting up as she waved at me. I waved back, a smile settling on my face as my heart warmed with the pleasure of reuniting with Tala after eight months that felt like eight years.

As I hastened up the stairs, she met me halfway, drawing me into a surprisingly strong hug, belying how deceptively fragile her slender frame appeared. I closed my arms around her, reciprocating her embrace before closing my wings behind her. She purred and rubbed her face in the crook of my neck where my down feathers were the fluffiest, and in a way she knew tickled me.

I chuckled and released her.

"Damn, I didn't realize how much I had missed those winged hugs!" Tala exclaimed in an overly dramatic fashion that had me laughing.

"I guess I'll have to make up for it over the next few days," I said teasingly.

"You better," Tala replied with false outrage. "It was about time you got your fluffy tail here. How dare you abandon me in this frightening place for so long all by myself?"

I rolled my eyes as she hooked her arm under mine and dragged me up the stairs.

"First off, you're not alone," I countered in a less-than-impressed tone. "Second, I was off on the mother of all internships. You would have plucked my feathers had I not taken it."

"Yeah, yeah, Miss I'm-so-well-connected. Always the same folks getting all the advantages," she replied with a theatrical pout.

I snorted and playfully elbowed her. "Don't hate, you diva. Keep hanging out with me, and you just might get connected, too!"

"Why do you think I'm friends with you?" Tala asked as if the answer should be obvious.

I pressed a palm to my chest, pretending to be deeply wounded. "What?! I thought it was for my winged hugs?"

"Well, that too," she added, waving a dismissive hand.

"I'm glad to hear it," I replied, making a face at her.

"Are you all settled?" she asked as we wove our way through the throngs to enter the main hall of the massive building.

"I still have some unpacking to do. I'll finish it tonight once I get back to my room."

"Nuh uh! Absolutely not tonight. You can take care of that shit tomorrow," Tala replied in a tone that brooked no argument.

"Why? What's going on?" I asked, intrigued.

"Echoes of Madness is playing," she said as she began giving me the tour of the campus.

I scrunched my face. "That sounds like a human hard rock band. I'm not really into that."

"It's not hard rock!" she swiftly countered. "Their style is more like grunge, alternative metal, and soft rock. And girl, let me tell you, when Kai starts singing a ballad, your toes are going to curl something fierce... Well, talons in your case."

I snorted again and opened my mouth to reply, but she continued singing the praises of the band—or rather of its lead singer.

"When he starts belting out a rock section, your ovaries will flat out explode. And that body...! The way he moves should be absolutely illegal. That hip thrust—"

"Tala, this is *way* too much information!" I interrupted, more amused than scandalized. "Honestly, it sounds to me like you want a one-on-one date with him, not a third wheel to rain on your parade."

"Not a chance," she said with a falsely dejected expression. "He doesn't like women."

"Oh, Kai is gay?" I asked, curious.

"I wish," a sexy male voice said behind me.

I jerked my head around to see a very handsome Edocit male walking past us. He winked at me, which had both of us chuckling as he continued on his way.

"Is he asexual then?" I asked Tala as we walked past the administrative offices towards the library.

She shrugged. "That's what the rumor says. He's been here two years and never dated anyone despite every possible type of galactic pussies being thrown at him."

"TALA!" I exclaimed, genuinely shocked, and my cheeks heating.

She grinned at me, a mischievous glimmer in her eyes as she further prodded me, taking great pleasure in my embarrassment.

"Feathery, scaly, hairy, fleshy," she enumerated, pinching the brown skin of her forearm as she stated that last word, "Mr. Kai wants none of it."

"Ooookay," I said, unsure as to what I should respond to this.

"Is it normal?" Tala asked, this time with sincere curiosity.

"Is what normal?" I asked, baffled.

"For Temerns to be asexual? You also never seem to be interested in anyone," she added, giving me an assessing look.

My brow shot up. "Kai is a Temern?"

"Yes."

"Oh wow, I had not expected that. But no, my people do not tend to be asexual, or at least not in a proportion different from any other species. We do get aroused, but we don't tend to do hookups or one-night stands."

"Why not? Is it a cultural or religious thing?"

I shook my head while giving her an indulgent smile. "Neither. But we're empaths. We feel what our partner feels. It can be quite awkward and uncomfortable when the other person has great expectations or develops a deep attachment that you cannot reciprocate. The guilt of causing them pain, distress, or discomfort can be quite the deterrent."

"Damn! So I guess none of us were good enough to make him want to cross that line," Tala said with a sad expression.

I frowned at her, although my amusement was still visible. "Don't you have a partner? Aren't you still with the lovely and very sexy Mares?" I asked.

"Yep!" Tala replied smugly.

"And you're drooling over a Temern?" I challenged in a slightly reproving tone.

She huffed. "There's no crime in enjoying the view and having one's ego stroked by attracting the attention of the popular guy."

I snorted. "I thought you didn't do beaks?"

"Girl, that guy would make *anyone* do *anything!*" she exclaimed as if it was self-evident. "Every rule has an exception, and he is all of them. I mean, you know how humans like kissing. But for Kai, we'd give it up in a heartbeat."

I burst out laughing. "After so many decades, centuries even, of cohabiting with humans, I would have expected you would all know by now that even species with beaks like mine are able to kiss."

She made a disdainful gesture. "You guys do the tongue wrestling dance. It's not the same as a proper, soft, cushioned kiss that people with lips can exchange."

"Fine, fine," I said, shaking my head at her. "But you know, fanning yourself over the fact that a Temern has a beautiful voice is a bit silly. Every bird folk can sing."

She pointed at the cafeteria as we walked past it and indicated the hallway that led to the labs and research departments before leading me down the right corridor towards the lecture amphitheaters.

"I'm aware of that. But Kayog is something different altogether. Beyond the fact that he's super-hot, he's an amazing singer and performer, the top athlete in multiple sports, and a genius in class."

"Sheesh, sounds like he's Mr. Perfect," I said with a hint of sarcasm. "But as we both know, there's no such thing. So what are his issues? Let me take a wild guess. He's entitled? Arrogant? A bully?"

She shook her head at each of my questions then made a weird face. "Kai is none of the above. His only flaw—if you can really call it that—is that he's a pretty hardcore introvert."

I gaped at her. Of all the answers she could have given, that one never featured on the list. "An introverted lead singer?! They're the biggest attention whores in the universe!"

Tala sighed, a frown creasing her brow as she guided me towards the hall where our first lecture would be held.

"It's complicated," my friend replied at last.

"Complicated how?" I insisted.

She chewed her bottom lip while reflecting on her answer. "I'm not sure how to describe it. Kai often isolates himself at completely random times. You'll see him hanging out with a group of jocks, then he'll suddenly take off in the middle of a conversation. A few times, he also walked out of class and didn't come back. In fact, he attends most of them remotely."

"And yet he's a top student?" I asked, the suspicion taking root in the back of my head audible in my voice.

"He's not cheating, if that's what you're implying," Tala said in a tone that brooked no argument. "Once you meet him, you'll see that Kai is genius-level smart. But come, class is about to start. We'll finish the tour after."

We stepped inside the lecture hall, and my eyes nearly popped out of my head. I had known Acadia possessed some of the largest classrooms in the galaxy, but this exceeded anything I ever witnessed. At a glance, it appeared to offer at least a thousand seats. Shaped like an amphitheater, it had multiple rows arcing in front of the stage. Three balconies offered even more seats with multiple giant screens strategically positioned to give a great view regardless of where you sat. Although I couldn't see any PA systems, I didn't doubt the room possessed the finest audio systems available.

To my surprise, Tala headed for seats about a quarter way into one of the ten front rows. While that suited me, I couldn't help casting an inquisitive look at my friend.

"Front row? I thought you loved hanging in the back to hide whatever shenanigans you were up to?" I asked teasingly.

"I am, but not on the first day," she replied in a conspiratorial tone.

"Oh? And why is that?" I asked as I settled in my seat, grateful for the adjustable backrest so that it wouldn't get in the way of my wings and tail.

"Yep, because it allows you to get a good look at everyone coming in, on top of enabling us to get out fast once they inevitably release us early," she deadpanned.

I smiled and nodded before letting my gaze roam around the room to see who all was in attendance already, and if I spotted any familiar faces. I waved at a few acquaintances and made a mental note of the people I recognized but didn't personally know yet. I would introduce myself later at an appropriate time. In the field I was pursuing, developing relationships with as many people as possible—especially among the elite—was vital.

Then a sudden hush fell over the room. Most of the discreet chatter ended as many heads turned towards the entrance.

"Oh my God!" Tala whispered with a thrill in her voice.

That reaction surprised me as I assumed the professor had entered, eliciting the sudden decrease in conversations. I glanced in the general direction that everyone was staring at only to freeze.

The most breathtaking Temern I had ever seen was walking up one of the main aisles, talking in a hushed tone to a human. He was tall—very muscular for our species, which tended to be lither—but not in a bulky way. His lean body put every defined groove of his abdominals and biceps on display. A pair of majestic wings hung on his back, the lustrous feathers the same dark maroon as most of his body. His front was a lighter beige color that seemed to emphasize the perfection of his torso. The golden down feathers of his chest spread to his stunning face, with a proud beak, and mesmerizing silver eyes. He walked with a grace that screamed of control and underlying power ready to be unleashed in the blink of an eye.

He suddenly stopped, frowned, and his head jerked towards me. Our gazes met, and it felt as if I'd been struck by a boulder straight to the chest. Time stopped. The silver sea of his eyes swallowed me whole. It hypnotized me even as it stripped me bare, leaving me feeling vulnerable and exposed.

Despite the shock that appeared to rob me of any rational thinking, I didn't miss the stunned, disbelieving, and almost awed expression on the beautiful stranger's face.

He started, breaking the magic, and he jerked his head away from me to look at his friend. He blinked, appearing to realize that his companion had been calling him while he'd been staring at me. After nodding at something his friend said, he stole another glance my way, his face unreadable. He then looked away and climbed the rest of the stairs granting access to the side balcony to my left.

Still dazed, I forced myself to avert my eyes, my heart beating at an insane speed. It took every ounce of my willpower to keep myself looking ahead instead of trying to steal another peek at him.

"What the fuck, Lin! He was staring at you!" Tala exclaimed in a hushed tone.

"Who is he?" I asked in the same hushed voice, still unsettled by the powerful effect he had on me.

"Mr. Perfect I've been telling you about! That's Kai!" Tala said as if it was self-evident.

A human female sitting in the row right in front of us turned around to look at us, curiosity plastered all over her pixie face covered in freckles.

"Do you know him?" she asked.

I shook my head. "No."

"Wow! He never stared at anyone the way he just stared at you," she replied in a voice dripping with envy. "I guess he's just into Temerns."

"Oh please!" Tala said in an outraged tone. "There have been plenty of other Temern females in Acadia, and he never spared any one of them a single look."

The woman shrugged, pinched her lips, and turned her back to us to face the teacher. I couldn't decide if I felt pity or annoyance for her as I skimmed over the emotions emanating from her. Although bitterness and jealousy dominated, I also perceived a great deal of resignation, sadness, and that unpleasant aura emitted by people who lacked self-esteem or wallowed in self-recrimination. I had no doubt she was thinking something silly like she had been foolish to think she ever had a chance with him because she didn't believe herself good enough.

As an empath, I always wanted to reach out and lift up people who involuntarily self-harmed with such negative thoughts.

"Fuck my life, you actually got him! I'm sticking to your ass forever," Tala whispered.

I snorted. Tala was something else. When you first met her, you could be fooled into thinking she was stuffy, overly proper, and quite the regal Nubian queen. But once she got to know you and dropped the mask her rigid upbringing required, you discovered the funniest, most mischievous, and irreverent rascal ever. And underneath all that, the most loyal and selfless friend one could ever wish for.

The teacher stepping up to the podium reclaimed our attention. For the first time in my life, I truly struggled to focus on a lecture. I hated that we were sitting in one of the front rows as I couldn't see Kai from this position without clearly turning my head towards him. And yet, I could feel the weight of his stare on me all the way from the balcony. I caught myself more times than I could count moments before I would try to steal a peek at him.

To my total dismay, I couldn't even get the slightest glimpse of his emotions. It was as if he had erected an impenetrable wall around himself. Temerns all possessed the ability to block our emotions from our peers for privacy. However, it was never fully sealed. You could still glean some surface information. But I got nothing from Kai. Although distance impacted our ability to read others, he wasn't so far that I wouldn't get at least something. That bothered me even more, further impeding my ability to focus.

Thankfully, as was often the case on the first day, the professor merely went over the syllabus for the semester, giving us an overview of the assignments we would have, the type of books, events, and subjects we should immerse ourselves in to further assist us in this course.

By the time the professor released us, less than thirty minutes had elapsed. As people started trickling out of the room, Tala didn't rush out as she initially hinted she would. As I slowly walked my way out of the row I had been sitting in, I could no longer resist the urge to glance at the balcony.

The dumbest wave of jealousy and disappointment swelled within me when I found him surrounded by countless groupies of all genders. To my shock, he immediately turned to look at me as if he had sensed my gaze on him. Stupidly feeling as if I'd been caught red handed, I averted my eyes only to peer back up and find him still looking at me. He smirked, something akin to triumph sparkling in his silver eyes.

That pissed me off and, pushing past Tala, I all but stormed out of the room.

"Fuck him," I muttered under my breath.

"Wait! Don't you want to meet him?" Tala asked, half jogging to catch up to me.

"No," I said in a clipped tone.

"Why not?" she asked, baffled by my sudden change in demeanor.

"Because he's an ass."

Tala recoiled then grabbed my arm to stop me and make me face her.

"What? What happened? What did I miss?"

"You didn't see his smug smirk?" I asked, feeling both annoyed and humiliated.

She hesitated before giving me an apologetic look. "Uh, beaks make it hard to see when you guys smile, let alone smirk."

I rolled my eyes, gently pulled my arm free of her hold, and resumed walking. "Well, *I* saw it."

Tala made a dismissive gesture. "I don't know what you saw —or rather what you *think* you saw—but I can assure you that you're wrong. And we'll settle that tonight."

"Absolutely not! I'm not going," I said firmly.

It was her turn to roll her eyes. "Aww, come on! Since when are you this emotional?"

I glared at her. "Don't call me emotional. And I've never been into rock bands."

She huffed. "You need to socialize, and that bar is the best place."

I gave her an incredulous look. "In all that noise?"

"It's not always noisy," she said in a tone that implied I was starting to try her patience. "Remember that everyone here are future ambassadors, special envoys, and intergalactic political and scientific elite. You need to make connections to help build your career. So pull that stick out of that fluffy behind of yours, and don't be a stuck-up brat. You already look snobbish enough."

"I don't look like a snob!" I exclaimed, outraged.

"Yes, you do," Tala said, this time without the teasing that could previously be heard in her voice. "You come across as even more stiff than I do with strangers. What you don't realize is that with your pristine white feathers, that fancy tail of yours which looks almost like a train, your melodious voice, and the graceful way you walk, you feel like royalty. People don't approach you because they feel intimidated or beneath you."

"But that's not the case!"

"*I* know that, but *they* don't. People need to see you actually chill and enjoy a good time in a laidback setting. You need to be seen as approachable to maximize your time here making connections," Tala continued in a big sister tone. "Anyway, Mr. Perfect never mingles with the crowd. Therefore, you'll be safe from his smirk."

I made a face at her, and she chuckled in response.

"Fine, you bully," I muttered.

She laughed, kissed my cheek, hooked her arm with mine, and led me to the other section of the campus I hadn't seen yet before our next class.

CHAPTER 2
LINSEA

I landed in front of the Iron Empire Club, folding my massive wings behind me as soon as I touched the ground. It was a remarkable architectural creation with a modern industrial gothic style. I walked up the stairs nodding at a few people in the crowd, some standing outside while a few others were also making their way inside. As I passed through the open heavy metal doors, I couldn't help being impressed by the interior design.

In my mind, I had pictured a dark, cluttered, and slightly claustrophobic space meant to force intimacy. Instead, a pleasantly elegant hall beckoned me, with sharp lines, exposed beams, the occasional cement walls, minimalist decor, and huge windows that let the place breathe. Although it was currently being used as a club and concert venue, it could easily serve for more formal events.

Any misgivings I previously had about coming faded away. Tala had been right about this being the perfect networking scene. It was classy and yet agreeably informal and relaxed. As was to be expected based on the type of students attending Acadia, the crowd comprised many different species, most of the people being the offspring of influential political, scientific, and socio-cultural figures. There was a reason Acadia had some of the strictest and most thorough background check requirements for admission.

With my family evolving in some of the highest ranks of the political and legal spheres, I was acquainted with many of the people present. However, I needed to turn these acquaintances into actual alliances and maybe even friends. Beyond the fact that I had too much pride to simply rely on my good name to open doors, personal relationships went a long way into helping us achieve goals that could be otherwise heavily challenged.

I made my way to Tala, who was having an animated conversation with Colin Wilson. It surprised me that he should be here. Being an over achiever, at the age of 35, Colin had already earned a position as Senior Director of the Enforcers—the galactic peacekeeping forces under the umbrella of the United Planets Organization.

The UPO acted as a moderator and protector to ensure the peaceful coexistence of its various member planets. It helped define and enforce the rules of conduct for fair trade, territorial sovereignty, guidelines on interacting and protecting primitive worlds, vetoed or approved colonization efforts of new planets, as well as helped navigate galactic disputes in all their forms. My mother worked as a negotiator for the UPO. My nan also worked for them but as senior legal counselor. Whereas my father was a criminal lawyer for the Enforcers. And I hoped to follow in the footsteps of the two most important females in my life by also joining the UPO but as an ambassador for the organization.

So yes, making friends and forging alliances among these people, many of whom would become my counterparts or future colleagues was of the essence.

"Good, you're here!" Tala said enthusiastically as I closed the distance with them. "I told Mares I was going to come drag you kicking and screaming if needed."

"You shouldn't make threats of bodily harm in the presence of a Senior Enforcer," I said in a playfully chastising tone while giving her a hug.

She huffed. "I've got connections, too. And Colin's got my back, right?"

He chuckled and bowed his head in agreement as I turned my attention towards him.

"I most certainly do, and anyway, I was a little too distracted to have heard anything," he replied in an overly innocent fashion that had me smiling.

"Traitor!" I said with false outrage. "Fancy seeing you here, though. What brings you to these parts?"

Before he could answer, Tala interjected, her face turned away from us as she seemed to look for someone in the crowd.

"If you'll both excuse me for a minute, I need to find my man out there. I bet you some bimbo is hogging him or trying to pluck a leaf from his hair."

We both snorted, and Colin waved a hand indicating for her to proceed. We watched her march resolutely in the general direction of the bar where Mares had gone to fetch them some drinks.

I glanced back at Colin, an attractive human male. At 6'2, he was barely an inch taller than me. He kept his black hair in a short, somewhat military style. Piercing gray eyes peered at me in his ruggedly handsome face, with a square jaw, and a Roman nose. The slight bump on the bridge hinted that it had likely been broken before. It wouldn't be surprising as he used to indulge in competitive boxing. Although muscular, he had more the fit body of a swimmer rather than a bodybuilder. Like many of the people in attendance, he was wearing casual chic clothes in darker shades.

Admittedly, I never quite understood why species who needed to wear clothes tended to pick dark colors. While I recognize that black held and undeniable aura of strength, I would want to adorn myself with a more joyful and exciting palette like Tala did.

"To answer your question, I'm here to assess potential recruits," Colin said calmly.

My eyes widened in surprise. "Who?"

He gave me an indulgent smile. "That would be telling, my dear."

I made a face at him before glancing around the room, trying to identify someone who could make an interesting candidate for the ultimate peacekeeping force in the galaxy. Pursing my lips, I gave him a suspicious look.

"You came to assess potential recruits here? Why not at a sports event, science fair, or debate? Those strike me as far more appropriate venues to evaluate candidates in the heat of action."

This time, his mysterious expression piqued my curiosity even more.

"You'd be surprised about where we go for recruiting. The best candidates are usually found in the oddest places. That said, I'm also here investigating."

"Investigating what?"

He smiled in a way that implied I should know better than to pry but still in a gentle fashion. "You'll hear about it soon enough."

Just as I was opening my mouth to ask another question, a swarm of people suddenly rushed in while those already inside hurried to the front of the stage.

"The main event is about to start!" Colin said in an amused tone.

"How do you and they know?" I asked, confused.

There was no specific schedule as to the start of the concert, only that the club opened as of 6:00 PM.

"Everyone came in because the singing heartthrob just flew in," Colin said with a teasing glimmer in his gray eyes. "Enjoy the show. I will see you later."

"See you," I replied distractedly, annoyed by the sudden flutter in the pit of my stomach.

A wave of excitement blasted my way, and I immediately recognized it as emanating from my friend. As an empath, I could passively feel the emotions of anyone within a fifty-meter radius, or up to a hundred meters if I focused on a single target. But as that would be overwhelming to constantly be flooded by people's feelings, Temerns could shut down that ability or only keep it active on a specific person. When I went out with friends, I kept a thin tether on them, excluding everyone else. In this instance, it made it easier to zero in on Tala's position amidst the throngs.

Tala hastened to my side, her boyfriend Mares in tow, holding a drink in each hand, one of which he extended to me. Mares was a stunning male. Typical of his Edocit origins—a dryad-like species—he had a beautiful brown skin—although on the darker end of the spectrum as they went from pale hazelnut to ebony. Embossed swirls adorned his arms, cheeks, and visible spots on his muscular chest. Those natural patterns called *yevins* marked an Edocit's lineage and could also serve as fingerprints.

Being an Utzac—one of the different breeds of the Edocits— Mares possessed a majestic set of antlers. Delicate leaves sprouted from the thin vines intertwined with his bluish-green hair. A few white flowers actually blossomed in his hair, an involuntary reaction that expressed happiness. Unlike other Edocit breeds, the Utzacs also had natural colorful leaves that strategically grew to hide naughty bits, shaped like a loincloth for males, and like a long skirt for females.

He smiled at me, his dark green eyes devoid of sclera or pupils, sparkling with excitement.

I genuinely liked Mares. More than once, I felt ashamed of the envy their loving relationship stirred within me. I wanted to meet someone who would look at me the way Mares looked at Tala. The emotions that radiated from both of them merely being in each other's presence was a gift in and of itself. They had been together for over a year now, and their love only seemed to grow. I didn't doubt they would eventually marry.

"He's here!" Tala said excitedly as I thanked Mares for the drink.

"So I heard," I replied, unimpressed. "It appears he wants to make the grand diva entrance."

"No," Tala replied with a stern look. "Stop hating on the poor male."

"I'm not hating," I said dismissively. "But that so many people were just hanging out outside waiting for him to arrive hints that this is a recurring thing. He just shows up at the last minute, knowing his fans are foaming at the mouth, ready to rush inside to see his *perfection*."

Shamed burned my gut at the disappointed look my friend gave me. I'd never been the snooty type. This snarky behavior over a mere smirk screamed how much he had gotten under my skin.

Even as those thoughts crossed my mind, I saw him grace-fully fly past one of the back windows then disappear behind a wall.

"Damn, girl, I've never seen you acting so judgmental towards anyone," Tala said in a chastising tone that had me even more embarrassed. "Like I said earlier, he is introverted."

"What does that have to do with anything?" I asked, confused.

"If he was a diva, and wanted that grand entrance you're claiming, he would have landed at the front door and strutted his way in through adoring fans before heading towards the stage," Tala explained in a calm voice. "Instead, he always flies in right before the show, gets in through the back door, sings, and then leaves. These are not the actions of a diva or an attention whore."

I couldn't argue with that logic. That was indeed the behavior of someone who didn't particularly want to interact with people and especially large crowds. How did that make any sense? Before I could dwell any further on the topic, the lights dimmed, the opacity of the windows shifted to create a more intimate setting, the ambient music faded, and the spotlights flooded the stage.

Excited shouts and clapping filled the room as the musicians stepped onto the stage. They were all handsome humans in the same age bracket as the rest of us, mid to late twenties. None of them looked familiar to me. The four men settled at their respective instruments, then Kayog made his entrance. The shouts went up another notch as he walked gracefully to the microphone in front. To my dismay, a thrill ran down my spine, and my stomach fluttered with far more excitement than I wanted to admit. I felt even more pathetic as I tried to convince myself that my reaction to him was only due to my empathic abilities picking up other people's excitement.

As soon as he put his hand on the microphone sitting on the stand, an electrified hush descended over the attendees. Although other species understandably struggled to see when species with beaks smiled, the one that settled on Mr. Perfect's mouth was undeniably perfect and seductive as fuck. However much of it the crowd perceived really didn't matter, they all melted regardless.

To my shock, his silver eyes zeroed in on me. Whatever hate or dislike lurked within me towards him instantly vanished. How in the world could he have so much power over me? Worse still, the smile he gave me held none of the arrogance I previously perceived in the lecture hall. It was tender, gentle, but also almost sad. That latter part didn't make sense.

And then he pinned his eyes at me.

It was a common practice among bird folks. Our irises enlarged while our pupils rapidly shrank. On instinct, I reciprocated this greeting, which expressed that we were pleased and even honored to make that person's acquaintance. His smile broadened, and only then did he shift his gaze away from me.

I realized I'd been holding my breath and felt both bereft and a little dizzy. Had he been as affected by this brief exchange as I had been? How was he able to so fully block his emotions from me?

When he picked up the mic from its stand, another excited cheer rose from the crowd. Thankfully, despite their excitement, the people present weren't the rabid type that would recklessly push to get closer to the stage and crush the poor souls in front.

"Good evening, everyone, and thank you for coming in such large numbers on the first day of class. We're thrilled to see so many familiar faces, and especially the new ones," Kayog said in a sexy voice that had goosebumps erupting all over me.

However, it was the meaningful glance he cast my way upon saying the last part of his sentence that had a swarm of butterflies taking flight in my stomach. My cheeks heated when a few heads turned my way as multiple people realized he had meant these words specifically for me.

Or at least so it seemed...

Even my wretched friend elbowed me discreetly, her excitement reaching peak levels through the empathic tether I had with her. Thankfully, Kai resumed speaking, drawing everyone's attention back to him.

"For those new to us, let me introduce you to my wonderful companions. Benedict Gibson on the drums, Devin Thomas on the guitar, Adam Cole on the keyboard, and Carter Fox on the bass. And I am your humble servant, Kayog Voln. Together, we are Echoes of Madness. And tonight, we will start with a brand-new piece inspired by an enchanting vision called Peaceful Dove."

He placed the microphone back on its stand and wrapped both hands around it. A deafening silence descended over the room. The lights dimmed further, and the spotlights focused on him. Another powerful shiver coursed through me as he closed his eyes. He began whistling a haunting melody in a cooing voice reminiscent of a mourning dove, but the sound was a little deeper, throatier. Only the keyboard and bass accompanied him with sustained chords that made the overall melody rounder without competing with him.

And then he began to sing.

You came like a whirlwind into my life
One look at you tore my walls down by half
The divine song of your soul mesmerizes me
Your mere presence makes me ache for what could be
You are my light, my quiet, my peaceful dove
Oh how I wish I was someone you could love

As soon as he finished singing that last line in a soft ballad, I nearly jumped out of my skin when the drums and guitar came in with a savage metal riff. Kayog ripped the mic off its stand, an angry expression descending over his gorgeous face. He flapped his wings hovering a meter over the stage, looking almost like a vengeful angel about to unleash his wrath against sinners.

But I'm crazy
Glimpse into my mind, and enter the mouth of madness
I'm crazy
A raving lunatic filled with nightmares and darkness

The guitar shifted to a slow riff, the drums went down to a low, steady roll, and both the keyboard and bass took on an ominous edge. However, while the keyboard played a high-pitched, haunting melody in a loop like one would hear in a horror movie, the bass went so low, you could feel it vibrate through the floor beneath your feet and all the way up in your chest. Kayog's voice became menacing as he stared directly at me.

Fly away my peaceful dove
Fly away while you still can
'Cause no power from below or above
Will free you once you enter the beast's den
Because I'm crazy

The guitar quieted down, and the drummer only used his bass drum and discrete cymbals to mark the beat. The keyboard and the bass shifted back to playing ominous sustained chords while Kayog resumed whistling.

"He wrote this song about you," Tala whispered, her eyes glued to the stage.

"What? No he didn't!" I whispered back, ignoring the little voice at the back of my head calling me a liar.

"Yes, he did," Mares said, giving me a sideways glance as his arms tightened around Tala's waist, who was leaning her back against his chest. "It would be too much of a coincidence for him to release a new song today about a peaceful dove."

"A white dove is the human symbol of peace," Tala reminded me.

"But I'm not a dove," I argued feebly, embarrassed by that pathetic response.

Mares gave me an unimpressed look. "No, but you are a white bird. He's warning you."

"About what, though? We've never even talked," I challenged.

"But he noticed you," Tala countered. "I bet he wants you but thinks that somehow he is bad for you."

"Why? Because he's crazy?" I asked in a slightly derisive tone, echoing the lyrics. "Whatever happened to him being Mr. Perfect?" I added teasingly to lighten the mood.

Instead of snorting or giving me *the look*, Mares frowned and took on a serious expression.

"I think he might be neurodivergent," he replied pensively.

It was my turn to frown. "Being neurodivergent doesn't make someone crazy," I argued sternly. "Plenty of people like that have very normal lives and relationships."

"*I* know," Mares said in a reasonable tone. "But *he* may not think so. After all, he systematically avoids people and has been single for as long as any of us have known him. Someone this handsome, charismatic, smart, and popular wouldn't be single unless it was by choice. But I somehow doubt he does so happily."

Too soon—or was it not soon enough?—the song ended to crashing applause. He smiled, bowed to the crowd, then briefly made eye contact with me again. That seemed to confirm that it had indeed been about me.

That utterly confused me. Did he genuinely like me but did not want to have a relationship? Was it his way of saying he wouldn't mind playing naughty with me but not to expect any form of commitment? Or were we all seeing something that wasn't there?

The concert went on for another forty minutes. The way his body moved as he traipsed around the stage, alternating between ballads and more up-tempo pieces royally messed with my head. Based on Tala's prior statements, Kayog was a top tier athlete. And his body certainly seemed to confirm it. He had a way of swaying his hips that had his muscular abs just screaming at us to reach out and touch him. The play of light and shadows on his chest emphasized each of the scrumptious curves and bulges.

At one point, he put the mic back on its stand and stared me straight in the eyes. His right hand tightly gripping the upper part of the stand felt almost as if it was gripping my throat in a possessive and controlling fashion. The fingers of his right hand glided down the length of the stand, and I could almost feel them running down my spine in a gentle caress. A fire lit in the pit of my stomach, and I started throbbing in places I shouldn't.

Once again, when he looked away as he went into the chorus, belting out the words with an intensity that had the crowd going wild, I felt almost abandoned. However, through the electric emotions sparkling all around me, a more potent one drew my attention. It took a second for my gaze to zero in on Colin. He was intently studying Kayog, his face unreadable.

As soon as the show ended, Colin headed backstage almost at the same time as the musicians did. One of the bouncers tried to stop him, but he whipped out his Enforcer badge. Although surprised, the bouncer bowed his head and let him through.

What in the world could he possibly want with Kayog?

Is he trying to recruit him? But for what?

CHAPTER 3
KAYOG

As we made our way into the dressing room, I couldn't help but smile at the excitement of my companions. They were almost talking over each other, commenting about the incredible response we received from the crowd. In the two years I spent performing with them, the popularity of the band had steadily grown. While our performances were usually well-received, tonight undeniably went to another level.

"Dude, you totally killed it!" Devin exclaimed, slapping the back of my shoulder with a huge grin plastered on his face.

I gave him a smug smile. "Of course, I did."

He chuckled and shook his head at me.

"That dove song was freaking chef's kiss!" Benedict said as we entered our changing room.

"Hell yeah, it was!" Devin replied while putting his guitar back on its stand. "To think I was giving you a hard time about squeezing it in at the last minute like that."

"I told you it was worth it," I said in an amused tone, counting the minutes before I could make a discreet exit.

"You sure did, and I agreed the minute you sang it for us," Adam said with a wink.

He grabbed that dreadful beverage called beer that humans enjoyed so much, passed a bottle to Carter, who gladly accepted it, then let himself drop in one of the two couches in the spacious room.

"So where did that come from? That hot Temern chick inspired it, right?" Devin asked, wiggling his eyebrows in a suggestive fashion. "I can't blame you. I'd fluff her feathers, too."

I never saw myself moving. One moment, I was staring at him as blind fury surged through me, and the next, I was grabbing him by the collar and slamming his back against the wall. The horrified and stunned expression on his face reflected the shock I felt. I'd never been one to settle matters through violence, let alone over some dumb horny male's comments. But this triggered me beyond words.

"Whoa, Kai! Chill man! It was just a joke!" Devin exclaimed, raising his palms in a surrendering gesture.

"Don't *ever* disrespect her," I snapped in a menacing tone.

"Everyone, relax," Benedict said in a soothing voice. "Kai, let him go, Brother. He didn't mean any offence. You know he's a moron. Let go," he repeated, gently tugging on my arm.

I reluctantly complied, surprised that I would even drag this for so long. Being the peaceful type, my current behavior made no sense, especially considering I indeed knew Devin said offensive things without actual malice simply because he had the dumbest sense of humor.

As soon as I took a few steps back and dropped any menacing stance, Ben turned back to Devin and smacked him in the back of the head.

"We don't disrespect women, remember?" Ben told him harshly.

Devin scrunched his face and rubbed the back of his head, glaring at the drummer then at the rest of us as if we were being overly dramatic.

"It was just a fucking joke!" Devin exclaimed.

"Stuff the dumb jokes," Ben replied sternly. "Don't ruin the best concert we've ever had just because you can't help saying stupid shit."

"Fine, sorry," he muttered.

Despite the grumpy way in which he stated his apology, his emotions clearly broadcast the sincerity of his embarrassment and remorse. I immediately felt bad for my excessive reaction. Devin genuinely wasn't a bad person. He just never thought before he spoke. Before joining the band, he'd always hung out with the type of toxic males who sought their peers' validation by demeaning others, especially females. He had come a long way since then but still had much work to do.

"Anyway, that Temern female is indeed very beautiful and classy," Benedict said with a friendly smile while giving my shoulder a gentle squeeze. "It's good to see you finally opening up to someone."

I snorted and shook my head. "I'm not pursuing her."

As one, all four of my companions recoiled.

"Why the hell not?" Devin asked. "She clearly likes you."

"Every woman does," Adam interjected teasingly, making the others chuckle.

"Truth!" Carter chimed in. "And you wouldn't have written such a beautiful song about her if you didn't feel the same."

"We're about to go mingle with all the influential brats out there," Benedict said. "This is the perfect time for you to talk to her."

"No thanks," I said in a gentle but firm tone. "You know that I don't do crowds."

"But you rock them!" Adam exclaimed with the same confusion he expressed every time I fled after a concert. "The fans worship you!"

"And there's a big label rep in attendance," Benedict added in a hopeful voice.

I frowned and gave him a reproving look while trying to silence the guilt surging deep within.

"Ben, you've always known the deal. I've been up front from the start that I'm only here temporarily. I have no desire to have a singing career."

"But you're the face of the band!" Devin said with a crest-fallen expression. "We're nothing without you. People come to see Kayog, not Echoes of Madness!"

"That's not true," I said with conviction, even though I couldn't deny the partial truth of his statement. "Your songs in and of themselves are magical. You guys composed the vast majority of our repertoire. There are tons of hot and charismatic singers out there who could join you and who would love to sing what you guys create. I may be the current fad but I'm very much replaceable."

"They won't be you," Adam countered stubbornly.

"No, and that's a good thing. They will be themselves with their own appeal. Remember that this is my last semester here. Now is a good time to really put the effort into finding a new lead singer. Talk to that label rep. I'm sure he has plenty of talented singers he could pair you with. Your songs and the depth of their messages are really what makes this band, not the singing bird," I said in a gentle voice.

Ben opened his mouth to say something. I didn't know if it would have been another argument or him ending the discussion as was his wont when it came to keeping the peace. However, a firm knock on the door interrupted him.

"Come in," Ben called out.

Narok—the Zamorian bouncer—poked his head in to look at us with an apologetic expression. It always blew my mind to see this gentler side of the giant, considering his overall intimidating appearance. Zamorian males were massive and averaged a height of seven feet tall. Their species had everything in double: four arms, four eyes, a second set of every vital organ, including the naughty bit. When they became angry, their eyes would take a frightening shade of orange that would have even the boldest feel a lot less cocky. Their insane strength, speed, and lust for blood made them among the fiercest warriors in the galaxy.

"Sorry to bother you, but Director Wilson from the Enforcers is here to see Kayog," Narok said.

"What the fuck?!" Devin muttered, echoing the thought that popped into my head as well as the expression plastered on our companions' faces.

"Let him in," I said, both confused and baffled.

A part of me also felt annoyed that I hadn't perceived his presence. Or rather that I had not singled it out among the other people broadcasting the same type of eager emotion that he did. His had a different, more calculated and determined edge that should have made it stand out.

I really don't need this right now.

I needed to go and could only hope this wouldn't take too long. If I didn't isolate myself soon, things would get ugly fast.

"I'm sorry to bother you, gentlemen," Director Wilson said to all of us in a friendly tone as he entered the room.

"Is there a problem?" Ben asked, taking a step forward in a slightly defensive stance in front of me.

My heart melted for the brawny human. Although he was slightly shorter than my own 6'4, Ben had broad shoulders and thick arms that had people think twice about messing with him. While he wouldn't hesitate to throw hands if needed, his sweet face truly was a mirror into the cuddly teddy bear that dwelled within. Still, I loved how protective he always was towards me and any person he believed to be in need or in danger.

It was all the cuter that if trouble truly arose, I was much better suited than he was to protect us.

"No, there's no problem at all," Director Wilson said reassuringly. "I would just like to have an informal talk with Mr. Voln. It's not easy getting in touch with you," he continued, turning to face me. "Do you have some time now, or should I leave a card, and you can call me whenever?"

How about never?

Naturally, I kept the rude thought to myself and gave him a polite smile. A part of me considered taking him up on his offer to call him later so that I could get out of here before the pain in my head grew any further. Another part deemed it better to get this done and out of the way immediately. Anyway, knowing myself, I would obsess over it until I knew what he wanted with me to begin with.

"Now will be fine," I said with the right level of distant politeness to make it clear I didn't want this to drag on longer than necessary.

"Wonderful!" Wilson said with an excess of enthusiasm that hinted at the fact he knew exactly where I stood. "Is there a private place we can go discuss?"

"You can have the room since we're heading out to mingle with the fans," Ben said begrudgingly before giving me an assessing look. "You're going to be okay?"

Once again, a wave of affection swelled within me. I would miss him greatly at the end of the semester once I moved on.

"Yes, Brother. I'll be good," I said with a smile.

He nodded stiffly then gave the Enforcer one last suspicious look before heading out the door, the rest of the band filing out in his wake. The Director repressed an amused smile. His emotions were quite fascinating. They combined the strangest mix of curiosity, anticipation, suspicion, and something I couldn't quite define. Nefarious wouldn't be appropriate as I didn't sense any threat from him or actual ill intentions. But I also got a strong sense that he had set goals that he planned on seeing through no matter how I felt about them.

I gestured towards one of the couches as soon as the door closed behind my friends.

"Please have a seat, Director Wilson. Would you like something to drink?" I asked as he settled in the large sectional couch made of dark brown leather.

He shook his head. "No, thank you. I won't hog too much of your time. I'm certain you have far more interesting places to be than talking with me. And please, call me Colin. I'm rather informal."

"Good, so am I. So you can call me Kayog," I replied as I sat on the cushioned stool across from him, which was a lot more comfortable for my broad wings.

"Kayog it is then! You have amazing talent! Your voice is exquisite," he said in a flattering tone that left me completely indifferent.

He was testing my responses to assess my personality, including if I could be bought or manipulated with compliments.

I shrugged. "All Temerns can sing. Compared to others of my peers, I would deem myself average, in no way exceptional."

"I don't know about average, but your charisma certainly isn't. You had the crowd eating out the palm of your hand."

I raised an eyebrow and gave him a stiff smile. "You're not wrong. People seemed to respond well to me in general. But what can I do for you? What did you wish to see me about?"

"I came here to get a better understanding of an ongoing investigation regarding potential terrorist attacks and a growing number of Good Samaritan incidents taking place in the area lately," Colin said in a matter-of-factly manner.

This time, both my brows shot up. "Do you believe me a terrorist?!"

He burst out laughing. "No, not at all."

"A Good Samaritan then?" I insisted.

He smiled, although his eyes narrowed ever-so-slightly. "Are you?"

"I don't know. As much as possible, I try to be helpful when needed. Why? Is being good a crime?" I asked in the same nonchalant fashion he questioned me.

He shrugged. "Obviously not, except if being a Good Samaritan turns into becoming a vigilante. Then it's a bit more problematic."

"I can see that," I replied in a noncommittal fashion. "But what does that have to do with me?"

"Nothing directly," he said in a mysterious fashion. "I was merely saying that I came to this planet to look into these two matters and figured I would seize the opportunity to pay you a visit while at it. You see, we always keep an eye out for potential Enforcer recruits. And we feel that you could be a perfect candidate."

I gaped at him, genuinely stunned. Of all the things he could have said, that one never featured anywhere in the list of possibilities.

"Me? An Enforcer?! Why would you want to recruit a singer?" I asked, baffled.

He gave me a 'don't be silly' look. "You're far more than a singer, Kayog. At only 27 years old, you already possess two master's and are on the way to finish a third one in just a few months. You're a very popular singer and performer, participate in pro level athletic competitions—including combat—and you speak five languages fluently without the assistance of a translator. You're single, charismatic, empathic, self-made, and with both a flawless record and immaculate reputation. You could be anything from an Agent to an Ambassador, and everything else in-between."

My mind raced as a billion thoughts pushed and shoved at each other. This wasn't some impromptu chat on the spur of the moment. Granted, he mentioned I wasn't easy to get in touch with, but this man had thoroughly investigated me in order to so confidently list this many of my achievements.

What else does he know?

By who knew what miracle, I managed to keep a nonchalant expression on my face.

"You flatter me, but I'm not really into galactic politics."

He huffed as if I'd said something to insult his intelligence. "Really? You're doing a master's specifically in that field. Your first master's was in xenobiology. The second one was in galactic history with a focus on primitive and developing species. And right now, you're doing one in intergalactic politics with your thesis debating the pros and cons of the Prime Directive. If that's not being into galactic politics, I don't know what is."

I waved a dismissive hand. "There is such a thing as simply pursuing knowledge for its own sake. That I love understanding things thoroughly doesn't mean I want to partake in the process."

"Right," Colin said in a voice dripping with doubt.

"Well, I thank you for your interest. But if there's nothing else, I will be heading out," I said, repressing the urge to rub my temples and my nape to lessen the pressure that sent increasing stabbing pain at the back of my head.

"Out to the party?" he asked with curiosity.

"No, I'm leaving."

He recoiled in genuine surprise. "Leaving? Why?"

"I don't do crowds," I said, my voice a little clipped by the growing pain his persistence forced me to endure.

"A performer and captain of two sport teams who doesn't do crowds?" he exclaimed disbelievingly.

"That's correct," I said, standing up with an expression that made it clear further insistence would now be flat out rude.

He stood up as well, his eyes narrowing as another wave of suspicion surged within him.

"What are you running away from?" Colin asked, the Enforcer in him seeping through.

"Absolutely nothing," I replied in a cool voice. "Now if you'll excuse me."

Without waiting for his response, I headed towards the door.

"Wait! Please take my card," he said, catching up to me and extending it towards me.

I glanced at the card and swallowed back the urge to tell him to keep it. Not wanting to give him another excuse to shackle me here any further, I simply took it.

"You truly are a fascinating candidate, Kayog Voln," Colin said pensively.

"I'm not a candidate," I said sternly.

"The UPO and the Enforcers can open the kind of doors for you that no one else can," he said in a strange tone that was both commanding and meant to be coaxing. "Call me whenever you want to know more about any possibilities for you within our ranks."

"Sure," I said absentmindedly before all but running out.

My stomach roiled with the nauseous feeling that preceded a monster headache. The horrible pressure behind my eyes nearly made me want to claw them right out of my head. I all but burst out of the back door and took flight.

Through the windows that had resumed their normal opacity, I could see the crowd happily mingling within. My chest constricted with envy at the thought of all these people, be they friends, lovers, acquaintances, and even random strangers who got to hang out in a common space, have fun, and simply enjoy their mutual company without a care in the world.

I both loved and hated my loneliness.

I actually liked people a lot. Given the choice, I would be the heart of the party. Sadly, I dreaded their emotions and how they wrecked me.

Why the fuck am I such a broken Temern?

Flapping my wings as hard as I could, I soared high into the sky and away from the populated areas towards the water. The farther I got from people, the more the brain-melting pressure torturing me decreased. The most painful part was losing the mesmerizing song of my beautiful dove. But the rest of the noise was too much for me to handle.

Memories of the breathtaking female filled my mind, dampening the enduring discomfort clawing at my brain. Watching me perform had aroused her. Every wave of her delectable emotions had set my blood ablaze, making me dance in an even sexier fashion. Her desire had fanned my own. A part of me felt embarrassed by the way I behaved on stage. I always made it a point to entertain without using sex or sending out the wrong signals to the fans, especially those who might be drawn to me in a romantic fashion.

But my dove changed everything.

I had wanted her to ache for me as much as I ached for her. A sadistic side of me I never realized lurked deep within actually took great pleasure in the fact that she couldn't decide if she liked or distrusted me. My competitive side enjoyed the prospect of breaking down her walls and making her fall madly in love with me. However, this was a challenge I shouldn't... couldn't take on.

She was my soulmate, an impossible dream I never thought could come true. But I meant every word of this song I wrote for her. I was crazy.

She could be my peace...

Unfortunately, as proven tonight, even my dove wouldn't be enough. The foul noises from the crowd almost buried her. As I completed the flight back home, the dark shadow that always seemed to hover above me swallowed me whole, casting me into a deep well of despair. I couldn't live on campus. In fact, I couldn't live anywhere that was remotely populated. Even the forest presented its own set of challenges.

As I landed on the small island far in the river running past the campus, I silently thanked the powers that be for its existence. It had required a lot of sweet talking and convincing to get the mayor to allow me to settle here, isolated from everyone. My cabin, custom made for my needs, had been a blessing. I rushed inside, closing the door. The noise immediately diminished by half.

Wings spread wide, I leaned against the door, the back of my head resting on the special padding designed to block most forms of communication signals, from radio frequencies to psychic waves. A shuddering breath escaped me. I couldn't tell if relief, sorrow, or a mix of both prompted it.

I slipped down the length of the door and sat on the floor. My legs folded against my chest, I wrapped my arms around them and rested my forehead on my knees. A dull ache stabbed my heart as the beautiful face of my dove danced before my mind's eye. As I waited for the debilitating pain in my head to fade, I hummed to myself the enchanting song of her soul.

I could dream safely of her, here in my home, my sanctuary... my prison.

CHAPTER 4
KAYOG

Over the following two days, I attended class remotely. Of late, my ability to tolerate the presence of others noticeably decreased. Where I once could attend a couple of classes in a row before I needed to isolate myself, now I could barely handle a single one. The swelling in my brain also took longer to go back down. Thankfully, although the university didn't know the full extent of my condition, they had given me leave to attend from home. My assiduity and excellent grades played a significant part in that special permission.

This morning, needing to resume my training for the upcoming canoe competition—not to mention my burning urge for physical activity—I flew back to the campus very early before the masses started stomping about. My stomach fluttered at the prospect that I might run into her. I both hoped and dreaded seeing her. My head told me that I should stay away, but my heart strongly disagreed.

I went to the hangar to retrieve my canoe. It was a sleek, single paddle vessel that I portaged to the river running alongside the university. On each side of the water, they'd built multiple rows of bleachers along the shore for the public to attend the various competitions that took place here. Although I specialized in the short 200-meter races, I actually excelled in the medium and longer races, especially the 1000-meter one.

I placed the canoe in the water, did a bit of stretching, and then embarked on my craft. It had a large open cockpit with a foam knee block upon which I knelt. The footrest had been modified to better accommodate the shape of my bird feet. While I didn't hate kayak racing, I much preferred the canoe as you steered with the paddle instead of needing a rudder. It required a lot more control, focus, and often using specific types of strokes to keep the craft moving straight—the type of challenges I loved.

I completed a first 800-meter lap, with some resistance bands on my craft and paddling at a leisurely pace to focus on my form, technique, and really establish that mind and body connection. On the return lap, I removed the resistance bands. I would do about thirty strokes at a set pace, before drastically increasing the speed for a short burst, then relaxing a little, and rinse repeat.

I then proceeded to a 1000-meter lap, at a leisurely pace. Taking position for the return lap, I set the timer of my bracer, and mentally prepared during the countdown for an all-out race. As soon as the signal went off, I paddled hard, even as I tried to pace myself so that I wouldn't run out of steam before the finish.

Barely a hundred meters in, I felt her.

I nearly lost my focus and rhythm from shock. The intoxicating melody intensified as she drew nearer. The urge to scan the shore in search of her burned deep in my gut, but once more, I forced myself to stay the course. However, any thought of properly pacing myself flew right out of my mind. Even though I couldn't see her, my dove had stopped by the bleachers on the east shore and was observing me.

Her emotions screamed just how impressed she was with my performance. They also hinted at arousal and above all at her excitement and nervousness at finding me here. The irresistible need to impress her took over any rational thought. I pushed myself hard, showing off my strength, technique, and stamina. My muscles and lungs started to burn, but I ignored them, too busy basking in her awe. It wrapped around me like the silkiest fabric, taking away the pain and infusing me with a jolt of energy that spurred me on well-beyond my normal limits.

I reached the edge of the river, panting heavily. Stepping out of my canoe on slightly wobbly legs, I puffed my feathers and fluttered my wings to create more airflow around my body and dissipate the excess heat generated by my exertion. Sometimes, I envied other species their ability to sweat to regulate their body temperature.

For a split second, I feared she would walk away. Her emotions loudly broadcast her hesitation as to whether she should go about her business or acknowledge me. My heart soared when she suddenly started clapping. Trying to act nonchalant, I calmly turned towards my dove. As I watched her casually approach, my pulse picked up in a way unrelated to the effort I just did. I bowed my head and did a little curtsy in thank you as she closed the distance between us. She chuckled, the sound delicate and musical like windchimes swaying in a soft breeze.

"Impressive," she said, stopping a short distance from me.

"Thank you," I replied, feeling incredibly self-conscious.

As a singer and athlete, I regularly received my fair share of compliments. But coming from her was something else altogether. The sincere admiration emanating from her seriously messed me up.

"This is my first time ever seeing a Temern paddler," she said pensively, her beautiful blue eyes going slightly out of focus as if she was searching her memory to confirm that statement.

I smiled.

"Our wings can be a serious impediment with the wind, not to mention the extra weight," I said in a gentle tone. "It just means we must hold a perfect form and use more strength than our rivals."

She gave me a slow once over that had my stomach quivering. It wasn't lurid or suggestive, merely assessing and admirative. Still, it messed with my head.

"Well, you certainly do not lack in the strength department. A talented singer and a highly skilled athlete... You put the rest of us, mere mortals, to shame," she added teasingly.

I burst out laughing, and lowered my gaze, feeling both delighted by her compliments and stupidly embarrassed. It took every ounce of my willpower not to squirm.

"Ahah, hardly. I'm sure you have your own amazing talents that have others drooling with envy," I replied. "By the way, my name is Kayog. Kayog Voln."

"I know," she replied with a mischievous smile. "*Everyone* knows. And you also said it at the concert the other night."

"Right, I did," I mumbled, feeling stupid.

"I'm Linsea Kenna."

Linsea... Beautiful name for a beautiful dove.

I wanted to sing her name at the top of my lungs, let it roll on my tongue, and savor every syllable. But I reined myself in.

"That's a lovely name. It's a pleasure to formally meet you," I said.

"The pleasure is all mine," she replied timidly.

Fuck me! Everything about that female truly did a number on me. The emotions swirling around her were quickly becoming an addiction. And that song...! The melody of her soul harmonized with mine in a way that transcended the divine. It almost felt like a physical caress to the very core of my being.

Linsea still didn't know how much she wanted to allow herself to explore the feelings I stirred within her. And that ambivalence only poked the hunter lurking inside me that wanted to capture her.

I shouldn't pursue her.

What future could someone as broken as I was offer her? And yet, we were soulmates. Some way, somehow, Fate intended for us to work out. Furthermore, turning my back on the greatest gift the universe could bestow upon anyone would be a crime. Anyway, I was already much too hooked—not to say obsessed—to let her get away.

I turned the canoe sideways away from me, slightly bent my knees, and pulled it onto the shelf thus created by my lap. Reaching with my left hand for the portage yolk, I rolled it towards me.

"Do you need help?" Linsea exclaimed, taking a step forward, but unsure what to do.

"No, I've got this. But thank you," I said gently.

I tilted the canoe and then lifted it above me before resting it on top of my head. My palms splayed against each of the inner sides kept it steady. Although this was the standard way I always portaged my canoe back and forth, seeing my female this impressed by the ease with which I lifted it had me preening a little.

"Wow, you really are strong!" Linsea whispered with awe, as if more to herself.

"Maybe a little," I replied with a wink.

She chuckled, her eyes sparkling with amusement.

"Will you walk with me?" I asked softly.

"Sure!" Linsea said, before cringing inwardly, no doubt berating herself for the overly eager way she agreed. "Someone has to make sure the most famous singer of Acadia doesn't hurt himself carrying a huge canoe on his own."

I snorted, impressed by her quick thinking. Although only the smartest and elite people could enter the school, the occasional privileged brats managed to worm their way in. Obviously, my soulmate could never be such an individual. But this first glimpse of the skillful fashion with which she wiggled herself out of what she perceived to be an embarrassing admission piqued my curiosity. I would greatly enjoy mentally sparring with her.

"To be honest, when I heard about you also being a top athlete, I expected you would participate in flying sports like Lazgar," Linsea mused aloud.

Lazgar was a game invented by one of our distant kins, the Zelconians. They were bird folks like us who lived on a primitive planet that still fell under many strict guidelines of the Prime Directive. While the local species had not yet achieved interstellar travel, off-worlders were allowed to land on the planet and interact with the natives in a limited fashion.

The sport, which took place in a special arena with looping obstacles that shifted overtime, involved groups of twelve to twenty people. The participants chased after Lazgar—a drone—in an attempt to capture it before the clock ran out. The faster you caught it, the greater your score. It had been created and named after a Zelconian brat named Lazgar who became famous for running away to dodge classes and being chased all over creation by every possible adult in town.

I smiled and nodded. "A fair assumption, and an accurate one. I actually hold the current record for the highest score."

She burst out laughing and shook her head at me as if I was a hopeless case. "Figures. Is there anything that you don't excel at?"

"Oh yeah! Far too many!" I exclaimed with an overly dramatic expression of discouragement.

"Really?" Linsea asked in a dubious tone. "Such as?"

"That would be telling," I replied teasingly. "Hang around enough, and you just might find out."

"Careful, I might take you up on that," she said in the falsely menacing fashion.

Saying it was sexy as fuck would be quite the understatement. The ease with which we communicated further cemented the fact that we were meant for each other. Despite my nearly non-existent personal experience with females, I wasn't so clueless as not to recognize flirting when it happened.

We entered the hangar located a short distance from the river. Dozens of canoes, kayaks, waterboards, jet skis, and various other crafts and water-based sport equipment were stored in neatly organized sections of the space more or less shaped like an H. I headed straight for the section with the canoes.

They each sat on racks secured by digital locks. Across from them, in the central part of one point of the H, a couple of washing stations allowed us to clean our crafts before storing them again. I settled my canoe on the left one.

"You're up early," I said while pulling the hose to start rinsing my canoe.

She nodded. "I like exercising in the park along the water. I got curious when I saw a lone paddler. So I came to have a peek."

"I'm glad you did," I said.

To my surprise, she gave me a strange look and tilted her head to the side while pondering her response. Based on her emotions, whatever thoughts were crossing her mind had nothing to do with her coming to investigate the lone paddler.

"You put on an amazing show the other night," Linsea said pensively. "I'm not really into rock bands—even though that's not really what yours is. But I can't deny that I really enjoyed it."

"Thank you. It pleases me."

"You vanished really quickly. The rest of the band mingled with everyone, yet you were nowhere to be seen," she said, her tone nonchalant despite the intensity in her eyes.

Although I expected that question would pop up sooner than later, I still fought the urge to squirm.

"I don't like crowds," I said, smiling at her confused expression. "Your reaction is normal. Everyone is baffled by this. Performing during a show is fine, but I'm really not too keen on what happens after."

"Why? Too many groupies?" Linsea asked with a taunting glimmer in her eyes.

I snorted then nodded. "At the risk of sounding vain, I have to say yes."

"That's the price of fame for you," she quipped, before taking a more serious expression. "There was a record label present that night."

My face immediately closed off. "That's a hard pass for me."

She frowned, unsure how she felt about my response. "What of the band?"

"I told them to find a new singer if they wanted to move forward with any potential offers," I replied while applying some soft soap on the canoe. "The guys always knew the deal from the beginning. It's not like I sprung this on them last-minute and blindsided them."

"But they undoubtedly hoped you would change your mind," she insisted.

"You're right," I conceded. "However, that's entirely on them. I made my stance crystal clear to them over and over again. If they decide to remain in denial, there's nothing I can do about it."

"Why don't you want to?" she asked with genuine curiosity. "You're very talented, with incredible charisma, and you seemed to enjoy yourself."

"I do enjoy singing, just like every other Temern. And I'm sure you do as well. But that doesn't mean I want to make a career out of it," I replied in a factual manner.

"Fair. Then what career actually appeals to you?"

I repressed a smile at this subtle get-to-know-a-potential-partner interrogation.

"In truth, I don't know," I said in all sincerity.

Right on cue, Linsea frowned. It was never a good look to have reached my age and still not know what we wanted to do, especially in an environment such as Acadia where everyone here was extremely driven and ambitious.

"But you're working on your master's, aren't you?" she

asked carefully, her confusion audible.

"I am," I confirmed. "But this will be my third one."

The shock plastered all over her face wrested an amused smile from me. That too was a common reaction whenever I revealed this to people.

A million thoughts flitted over her beautiful features. She was weighing which question might cross into the realm of inappropriate while also wondering how to sate her curiosity.

"That's quite expensive," she said at last.

I snorted. "Technically, you're correct. However, beyond the fact that I can afford it, I've also been lucky enough to receive scholarships that have covered the cost for all three of them."

Her brows shot up with a mix of shock, awe, and persisting confusion.

"So you're some kind of Whiz kid, as the humans like to say," she replied, still circling around the question she truly wanted to ask.

I shrugged as I began to rinse the soap off the canoe. "Not really. I'm just very curious, and I love to study. As I can't stay idle, I'm constantly on the lookout for a new passion to capture my attention that will also give me a better understanding of our world. Since I'm an overachiever, I always strive to excel at whatever I do. In return, it's given me some great opportunities such as these scholarships."

"Considering how hard they are to obtain, I think you're being excessively humble, which is pleasantly surprising. Lead singers and guitarists in bands usually have the reputation of being very hungry for attention and praise," she said in a slightly teasing tone, although her curiosity remained unsated.

Under different circumstances, I believed she would have pried a lot more openly. As this was our first real interaction, Linsea would likely continue to test the waters for a while longer. I wanted her to simply be blunt. Saying I had nothing to hide would be a lie. However, if I ever hoped to have a chance at a future with her, sooner than later, I would have to reveal the freaky side of me that forced me into this hermit and asocial life.

"But to answer your question, I suspect I'll eventually end up at a desk job drafting laws and articles around the Prime Directive and vulnerable species," I said nonchalantly.

"A desk job?" Linsea echoed with an almost horrified expression. "You're far too charismatic to lock yourself up in some sterile room typing up articles of law."

I shrugged. "Time will tell, I guess. What about you? What exciting career appeals to you?"

She clicked her beak in that typical fashion that expressed reflection for us, a bit like when humans chewed their bottom lip before answering a sensitive question.

"Initially, I wanted to do charity work. But I've been seriously reconsidering it," Linsea said pensively.

It was my turn to look surprised as I turned off the water and activated the fans around the base holding my canoe so that it would start drying it.

"Why? What changed your mind?"

"Control," she replied in a self-evident manner. "I just finished an internship, which is why I missed the previous semester. One of the things that became painfully obvious was that charities are constantly begging and hoping they'll receive some crumbs. The main way things move forward for them is if they have allies and advocates in high places. If I become an ambassador or political envoy, I can put pressure on the right people to make things happen."

An almost predatory smile settled on my face.

"Well, well. Someone isn't a goodie-two-shoes, like Benedict loves to say. For some reason, I expected you to be the type to avoid making waves. So I'm quite pleased to see you're an assertive female and a go-getter, who knows exactly what she wants and takes the steps to achieve her goals."

"I try," she retorted with a smug and coquettish expression

that had me chuckling.

With the dryers having completed their task, I picked up my canoe and brought it to its reserved rack before locking it. I glanced at Linsea, her emotions broadcasting the same hesitation I felt. We weren't ready to part ways but didn't quite know how to take the next step.

"Do you want to have breakfast?" Linsea suddenly asked.

Despite the casual way in which she spoke those words, and her relaxed demeanor, every fiber of her being was tense, bracing for a rejection. The silly female didn't realize that I was already hers.

"I would love to, but I would need a few minutes to take a quick shower," I said in a sheepish tone. "I'm musty."

"Oh! No problem at all. I can wait... Unless you have other plans?" she asked carefully.

"None. I'll be quick," I said with a smile, before frowning. "Hmmm, maybe we should avoid the cafeteria?"

She slightly recoiled at this unexpected request. "Why?"

I shifted on my talons, feeling a little self-conscious. "Not to brag, but if we're seen together, people will probably start bothering you."

Linsea's face closed off. Although most people would deem it a neutral expression, her emotions screamed loudly her blossoming suspicion. It made me chuckle again. A part of me felt guilty as she had no idea that every Temern's innate ability to block their emotions from others didn't work with me. She was an open book to me, while I was entirely closed to her...

... for her own sake.

"I'm not hiding a secret girlfriend, if that's what thought is currently crossing your mind," I said teasingly. "This is genuinely to protect you as people can be quite invasive. I'm used to people ogling me nonstop, and it no longer bothers me. As you said, it's the price of fame. But if you're fine with it, then it's no problem."

"I'm fine with it," she replied firmly.

"Then the cafeteria it is," I replied with a smile. "I'll be right back."

Obviously, that wouldn't have been my choice. At least, it was early enough that there wouldn't be too many people present, which would make the crowd bearable, or at least manageable. I turned to leave, but before I could get even five steps in, Linsea called out to me.

"Actually, wait! You make a good point about your groupies being fairly hardcore. Let's go somewhere private so that we can eat in peace. Come to think of it, having people staring at me while trying to enjoy my meal would be rather awkward," she said, making a face.

I laughed. "I can promise you that it is. But like I said, we can do whatever you wish."

"Private it is. By the way, I could go get food for us while you shower," Linsea offered.

"Sure!" I said, thrilled at the idea not to have to expose myself to the masses earlier than necessary.

"What do you want?" she asked.

"I would love the athlete's breakfast number two," I replied while reaching for my bracer on my left forearm to transfer her some credits.

Moving at surprisingly fast speed, Linsea grabbed my wrist, stopping me, before frowning at me with a somewhat outraged expression.

"No! I got it," she said.

"What the fuck?!" I exclaimed, with an even more offended expression, too stunned to even properly enjoy the wondrous feel of her hand on me.

She released my wrist, and I almost whimpered at the loss of her contact.

"You can buy me breakfast another time," she said dismissively.

I almost argued. However, beyond her stern look warning me not to, her offer pretty much guaranteed a second date. Only an idiot would pass up that opportunity.

"Fine, but it is dinner that I will buy you," I said in a slightly grumpy tone.

She immediately relaxed and chuckled. "Or that works, too."

"Pinky swear," I insisted.

This time, she burst out laughing while giving me an incredulous look.

"What?!" she asked.

"I said pinky swear," I repeated in an unrepented fashion. "If I recall properly, it is a human pledge."

"Yes, it is. And I'm quite familiar with it. I just never expected to hear it from you," she said with an amused expression.

"Good. Glad you're familiar with it. And never assume anything about what I would and wouldn't do. You will get whiplash from all my unexpected behavior," I said in a mysterious tone laced with a hint of smugness. "Now swear."

She shook her head at me, the joyful aura emanating from her wrapping around me in the most wondrous fashion.

"Fine, you bully. I pinky swear," she said with pretend displeasure, as she raised her pinky finger towards me.

"Good girl," I purred as I wrapped my pinky finger around hers, hooking them together for a second before dropping my hand. "Meet at the picnic table near the gazebo?"

She nodded. "Deal."

I smiled, my heart soaring with excitement. "See you soon, then."

"See you soon," she replied before turning around and exiting the hangar.

My gaze lingered on the perfection that she was as she gracefully walked away. Yeah, no matter how crazy I was, I could never let her go. Linsea was my soulmate.

CHAPTER 5
LINSEA

My cheeks burned with embarrassment as I forced myself to exit the hangar with poise and at a relaxed pace. I could feel his gaze boring holes in my back. What thoughts were crossing his mind? He seemed totally taken by me, even flirting a few times, subtle though it had been. But why the fuck could I not read even the smallest sliver of emotion from him? With a certainty I couldn't explain, I believed he somehow managed to read mine. That shouldn't be possible, and yet there it was.

Thinking of how many times I got turned on or aroused by him had me beyond mortified if he was indeed able to perceive everything I felt in his presence. Even the most powerful Temerns among us always leaked a bit.

As I flew to the main building on my way to the cafeteria, my wretched mind remained stuck on Kayog. Knowing he was currently showering had the naughtiest fantasies playing in my head. I could see the water trickling down the perfection of his body, each drop gliding over his broad chest, between the chiseled grooves of his abs, and down to his muscular thighs.

I wanted to be right there with him gently raking my nails along the small down feathers that lined the junction between the base of his wings and his back. A dull throbbing manifested itself between my thighs as I imagined the throaty sounds he would make as I teased this sensitive spot.

During the concert, I memorized the sinful way his body moved and the sensual expression on his face when he leaned forward towards the mic, his fingers running down the stand. Would he look the same in the throes of passion? Would his body rock over mine with a similar animal tension barely repressed and eager to be unleashed?

By the Maker! Control yourself!

I'd never been one to be so easily affected by a pretty face, a hot body, or a seductive smile. And I certainly never let my hormones control my better judgment. But right this instant, I couldn't stop thinking about how badly I had wanted him to throw me onto the grass, right next to the river, extrude what I instinctively knew would be a massive cock, and fuck me senseless.

ENOUGH!

Tala would never let me hear the end of it if she knew even just a fraction of how insanely I'd become obsessed with Mr. Perfect. And so far, he was truly turning out to be perfect.

Really?

That thought gave me pause. Yes, Kayog was an over-achiever who excelled at everything and made it look easy. For that alone, he would have every right to boast and strut about. However, he turned out to be oddly humble. I liked that. Nothing turned me off as much as people with overinflated egos, brag-garts, and those who thought themselves better than others, whatever the reason for it.

That said, I also worried about him possibly being flaky and unreliable. Sure, he dominated in things that had set rules and guidelines, like sports and school. But why didn't he have a clear career path in mind? Was it the fear of commitment? Of the unknown? Of proving himself in a space that wasn't rigidly controlled? And why so many masters? Lack of ambition? Fear of success?

For a split second, I almost latched onto that last speculation. Yet even that didn't work. His competitive nature belied that possibility. He liked winning. So why was he wavering so much?

Then there was the question about his current focus on the Prime Directive. Why center his galactic politics master's around that specific topic? Did altruistic sentiments fuel his interest in protecting the weak and vulnerable, or were more nefarious and materialistic goals driving him? Someone with thorough knowledge of the strength, weaknesses, and resources of primitive species could obscenely enrich themselves by exploiting the loopholes in the Prime Directive.

So many questions and so few answers...

As I landed in front of the building and made my way to the cafeteria, I kept speculating about the male who had me every shade of messed up. I didn't want to come off as too aggressive, but I needed answers and to get a better sense of who I was dealing with. Judging by my reactions to him, I suspected I would quickly fall head over heels for him. Therefore, I needed to do my due diligence before I got in too deep.

As I stood in front of the counter, I glanced at the menu, zeroing in on the one Kayog requested. Being a creature of habit, I never bothered to look at the vast variety offered to cater to the needs of the diverse species that lived on campus. Usually, breakfast for me would be natural yogurt with fresh fruits and grains. But his choice actually appealed to me.

The athlete breakfast number two was divided with half of it being carbs, and the other half equally split between lean proteins and fruits. That specific one offered grilled chicken skewers, trail mix crackers, mixed fruits mostly comprised of berries, and a bottle of flavored water.

Over the years interacting with humans, I had grown quite familiar with their food, and especially their love of chicken. We had the equivalent on our homeworld, but they didn't thrive and adapt as easily to other climates and environments as chickens did. Deciding to emulate Kayog, I ordered two portions of that breakfast. Just as I was reaching for the bags, I felt the familiar waves seconds before my friend called out my name.

"Hey, Lin!" Tala shouted, clinging to Mares' arm as she approached with a big grin. "We didn't see you in the park and thought you might have decided to sleep in. Want to join us for breakfast?"

I turned around. Before I could put in a single word, her eyes locked on the two bags in my hands.

"Wait. Food for two?" She released Mares' arm and put her fists on her hips in that outraged fashion that hinted I better give her a good explanation if I wanted to avoid getting in trouble. "You replaced me already?"

I snorted and shook my head. "Of course not, silly woman."

"Then who is it for?" she insisted.

The way I scrunched my face sufficed to tell her everything. Her eyes slowly widened as her mouth gaped in an almost comical fashion.

"Nooooo! For real?"

I shrugged, feeling a little self-conscious, while Mares chuckled, looking both amused and a little surprised.

"I just ran into him while training," I said a little too defensively.

"You tramp!" she whispered, the excitement in her voice belying the otherwise harsh word.

"Hey!" I exclaimed, not offended in the least as I knew there was no malice behind it.

"I knew it, acting all uninterested, hating on him, and pretending he was beneath you. Told you you'd fall for him," Tala said smugly.

"We're just having breakfast. And I wasn't hating," I muttered.

"Sure, sure. Whatever. Go get your man, and then I want all the juicy details!" Tala said, while Mares shook his head at her.

"Absolutely not!" I said in a stern voice.

"You should run before the throngs notice," Mares said, his dark green eyes sparkling with amusement.

"Yeah, good point," Tala concurred. "But I still want deets! Now go have fun, and for once, forget about being so damn prim and proper."

I laughed and hastened outside before taking flight. Sure enough, a lot of people were slowly making their way in, some of them grabbing food, others just congregating outside, and a few hastening about whatever business called them.

As I flew towards the gazebo—which was a respectable distance away from the masses—I congratulated myself for agreeing not to eat in the cafeteria. The privacy of the park would allow us to be ourselves as we got to know each other. While his initial suggestion had indeed made me suspect he had some secret affair going on, and that he wanted to keep any potential involvement with me hidden, the sincerity with which he offered me a choice silenced that fear. However, it shamed me to admit that I first insisted on going to the cafeteria because I wanted us to be seen together.

I didn't consider myself the possessive or insecure type. Flaunting my relationships also held no appeal to me. But for some reason, I wanted to stamp this male as mine, be publicly claimed by him, and make it clear to all the groupies that he was off the market. Considering we'd only officially met not even an hour ago and spoken for the first time for barely half an hour, my reactions were disturbed. The reality was that I didn't know him at all, aside from the fact that he was hot as fuck, crazy smart, athletically skilled, and so far, seemed like someone whose companionship I could really enjoy.

To my shock, I spotted Kayog sitting in the grass, meditating in the lotus position. I almost stopped, wondering if I should interrupt this moment of introspection. Even as that thought popped into my mind, his eyes suddenly opened, and he looked at me. Considering how far away I still was, he couldn't possibly have felt me... right? He stood up and smiled warmly, spurring me to complete my approach.

"Sorry, I didn't mean to interrupt," I said sheepishly as I landed near him.

"You didn't," he said in a reassuring tone while freeing me from the bags.

"So you're into meditation?"

He nodded. "I do it quite often."

"That's nice," I replied, once more baffled by this unusual male.

A million questions pressed themselves on my tongue, but I squashed them, not wanting to pry. Although I intended to get around to it at some point, I didn't want to scare him away by coming across as if I was interrogating him. A part of me also wanted him to freely open himself up because he wished me to know him, and not because he felt pressured to reveal more than he was ready to.

We settled at a picnic table under a tree near the gazebo. We opened our respective bags and started eating. The first bite of the trail mix crackers had my eyes nearly popping out of my head.

"Oh wow! These crackers are amazing!" I exclaimed before greedily shoveling another one into my mouth.

Kayog chuckled. "They truly are. I'm embarrassed to admit that I'm a little obsessed with them."

I smiled at how adorable he looked whenever he took that sheepish expression. Every assumption I had made about this male was falling apart, one after the other. He truly seemed to be humble, sweet, and unpretentious. Nothing like the entitled rock star I kept imagining. Maybe Tala was right after all about me mistaking his smile for an obnoxious smirk that first day.

"So tell me about yourself," he said while picking up one of the chicken skewers. "Do you have any siblings?"

I shook my head. "Nope. You could say that I am my parents' spoiled little princess. Although, technically, my nan mostly raised me."

His eyebrows shot up, a mix of sympathy and curiosity shining in his silver eyes. "Why is that?"

"My parents travel extensively," I said in a wistful manner. "My father is a criminal lawyer for the Enforcers, while my mother is a negotiator with the UPO. So they're constantly traipsing all over the galaxy to deal with whatever mandate they've been assigned to."

"Damn! That must be quite hard on their marital life," Kayog said with empathy.

I smiled. "Actually, they make it work by travelling to each other. They never spend more than a week apart. In many ways, it's comparable to being married to a truck driver or traveling salesman. You're gone for a few days but always return home after a short absence."

He slowly nodded as he weighed my words. "I can see that."

"They also have daily vidcalls with each other," I continued. "Growing up, they regularly communicated with me and visited at least once a month for a few days. So they were active in my life."

He tilted his head to the side while giving me an assessing look. "Did you resent it?"

I smiled and shook my head before taking a sip of the flavored water. "Not at all. In fact, it was my choice to stay with my nan rather than with them."

His stunned expression made me chuckle.

"In order to stay with my parents, I was homeschooled," I explained. "As a young child, I didn't mind so much. But once I turned eight, I started resenting not having the ability to form long-term friendships with people as I would have to part with them after a few weeks. Staying with my nan gave me the stability that I longed for with a permanent school where I could play with friends and lay some roots."

"How did your parents feel about it?" Kayog asked softly.

I loved how respectful he was when addressing what could potentially be a sensitive topic. Above all, the genuine interest in understanding how I lived that part of my life touched me. Too often, people would have these types of conversations only out of politeness because it was expected. With him, even though I still couldn't read his emotions, I felt seen and like I was fascinating to him.

"They were sad to part with me but also understood that their lifestyle didn't meet my needs," I said, my heart filling with affection for my parents. "Obviously, as empaths, they could feel my growing displeasure and had an open discussion with me about it. My happiness was the most important thing for them. They even offered to ask for a reassignment to more sedentary roles. That's what sealed it for me."

"How so? I would have expected you to seize the opportunity," Kayog said with curiosity.

"I'm an empath, too. They wouldn't have hesitated to do it to make me happy, but they would have been miserable on the career front. I loved them for being willing to sacrifice what they had spent their entire lives building for my sake. But the work they were doing was important. They were changing lives for the better, and it made me incredibly proud. So I insisted on going to live with my nan. That was the best decision."

"How did she feel about it? Grandparents usually love having their grandchildren around but only for a few hours or a couple of days, not to inherit the full responsibility of raising younglings all over again," he said in that same gentle fashion.

"She was over the moon," I said with amusement, my heart melting with affection for the elder lady. "Her colleagues call her the dragon, even though it doesn't make much sense considering we're not reptilian. But she is undoubtedly a force to be reckoned with."

"What does she do?"

I shifted my wings, the soft breeze rubbing against the down feathers at my nape in a way that was starting to tickle.

"Nana Arika is the Senior Counselor for the UPO's Intelligence Division," I said, the pride I felt audible in my voice.

Kayog slightly recoiled, and he gaped at me in shock. He quickly regained his composure but continued to stare at me in awe.

"Wow, your family is truly connected at the highest levels," he said, impressed.

I shrugged, trying to act nonchalant. "Just like the families of more than half the students here. I'm not that special."

A strange expression fleeted over his features, piquing my curiosity.

"What?" I asked, intrigued.

"Many students come here because their families expect them to pursue their legacy," Kayog said carefully. "Did you come here to follow in the path of your parents or grandmother?"

I smiled. "Yes and no. I didn't go into galactic politics for my parents, but definitely *because* of them and my nan. My entire life, I've been exposed to the many things I can help change if I enter this field. My nan wanted me to become a counselor like her."

"I bet," he said with an amused smile. "Frankly, I'm surprised she didn't convince you. Arika Sorek is extremely well-known as a fierce and no-nonsense advocate who you do not want to go up against. She'll chew you up and spit you out without you ever even understanding what hit you."

"That couldn't be more accurate," I said with a laugh. "But I couldn't see myself spending my life in boardrooms dealing with the same handful of high-ranking idiots and counselors. I want to travel the galaxy like my parents and have a direct impact on the lives of the most vulnerable."

"An admirable objective," Kayog said, his eyes brimming with an approval that had me tingling all over.

"So that's me in a nutshell. What about you?" I asked. "Any other genius siblings like you? Is your family in the same field?"

An unreadable expression crossed his face. For a split second, I believed he was going to deflect and avoid answering the question. To my pleasant surprise, he didn't.

"I don't know, and I doubt it," he said with a shrug before tossing his last trail mix cracker into his mouth.

"Huh?" I asked, baffled.

He smiled. "My parents ditched me when I was an infant. So I have no idea if I have any siblings or what field they worked in."

I pressed my palm to my chest, my heart breaking for the baby he had been. "Ditched you?" I echoed, crestfallen.

He nodded, his reassuring smile making it clear he held no trauma or distress over it.

"I was put in stasis inside a child emergency pod. It was sent directly to an orphanage in the small town of Voln," he said factually.

My eyes widened. "Voln?" I repeated.

He gave me an approving smile that I had picked up on it.

"Yes. I was named after that village on Daelynn, the home-world of the Darwandir."

"Oh Maker! Did their ship crash? Or were they attacked by pirates?" I asked, trying to make sense as to why parents would discard their newborn child like that.

If they had access to an emergency pod built specifically for a child, then they had access to all the technology and services available to support parents who chose not to keep their child. There was no shame or stigma associated with renouncing one's rights to their offspring. Better they be placed in a safe environment that could nurture their growth than keep them forcefully in a situation where they weren't wanted and made their guardians miserable.

"Nothing like that. The pod was launched from a forest located 75 kilometers away. They included a note with my first name in which they apologized but stated that my needs exceeded their capacity to handle."

"Your needs?!" I exclaimed, both outraged and baffled. "What needs could you possibly have as an infant that would overwhelm them to the point that standard family support and advanced technology couldn't help cater to?"

Kayog gave me an indulgent smile. "I was a very... difficult child."

"Difficult how?" I insisted. "And how old were you?"

"I was four months old."

"What the fuck?!" I exclaimed, anger seeping into my voice.

He chuckled and gave me a reassuring smile. "It's okay, Linsea. As bad as it looks when you hear this, I cannot blame them. I had some significant... health issues. Any parent in their situation would have probably resorted to the same thing."

My tongue burned with the urge to drill deeper and make him go into extensive details as to what condition an infant could possibly have to justify being abandoned the way he had been. However, that he kept it vague indicated that he wasn't ready to expose what had to be very personal medical history. After all, we were still strangers.

The glimmer of gratitude that flashed through his eyes confirmed I had made the right decision by not forcing the issue. The last thing I wanted was for him to close himself off because I was being too nosey.

"For the first couple of years, I was shuffled around a lot," Kayog continued, his face taking on a faraway expression as he reminisced. "Nobody wanted to keep me. I cried too much, and nothing they could do ever appeased me. Everyone was at a loss as to what the problem could be."

"Although it is a member of the UPO, Daelynn isn't the most advanced planet. Their doctors may not have been best suited to deal with a Temern infant," I said carefully.

"The first thing they did was contact a Temern. Apparently, that didn't go too well, and they decided to pursue different avenues."

Something in the way he said this raised many red flags. What had the Temern seen or said that would make them not want to further retain the services from one of ours?

"Eventually, a couple took me in. They kept me until I was old enough to leave."

"That's wonderful!" I exclaimed. "How did they solve your problem?"

He stared at me for a few seconds. I couldn't tell if he was looking for the proper way to word it or whether to answer me at all.

"They placed me inside an isolated bunker two hundred meters away from the main house. It had its own bathroom, bedroom, and a small office space. They brought me food and anything else I needed," he said, matter-of-factly.

"WHAT?!" I shouted, jumping to my feet, horror and outrage coursing through me. "Why and for how long?!"

"Please, Linsea, sit down. It's okay," he said in a soothing voice.

Embarrassed by my outburst, I settled back down on the bench, my mind reeling, and my blood boiling with anger that he should have been subjected to such abuse.

"I remained there from the age of three until I was fifteen," he said calmly.

"What the actual fuck?!" I hissed. "How did you get free?"

To my shock, a glimmer of amusement sparked in his eyes.

"I applied for my first master's," he said in a mischievous

tone, then burst out laughing at my stunned expression. "I had nothing else to do in that bunker, so I studied."

"And then what happened?" I asked, stunned by how nonchalant and unfazed he seemed to be about the whole situation.

"As a part of the process, I had to do an in-person interview and evaluation. Unfortunately, while waiting to enter the meeting room, I had a major panic attack in public," he said grimly.

"No shit!" I exclaimed. "You've been trapped in solitary confinement for twelve fucking years! It's a miracle that you haven't gone insane. Of course, you would have a mental break-down after suddenly finding yourself surrounded by so many people."

Suddenly, his distaste for crowds totally made sense. What other trauma was he still carrying from those dreadful days?

"The truth about my living situation came out, and things got ugly," Kayog continued.

"I hope they got arrested!" I growled.

His hesitation had me on the verge of losing my shit again.

"It's complicated," he said carefully.

"In what way?" I exclaimed in a self-evident tone. "They locked you up and abused you for more than a decade. They deserve a one-way ticket to Molvi!"

He snorted and shook his head. Molvi was not something you wished upon anyone except the foulest of people. The prison planet was the harshest punishment one could get. Being sent there pretty much equated to a death sentence.

"I know how it seems, but they didn't mistreat me. Growing up there helped me cope with my condition," he said softly as I stared at him in disbelief. "As shocking as this may sound to you, I don't hate them. In truth, I am grateful. They didn't love me, but they also didn't wish me harm. The entire time I lived with them, I wanted for nothing. Anything I needed or asked for, they provided."

"Why am I getting the feeling they didn't face justice?" I asked, struggling to reconcile what he was saying with the fact that they caged him for his entire youth.

"They were indicted, but I challenged the charges against them," Kayog said. "Due to my condition and how what they did genuinely helped me survive a difficult youth, the courts agreed to drop the charges. However, I received a huge settlement as they deemed that the Child Protective Services failed me."

My eyes widened in sudden understanding. "You hinted about being financially comfortable. Is that the source of your wealth?"

He nodded. "Mainly, yes. But where school is concerned, I received substantial scholarships, so the settlement credits remain almost entirely untouched."

"That's great!" I said, pleased that he still got something good out of this whole ordeal. "Do you still talk with your foster parents?"

"No. We parted ways on good terms, but the relationship had more than run its course," he said with an expression that clearly stated that this was a done deal, and not necessarily one he would want to revisit.

And yet, there was no animosity from him. He truly seemed to harbor no ill will towards the people who 'raised' him.

"I understand how you became an ace student, but how did you also become a top athlete?" I asked, still struggling with the difficult childhood he endured.

"I lacked proper physical activity," he said with a wistful smile. "A part of my 'rehabilitation' included seeing a psychologist and a physical trainer. I wasn't fat or anything along those lines, but I had no muscle, little stamina, and was overall low energy."

"Let me guess, you took a liking to it."

"Did I ever. Just like studying, it gave me something to focus on. However, it went even further as I could feel my body change and grow in a way that I really liked. It provided me with a sense of control that I never had before. My work and dedication could yield the results I wanted. For once, I was no longer a passive bystander when it came to the behavior of my own body. Then I discovered that I had quite the competitive streak, so that pushed me even further into wanting to excel in the disciplines I chose."

I chuckled at the cute way with which he scratched the beautiful golden feathers near his nape. It struck me as a nervous tic whenever he felt embarrassed or self-conscious.

"So how did you transition into being able to handle crowds?" I asked softly.

"It was... a slow and gradual process," he said hesitantly. "But to this day, I still mostly live isolated."

I frowned and studied his features as if they could reveal the answers to the countless questions bubbling in my head.

"May I ask what your condition was... or still is, if it hasn't been resolved?" I inquired in a gentle and somewhat apologetic tone.

He stared at me with the strangest expression. A sense of unease washed over me as he stretched his neck, his right hand slightly twitching before he closed it into a fist.

"I'm crazy," he said at last.

"No, you're not!" I exclaimed in a tone that brooked no argument.

"Yes, Linsea, I am," Kayog said with a finality laced with resignation that left me reeling.

I held his gaze unwaveringly, my mind racing.

"Is that what your new song was all about?" I asked, tension seeping into my voice.

"Yes," Kayog said in a factual manner, his face devoid of any emotion.

"Am I the dove?" I insisted.

Once again, he acquiesced with almost robotic stoicism. "Yes."

However, something had changed in his demeanor. It had been building for a while, but my brain was only now registering it. A nerve was ticking on his temple, his hands—especially the index fingers—occasionally twitched. His back was stiff, and his majestic wings were increasingly pressing closer to his body, in that involuntary way bird folk often did when afraid or in pain. It was an instinctive response to protect our bodies from harm.

As I didn't know if these were normal tics for him that I had not noticed before as I'd been too busy drooling and fantasizing over him, I decided to keep quiet about it for now. If they were standard for him, I didn't want to point out something he might feel self-conscious about.

"The song said that I should run far away," I continued in the same controlled and non-confrontational tone. "Is that what you want? For me to stay away from you?"

"No," he said firmly, the sincerity in his voice acting like the sweetest balm on a wound I didn't even realize I felt at the prospect of him not wanting to have anything to do with me. "But you probably should."

"Because you're crazy?" I asked.

"Yes."

He stretched his neck again and glared in the general direction of the university. I followed his gaze, assuming there was someone passing by that he either disliked or who was doing something inappropriate. But we were still pretty much isolated, although quite a few clusters of people were now congregating near the entrance of the campus, as well as scattered in various areas around the building. Nothing and no one stood out in a way that could explain his reaction.

I glanced back at Kayog to see him retrieving a small pill from a secret compartment in his bracer. He popped it into his mouth, and seconds later, his pupils dilated. Some tension gradually bled out of his shoulders. He still seemed tense, even opening and closing his hands like one would after they'd gone numb.

I gaped at him in horror, refusing to let the thought creeping its way into my mind take root.

"What was that?" I asked in a much harsher tone than I meant to. "Is this some kind of medicine?"

My heart sank when he didn't instantly say yes.

"No, but for me, yes," he said, his face closed off and all warmth fading from his eyes.

"No? Then what is it? Are these drugs? Do you suffer from addiction? Is that why you say you're crazy?" I blurted out, anger seeping into my voice.

I hadn't meant to bombard him with so many questions nor to come at him in such an aggressive manner. But the disappointment that he might in fact share some of the big flaws often linked to performing artists' lifestyle hit me hard.

"No, I'm not a drug addict," he said in a clipped tone, his face hardening.

Yeah, right. That's exactly what a junkie would say.

Although I kept that less-than-charitable thought to myself, I didn't let go.

"What is it then? And why are you taking it?" I challenged.

He clicked his beak with annoyance and cast an almost murderous glance towards the university. What the fuck was his problem with the school? None of his behavior made sense, and my own aggravation at him refusing to give me clear answers kept growing.

"What is it?" I repeated more forcefully.

Kayog snapped his head back towards me, this time, an angry expression settled on his face. To my shock, his sclera appeared to be bloodshot. He didn't say a word, his gaze leveled on me, his hands fisted as if he was struggling to rein himself in.

I took a deep breath, berating myself for handling this whole thing so poorly. Antagonizing someone struggling with substance abuse was the best way to drive them away.

"Please, just talk to me, Kayog," I said in a soft and appeasing tone.

"I should go," he said sharply, putting the empty wrappers from his meal back into the bag.

"No, wait!" I exclaimed, panicked. "Look, there's no shame in dealing with addiction, especially considering the rough upbringing you had. There are plenty of programs that—"

"I'M NOT A FUCKING ADDICT!" he shouted.

I recoiled and stared at him in shock. Despite his visible anger, I didn't fear he would harm me, but my heart broke that he should be in such denial. You couldn't help someone who refused to acknowledge they had a problem to begin with.

He snorted and gave me a disgusted look that cut deep.

"You know, Linsea, you're cute, but you're pretty fucking judgmental. You don't know me."

"I don't, but I'm trying to," I said in a soft voice.

"It seems clear now that you shouldn't," he snarled.

"But—"

"ENOUGH!!" Kayog yelled, slamming his fist so hard on the wooden surface of the table that it cracked.

I gasped, my heart nearly leaping out of my chest. This sudden violence hadn't been aimed at me. Kayog was staring at the school with murder in his eyes. My blood turned to ice when they appeared to glow. A Temern's eyes should never glow. Then, with an angry growl, he jumped onto the bench before taking flight.

I sat there, frozen in shock as he dashed away like a vengeful god on a mission. Then suddenly snapping out of my daze, I absentmindedly grabbed our empty bags and flew after Kayog to figure out what might have prompted this irrational reaction. He appeared to have been infuriated by something or someone. But we were much too far from anyone for him to have perceived their emotions, let alone for them to anger him this much.

At a glance, I hadn't noticed any earbuds or other communication devices from which he could have received some sort of message. Although he likely had a translation implant—like most people part of an advanced species—those devices couldn't be used for remote communication. So what in the world just happened?

He did say that he was crazy...

Was Kayog hearing voices? Could he be having some sort of psychotic episode? There were a great number of non-medicinal or natural substances that were known to help people dealing with mental issues caused by chemical imbalances. Kayog claimed the pill he popped wasn't medicine, but that for him, it acted as such. Could that be it?

Any further speculation faded from my mind when Kayog didn't go for the main entrance but darted instead towards a secluded part of the gardens lining one of the eastern buildings of the campus. A few people noticed him. Their emotions loudly broadcast their curiosity as they started moving in the direction he was heading. I could only presume that his facial expression alerted them to the fact that something fishy was happening.

To my dismay, the students' confused curiosity quickly shifted to a mix of anger from some, and morbid excitement for others. Whatever the cause, it couldn't be good. Sadly, from this angle, I couldn't see whatever lay around the corner of the large building. Kayog vanished behind the wall as he swerved right, and a loud, angry shout reached me, but I couldn't make out the words.

The scene finally appeared in my line of sight just as Kayog landed in front of a group of three human males. It took me barely a second to understand what had been happening when I spotted a terrified Nazhral female pressing her back against the wall.

How in the world did he feel this all the way from the gazebo?!

"Hey, mind your own fucking business!" a man with short black hair shouted, advancing menacingly towards Kayog.

Not wasting his breath on the fool, Kayog grabbed him by the collar and flung him like a ragdoll across the lawn with mind-boggling strength. The dark-haired man flew at least ten meters before landing hard on his back. Lucky for him, it was grass and not the hard pavement that graced the front entrance and terraces around the campus. But that still appeared to knock the wind out of him.

The two other men—one blond, one with dark brown hair and a scar on his forehead—stood together in front of Kayog.

"Leave, and don't ever harass another person—let alone a female—ever again, if you know what's good for you," Kayog hissed.

"Stay out of it, Temern!" the blond male snarled. "That thieving bitch and her fucking people are the reason my family nearly went bankrupt."

I landed at a safe distance away, countless other students gathering around to witness the altercation.

"Last warning!" Kayog repeated.

"Fuck you!" the scarred man shouted before charging forward.

He threw a meaty fist at Kayog, who easily dodged it. I gasped when he immediately swiped his left wing at him, striking him hard enough to throw him onto the ground with a loud thud. That was a very dangerous thing to do unless you fully mastered that kind of move as our wings were fairly fragile. One blow at the wrong angle could dislocate it, break some of the bones, or damage our feathers in a way that would severely impede our ability to fly straight.

The scarred man groaned painfully even as he rolled to the side in a fetal position. Unlike his first buddy who had been tossed onto the grass, he hadn't been so lucky, getting slammed instead on the hard stone pavers. I doubted he'd broken anything, but this couldn't be pleasant.

The blond man emitted an enraged cry and also tried to throw a flurry of punches at Kayog. Although he effortlessly dodged or blocked them, Kayog was growing increasingly furious at the human for not backing down. In between two parries, he rammed the flat of his palm in a powerful blow against the man's chest, who stumbled back, nearly falling on his ass. In extremis, the blond man managed to remain standing by leaning against the back wall a couple of meters away.

An alarmed cry rose from the crowd as the first man with the short dark hair got back up and ran from the grass with an almost demented look on his face as if intending to tackle Kayog. I shouted his name in panic when he just stood there, staring at the incoming attacker with a terrifying expression.

My mind froze when he raised his left palm, his much longer arm allowing him to reach his attacker long before the human could strike him. Kayog covered the man's face with his hand and shoved him back. For some insane reason, I could have sworn his palm glowed. It stopped the aggressor dead in his tracks, but carried by his momentum, his feet flew up, and he banged the back of his head on the hard pavement.

A horrified gasp rose from the crowd. Although no blood pooled around him, the man's eyes rolled to the back of his head, and he remained still. My stomach roiled at the thought that the force of the impact might have broken his neck. But the female Nazhral screaming reclaimed all of our attention.

Realizing that things weren't going his way, the idiotic human lunged for the female, likely intending to use her as a meat shield. But he never got to her. She ran even as Kayog rushed him.

"I SAID ENOUGH!" Kayog shouted in a booming voice.

He grabbed the human's wrist, who tried to punch him in the

throat. Kayog dodged to the right, then backhanded him with such force it resonated like thunderclap. Blood exploded at the corner of the man's mouth. His knees buckled, and he barely managed to remain standing. With an almost feral roar, Kayog took flight, holding the human by his wrist.

"Kayog, no!" I whispered, even though I didn't quite know what he intended to do.

A handful of people ran to the scarred man, who was thankfully coming to. But I only had eyes for Kayog. My blood turned to ice as sudden understanding of his intentions dawned on me. He flew a short distance to a tall, ancestral tree and soared to its summit, at least ten meters high, before letting go of the man's wrist.

The poor human screamed, the sound quickly dying as he hit many of the countless thick branches on his way down, until he crashed heavily onto the ground. Although the branches had slowed his fall enough to spare him guaranteed death, he'd nevertheless sustained some significant damage. He curled on the ground moaning, his clothes torn and visible lacerations on his skin.

To my horror, Kayog landed in front of him, a murderous look on his face. On instinct, I flew towards them, terrified of what might follow. As I closed the distance, I heard the man begged Kayog through tears and pained moans not to hurt him anymore. For half a beat, I feared I would be too late when Kayog's claws extruded.

Without thinking, I landed in front of him, almost on top of the human, and placed my palms on his chest.

"Kayog, please don't hurt him. It's over!" I pleaded, my mind vaguely registering that I had dropped our bags at some point, probably after the fight had begun.

He rolled his neck before looking at me. A sense of dread washed over me as I gazed at his face. I could barely recognize him. His eyes were so bloodshot, red veins zigzagged his sclera like Tesla coils. In fact, he almost looked as if bloody tears were welling in his eyes.

I recoiled and subconsciously yanked my hands away from his chest as if its mere contact burned me. For the first time, I was truly scared of him. A wave of anger twisted his features. He stared at me with a hurt, sad, and almost betrayed look before soaring with one powerful flap of his wings.

Numb, scared, and confused, I watched him fly away while people around me rushed to the injured male.

What the fuck just happened?

CHAPTER 6

KAYOG

I felt her approach long before she landed. A wave of gratitude swelled within me, even as I drowned in sorrow. The subtle knock on the door before she entered wrested a reluctant smile from me. She'd always been overly respectful, even though she knew I was fully aware of her presence. I didn't have to bid her come in for her to open the door.

Without a word, Isobel walked to the center of the living area where I was sitting on my haunches in my failed attempt at meditating. She stopped a couple of steps in front of me. I just drew her closer as I propped myself up on my knees, wrapped my arms around her waist, and pressed my cheek against her stomach.

Still silent, she caressed my head as tears trickled down my face. She didn't need me to speak to understand after years of trying to help me find a peace that never came. I couldn't say how long we remained like this before I finally released her. I sat back down on my haunches and wiped my tears. Through the years, I'd often gone through hard times, but I couldn't remember ever feeling this defeated.

Isobel knelt in front of me and wiped out the lingering moisture from my face with two fingers.

"Are you feeling a little better?" she asked at last.

Crushed by despair, I shook my head. "I'm tired, Isobel. So very tired... I don't think I can do this anymore."

"DO NOT speak that way or even think such things," she said sternly. "You have fought too long and too hard to give up now when you have so much to live for. You're stronger than this."

"I'm bruising way too fast now," I said. "At this rate, I will soon have to completely isolate myself to even be remotely able to function."

Isobel pursed her lips as she reflected on my words then nodded slowly. "So it seems."

"I think it's her causing it," I replied, my throat painfully constricted.

"Your peaceful dove?" Isobel asked in a gentle voice.

I nodded. "Yes. Her name is Linsea. Her song is so incredibly beautiful. I want to wrap myself in it, and lose myself in her, shut out anything other than her. But being near Linsea is like opening the floodgates. I feel and hear too much. It's like I'm being bombarded from every angle, and my brain is scraped raw all the time."

Isobel frowned as I took a shuddering breath. Even now, the pounding in my head remained relentless, and a sharp pain continued stabbing at my brain, especially behind my eyes.

"Have you tested your levels?" she asked, studying my face.

My shoulders slouched. "Yes. And they're off the charts. Nothing I do improves my situation. It's been steadily getting worse over the past two years, but now it's completely out of control."

She reached for my right hand and gave it a gentle squeeze. Despite her efforts to keep her emotions positive, the helplessness and despair within her shone through and echoed my own.

"She thinks I'm a savage beast and a junkie," I said bitterly, the disgust and disappointment my actions had awakened in Linsea still cutting me to the core.

"You're not!" Isobel exclaimed, offended on my behalf.

"Really?" I asked with a hint of challenge.

She recoiled and gave me a shocked look. "Kayog, how can you say such a thing? You know perfectly well that you're not a junkie. This is not an addictive drug, and you only take it in extreme cases as needed. I can see why she might have misinterpreted what she saw. The main question is whether you told her."

"That I'm crazy?" I asked, dejectedly. "Yeah, I did."

"You're not crazy," Isobel replied sternly, the disapproval in her voice striking me hard.

She had been the only one to have always seen me as a person, not a broken freak, not an abomination to be wiped out. In the six years since I had met her, Isobel had turned every stone and used any resources she could to try and help me. She was more than a friend. To me, she was the sister I never had, and at times almost a mother figure—despite us being the same age.

"Why can't I be normal?" I asked in a broken voice. "Why can't I be with her?"

"You *can* be, Kayog," Isobel said forcefully. "But you *must* talk to her. Once you explain your condition—"

"I can't be fixed, Isobel!" I snapped. "We've tried everything!"

She waved a dismissive hand. "Millions of people across the galaxy live with their disabilities. There's no reason for it to be any different for you. In the meantime, we continue to look for a solution for you. But talk to her, Kayog."

I slowly shook my head, my gaze going out of focus as I replayed the scene in my head.

"You didn't see how she looked at me or how she felt after I dropped that human down the tree. In that instant, Linsea was afraid of me. She thought I looked like a monster," I said, a stab-bing pain slashing at my heart.

Isobel sighed and caressed my forearm in a soothing fashion.

"I can see why. In her place, I might have reacted the same if I didn't know the truth about you. But you said she's your soulmate."

"She is," I said in a tone that brooked no argument.

"Then talk to her!" Isobel exclaimed as if she wanted to smack me for being irrationally stubborn. "The Maker didn't pair you for nothing. Linsea entered your life because you are meant to work out somehow. Fate intended for you to meet now when things are reaching their critical point. Together, I have no doubt you will find the solution I failed to provide for you."

"You didn't fail," I countered passionately, guilt twisting my insides that I might have made her feel inadequate or like I wasn't grateful for all that she had done. "Your friendship and support are what gave me hope and kept me going this whole time."

"Then let me continue to support you through this by heeding my advice. Talk. To. Her. You deserve to be happy, Kayog. You are the kindest soul I know."

I snorted with self-derision. "Yeah, well this all might be a moot point. I will likely get expelled after my stunt."

Isobel shook her head with a conviction that took me aback. "You won't. Celeste—the Nazhral female you rescued—vouched to the fact that you were saving her. All the witnesses concurred with her statement. Sure, you might get slapped on the wrist for excessive force, but it was three against one."

"They're still likely the children of very influential parents," I countered. "They don't just let anyone into Acadia. Surely their parents are going to demand some form of justice."

"Nope," she said with an unusual smugness laced with a hard glint in her eyes. "Those three boys have been problematic from the beginning. Yes, their parents are influential and the only reason they actually got in. In truth, you did the school a favor by giving them the excuse they needed to potentially expel them. But you're going to be fine. I confirmed it before coming here."

Despite my current predicament, a wave of relief washed over me. I didn't know how to move forward from here. But I liked that the choice hadn't been taken out of my hands as would have been the case had I been expelled.

"For the record, Director Colin snooped around and meddled quite a bit after the incident," Isobel said pensively. "I think he may have put his thumb on the scale in your favor."

"Really?" I asked, stunned. "What did he tell them?"

"No clue," she replied in an apologetic tone. "But he's extremely curious about you. When he questioned the other students about the incident, he also drilled them about you as a person."

"Fuck," I muttered. "Now he's going to be even more on my ass. He thinks I'm the Good Samaritan."

"Are you?" Isobel asked, her face unreadable as she held my gaze unwaveringly.

Any other person staring at her would have had no clue as to what thoughts crossed her mind. With my empathic abilities, I could read clearly that she believed I was. Although she didn't approve of vigilantism or violence in general, she also didn't condemn me for whatever measures I might have used to protect the innocent.

I didn't answer but didn't avert my eyes.

She snorted. "Figures. I suspected as much from the first time I heard of a timely rescue."

"I fly around a lot at night when I can't sleep," I said in a non-committal fashion.

"And your emphatic abilities conveniently lead you to stumble on the damsels in distress?" Isobel asked in a teasing tone.

I smiled. "Actually, it's more like 'dudes' in distress, as humans like to say. But who's keeping count?"

She chuckled and shook her head affectionately at me.

"For what it's worth, I cannot take credit for every instance of timely rescues. There are others out there who aren't okay with innocents getting harmed," I said.

She tilted her head to the side and gave me an assessing look. "Enforcers are extremely resourceful and spare no expense for the welfare of their troops. Have you considered joining them?"

I shook my head with conviction. "The minute they find out more about me, they'll probably have me committed or turn me into some sort of lab rat. I've had it with institutions."

She pinched her lips into a disappointed but resigned expression. "Yeah... I get it."

By the look she gave me, Isobel appeared to want to say something else but thought better of it. Reaching for my face, she peered into each of my eyes, likely assessing just how badly they had to be bloodshot right now. My friend then pushed back up onto her feet and ran the scanner from her armband over my head. The way her brow creased as she examined the result on the interface told me everything I needed to know.

"There's still a great deal of swelling. Take another pill and then we can meditate together," Isobel said in a commanding tone.

I nodded, lobbed another pill into my mouth, and assumed the Lotus position as my friend did the same. It wouldn't fix me, but it would help bring some peace into the endless chaos of my mind.

CHAPTER 7
LINSEA

S hame burned my gut as I caught myself yet again glancing at the door. It was dumb of me since Kayog often attended class remotely. But I couldn't help hoping he'd show up against all odds. I still didn't know how to feel about the event that went down yesterday.

"He's not going to come," Tala said in a soft voice after I peered at the door again.

My cheeks heated with embarrassment that I'd been so obvious she noticed.

"Ugh. I'm so pathetic," I muttered.

"No, you're not," Tala said firmly. "You're very drawn to Kayog, and it's clearly reciprocal. Shit happened, and it's only fair that you would be confused about it. But he's not a violent male."

"Huh?! You didn't witness what went down!" I exclaimed disbelievingly.

"I didn't need to. Kayog protected Celeste from a group of bullies," Tala said in a calm and self-evident manner that threw me for a loop.

"By dumping that idiot through a tree?!"

She shrugged. "It slowed the said idiot's fall. His ego is a lot more bruised than his body. And he deserved it."

I shook my head, unconvinced, a shiver coursing through me as I replayed the whole scene in my mind.

"There's more to it, too. Kayog's eyes glowed, and I think that his hands did as well. He was like…" my voice trailed off as words failed me.

"Like what?" Tala insisted softly. "Like he was possessed?"

I shook my head. "No, but…"

"But what?"

I heaved a sigh and shrugged. "Honestly, I don't know. All I can say is that, for a brief moment there, he really scared me. I wasn't really scared *for* myself, but I didn't know who I was looking at. Maybe possessed isn't a bad word after all."

"Talk to him," Tala said firmly.

I scrunched my face, feeling torn. "Or maybe I should just listen to his advice and run while I can. And yet, another part of me doesn't want to. Above all, I really want to understand what happened, what triggered that reaction, and why the fuck his eyes glowed. Temerns don't have abilities like that. But he really feels like a lot of trouble that I might be wiser to steer clear of."

"Girl, talk to your man. You owe both of yourselves to at least find out what's going on so that you can make an enlightened decision. No one writes a song like this about a female they just met if they weren't serious about her. Give yourselves a chance," Tala said.

"Yeah, assuming he ever shows up again," I said in a grumpy tone. "For all we know, he might have gotten expelled. Acadia has strict rules regarding violence."

She made a dismissive gesture. "Nah, he won't be. We would have heard about it by now. Plus, everyone hailed him as a hero. The school would have a lot of disgruntled people to deal with if they punished him for protecting someone in danger."

"Hmmm, okay," I said in a non-committal fashion, just as confused now as I was at the beginning of this conversation.

Although I expected it, I still felt utterly disappointed when Kayog didn't show up. Focusing on the lecture rivaled the most grueling Olympian feat. By the time we were dismissed, I'd changed my mind on my next course of action at least a billion times.

"Excuse me! Are you Linsea Kenna?" a soft female voice called out the minute Tala and I walked out of the lecture hall.

I turned my head in the direction of the voice, stunned to see a slender, young human woman swallowed up in a long robe with runic symbols that I recognized as representing most of the main religions observed by the various species members of the UPO. She had long, dark blonde hair, olive skin, and dark green eyes that examined me with kindness. And yet, intense nervousness radiated from her, as if she feared my reaction to her approaching me.

"Yes, I am," I responded, curious.

"Could you spare me a moment to talk?" she asked, her nervousness cranking up another notch.

"Sure," I said, fully turning to face her.

"It is for a private matter," she added, casting an apologetic glance at my friend.

Although clearly bummed out to be excluded, Tala nodded and gave me a friendly smile. As much as she shamelessly loved good gossip, my best friend was also the most trustworthy person I knew. She would never pry about private matters and would never reveal a secret that had been confided in her without express consent.

"I'll be in the eastern garden when you're done," she said before walking away.

I gratefully smiled at her before turning my attention back to the stranger. She waved towards a discreet alcove where we could speak more freely, and I followed in her wake.

"What can I do for you?" I asked, intrigued when we stopped.

"My name is Isobel Biondi. I am Kayog's closest friend."

I recoiled, shock and betrayal slamming into me. "You're his girlfriend?!" I blurted out, immediately annoyed by my stupid mouth running away with me.

She burst out laughing and shook her head. The sincerity of her reaction and emotions instantly crushed whatever doubt I might have had. This further increased my mortification that my mind should have gone straight there when he had given me no reason to suspect foul play.

"No," she said in an amused tone while waving at her outfit. "This robe marks me as a doctorate student in the galactic clerical program. As part of our training, we must remain celibate for five years. This is only the second year. So no, there's no romantic involvement between Kayog and me. He's just a really good friend, who I consider pretty much a brother."

"I see," I replied, although I didn't actually see anything. "Did he send you to talk to me?"

Seeing her flinch took me aback.

"No, he didn't. In fact, he'll probably kick my butt once he finds out," she said sheepishly.

I frowned, always instantly suspicious of anyone who would betray or act behind the back of someone who trusted them.

"Then why are you?" I asked, my voice a bit cooler.

"Because he's my friend, and he's in an incredible amount of pain. In the six years I've known him, he's never spared any female a second thought. The moment he met you, he hasn't been able to stop thinking about you."

My cheeks heated, and I shifted on my talons, feeling both flattered and embarrassed.

"Kayog says you're the one, his soulmate," Isobel continued with a conviction that left me reeling. "But he also believes that he's not worthy of you."

"What?!" I exclaimed, flabbergasted by both her statements.

"He thinks he's crazy, but he's not," the priestess said in a tone that brooked no argument.

"He said as much," I conceded pensively. "Why does he think that?"

She hesitated then gave me an apologetic look. "As much as I would love to answer your question, it is not my place to say. He needs to tell you himself."

I clicked my beak in annoyance, even though I appreciated that she would extend him that respect.

"As an empath, I can sense that you mean every word you've just spoken. But Kayog doesn't know me. So his claim that I'm the one seems extremely farfetched. After all, we spoke for barely an hour for the first time yesterday," I replied, choosing my words carefully not to say that it in fact sounded crazy.

She smiled in an indulgent fashion. "With anyone else, I would agree that such a statement would be outlandish. But Kayog sees and hears things in a way that no one else can. I assure you that he's not crazy. He's just unique."

"You mean the same way that autistic people can perform insane mathematical equations in seconds?" I asked.

She pursed her lips as she weighed my words for a couple of seconds before hesitantly nodding.

"It shares some similarities, I guess. But like I said, Kayog is unique in a way I've never seen before," Isobel replied carefully.

"So he *is* autistic or neurodivergent?" I insisted.

The priestess shook her head firmly. "He's not. Kayog has simply been misdiagnosed his whole life."

I nodded slowly. "Considering that he was raised in a Darwandir colony, I can definitely see how that could happen."

Isobel recoiled, and her eyes widened in the strangest mix of shock and hope.

"You know about that?!" she exclaimed.

I shrugged. "Yes, he told me."

"Everything?" she insisted, her gaze intense.

"Not about the specifics of his illness," I conceded. "He only mentioned that the one time he was seen by a Temern doctor, there was reason to believe that he might try to hurt him."

"Not hurt him but flat out kill him," Isobel corrected, her voice and expression hardening with lingering anger towards the doctor.

It was my turn to recoil. "What?! Why in the world would someone sworn to heal people want to harm them instead? And especially one of our own?!"

I didn't want to believe what she said, but the emotions swirling around her made it clear she was totally being honest based on the facts she knew.

Isobel opened and closed her mouth a couple of times before sighing with frustration.

"I've said as much as I can on this matter. All I can do is beg you to please, please talk to him. You are well-connected. Maybe you can help get him the medical assistance he needs," she said in a pleading tone.

I ran a nervous hand over the soft feathers on my head and shifted my wings to release some of the tension building in my back.

"I haven't seen him since the incident yesterday, and he rarely comes to class," I said.

"He will do his canoe training tomorrow," the priestess replied swiftly. "It helps him focus. Please, I don't know how else to help him. This whole thing is breaking him both physically and mentally. I believe with all my heart that the Maker sent you here to save him. I can feel it in my bones!"

Overwhelmed, I rubbed my nape, too many thoughts swirling inside my head. But even then, I already knew that I would do whatever was in my power to help him. This woman genuinely believed that he was in distress, and that I could tip the scale. As she stated so accurately, I was well-connected. If whatever was affecting Kayog was medical in nature, we would find a cure.

"Are you in touch with him, or do you see him?" I suddenly asked.

She nodded, hope shining brightly in her dark green eyes. "Yes, I do."

"Then the next time you speak to him, tell Kayog he still owes me dinner."

She gaped at me for a few seconds before bursting out laughing, all tension bleeding from her shoulders. Then the warmest wave of gratitude emanated from her and slammed into me. Whatever doubt I might still have had about her feelings for him faded in that instant. Isobel truly loved him like a brother, or even in almost a motherly fashion.

"I can see why he loves you. Thank you for giving me hope of his imminent salvation. The Maker sent you."

She gently caressed my arm in a gesture that combined friendship and gratitude before turning around and walking away.

I paced my living room restlessly, glaring at my vidscreen every other second as if it was responsible for my nan not calling me. My impatience was unjustified as we were still four minutes away from the agreed time. One thing that could always be relied upon was Nana Arika being exactly on time, not a little before or after, but right on the dot.

And yet I couldn't help but inwardly curse the clock for not moving faster.

Right on cue, an incoming message popped on my screen at exactly 5:30 PM. I all but threw myself onto the couch as I accepted the call. My grandmother's gorgeous face immediately appeared. I was her spitting image, except that where I was completely white with a few dark specks on the fluffy down feathers of my chest, my nan was completely black with white specks. We often joked that she was the Ying to my Yang. And yet, our personalities were disturbingly similar.

"Hello, my darling," she said in that loving tone that always felt like a warm blanket.

"Hi, Nana," I replied affectionately. "I'm so sorry for bothering you while you're in the middle of that big mandate, but I really need your help."

"Regarding that Kayog Voln?" she asked in an overly nonchalant tone that didn't fool me in the least.

I stiffened, my mouth gaping as my mind raced to figure out how she already knew about him. I hadn't spoken a word yet regarding Kayog as we didn't officially have any kind of relationship. And then it hit me.

"Did Colin say something?" I asked.

She shrugged her left shoulder, her face still noncommittal while her blue gaze, identical to mine, remained intense.

"Maybe," she replied in a mysterious fashion.

My temper instantly flared. I knew this was her professional instinct kicking in to draw as much information from the other party without giving away too much of what she knew. But right now, I needed an ally, not a prosecutor.

"What did he say?" I asked in a clipped tone, annoyed that I couldn't read her emotions through the screen.

She narrowed her eyes at me, my reaction making her even more suspicious.

"You know that I'm not one to reveal what has been confided in me. However, you got yourself an interesting friend, if a little violent," she replied in a neutral tone as she studied my responses.

There was no question my nan also wished she could read my own emotions right now.

"He's not violent," I replied firmly, shocked by my own conviction as I spoke those words.

This very morning, I'd been uncertain how I felt about the brutal display he'd put on just yesterday. But that one conversation with the priestess had completely flipped everything on its head.

"Really?" Nana Arika asked, her dubious eyebrow reflecting the disbelief in her voice.

I nodded. "I know how it looks," I conceded. "Truth be told, I had some reservations about him. But he was in fact protecting a victim against three bullies. Clearly, he had the strength and skills to inflict grievous damage to all of them, but he didn't. That said, I'm not calling you about that incident but to request some medical help and your word that it will not be discussed with anyone we can't fully trust."

This time, my nan straightened, and the slightly distant expression that screamed careful reservation faded. I never made this type of request, so she knew something serious was happening.

"Of course, sweetie. You have my word."

"Thank you," I said with sincere gratitude. "The reason for this request is that Kayog is suffering from some kind of rare condition. I don't have all the details yet, except for him telling me that the one time he consulted a Temern doctor, his life and welfare were endangered."

My grandmother recoiled, and a troubled expression flitted over her features.

"A Temern doctor wanted to hurt him?" she insisted, her majestic wings stiff with tension.

I nodded then proceeded to recount everything that happened since meeting Kayog, including his song, everything he said while we shared breakfast, the incident with the bullies, and Isobel's revelations.

Seeing my grandmother almost slump against the backrest of

her chair as if in need of support had every single one of my senses going on high alert. Her eyes flicked from side to side as her mind raced, countless conflicting emotions pushing and shoving each other over her face. My tongue burned with the need to question her, but I didn't want to break her concentration as she sorted out all that I had confided in her.

"How old is your friend?" she suddenly asked.

"Kayog is twenty-seven," I replied, my back stiff with anticipation and nervousness.

She frowned and shook her head with an air of confusion.

"What?" I asked, getting aggravated. "What are you thinking?"

She shook her head again as if unable to make peace with the thoughts bubbling in her head.

"I know of only one specific situation where Temern doctors would want to kill one of us, and in fact be expected to," she mused aloud, still seeming to struggle to reconcile whatever was going through her mind.

"Expected to?!" I exclaimed, outraged. "Whatever happened to their oath of doing no harm?"

"Like I said, there is a very unique situation that warrants it. But Edals are never that old."

"Edals?" I echoed. "What is that? And what could possibly warrant murder?"

"Edals are Temerns who suffer from an extremely rare mutation," Nana Arika explained carefully. "It's a case of madness where the child is born rabid."

My blood turned to ice. "Rabid? But how? Why?"

"They have abnormal pineal glands, which is what controls our empathic abilities," she replied.

"And that gives them powers, like that glowing energy around Kayog's hand?" I asked, my mind reeling.

She shook her head. "I can't say whether they do or not. From what I read on the topic, their EEG readings are through the roof. Most of them die in the womb or are terminated the moment they're diagnosed as Edals. The rare exceptions who make it through birth show absolutely no visible sign during gestation. Then the moment labor starts, it seems to trigger some sort of activation of the mutation within their pineal gland, and they just come into the world screaming non-stop. They claw at everything and everyone, including themselves. They have to be restrained not to severely self-harm. In most cases, they die from an aneurysm or full-on cerebral hemorrhage."

I clasped my hands in my lap to keep them from shaking as I replayed my conversation with Kayog in my mind. When he first told me about his story, I wondered what kind of monstrous parents would just put their newborn in stasis, stuff him into an emergency pod, and ship him to a species that knew nothing of his anatomy just because they couldn't handle his crying. Now, I couldn't help but wonder if they had in fact sent him away to give him a chance at life and spare him from our doctors' euthanasia.

"What is the oldest Edal recorded?" I asked in a whisper.

"If this is what your Kayog is—and so far it sounds like he might be—then he undoubtedly is the oldest. They usually die within twenty-four hours. The oldest on record passed away within a week of sheer agony. They never make it to twenty-seven."

"Maker!" I breathed out, pressing my palms to my cheeks before giving my nan a confused look. "How come I've never heard of Edals? This seems like such a tragic and extreme condition that it should be broadly talked about."

She shook her head. "Like I said, it is an extremely rare condition, and we only have one or two cases every century or so. As the solution is quite controversial, it was deemed better to keep it a secret and only address it with the parents."

"But why? Killing the fetus or newborn child seems a bit extreme. With all our technological advances, surely something could be done for them? If I had an Edal child, I'd want them put in stasis so they don't suffer while doctors work around the clock to find a cure."

She gave me an indulgent smile. "Like I said, Edals are an extremely rare occurrence. Based on our history, such a defect would be deemed very harmful to a house's reputation. The family would want to keep it a secret so that the entire bloodline wouldn't be shunned for fear they might taint others. This guideline dates back centuries ago. It was never updated since there was no reason for anyone to believe such a child could be saved. And we don't know that your Kayog is an actual Edal."

"If he's not an Edal, why else could a Temern doctor possibly want to kill him? And either way, a child self-harming shouldn't be a justification for such extreme measures. Plus, in Kayog's case, he was already much older and not self-mutilating when a Temern doctor found out about his existence. So what other motive could there be?"

She shook her head. "I cannot think of any other reason for them to do so. At least, nothing that I am aware of."

"And what if he is an Edal?" I challenged.

"Then he will have single handedly changed everything. We need him examined by our top doctors as soon as possible," she said in an imperative tone.

"I will not have him turned into some sort of lab rat. He's a person, not an experiment!" I said sternly.

She chuckled and her gaze softened, even though I didn't miss the serious glimmer that still lurked within.

"Before we speculate further, we need to find out more about him," my nan said in a factual tone. "Based on the security recordings of the campus, Colin confirms that Kayog's hands and eyes definitely glowed. They also recorded a significant kinetic power surge. Whatever he is, your boyfriend is something else we've never encountered. The question is whether he's a threat."

"No, he's not," I said with a finality that had my nan raise her eyebrow with a hint of amusement. "Tala said that he is extremely protective of people."

To my surprise, my nan nodded. "That is indeed what his record states. But we also have very strong reasons to believe that he is the vigilante striking on Mazeria, or at least one of them. In which case, he might be a psychopath who channels his need for violence that way."

That gave me pause. While my gut screamed that he was not a violent person or a threat to society, it would be completely irresponsible for me not to at least consider that possibility.

Feeling a little defeated, I glanced at my grandmother with an almost pleading expression.

"I like him, Nana. I really, *really* like him. No one has ever made me feel the way I do around him, and every fiber of my being says that he's a good male who desperately needs help. But I'm scared and confused. I don't want to make bad decisions based on emotions."

She gave me an affectionate smile. "You were never reckless, my darling, and least of all the type to go boy crazy. I have concerns about that male, but your affection for him tells me that he must truly be an exceptional person. The Enforcers are heavily investigating him to determine if he is a danger or an asset. I will do everything in my power to protect him, but he must come in for tests. We have to know whether the power he displayed on that campus is all he has, or if there is far more that could be used as a weapon of mass destruction."

"I understand, but I will not let him be turned into a lab rat," I reiterated.

"Honey, if he's an Edal, he will have no choice but to volunteer to be one, if we ever want to find a cure. But it can be done in a respectful and empathetic way. What I can promise is that so long as he is not a threat, I will see that he is afforded the same

93

freedom of choice any other civilian would when it comes to their healthcare."

Although it wasn't the answer I had hoped for, it was honest and reasonable. I gave her a stiff nod.

"Be careful sweetie. I love you."

"I love you, too, Nana. And I promise I will be."

CHAPTER 8
KAYOG

I slipped three more dipramine pills into the secret compartment of my bracer. It was a tricyclic antidepressant that had long been discontinued on most planets. It was not an ideal medication. But it was the only one that somewhat worked to slow—and sometimes even stop—my pineal gland from functioning. When it kicked in, the drug helped numb the noise and the unbearable headaches that drove me insane.

A massive influx of joyous emotions was fine. For that reason, I had no problem participating in sports events or performing a concert. I loved the physical pain and focus that athletic endeavors provided. The same could be said about being surrounded by the cheers, excitement, and thrill from the crowds attending my shows or competitions. It was once they ended that everything went downhill.

Once the dust settled, people reverted back to their less pleasant emotions such as anger, jealousy, sorrow, and hatred—all of which individually felt like being stabbed by a dagger. And once all of them mixed into one chaotic maelstrom, it subjected me to sheer agony. So many times, I fought between the urge of gouging my eyes out or destroying the source of the pain—the people broadcasting those foul emotions. And that made crowds a true nightmare.

Still, today I could potentially see my love again. My innards painfully twisted every time I contemplated the possibility that I would see fear and disgust in her eyes. The only thing that gave me hope was Isobel telling me that Linsea was still waiting for that dinner I owed her.

The anger I initially felt about the priestess approaching Linsea on my behalf quickly faded. Beyond the fact that she had done it out of genuine love for me, it had also been the boost I needed to stop being so pathetic about being honest with my soulmate. If I couldn't be truthful about myself with her, then we weren't meant to be together. By talking to my dove, Isobel made her more receptive to what revelations I had to make.

My pulse racing with trepidation and anticipation, I flew to the campus and began my canoe training. My disappointment at not seeing Linsea show up at all turned into sorrow when I finished and entered the hangar to wash then store my canoe. I took double the time to complete that task in the hope that she might have slept in or been otherwise detained. Heartbroken when she still failed to appear, I went into the shower, trying to come up with any rational reason to explain her absence. Based on Isobel's comments, she believed Linsea would come to my training. However, in retrospect, my friend never claimed that my mate had confirmed she would.

And then I felt her.

My heart leapt in my chest, and I nearly slipped and broke my neck in my haste to finish washing and rinsing myself for fear she would leave, thinking she had missed me. Other Temerns would simply lower their psychic walls enough to allow their counterpart to perceive their emotions and thereby confirm their presence. I couldn't do that without causing significant distress to my mate.

I forced myself to come calmly out of the showers. Fuck me,

she was beautiful! Standing next to my canoe, she was gently running her fingers over the edge. The most irrational jealousy surged through me as I wished she was caressing *me* that way.

She jerked her head in my direction, a timid and slightly hesitant smile blossoming when she saw the expression on my face. Only once she turned to fully face me did I notice the two bags in her hand. I snorted and shook my head at her as I closed the distance between us.

"Hey! I thought *I* owed *you* dinner?" I said with false outrage.

She glanced at the bag in her left hand before peering back up at me with a mischievous expression.

"Oops! You make a fair point," she said with pretend dismay before shrugging. "I guess that means that you now owe me *two* dinners."

I laughed and bowed my head in concession, my heart filling to bursting with joy. My wretched mind had imagined a billion different nightmarish ways in which our next meeting would go. But just like that, my dove had made it so easy and painless. She was truly my soulmate.

"Deal," I said with a grin.

"How are you?" Linsea asked softly, the genuine concern she felt for me seeping into her voice.

That, too, had a pleasant warmth spreading through my chest.

"I'm doing good. Much better, thank you," I said in a gentle tone.

Although I intended to go into far more details, I didn't want to do it here.

"I'm glad to hear it. I figured you might be hungry after the type of intense training you perform," Linsea said sheepishly, showing me the bags.

"I'm absolutely famished," I replied sincerely.

I'd barely eaten since the incident, feeling too distraught to be able to stomach anything.

"Do you want to eat off campus?" Linsea offered.

"That would be great, if you don't mind," I said, my heart soaring.

"I don't mind. Is there any specific place where you feel comfortable?" she asked, her emotions loudly broadcasting that she truly wanted me to be at ease, and not out of some misplaced sense of obligation.

I shifted on my talons and chose my words carefully before speaking.

"Truth be told, the most comfortable place for me would be my house. But I don't want you to think I'm some sort of creep if I invite you there," I said, tension audible in my voice.

To my shock, Linsea smiled, her aura radiating something akin to relief, as if she had hoped for that very answer... which didn't make sense.

"Your house it is, then," she said in a factual manner.

I gaped at her, flabbergasted by the ease with which she agreed.

"Are you sure?" I asked, uncertain.

"Yes, Kayog," Linsea said firmly. "I trust you not to harm me."

A powerful emotion nearly choked me as I basked in the divine light that emanated from her.

"Never, my dove," I replied, shocked to even be able to form any word.

Before I could flinch inwardly at using the term of endearment, the wave of pleasure emanating from Linsea both appeased me and whipped the possessiveness I felt towards her into a frenzy. It tickled me pink that she was still responding so positively towards me, especially after how much I dreaded that this reunion might turn sour.

After relieving her of the two bags, I took flight, happy to leave behind the painful chaos of the campus stirring to life as more and more students started their day. There was something magical about flying next to my mate. My mind swirled with images of our nuptial flight, of countless adventures of us soaring through the skies surrounded by nothing but pristine nature, the caress of the wind, the warm rays of the sun, and the enthralling aura of our love swirling around us. I wanted this so badly I could taste it.

Linsea gasped as we approached our destination, and she finally noticed a lone house sitting by itself in the middle of a tiny island in the river.

"Is this your house?" she exclaimed, flabbergasted.

"It is," I replied smugly.

"You own an entire island?!"

I chuckled. "Technically, this is too small to be called an island. It's actually an islet measuring a little over sixty square meters. And sadly, no, I do not own it. Normally, you cannot build a residence here. But the mayor was kind enough to grant me a special permit to temporarily settle here for the duration of my education," I said as we began our descent.

From a bird's eye view, the house was shaped like a cross with slightly slanted dark roofs. They were all solar panels which allowed me to enjoy most standard creature comforts without having to be connected to the city grid.

"It is a deployable home, designed specifically for my needs. So it's perfect for me to travel anywhere with it," I explained as we landed.

Although not perfect, this home was my haven. Over the years, it had been the only thing that kept me from going entirely insane. If I could go back in time, I would have made a few additional tweaks, but this was more than good enough. I loved the huge reflective windows all around that always had light flooding in, while affording me the privacy I craved... Not that anyone ever came here.

I opened the door and waved her in before following her inside. Even with the door still open, the dampening effect of the house almost had me moaning with relief. Entering the shelter of my home always made me fully grasp how painful things had been. Considering people were only just getting up, it distressed me to realize how insanely sensitive I had grown of late.

However, while coming home elated me, I immediately felt the shift in Linsea. I wouldn't call it discomfort, but it affected her not in the most positive way. It was to be expected for anyone unused to this type of environment.

"Whoa!" Linsea whispered to herself, frowning slightly as she looked around the room, trying to figure out what exactly unsettled her. "This feels weird."

"Yes, that's normal," I replied in an appeasing tone.

Her eyes widened in sudden understanding.

"Oh wow! This feels like an anechoic chamber! It's like there's no echo!" she exclaimed.

My smile broadened. "It is kind of the same principle, but it's not for normal sound. This house is designed to block psychic signals."

She slightly recoiled, confusion settling on her beautiful face. "Psychic?" Linsea repeated.

I nodded. "There are quite a few things I need to explain to you. But first, let me give you a quick tour. Then we can settle at the table and talk while we eat."

"Sounds good," she replied, the relief and excitement radiating from her confirming she had hoped I would come clean about certain things.

As much as I had dreaded it—and still did to a certain extent—it finally sank in that this was the right thing to do. Isobel had been correct in stating that I should be able to discuss anything with my soulmate. It couldn't be a coincidence that Fate sent her my way at the very moment I felt on the verge of throwing in the towel. Linsea was giving me a reason to hang on to a miserable life I no longer had the strength to endure.

I gave her a quick tour of the house, which featured one

bedroom with its en suite bathroom, the second bedroom which I used as an office, the living room which also served as my meditation room, and the adjoining kitchen dining area with a small water closet by the entrance.

"This is a really beautiful house," Linsea said with sincere admiration. "I love the earthy color palette you chose. For some reason, I expected your place to either be all black and dark grays, or the typical white and brown that males often go for. But I adore this forest-green, midnight-blue, oranges, and deep-reds that you used. It's warm, joyful, and inviting without being over the top or aggressive. I also really appreciate how you balanced making the place feel homey but not cluttered."

I puffed out my chest a bit more with each of her words. As I never entertained guests aside from Isobel, I had no idea how my female would have perceived my decor aesthetic. Saying her response pleased me would be a major understatement.

"I'm glad you like it. As I spend most of my time here, I need it to feel warm and inviting."

Although I spoke those words in a cheerful way, I didn't miss the sliver of sadness they triggered in her. Like most people, she would deem this house a prison rather than a haven. In more ways than one, it would be an accurate assessment. But for me, the protection it provided outweighed any negative connotation that came with it.

"This place must have cost a fortune," Linsea said pensively as I guided her to the dining table large enough for four people.

"It wasn't cheap," I conceded, "but the settlement covered all of it with plenty left," I said as I stopped right next to the table.

"That's amazing!" she said with a smile, her gaze roaming over the house one more time before settling on me. "I truly love your home. It's very reflective of you."

I tilted my head to the side and gave her an inquisitive look. "Reflective of me?" I echoed. "What do you mean?"

"It's comforting, sweet, colorful, powerful, and yet humble

with the right level of sober to make it inviting instead of suffo-cating. While the dampening effect is unsettling at first, it quickly fades into the background. And you just want to wrap yourself with the warmth of your home," Linsea replied pensively, rather than answering me as if speaking to herself.

Each of her words had me melting from the inside out. On instinct, I caressed her cheek. The softness of her feathers against my palm nearly had my knees buckling. To my shock, my female leaned into my touch, and she blasted a wave of tenderness at me. Unable to resist, I drew her into my embrace. Linsea came willingly, pressing her slender body against mine, and burying her face in the crook of my neck.

"My dove," I whispered, my throat constricted.

A violent shiver coursed through me, and my nerve endings tingled while my skin heated. I'd never had such a potent reac-tion to anyone. It wasn't lust fueling this response, but a deep sense of rightness, of belonging, of finally being whole.

I slipped my arms around her waist, tightening my hold. She flattened her wings against her back, and I wrapped mine around her. A deep, rumbling coo vibrated through my chest and up my throat. Another shiver ran down my spine when Linsea joined her voice to mine as she rubbed her face against the down feathers covering my neck and chest.

In perfect sync, as if a silent communication had passed between us, we stopped cooing. I slightly released my hold, and Linsea lifted her head to lock gazes with me. I drowned in the crystalline blue sea of her eyes, an incredible sense of well-being and of perfect communion descending over me. After a few seconds—or countless minutes—I leaned forward and rubbed my beak against hers in a soft kiss, which she reciprocated.

Her nails gently scratched the down feathers lining the base of my wings, near my spine. Under specific circumstances, it would be deemed an erotic gesture, as this spot was quite eroge-nous for us—and for bird folk in general. However, it could also be a soothing gesture or mark of affection, especially between mates. That Linsea would do this indicated that she believed our relationship was moving towards something more serious and exclusive.

With much reluctance, I took a step back, freeing her of my embrace. But we held both hands for a few moments, our gazes still locked. In that instant, something settled in my chest, further fueled by her emotions swirling around me in a gentle caress, and the enthralling song of her soul healing the deep wounds in my messed-up brain. Linsea and I were meant to be. Some way, somehow, we would figure it out together.

Still holding one of her hands, I helped my mate onto her seat before settling on the other side of the table. It sat across the lab kitchen and right in front of the large patio doors that gave onto the right side of the house, with access to the river less than ten meters away. It offered a peaceful and amazing view, especially with the luxuriant forest on the opposite shore with the mountain peaks soaring in the distance.

As we began to eat, I couldn't help an amused chuckle when I noticed that my mate had brought herself a double serving of the grain crackers. I filed away that information so that I could get her an exclusive gift box filled with an expansive variety of flavors and grains that were not available in the cafeteria.

After a few bites, I took a deep breath and launched into revealing everything about my condition.

"Right from birth, it was obvious that I wasn't a normal Temern. Despite extensive training, I'm unable to shut out people the way the rest of you do. Except, I don't just feel people's emotions as sensations like you. To me, they also translate as sounds."

Linsea froze, halfway through bringing a cracker to her beak. She stared at me with a stunned expression.

"As sounds?" she repeated, confused.

I nodded. "Souls have songs, unique melodies for every individual, pretty much like a psychic fingerprint. But emotions have sounds. For example, to me, anger is a very grating sound like a loudly squeaking door. Joy is like a very light windchime. Sorrow is high-pitched and one of the worst ones out there. The deeper the sorrow, and the more aggressive it becomes. It turns into something akin to a screech or nails on glass," I explained.

My mate gave me a horrified expression. "Maker! That must be horrible."

"It definitely is," I said in a dejected tone. "Jealousy and envy come across as a sustained growl. But they also have sensations. Anger is like a crawling sensation. Sadness feels like suffocating or being choked. Jealousy is just slimy and makes my skin itchy. Whereas fear is more like that unpleasant pins and needles sensation after one of your limbs has gone numb and is now reawakening."

"Wow! I never would have expected this. But what about joy? What does it feel like?"

I smiled. "It's warm and comforting, like a gentle summer breeze. But love is the best. It's the embodiment of peace, that groggy feeling and sense of well-being you get while getting a massage at the spa."

"That's amazing!" Linsea said with a hint of envy. "If I was able to get that just from hanging around people in love or who expressed that emotion, I would latch onto them around the clock."

I chuckled. "Being near such people is indeed wonderful. Sadly, I cannot just focus on them in isolation. I feel everything from everyone, all at once. Always," I said, bitterness seeping into my voice.

My mate pressed a palm to her chest with a shocked expression. "What do you mean by everyone?" she asked carefully.

"Absolutely everyone. The entire campus and the surrounding areas. That's why I can only stay near crowds for very short periods of time before it gets overwhelming. It's especially hard when people feel extreme emotions."

"And you say that you cannot block them?" Linsea insisted, shock and empathy warring within her in equal measure.

"I absolutely can't, and it's not from lack of trying," I said with resignation. "Naturally, the more people are present and awake, the louder it gets. Between their various emotions, the sounds they produce, and sensations they create, I'm cast down into a deadly chaos that drives me to the edge of madness."

"Is that why you systematically block your emotions from me?" she asked in a careful tone.

I shifted my wings uneasily before nodding. "It would be very painful for you or other empaths to feel my emotions."

"Show me," she demanded.

"No! I just told you that—"

"And I heard you," Linsea interrupted in a gentle but determined tone. "But I want to fully understand and know you. Which means getting a glimpse of what you feel as well. A bit of pain doesn't scare me. And we're in your house. What better place than here where you are the least affected by others thanks to the dampening effect?"

Although my female was making a good point, my gut screamed that this was a bad idea. Yes, the house significantly diminished the noise in my head, but it didn't squash it. What if I hurt her?

And what if I don't, but her perception of my emotions turns her off?

No one had ever felt my emotions... at least not since I had been old enough to figure out how to erect my protective walls. The prospect of having someone else read me was beyond terrifying. I felt vulnerable, exposed, and utterly self-conscious. At the same time, denying Linsea what I greedily plundered from her would not only be disrespectful, but could also be construed as a lack of trust. The point of this whole conversation was to lay out the truth, not keep further secrets from her.

"Very well," I said with much reluctance, trying to ignore the loud voice at the back of my head screaming for me not to comply. "But I will only give you a small glimpse at first to see how you handle it. And if all is fine, I'll further lower my walls. Okay?"

I braced for her to argue. To my utter relief, she smiled and nodded. The gratitude emanating from her made me feel like an idiot. Although Linsea initially made that request out of pure curiosity, it had shifted into something deeper. In that instant, I realized that she wouldn't have pushed further had I declined. But she wanted—maybe even needed—for me to put my walls down, open myself to her willingly, and trust her.

"Alright," I said, my worry still audible in my voice. "Here goes."

Heart pounding, I slightly lowered my protective wall.

"Aaah!" Linsea shouted almost immediately.

She slapped both hands to the side of her head, her eyes closed tightly, her face constricted with a painful expression, while she pressed her temples.

"Linsea!" I exclaimed, slamming my psychic walls shut as I rushed to her side. "Are you okay? I'm sorry! I'm so sorry!"

She blinked and took a couple of deep breaths before looking back at me. I cupped her cheeks, studying her face to assess the extent of her distress. My mate placed her palms on my chest. For a split second, I feared she would push me away, but she leaned on me for support instead.

"I'm... I'm okay," she said, her voice a little shaky. "What in the world was that?! Is this what you feel?"

"Yes. I'm so sorry. I should have known better..."

"Don't apologize, silly male," she said in a slightly chastising tone. "I insisted you did. But... I thought you said your house dampened the effects of your abilities?"

"It does. This is the bearable level," I said carefully, still examining her to make sure she was unharmed.

Her eyes widened. "That's what you call bearable?! You mean it's normally worse?"

I nodded grimly. "Yes. It's normally three to four times worse when I'm outside."

She gaped at me. A flurry of emotions flitted over her features, from shock and disbelief, to pity, sorrow, and a grim determination laced with anger. It was as if she'd found a new enemy she fully intended to take down.

"How can you tolerate it? This is sheer agony! How did you manage not to go insane?" she asked, flabbergasted.

"By living in the bunker," I said with a hint of self-derision, settling back in my chair now that I was reassured she wasn't harmed. "Actually, it was an accidental discovery. Evelyn—my foster mother—was at the end of her rope. I had been screaming nonstop from the pain of the constant psychic assault from everyone that I could perceive over a much-too-wide radius outside the house. She'd been crying from exhaustion from what I'd been putting her through and desperately needed a break. So she put me there for an hour just so that she could gather herself."

"Poor female," my mate said with sympathy. "I cannot begin to imagine what it must have been like, especially if they didn't fully understand what was happening with you."

I nodded. "It was especially hard for her because she also had to keep an eye on me as I was quite strong and constantly trying to maim myself to end the pain. She came back into the bunker, apologizing profusely for abandoning me there. So you can imagine her shock when she found me quiet, and I smiled before hugging her. At first, she thought it was my way of trying to mollify her to make sure I would never be 'punished' like that again. Instead I told her that I loved it there."

"What?! You were the one who asked to live there for the long haul?!" Linsea exclaimed, stunned.

I chuckled. "Yes, I most certainly did. Evelyn argued with me quite a bit to make sure it truly was what I wanted. But I had never been this quiet for so long, not screaming and writhing in pain. So clearly, something in that bunker was agreeing with me. So she consented. Along with her husband, William, they improved the place to provide me with all the comfort I needed."

My female leaned against the backrest of her seat, a mix of disbelief and comprehension flitting over her gorgeous face.

"Wow, I'd totally misconstrued the entire ordeal. No wonder they didn't file abuse charges against them," she mused aloud.

"Correct," I said with a smile.

Her brow creased. "But then, why did you get a hefty settlement?"

"Because the state failed me. My foster parents pleaded many times for help, but were ignored, given the run around, or redirected left and right because nobody knew what to do or simply couldn't be bothered," I explained with a shrug. "In the end, it served me well as the settlement has allowed me to buy this home and to pretty much live anywhere I want without going insane."

She slowly nodded, her blue eyes flicking from side to side as she reflected over the whole situation. However, the main thought that dominated for me was the fact that not once had she seemed turned off, disgusted, or repulsed by me or anything I had revealed. It shamed me that I ever doubted that my soulmate would be able to accept me with my flaws, severe though they were.

"That pill you took the other day, is it to combat that noise?" she asked carefully.

"Yes," I replied without hesitation. "It's called dipramine. It slows down my pineal gland, which in turn blocks part of my ability to feel people. Sadly, it's not a full shutdown."

Linsea stiffened, and she leveled an intense stare at me that had all my senses on high alert.

"You said your pineal gland, correct?"

I nodded. "Yes."

"It's malfunctioning?" she insisted.

"Not exactly. It didn't form properly."

My mate's sharp breath intake freaked me out, especially since her emotions appeared to be all over the place.

"What is it?" I asked.

She shook her head. "In a minute, I will tell you. But please answer one more question for me first. Have you tried psychic disruptors to shield you from people's thoughts and emotions?"

I made a disdainful gesture. "I did. Every possible model out there, but none of them work. I produce excessive amounts of melatonin, but mine is… unusual. It's melatonin, and yet it's not. The doctors said it was abnormal, but they couldn't quite explain how. Why do you ask?"

She took a long sip of her flavored water before answering.

"I asked my nan if she had any idea why a Temern doctor might want to harm you."

My back immediately stiffened, and a sense of dread washed over me. Noticing my reaction, Linsea reached across the table to squeeze my hand in a reassuring fashion.

"Don't worry, Kayog. My nan is absolutely trustworthy. She believes that you might be an Edal."

I blinked. "What is that?"

She gave me a detailed description of everything her grandmother shared with her. Although there were undeniable similarities, the differences struck me as too significant for me to qualify.

I shook my head. "Those are fascinating revelations. However, that cannot be my case, if only for the fact that I grew to be this old."

My mate nodded. "That stumped her, too. But there are too

many signs pointing in that direction. Maybe the time you spent in that stasis pod played a role. Maybe your parents did something before they resorted to letting you go that helped you survive those first few critical days. There are too many unknowns for us to truly assess whether you somehow benefited from something the others didn't, which saved you. Would you consent to a medical exam?"

"No," I said in a tone that brooked no argument.

Although she had expected that answer, I hated the disappointment that emanated from her. Despite that, the stubborn determination lurking underneath made it clear she wasn't ready to give up. I didn't quite know how I felt about that. A part of me loved that she clearly wanted to help me while the other dreaded that she would attempt to coerce me into something I wasn't comfortable with.

"I understand your very valid concerns based on previous experiences," Linsea said in a reasonable tone. "But there has to be a cure or a way to fix whatever is ailing you. For this, we need the assistance of top medical professionals."

"I don't trust them," I said forcefully.

"Fair, but you could sense if they had ill intentions," she countered.

"True, but by then it might already be too late for me. They could have me trapped and unable to escape whatever they have in store for me," I argued, hating that I sounded excessively paranoid.

To my surprise, Linsea rose from her chair and circled around the table to come next to me. I slid my chair back and welcomed her when she settled in my lap. My chest instantly warmed, and the sense of peace I always felt in her presence cranked up a notch.

"Do you trust me, Kayog?" she asked in a soft voice.

"Yes," I replied without hesitation.

"Then I need you to trust that I will never let anyone harm

you, let alone a medical doctor. You say we are soulmates. Although I cannot perceive things the way you do, I cannot deny that there is a strong connection between us like I've never felt with anyone else before. If you're mine, I will raze this world and any other to the ground before I let anyone take you from me. I refuse to let you continue to live at the edge of life because of something that could possibly be cured."

A powerful emotion constricted my throat. I had to swallow hard a couple of times before I trusted myself enough to speak.

"There are no ifs about it, my dove. I *am* yours. No one in any universe can ever complete me the way only you can."

"Then let me take care of what's mine. Let me take all the steps necessary to fix this," she said in a slightly pleading tone.

Years of fear and distrust shouted at me to stand my ground and turn down her offer. But beyond the fact that I genuinely trusted her, I couldn't continue living this shadow of a life filled with pain. I owed it to us to try everything possible for a chance at the kind of future my beautiful dove deserved.

"Very well, my Linsea. I will trust you to do what you think is right."

The emotion that welled within her in response to my words wrecked me. We weren't in love with each other, but we might as well have been. The songs of our souls intertwined in such a beautiful crescendo that it nearly had me in tears. What I wouldn't give for her to be able to hear how we harmonized the way I did.

She leaned forward and rubbed her beak against mine. I reciprocated, my hand gliding in a gentle caress down her back and the length of her slender waist. Her mouth parted, and I instinctively responded in kind, my tongue timidly poking forward before making acquaintance with hers. A bolt of fire lit in the pit of my stomach as we deepened the kiss.

Her pleasure mingling with mine quickly had me throbbing in a way that I didn't want to… at least not so soon. That I clearly perceived her own arousal didn't help my inner battle for restraint. With this being her first time coming to my house, I didn't want to let things go too far so that she wouldn't wonder if I had brought her here specifically in the hopes of taking advantage of her.

Instead, I broke the kiss and nudged her up. Although a little confused, she complied while casting an uncertain look my way. It had to be confusing for her not to be able to feel anything from me as empathic abilities were an intrinsic part of a Temern sensory system. It would be like losing the ability to see or hear for someone else.

With a vocal command, I activated some soft music, the type I often listened to in order to relax. The happy smile Linsea gave me was all the confirmation I needed. I drew her back into my embrace. For the next eternity, we swayed to the music, exchanging tender kisses and gentle caresses as we basked in each other's presence.

Whatever the cost, I would marry my dove.

CHAPTER 9

LINSEA

S tanding on the front lawn of the university after class with
Mares and Tala, I struggled with my mind constantly
wandering back to Kayog. I wanted to feel guilty about skipping
classes yesterday as I ended up spending pretty much all of it
with him. It disturbed me how hard and fast I was falling for that
male. We'd only met a few days ago and had spoken far too few
times for me to know him. And yet, with a certainty that couldn't
be denied, I knew that I was falling in love with him.

There was no question that I would marry him someday.

But first, we had to fix him. The fact that he allowed me to
take whatever measures were necessary to get the medical
assistance he needed moved me to my very core. As much as it
frustrated me not to be able to sense his emotions, I understood
his reluctance to being treated. His dread of the medical staff had
almost been palpable as we talked. He was taking a massive leap
of faith in me, and I would be damned before I let him down.

I already had a few things in motion with the blessed help
from my nan. Tomorrow, I would receive a special scanner that
would allow us to get the type of advanced data standard hospi-
tals couldn't provide. To the extent possible, I would provide the

specialists with the samples they needed without exposing my mate to them until it became essential.

That said, it would be a lie to pretend his medical condition hogged my every thought. The memory of his arms around me, of his muscular body pressed against mine, the gentle and respectful way in which he touched me, and the tenderness of his kisses had me tingling in all the right places.

More than once, I wished he had grown bolder and carried me to that wondrous bedroom of his with the breathtaking view of nature, and the massive bed which seemed to have the most comfortable mattress in the universe. At the same time, I loved the restraint he displayed.

Although our males retracted their naughty bits inside their bodies, we could feel when they were aroused if rubbing against them the right way. In some cases, you could even see the bulge beneath the thin layer of feathers on their crotch. As we danced, the state of his arousal had been loudly expressed. Too many times to count, my fingers itched with the urge to venture south and gently stroke that intimate part to coax him into extruding.

I wanted to feel embarrassed by the lascivious thoughts that he stirred within me. With any other male, I probably would have felt dismayed to be so eager this early after meeting. But with Kayog, everything felt right and fated. Still, I loved that he showed me in both words and action that I wasn't some fling or another conquest to add to his record.

"Stop fantasizing about your man and tell us how breakfast went with him—not to mention the rest of the day with Mr. Perfect," Tala demanded, wiggling her eyebrows in a suggestive fashion.

"She didn't have breakfast with me," Mares interjected with pretend confusion that had both of us chuckling.

"She had better not," my friend replied with false severity. "As much as I love her, should she come sniffing anywhere near you, I'll have to pluck her bare."

I burst out laughing. "I'd tell you to bring it, but as much as I appreciate your man, I'm already taken."

"Taken?!" Tala said, opening her eyes wide as she spoke the word in a manner heavy with raunchy undertones. "Do tell!"

"I already told you that I don't kiss and tell," I deadpanned.

"Oh, my God! So you did kiss?!"

I hadn't meant it that way, but my cheeks heated, and my embarrassed expression to have thus tattled on myself erased any doubt she might still have had.

"Let's freaking go!" she exclaimed, clapping her hands excitedly. "I want all the deets!"

"Tala," Mares said in a disapproving tone.

"But baaaabe!" she said in a whiny tone.

"No buts, my love. We do not pry into people's personal lives," he said in a gently chastising voice.

"Bah, you two are no fun," she said with an exaggerated pout that clearly indicated she was just playfully being a brat. "So when are you seeing him again?"

I scrunched my face and shrugged. "I don't know," I said sheepishly.

Their troubled expressions laced with a hint of pity— although quickly hidden—stung quite a bit. It didn't take a genius to know they were wondering if I was being played. At the same time, I could feel their inner struggle about it as they both strongly believed that he was serious about me, if only because they'd never seen him show interest in anyone else.

"I believe we'll see each other again either later today or tomorrow."

Their instantaneous excitement touched me deeply. They wanted to see me happy.

"You really like him," Tala said in a gentle voice devoid of her usual mischief.

"I do," I said with a timid expression. "He's so sweet and

respectful. But he has some substantial challenges that I hope I can help him with."

"Is he neurodivergent, as we speculated?" Mares asked.

I gave him an apologetic smile. "It's not my place to discuss his personal matters. But we had a long discussion yesterday, and it explained a lot of things. Honestly, I'm thoroughly amazed by him. The things he has overcome, all the challenges he faced and not only prevailed, but grew into such a good person is just awe-inspiring."

"Damn, someone is falling hard!" Mares said in a gently teasing tone.

"I am," I admitted shyly.

"Well he couldn't have gotten himself a better partner than you," Tala said affectionately.

"That's right," Mares said, puffing out his chest as he drew Tala into his embrace. "Because I already got the best one there is."

"Aww, why are you always so sweet?" Tala asked, melting against him.

My chest warmed for my friends, even as a sliver of envy flashed through me.

"You two are incredibly cute," I said with a smile.

"Of course, we are," Tala said, flicking her hair in a pretend diva fashion that had her mate and I laughing.

"We were thinking of going on a Nordjarimm ride," Mares said, sobering. "Would you want to come with us?"

"Better yet, could we make this a double date?" Tala suggested.

I hesitated. "You know, us winged folks usually prefer flying ourselves rather than riding flying mounts."

"Show off," Tala said, making a face at me.

I chuckled.

"Fair enough, but you could fly alongside us," Mares countered. "Their flight path is supposedly absolutely breathtaking."

I nodded. "Yeah, so I heard. But didn't they announce an incoming storm in that area?"

"Hmmm. Let me check," Mares replied.

He released his mate and walked a few steps towards the ancestral tree under whose shade we'd been standing. He placed his palm against the trunk, and his *veris* immediately extruded. Those vines ran just below or above the skin of Edocits both on their hands, feet, and intertwined with their hair. They allowed his species to connect with any plant, tree, and even the ground itself. On their homeworld, animals, fish, and birds also possessed their own *veris*, allowing Edocits to communicate directly with them.

In this instance, Mares was connecting with the tree, which would allow him to transfer his consciousness through any interconnected flora, giving him an open window into the remotest region of the planet. Naturally, the farther his consciousness traveled, the longer it took for him to return. Therefore, Edocits always carefully chose where they used that ability as their bodies remained vulnerable to attacks during that time.

His face went slack as his *veris* sank into the grooves between the bark of the trunk. Unlike on his planet, these trees did not have *veris* of their own, which made the connection a bit weaker.

"Man, you aliens have all those freaking cool powers and insane strength while us humans just suck," Tala mumbled.

Although she was saying it in a playful manner, there was in fact a hint of envy lingering within.

"Humans don't suck, least of all you," I said before gently squeezing her shoulder.

"Pfft, don't try to mollify me. You're too cool to need a flying mount because you have those amazing, badass wings. You can read people's emotions and are probably inwardly rolling your eyes at all the petty jealousy I'm broadcasting. And you could fling my whiny butt halfway across the yard with a flick of your wrist."

I couldn't help but laugh at the overly dramatic way in which she spilled all of that. She then playfully glared at her mate, who was still oblivious to what was happening here as his consciousness traveled the world.

"And he could survive for months simply feeding by photosynthesis. He can use his vines and *veris* tentacles to project his mind throughout this whole freaking planet. Mares can communicate with both the flora and fauna in his world. AND to add insult to injury, my plant man can grow some awesome, safe, and totally non-addictive recreational drugs in his hair. But humans, we just get bitchslapped by everything and everyone."

A wave of guilt surged through me for laughing. But Tala had a way of making anything sound absolutely hilarious. I hoped that wherever our careers led us, we would be able to remain in close contact, or to at least make sure that distance didn't kill our friendship. She was a breath of fresh air and a ray of light I wanted to keep forever in my life.

"While everything you said about Edocits and Temerns is technically true, humans still do not suck," I said in an indulgent tone. "Humans are without a doubt the most adaptable species in the entire galaxy. What you lack in powers and abilities, you compensate with ingenuity. The human race has developed incredible tools and technologies that allow you to rival—and in some cases even surpass—some of the most powerful races out there. There's a reason that you are the only species to be part of both galactic alliances of the known universe. Everyone wants you."

She pursed her lips in the most adorable pout, even though my words had touched her.

"Fine, but we're still weak."

Mares laughing in an affectionate fashion drew our attention. The sneaky male had returned to his body while we were talking.

"You're not weak, my love. What you are is fabulous, and you make me happy," he said, pulling her back into his embrace before kissing her forehead.

She snuggled against him, their love shining with the strength of a thousand suns. To my surprise, Mares turned to me with a taunting glimmer in his eyes.

"And your sexy birdman is also on his way."

My heart skipped a beat. "Really?!"

He nodded. "I saw him flying over the river on his way towards the campus. I guess he couldn't wait any longer to see you," he said with a wink.

"Ooh goodie! Then I get to ask him directly since you won't give me any details," Tala said with a shameless grin.

I shook my head at her in a way that clearly indicated I believed she was hopeless.

"As for the Canyon, it's a go!" Mares said. "It's a clear blue sky ahead and the perfect weather. We just need to convince your boyfriend to tag along."

I almost instinctively said that he was not my boyfriend—more out of principle than out of actual conviction—but decided to keep my peace instead. Truth be told, I didn't really know where we stood. In my heart, we were officially an item. But as we had not explicitly discussed the matter, I didn't want to be too presumptuous. How embarrassing if I were to act possessively with him only to have him put me back in my place publicly.

Moments later, I saw him flying in the distance. My pulse picked up when he headed straight for us, not with that hesitant way people often behaved when they were uncertain as to where to go. Kayog flew with a purpose, his extremely acute powers allowing him to pinpoint my exact position effortlessly.

I hated my inability to block my emotions from him as he began his descent. He was magnificent, the rays of the sun hitting every defined muscle of his body at just the right angle as he glided into a graceful landing a few meters in front of me. All worries about him being amused by how infatuated I was with him faded the moment our gazes met. The tender and possessive glimmer in his silver eyes had my stomach fluttering and my knees wobbling.

Despite that, I didn't know how to greet him. Every cell of my body screamed for me to throw myself into his embrace. But there were dozens—maybe even a couple hundred—other students surrounding us in clusters of varying sizes scattered around the lawn and the large path leading to the main entrance.

As he closed the distance between us, Kayog extended a hand towards me. My stomach did a somersault as I immediately placed mine in his. He drew me to him, and I went willingly, melting against his chest. He held me with a possessiveness that had me tingling all over. I slipped my arms around his waist and gently scraped the down feathers at the base of his wings. He shivered against me, and I barely repressed the urge to coo in victory. It was a sensitive spot, but also one that you only touched on someone you claimed as yours.

He did say he was mine yesterday.

And this public display from him made it official. He leaned down and rubbed his beak against mine. To my surprise, instead of pulling away, he brushed the side of his beak alongside my cheek, then down my neck, then nipped at the crook. It felt as if lightning had struck the base of my spine, and my knees nearly buckled. I gasped, and my fingers dug slightly into his back. His smug chuckle should have pissed me off, but it just got me throbbing something fierce. He rubbed his face in my neck, inhaled my scent, and only then did he release me.

Although he kept his eyes locked with mine as he caressed my cheek, he suddenly addressed my friend.

"Stop gaping, Tala. Or you just might swallow a bug."

I barked a laugh, immediately repressed.

"Kayog!" I exclaimed with a disapproving look.

"What?" he asked with the least sincere air of innocence. "I'm merely trying to be helpful."

"Oh, my God, Lin! Leave him be! He actually knows my name!" Tala exclaimed, clinging to Mares as if her legs could barely hold her while she fanned herself in a dramatic fashion with her hand.

I facepalmed while Kayog burst out laughing.

"Of course I do. I know the people my dove loves," he said in an amused tone before turning his attention to her mate. "Hello, Mares."

To my dismay, the Edocit pressed his palm to his chest as if he feared getting a heart attack, while an excessively shocked expression descended over his features in a performance that would put even Tala to shame.

"By the Gods! He knows my name, too! I'm so going to strut all over campus, flicking my vines like no one's business."

"You guys are hopeless," I said in a discouraged tone between two chuckles.

Still, I truly loved that he knew their names. I hadn't spoken to him about them. With his celebrity status on campus, he had to know this acknowledgment would touch them. I loved that he would show this consideration to the people dear to me.

"Well now that we're done fawning all over you, can we lure you into joining us on a trip to the Xilqen Canyon? We've been dying to take the tour and ride the flying mounts," Mares said.

Kayog scrunched his face.

"Flying mounts? No offense, but I much rather use my own wings."

I snorted and made a mocking face at Mares. "Told you!"

"But I would be happy to fly alongside their mounts if you want to go," Kayog said to me.

"Really?" I asked, taken aback. "You would be comfortable going?"

The gratitude with which he smiled did funny things to me.

"Yes, my dove," he replied in a reassuring fashion. "The Xilqen Canyon is actually very quiet and isolated. Plus it's incredibly beautiful. In fact, I can show you a secret lair that will blow your minds as to the wonders of this world and of its original inhabitants."

"Oh, you've got yourself a deal!" I said, my voice bubbling with excitement.

"Can you show us as well?" Mares asked in a hopeful voice.

Kayog gave him a haughty look that had me snorting again. "I don't know. Your wingless butts should probably stick to the trail."

"Hey! That's not nice, you party pooper!" Tala said. "You know you want to take us. Otherwise, we're going to beat your girl's ears down about how unloved and discarded we felt."

Kayog laughed. "Wow, your shamelessness commands respect. Fine, you win. I cannot have my mate's best friends bullying her because of me."

"Good boy!" Tala said smugly.

"I aim to please," Kayog replied with a flourishing bow.

Maker, how I loved seeing this relaxed and lighthearted side of him. Considering how many people were nearby—and failing miserably at not spying on us—I feared he would be quite uncomfortable.

"You know, you're way cooler than I thought you would be," Mares said pensively.

Kayog's brow shot up, his curiosity echoing mine.

"Is that so?" he asked.

Mares nodded and gave him a sheepish smile. "I expected you to be a little stuck up and slightly cold, not to say borderline haughty."

Kayog snorted. "Appearances are often deceiving, my friend."

"I know," the Edocit conceded. "It's just that you're just so... aloof and distant that I didn't expect this type of laidback humor from you. But it pleases me a great deal. As you can see, Tala and I are two goofs. And I need to stop letting her ruin me with her weird human expressions."

We laughed as Tala playfully elbowed him.

"Most people have a very inaccurate perception of who I truly am," Kayog said in a more serious fashion. "It is hard for me to be playful around people with unpleasant auras or who love to wallow in negative emotions. But both of yours are awesome."

Both Tala and Mares stiffened in surprise, although they also felt deeply touched by the compliment.

"Really?" Tala asked.

"Mmhmm. The most beautiful emotion in the world is true love. The song of two soulmates reunited is enthralling. It's like a flood of divine light shining down on you. You want to wrap yourself in it," Kayog said.

Mares frowned, his confusion reflecting the one Tala felt.

"A song?" Mares repeated.

Kayog nodded. "Every soul has a song, a unique melody. The songs of two soulmates vibrate in perfect harmony, like yours. It's absolutely beautiful and makes it extremely pleasant for me to bask in your aura."

"Are you saying they are soulmates?" I asked, happiness filling my heart.

"Yes, they are," Kayog replied with conviction.

"Really?" Tala asked in a hesitant voice.

"Yes, undoubtedly. Congratulations to both of you for finding each other," my mate said with a smile.

Mares and Tala exchange an uncertain look before looking at Kayog and me in turn, their emotions loudly broadcasting their confusion.

"Is that a joke, or…?" Mares asked.

"I never joke about that," Kayog replied in a tone that made it clear he wasn't playing. "You two absolutely are soulmates. But you've been aware of it for a while."

My friends exchanged another look, but this time, love laced with a hint of shyness dominated. They exchanged a kiss before glancing back at Kayog.

"So, what you're saying is that you're able to see when two random people are soulmates?" Mares insisted.

"Essentially, yes," Kayog said with a shrug.

"Damn, my friend. If you can 100% match people with their soulmates, you should start some kind of mating agency. People throughout the galaxy are fed up with crappy dating apps and websites."

We all burst out laughing.

"Kayog, the matchmaker," my mate said with a disbelieving expression. "And you say I'm the one with a sense of humor?"

Mares shrugged. "I think it would be a blast to be able to provide people with their happily ever after. That would be a lot better than the countless crappy jobs out there that no one wants."

"True. But I believe I'll pass. Interesting suggestion, though," Kayog said teasingly.

"I aim to please," Mares retorted, imitating the flourishing bow Kayog had performed when he spoke those same words earlier.

We laughed.

"Come on, you overpowered, silly aliens. Let's get going. I have a cool winged mount to ride!" Tala said.

"Lead the way, my love," Mares replied.

We hopped into Mares' personal shuttle to complete the thirty-minute journey to Xilqen Canyon. It was a majestic, protected land where the native species of Mazeria thrived for centuries before their extinction. Guided tours were offered riding a winged mount that followed a specific trail through the large territory that the Syllens had occupied.

Tala compared it to the Grand Canyon on Earth, but with the stony ridges clustered far closer together with narrower passages in between. Furthermore, Xilqen Canyon didn't have the burnished red and ochre color of her homeworld. Instead, the ridges all boasted grayish stones covered in moss or luxurious vines and other greenery.

We went to purchase our tickets, Tala and Mares each picking the mount they would ride. The Nordjarimm were magnificent creatures, half birds, half mammals. The four-legged mounts had cleft hooves on their back legs, and reptilian talons on their front paws. According to Tala, their bird heads looked like a mix of a puffin and a golden pheasant, both creatures from her homeworld. The golden tuft of hair on top of their heads and the long beard-like strings dangling from each side of their beaks gave them a wise and elder look. A soft brown fur covered their bodies with two majestic, feathered wings. Although they were pacific creatures, their rumps extended into a set of very long twin tails. They were tipped with a leaf-shaped, reddish appendage with ridged darts, which could stab or electrocute any predator that threatened them.

The human manning the rental counter gave us each a set of virtual guides. The tear-shaped, small magnetic devices attached to our temples with a simple pressure. Once we took flight, they would activate holographic displays, with personal audio explaining what we were seeing, including virtual overlays projected directly on the environment to show us a recreation of the indigenous people in their daily lives or during historical events. As they were individual guides, they wouldn't impede or overlap with what the others were seeing.

"Are you going to be okay using these?" I asked Kayog, worried as he pressed the first pod to his right temple.

He smiled reassuringly. "Yes, my dove. These won't harm me. They operate on a different frequency and target a different section of my brain."

"Okay, good," I said with relief.

He rubbed his beak against mine in a gentle kiss. Even though I couldn't read his emotions, it was obvious that he loved that his welfare mattered to me.

After helping his mate onto the saddle and making sure the security mechanisms were in place to prevent any guest falling off their mount mid-flight, Mares hopped onto his own mount and patiently waited for the clerk to do his own security check. It melted my heart to see how protective and attentive Mares always was where Tala was concerned.

We took flight and accompanied our friends along the preset trail the Nordjarimms were trained to follow. A tall hill hid the view of the canyon behind it. But as soon as we flew over it, the beautiful land beyond took my breath away. Although I had seen images of it, nothing could have prepared me for the magnificence sprawled before us.

Gigantic statues in the effigy of the long-lost Syllens—a dryad species—had been carved directly into the rock faces of the canyon. They were easily twenty meters high, their width varying based on the pose or hair of the statue. I now understood where Acadia had taken its inspiration for the design of the campus, with the corners of the buildings vaguely shaped like Syllen faces.

Their unique features mesmerized me. Centuries ago, the advanced Sikarians—a merfolk species—had colonized Mazeria. Although they had built their own cities a great distance away from the primitive natives, crossbreeding eventually occurred. The merfolk traits could now be seen on their faces, with the finned ears, gills in their necks, and smattering of scales on their foreheads.

The powerful emotions emanating from Mares had my skin erupting in goosebumps. In a way, the Syllens would be deemed distant cousins of the Edocits, even though they had evolved in a different direction.

The virtual guide went into great details as to how the primitive species achieved such phenomenal architectural feats. Although Sikarians had joined their tribes, they always observed many rules of the Prime Directive during their colonization era by not introducing their more advanced technology to their new people. That didn't prevent them from achieving great heights.

That said, unlike the Sikarians, the Syllens didn't turn their legs into tails when they went into the water. They always kept their legs, but had webbed feet and hands, as well as a long, fanned tail.

The icing on top? Like Mares, they also possessed *veris*.

Intricate pathways circled around the wide chasm between the rocky elevations of the canyon. The guide expressed that they sadly didn't have any writings or other records of the lost species to explain why they built their villages in the canyon and in such heights when they were hybrid dryads and merfolks. Them settling into a forest near a large body of water would have made more sense.

Still, it fascinated me to see how they integrated their natural environment with the sculptures. My favorite one had to be that giant face with its mouth open from whence a waterfall cascaded down into its open hands, creating two different pools and plateaus in which people could swim.

Sadly, as was too often the case with lost civilizations, the meddling of off-worlders totally derailed the future they'd been building. The visitors attempted to settle here. However, unlike the Sikarians, they came here with hostile intent, the main one being to convert the locals to their faith. Naturally, the Syllens resisted. In retaliation, the settlers destroyed their temples to coerce them into converting. And massive bloodshed ensued.

The settlers who didn't get massacred fled the planet. But the damage was already done. The local population got sick and slowly died off. History doesn't know for certain what was the source of the sickness that wiped out the local population. Some speculate that the settlers brought some sort of virus that the Syllens weren't able to fight back. Others believed that, out of spite, the settlers poisoned the land, their food reserves, or the water. We would likely never know.

However, the deeper we got into the canyon, the stronger I could feel something strange, as if the entire area was alive. It made no sense as only stones and vegetation remained. And yet, there was an undeniable flow of emotions, almost like a discreet sigh in the background.

I cast a concerned look towards Kayog who was gliding next to me, his broad wings spread wide as he rode the air currents. With his heightened sensitivity, I feared that the inexplicable emotions I perceived might be a painful cacophony for him. But he had a peaceful, almost dreamy expression on his face. Sensing my worry, he turned his head towards me and gave me such a joyous smile that all the tension I felt faded away. He closed the distance between us and reached for my hand.

With our wingspan, it required us to be more careful in how we flew to avoid crashing into each other. But with decades of experience flying, we instantly adjusted to each other. The gentle way he squeezed my hand before caressing its back with his thumb melted me from the inside out.

That male truly cared about me.

In that instant, thoughts of our nuptial flight flashed through my mind. It was much too early to think in those terms. But I didn't doubt that day would come.

Too soon, the tour came to an end in a large valley next to a huge body of water. Various breeds of Syllens were holding an annual fair where neighboring tribes would visit and celebrate together. Watching them dance and sing with the virtual overlay enthralled me. Obviously, these were only speculations derived from all the artifacts the archaeologist and historians found. But it still gave a fascinating glimpse into the amazing people they had been.

The virtual guide informed us that the Syllen segment of the tour was done. We would return to the visitors center through a slightly different path. It would cover more general topics about the flora and fauna of Mazeria. Kayog released my hand and hastened in front of our friends. He gestured for all of us to follow him instead, prompting Tala and Mares to take the reins to redirect their mounts away from their preset path.

At first, I feared that they would refuse the command. Technically, riders had some control over their mounts, especially if they wanted to revisit a segment of the tour or wanted to get a little closer to the structures. They could also land in various safe areas, so long as they didn't attempt to leave the Xilqen Canyon with their Nordjarimm or seek to enter areas that were clearly marked as forbidden.

To our collective surprise, Kayog led us back to the waterfall statue with open hands. He flew directly towards the lower hand and then vanished behind the cascading water. I raced after him, and to my shock, the entrance of what seemed to be a temple revealed itself behind the curtain of water.

The beautiful doorway had to have been carved, and yet the intricate, swirling patterns felt extremely organic. It was as if huge wooden vines, the size of thick tree branches, had emerged from the ground and hugged the gray stones in a deliberate but artistic fashion. Lush leaves sprouted over them, and small green vines dangled in some places. However, it was the delicate flowers with glowing pistils adorning them that took my breath away. To my chagrin, the virtual guide had gone silent, depriving us of additional information about this secret place.

I landed and walked up to Kayog, who had stopped a few meters in. The air of peace on his face reflected the one I felt. This place was sacred and radiated with the divine. Tala and Mares landed moments later, displaying an air of pure awe as they dismounted their Nordjarimm. The creatures refused to follow them inside when they both tugged on their mounts' reins.

I didn't perceive any fear from the creatures, only the firm resolve of pets who had properly been trained not to do certain things.

"It's okay," Kayog said in a reassuring tone. "The Nord-jarimms are not allowed to enter the temple. But they will patiently wait for us to come back out."

"Are *we* allowed to enter?" Tala asked in a slightly wary tone, echoing the thought Mares and I clearly shared.

Kayog smiled. "Access is not forbidden to visitors, but it is not advertised as they prefer to limit who enters it. In a moment, you will understand why. But just so you know, there are numerous protective mechanisms hidden in plain sight. Should anyone attempt to desecrate this place, they will be paralyzed, and the guards will be alerted."

"Okay, I'm glad to hear it," Mares said, relief and excitement audible in his voice. "This is mesmerizing. I can almost feel this place talking to me."

"It's not surprising," Kayog said with a smile. "The Syllens share many similarities with your species. It is heavily specu-lated that you have a common ancestry, although it is uncertain how that came to be. Come, you will want to see this."

The emotions emanating from Mares grew steadily as we walked through the wide corridor towards what appeared to be a massive cave. A shallow recess in the middle of the corridor—maybe two feet wide, and one foot deep—ran its entire length, allowing water to pour into the cave.

My jaw dropped as we reached the end of the corridor. A humongous chamber greeted us. The statue of a Syllen female dominated the room. She'd wrapped her arms around the shoul-ders of the two children flanking her—a male and a female—who were looking up at her lovingly. But where their faces expressed trust and serenity, hers sent a cold shiver running down my spine. It wasn't her expression, but the fact that a red liquid resembling blood poured out of her eyes in steady streams that trickled into the pond occupying the center of the cave.

All around, countless giant trees intertwined their branches into a continuous circle, almost like a Celtic knot. They didn't have any leaves, just a few vines interwoven in their thick branches, like the ones adorning the entrance of the cave. However, it was the giant knots all over their trunks that took my breath away. A golden dome, seemingly made of amber, covered the large opening of the knots. And within, people in fetal positions appeared to be sleeping.

Mummified Syllens...

"Ancestors," Mares breathed out as he advanced almost in a trance towards the trees.

Horror hadn't prompted that reaction, but pure marvel.

"Is this blood?" I asked hesitantly while staring at the red water gushing out of the statue's eyes.

"No," Tala said with a conviction that took me aback. "At least, I highly doubt it. There's no coagulation at the edges of the pond, and there isn't that distinctive smell of blood. I believe it's the same phenomenon that occurs on Earth at Blood Falls. It's a waterfall in Taylor Glacier in Antarctica. The underground water trapped beneath it is excessively saturated with iron. As soon as it comes out, the iron instantly rusts upon contact with air, which gives it that blood-like red color."

"You are correct, Tala," Kayog said approvingly. "Based on recovered texts, a Syllen prophecy claims that the day Etreya stops crying blood, the Syllens will be reborn."

"I'm assuming that statue is Etreya?" Tala asked.

Kayog nodded. "She's the Great Mother, the goddess of land, home, family, fertility, and love. According to the archeologists, that legend might actually be true."

"What?!" Tala exclaimed.

"Recent studies of the underground streams indicated that the iron levels have been steadily decreasing," Kayog explained, his voice bubbling with excitement. "They believe that in thirty to forty years from now, they will have diminished enough for clear water to stream down her face instead."

"But how will they be reborn?" Tala asked.

Her tone clearly expressed that she was struggling to accept what she presumed his answer would be. The troubled glance she cast towards the trees seemed to confirm it.

"These Syllens will rise again," Mares whispered in Kayog's stead before carefully placing his palm against the trunk of one of the trees, a few centimeters from one of the knots inside which a mummified Syllen lay.

His *veris* extruded and sank between the grooves of the bark, just like he had done with the tree outside the campus. In seconds, an air of pure bliss descended over his handsome face. His lips parted and slightly quivered, as if he couldn't decide if he wanted to smile or cry. The Edocit's eyes glistened and then tears began to trickle down his face.

"Mares, are you okay?" Tala asked, taking a nervous step towards her mate.

"Yes, Tala. He's fine," I said in a reassuring tone.

While I couldn't see or feel whatever Mares was currently experiencing, his emotions shouted loudly a deep joy and infinite love.

"Mother…" Mares whispered at last in a quivering voice.

I gasped as countless blue flowers with glowing pistils suddenly bloomed along the vines adorning the intertwined branches of the trees. It was like a domino effect, starting from the tree Mares was touching and spreading to all the other ones. It almost gave the impression that a starry night had appeared inside the dimly lit cave.

In response, the flowers in Mares' own hair bloomed. It was an instinctive reaction that Edocits had no control over, and which expressed extreme happiness.

"They're alive. All these Syllens are alive… just dormant,"

Mares said with wonder. "These trees are almost like our mother trees. But instead of merely sheltering the Syllens during their gestation like ours do, they are preserving their children until the time of their rebirth comes."

"Really?" Tala asked in a hushed tone, flabbergasted. "Didn't their species vanish more than two hundred years ago."

Kayog nodded. "Correct. But they have been in this semi-stasis state ever since. They appeared mummified simply because they shed all the water from their bodies. This halts their metabolism and makes them extremely resistant to dehydration, radiation, and major temperature variations until their environment is safe again. It is a deep state of hibernation similar to tardigrades on Earth."

"Wow, that is amazing!" she said with awe.

"It is," I concurred. "During our entire flight, I could feel their presence but couldn't figure out who was emitting those soft emotions. Never in a million years would I have expected this."

"You can feel the dormant Syllens?!" Tala exclaimed, stunned.

"Yes," I replied, while Kayog nodded.

"Yes," Mares said, wistfully. "They dream while the Mothers watch over them."

"You guys seriously suck with all your cool powers," Tala said with envy as she gazed upon the trees with wonder.

Mares chuckled. "Don't be sad, my love. Come, let me introduce you to Mother," he said, extending a hand towards her.

Although taken aback by his request, she went to him willingly. He took her right hand and pressed it against the trunk of the tree. Tala licked her lips nervously and cast an uncertain look at her mate. He gave her a gentle smile.

"You cannot feel her right now, but she can feel you. She loves you a lot and made me promise that once you and I are mated, I will bring you back so that you can properly be introduced. You will have your own *veris* then."

"I would like that very much," Tala said in a voice choked with emotion before glancing around the room with a frown. "This temple must be protected at all costs. As grateful as I am that you brought us here, no one should be able to enter this sacred place. While we may have good intentions, the same could not be said of any other random person."

"I agree," I said, casting a questioning look at Kayog.

"The Syllens are safe," he said in a reassuring tone. "Beyond the security systems I mentioned before, these trees are not helpless. Should anyone with evil intentions try anything, the trees can extrude some vicious spikes that will impale the fools who dared try anything. These pretty flowers can also release deadly spores that will wreck you in seconds and even kill you if exposed for more than a minute."

"Don't mess with a mother," Tala said, impressed, caressing the tree's bark one last time before dropping her hand.

Kayog nodded. "However, they're not as fully protected as I would like. I hate that this great nation was destroyed by off-worlders. And now, another greedy group wants to make sure they don't come back."

"What?!" I exclaimed, my shock reflected on the faces of my friends. "What do you mean?"

"There is a conference happening in a few days in the capital city's Convention Center," Kayog explained.

"A conference about what?" Mares asked, tension and preemptive anger seeping into his voice.

"About construction and touristic development projects in the canyon," Kayog replied with disgust and anger. "The organizer is a man named Connor Harmond. He represents multiple real estate development conglomerates. For years now, they've been trying to get construction permits and purchase some of the land in and around the canyon by claiming that the Syllens have been dead long enough."

"Clearly they aren't dead!" Mares exclaimed with outrage.

"The conglomerate argues that we are confusing the trees being alive as proof of life of the desiccated corpses they hold. They claim that invaluable resources are going to waste over wild flights of fancy and old wives' tales," my mate said with contempt.

"What resources are they after?" Tala asked, her voice hard.

"The area is rich in rare minerals," Kayog explained. "The lands are fertile and the iron concentration in the phreatic bed allows unique crops to grow. For years, the conglomerate has been trying to get the protective laws repealed. Advocates for the Syllens are pushing for Prime Directive laws to be instated for the region."

"How could that possibly happen?" I asked with a frown. "As much as I would love it, Mazeria has been colonized by humans for more than a hundred years."

"Yes but we're not asking for the expulsion of the humans," Kayog said with an indulgent smile. "We simply need to return this region and all connected lands back to its people and grant them the Prime Directive protection until they reawaken."

I clicked my beak pensively and slowly nodded. "If the estimates are accurate, thirty to forty years is more than enough time to prepare for their return and for the companies who built their businesses in the area to slowly move out. The museum and visitor center can recreate this whole experience via holodeck. It won't be difficult to scan and reproduce the entire region to a high level of realism."

"Exactly!" Kayog said with fervor. "Visiting this place while I was finishing my previous master's incentivized me to pursue my current degree. We need stronger Prime Directive enforcement to protect worlds and species such as this one. They deserve a chance to thrive and reach their full potential without being plundered by greedy corporations."

I smiled, thrilled to finally understand what was driving him. His talks about potentially going for a desk job for the UPO writing laws about the Prime Directive now fully made sense.

"Wow!" Tala said. "You're truly passionate about this."

"I definitely am," Kayog said firmly before taking on a sheepish expression. "That said, as much as I want to keep advanced species like ours from interfering with the daily lives and evolution of primitive species like this one, I'd give anything to meet them and get to know them. I'll have to be content with helping them thrive from the shadows."

"And that is a great reward in and of itself," Mares said in a soft voice. "Thank you for allowing us to share this incredible experience. Should you ever need my help with this project or anything else, never hesitate. This is the greatest gift you could have ever given me."

"You ladies are witnesses!" Kayog said teasingly. "Remember you offered when I will shamelessly come collecting."

Mares snorted and mumbled something about his wretched mouth always getting him into trouble. After a last farewell to the mother trees and the dormant Syllens, we exited the secret chamber, the almost divine peace of the temple still wrapped around us as we completed the tour on our way back to the visitors center.

CHAPTER 10
KAYOG

The past week turned out to be the happiest time I could recall in my entire life. I couldn't get enough of my mate, of her soothing presence, luminous smile, and the enthralling song of her soul. I never imagined I could be in such perfect harmony with someone. She didn't need lengthy explanations to get me. Our views on the world and the goals we wanted to achieve couldn't have been more aligned, even though we wanted to tackle them from slightly different angles.

Being with her just made me happy.

But her gift had not ended there. My Linsea had also brought Mares and Tala into my life. After nearly three decades spent mostly in isolation, I thought I had come to terms with being by myself. These past few days showed me how painfully lonely I had actually been. They were beautiful souls who systematically put a smile on your face. Their playfulness awakened the one that had been lurking deep inside me, just waiting for a chance to express itself. I loved that side of myself that never truly had a chance to fly free.

Seeing my dove also form a close bond with my chosen sister Isobel filled my heart to bursting. The priestess had been the only person I truly could have called a friend and who helped keep me grounded in my isolation. However, her clerical vocation made it difficult for us to spend much time together as she was often on pilgrimages, attending spiritual retreats, or away on study within isolated religious communities or cults.

I couldn't recall ever having people over at my place for a game night, least of all as a double date. And yet, here we were, playing a strategic board game in teams. Without going into extensive details, I had given them a slight overview of my condition which kept me from going to crowded places. The empathy and respect with which they received that information moved me to my core. It felt good being able to be honest and just be myself.

It also made me question if maybe, in my fear of being seen as a freak and an abomination, I hadn't been the architect of my own sorrow by keeping everything so heavily guarded. At the same time, my self-preservation instincts continued to believe that it had been the wisest course of action.

Anyway, there was a reason we weren't friends with just everyone and anyone. We gravitated towards people who shared our energy, but also whose auras made us feel good. Toxic and negative people naturally repelled others. While most species often couldn't say specifically why they didn't like hanging out with a specific person, empathic species perceived more precisely that unpleasant energy.

Mares and Tala radiated the type of emotions I wanted to wrap myself in. The couple and my mate attending my concert again last night had made the entire experience far more enjoyable. Our new relationship created a bond. And their affection towards me sent heightened levels of positive energy as I performed. In turn, this further drowned any negative waves that came at me.

After we concluded the last round—which my mate and I won by the skin of our teeth—I felt genuinely sad to see our friends leave. At the same time, I could never complain about private moments with my soulmate.

While I put away the game, Linsea brought a flat box with a handle to the living area. She had placed it in the closet when she arrived earlier. A sense of unease settled in the pit of my stomach. I knew exactly what it contained.

She gave me a sympathetic smile and gestured for me to sit on the couch. I complied, and she sat in my lap facing me, the box lying on the cushion next to us.

"Do you trust me?" she asked softly.

"Of course, my love," I said in a self-evident voice. "It's *them* who worry me."

"Then rest assured that I will only give anything concerning you to trustworthy people," she said in the same soothing voice.

"I'm sorry. This whole thing just has me really nervous," I said sheepishly.

"There's no need for you to apologize. I couldn't even begin to imagine how difficult this must be for you. I'm just grateful that you are agreeing to it, despite your valid reservations."

"Only for you, my dove."

Linsea rubbed her beak against mine in a soft kiss, then leaned to the side to remove a silver, hollow disc from the box. She held it over my head and paused, making eye contact with me to get my final assent. I smiled—although a bit stiffly—and nodded for her to proceed. She smiled in return and activated the device before releasing it.

It hovered with a soft hum and began to glow. The ring parted into two crescents, one on each side of my face, as they slowly glided down, scanning my head all the way to my clavicles before hovering back up for a second pass. I forced myself to remain as still as possible and to clear my head to avoid extreme emotions messing with some of the data. As soon as the two halves fused together again, my mate took the scanning device and tapped a few instructions on its small interface.

I tried to silence the unease wanting to rear its head knowing that she was likely transferring the data to her grandmother or medical contact.

"See? Quick and painless," Linsea said in that overly sweet way doctors addressed fussy young children unhappy about getting their vaccination shots.

I scrunched my face at her, which made her chuckle. However, she quickly sobered and caressed my head with a very serious expression on her stunning face.

"Your trust in this means more to me than you'll ever know. I like you a lot, Kayog. And I truly mean *a lot*. Whatever lies ahead for us—or with these results—I will never let anyone hurt you under my watch. Do not be fooled by my apparent sweet disposition. I have talons and have no qualms using them on anyone who crosses me or those I love."

My chest warmed with the love that had been steadily growing in my heart for my soulmate. I wanted to say something deep and meaningful, but my stupid mouth decided to take the lead.

"Then I better make sure you keep watching over me forever," I said teasingly.

She snorted. "You're rather easy on the eyes, so you might not have too much of a hard time convincing me to do so. Anyway, a certain birdie told me that we were soulmates. Therefore, any way you cut it, we're stuck with each other."

"We are," I said forcefully. "And on that front, that birdie is never wrong."

She smiled, her fingers fiddling with the down feathers on my head and temples in a way that made me want to coo.

"How's your head?" Linsea asked with genuine concern.

I shrugged in a nonchalant fashion. "Same old. But being with you helps tremendously."

She frowned, far from mollified. "Are you sure you want to go to that conference tomorrow night?"

That question took me aback. "Yes. You know how passionate I am about protecting the Syllens and their lands. The conference will not be broadcast anywhere, so the only way to get an accurate account of what will happen requires me to be physically present."

She absentmindedly clacked her beak in a way that equated with humans pinching their lips when they weren't pleased with something.

"It's just that you had a concert last night, spent the evening with the three of us tonight, and then that massive conference tomorrow feels like a lot for you, back-to-back," Linsea said carefully.

I tightened my hold around her waist, drawing her a little closer against my body. Fuck, it felt amazing to have someone as wonderful as she was genuinely caring about my welfare.

"The concert and spending the evening with all of you were fine. I actually thrive in the positive energy from the fans during a performance. And I left immediately after, before I could get distraught by their other emotions. And being with the three of you is no hardship at all, quite the opposite. I wish you could hear and feel how amazing it is to be surrounded by people who radiate pure love. You and your friends not only bring me peace, in many ways, you're even healing me."

"You know, if you're trying to make me like you, you're doing a mighty fine job of it," Linsea said in a taunting tone to hide how touched she was by my words—not that she could fool me.

"No, my dove. I'm not trying to make you *like* me. I want you to be madly in love with me."

"If you keep this up, it could very well happen," she deadpanned.

"Not *could*, but *will*," I countered with a hint of arrogance.

She chuckled and shook her head at me. "Challenge

accepted. But that doesn't make me any less worried about you for tomorrow."

Her words touched me in the most wondrous way. "I don't intend to linger very long over there. I just want to get a sense of where things are headed, and what his current plans are. And then I will leave early."

Linsea slowly nodded as she weighed my words. "Do you want me to come with you?"

My heart leapt, and I barely fought the urge to shout a resounding yes.

"Only if you want to," I said carefully.

She gave me an unimpressed look. "That's not the question I asked. Do you want me to come with you?"

I made a face at her. "You shouldn't even have to ask that question. I *always* want you by my side. So, if you truly want to go—or at least don't mind tagging along—then yes, I would absolutely love having you there with me."

"For some weird reason, it seems that I, too, like being with you," she said with a long-suffering sigh that made me want to spank her.

"Then we have a deal," I said with a shameless grin.

"Then we have a deal," she echoed, her eyes locking with mine.

In that instant, something shifted. I couldn't say what prompted it. One moment, we were talking. Next, we were kissing. And a volcano suddenly erupted between us.

In the past week, we had indulged in some increasingly heavy petting, reining ourselves in right before our passion flared to overwhelming levels. Today, our self-imposed shackles collapsed, and we gave in to the desire that had steadily been building between us.

Linsea's hands glided down my sides with a possessiveness that sent a delicious shiver down my spine. My palms settled on her rump and caressed its generous curves. The soft feathers of her tail fluttered, grazing the back of my hands as if to express their approval.

We deepened the kiss, our tongues mingling in a sensual dance that set my loins ablaze. Linsea's arousal was the biggest turn on imaginable. It all but screamed at me to proceed, to have my wicked way with her, and to do to her all the things I secretly fantasized about. She pressed her chest against mine, the heat of her body seeping into me.

I broke the kiss and gently tilted her back, my left hand holding her nape for support, while the other still firmly grabbed her behind. I greedily feasted my eyes with her beauty, and my mouth watered when I stared at her pelvic area resting against mine. Her stomach quivered, and she involuntarily blasted me with another wave of lust that echoed directly into my groin. I wished I could share with her the emotions she stirred within me. But nothing would ruin this moment.

My eyes flicked back to hers. No words were needed. With a smile laced with sexual tension, Linsea gave me her blessing. Without a word, I stood up, still holding her in front of me. My female wrapped her legs around my waist as I carried her to my bedroom, our gazes still locked.

She spread her wings wide as I carefully laid her down on the mattress. I didn't immediately join her and took a moment instead to admire her beauty. The dark blue blanket covering the bed acted as the perfect canvas for the masterpiece that was my female.

I knelt on the bed and gently grazed the tip of my beak over the tiny scales of her feet right before they gave way to the soft feathers of her calf. Linsea shivered, and her talons twitched as I pursued a path upward, my right hand caressing her other leg in the process.

Fuck, she was so incredibly soft!

I rubbed my face against her pelvis, my fingers weaving into the delicate down feathers along her inner thighs. A violent shiver coursed through her as I partially extruded my claws to gently scrape at the sensitive skin beneath them.

A smug chuckle escaped me. It had been involuntary, partially fueled by a hint of relief. From the moment things started to evolve towards something more serious between us, I worried about how our first time together would be—assuming we got that far. Due to my condition, I'd never pursued a relationship with anyone and therefore had never been intimate with a female. While I tried to reassure myself that things would naturally fall into place with my soulmate, I couldn't silence the pesky little voice nagging me about all the ways I would fail.

But I didn't account for my empathic abilities.

Initially, I tried to analyze her responses as I explored the perfection that she was, only to realize I was overthinking it. My mate was telling me what she wanted and needed, I only had to listen... and then insert my own little flavor to it.

I could feel her aching for my hand to venture towards her forbidden treasure. And fuck, did I also want to. But I continued to tease her, my fingers roaming around her pelvic area as I continued to fluff the feathers of her abdomen and chest with my beak and also peppered careful pecks along the way.

Linsea whispered my name, the needy sound sending blood rushing to my groin. My cock strained painfully against my protective pouch, begging me to extrude. I silenced it and focused instead on the wondrous feel of her hands caressing my head and sliding down to my shoulders. I nipped at the crook of her neck, close to her nape, in that spot that always drew a strong reaction from her. Right on cue, she shivered and released the sexiest moan.

I lifted my head to look at her. Fuck, she was beautiful, her beak slightly parted, her blue eyes darkened with desire as she locked eyes with me. Holding her gaze unwaveringly, I finally slipped the hand teasing her pelvic area between her thighs.

Linsea's breath hitched. I rubbed my palms over her sex, still hidden from view.

"Open for your mate," I whispered, my voice low but commanding.

Another shiver coursed through my female. She wasn't submissive, and that order cranked her arousal up a notch. For the tiniest split of a second, I believed she considered challenging me, if only to see how I would react. But her need to be touched outweighed her desire to test me. In the future, I didn't doubt for one second that we would spar in the sexiest exchanges of power.

Her protective flap parted, revealing the already glistening seam. The intoxicating scent of her musk wafted to me, making my cock throb with impatience. I wanted her heat wrapped around my length, squeezing it from all sides as I plowed into her, over and over again. But that, too, I silenced. I would see my female fall apart for me before I sated my rabid hunger.

Linsea inhaled sharply when I sank a finger inside her, and then a second. I zeroed in on the ridges that lined her inner walls like rings. Each one acted like a G-spot in Temern females and were impossible to miss, giving them intense pleasure both while their partners went in or out. A strangled cry escaped my female when I gently rubbed the first two rings that I could reach. She lifted her pelvis, as if to help me penetrate her deeper. I started moving my fingers inside her, gradually accelerating the movement.

Soon, the sound of her moans filled my ears as she gyrated in counterpoint to my movements, chasing after the climax looming on the horizon. I reclaimed her mouth, swallowing the sound of her pleasure while also letting it infuse every cell of my body through my empathic abilities. Fuck, I could reach my own climax by just feeding off her pleasure. Linsea raked her nails down my back before sinking them almost savagely in the highly erogenous spot at the base of my wings.

I didn't believe she'd planned on doing it with such force. As she knew how it turned me on when she did that, Linsea had likely only meant to reciprocate the pleasure I was giving her. But her orgasm slammed into her at that very moment.

We both cried out at the same time. Ecstasy swept her away, while her claws on my back hit me with the most insane mix of pleasure-pain that had my cock nearly punching through my protective pouch as it extruded with a will of its own. My loins were ablaze, and my stomach contracted spasmodically as my seed raged with the need to erupt.

I wrapped my hand around the base of my shaft, squeezing it brutally to stem the flow before it could rush out. My face buried in my female's neck, I nipped at her with soft kisses, while my fingers continued to make love to her. Focusing on her blissful state and on keeping her flying high helped me regain some of my frayed control.

As Linsea started settling back down, I resumed my exploration of her, filing away each of her sensitive areas like nipping the crook of her right elbow, gently clawing the skin right at the base of her spine where her tail began, and licking her navel, to name a few.

When my face journeyed back to her nether region, Linsea tensed with the strangest mix of anticipation and disapproval. It baffled me for a moment, before I realized she was displeased that I was once more focusing on her pleasure instead of allowing her to take care of me. As she couldn't feel my emotions, she couldn't know how much tending to her was also keeping me flying high. And truth be told, I was still too greedy in wanting to discover everything about her.

Before she could protest or deny me the treat that had my mouth fiercely watering, I dove between her legs like a starving male. After one long lick of her slit, I sank my tongue into her. My mate cried out, and her hands latched onto my head with something akin to despair.

Gotcha!

Her voluptuous moans poured out in a steady flow as I devoured her. I would never tire of her tart taste and of the wondrous sensation of her inner ridges rubbing against my tongue as I dipped it in and out of her. I could feel her cresting again. I sped up my ministrations, swirling my tongue around within her to increase the friction on her ridges. When my mate lifted her pelvic area as she prepared to topple over again, I reached around her rump and raked my claws on the sensitive spot at the base of her tail.

Linsea instantly fell apart. The powerful orgasm that slammed into her also hit me like a boulder. Throwing my head back, I released a loud shout as my fingers dug into the mattress. A few drops of my seed spilled out, and I ground my beak as an almost bestial growl vibrated through my chest. I felt dizzy, my body tense, my wings stiff as I battled against the climax trying to engulf me. My female's hammering me with waves upon waves of bliss made it nearly impossible.

Still half-dazed, Linsea latched onto my shoulders with both hands and drew me over her. She spread her legs wide and stared at me with a lascivious expression. Her pupils were so dilated they nearly swallowed her irises. I settled on top of her, my cock throbbing loudly in sync with my pulse. My female rested her palms on my behind, giving each cheek a tight squeeze.

I rubbed my beak against hers before kissing her deeply. The tender emotions radiating from her were wrecking me.

"Do you accept me, Linsea?" I said, my voice almost pained from repressed desire.

"Yes," she whispered in a breathy voice.

"Are you mine?" I insisted for a reason I couldn't explain.

"Yes," she breathed out again.

"My mate," I said like a prayer, full of love and devotion as I began to push myself into her.

I'd barely gone in a couple of centimeters before I had to

stop. Eyes tightly closed, my jaw clenched, I once more battled the urge to come undone. The searing heat of her inner walls pressing against my highly erogenous *ganacs* had me on the verge of spilling. Her tight sheath squeezed those sensitive bumps on the head of my cock, sending electric bolts of sheer pleasure coursing through my veins.

Considering my girth, I should have been the one easing her through the discomfort of my penetration. Instead, Linsea was the one cooing at me, caressing, and kissing me in a soothing and encouraging fashion as I struggled not to lose control. One centimeter at a time, I gradually inserted myself into the blissful haven of my female. Once fully sheathed, I nearly collapsed on top of my mate, my body trembling from the effort and over-whelming sensations setting my blood ablaze.

The smugness emanating from her pissed me off at the same time as it amused me. It was only fair that she should have me in a complete puddle after I'd already wrested two orgasms from her while denying her the possibility of reciprocating.

After what felt like a shameful eternity, I regained enough of my composure to start moving. Maker take me! Each stroke was driving me insane with bliss. As if the friction against my *ganacs* hadn't been enough, the ringed ridges lining her inner walls stroked and squeezed me with each rocking motion.

I couldn't even recall picking up the pace. One moment I was clenching my jaw not to spill my seed as I took my female with slow and careful thrusts. The next, I was pounding into her with reckless abandon.

Linsea was writhing beneath me, her hands feverishly roaming all over me as sighs of delight tumbled out of her throat. An inferno was raging inside me. I was burning from within, needing more, wanting more, even as my mind threatened to shatter. Nothing mattered anymore but the feel of my female's soft body beneath me, her tight sheath around my cock, and her tender arms wrapped around me in a possessive and passionate

148

hold. I wanted this to last forever, to lose myself in her and never return to the mortal world.

Linsea's orgasm came at her with the speed, suddenness, and devastating strength of a tidal wave. I didn't try to resist it as it also swept me away, her incommensurable pleasure crashing into me, compounding my own.

As one, we cried out. Her back arched over the bed, her wings spread even wider over the mattress, their tips stiff. I slammed myself home as I roared in ecstasy, my head thrown back, and my tail jerking up. My seed shot out of me in an almost painful flood, each spurt feeling like countless lightning bolts going off in my groin.

I felt faint, the room spinning around me, as my body instinctively resumed rocking in and out of my mate until my seed was spent. Still buried deep inside Linsea, I collapsed on top of her, tremors of bliss shaking me from head to talons. Half dazed, I rolled to the side, careful not to crush her right wing before drawing her on top of me. She was slightly trembling, her breathing labored as she slipped her arms around me, holding on as if out of fear I would vanish.

I cradled her in my arms, my body thrumming with infinite pleasure, my heart filled to bursting, and my mind enraptured in the divine song of our souls soaring in an endless crescendo. Linsea owned me... all of me. Whatever the future held for us... for me... this moment, right here, right now, made my lifetime of misery worth living.

CHAPTER 11
KAYOG

For the billionth time, I questioned the wisdom of attending the conference. I desperately wanted to be in that man's presence and hear his words to get a better sense of the threat he posed to the Syllens. I also needed to assess who his silent partners and allies were. Over the past three years, I had gotten increasingly involved in the protection of primitive worlds. In so doing, I discovered the identities of the secret puppet masters pulling the strings in the shadows by merely showing up at these types of events.

People could lie in the most convincing fashion and cover their trails perfectly. But their emotions didn't lie. More than once, my abilities allowed me to anonymously expose those wealthy manipulators. The public backlash sufficed to either force them to pull out or to cancel the more harmful aspects of the policies they were pushing or financing. I hoped to accomplish something similar in this instance.

And yet, my sense of unease about the whole thing steadily grew all day. Even now as Linsea and I were flying towards the Convention Center, my stomach knotted with apprehension. I could have stayed home instead with my female, basking in her affection, and maybe even playing naughty with her again. It shamed me that I should still be so hungry for her considering how voracious I had been throughout the night, and once more less than half an hour ago.

My mate truly owned me in every way. I still couldn't believe she was mine voluntarily despite how broken I was.

The pressure already building at the back of my head while we were still ten minutes away from the event made me seriously reconsider. The news warned of many protests happening all day in the capital city. A large, angry crowd marched through the streets and reached their rally point set at the entrance of the Convention Center thirty minutes before the meeting would begin.

I retrieved a dipramine from the secret compartment of my bracer and tossed it into my mouth. Although I still blocked Linsea from perceiving my emotions, she caught the gesture and immediately worried. I gave her a reassuring smile and plowed forward. Since we were almost there, it didn't make sense to me for us to back out now. Anyway, I only needed a couple of minutes inside to get most of the answers I sought.

As we glided over the insane number of loud and angry people, I inwardly congratulated us for deciding to fly rather than ride a shuttle. The parking would have been a non-negligible distance away and required us to try to weave our way through the throngs. Instead, we shamelessly flew right to the entrance before landing near the guards. Two of them instantly converged towards us with belligerent expressions, their hands hovering a little too close to their blasters for comfort. Granted, their weapons were set to stun, but getting shot didn't feature in my plans for the evening.

Before they could speak a word, my mate and I showed our attendees tickets. The guards immediately relaxed, further tension bleeding out of their shoulders after they scanned our tickets and confirmed their validity. With a stiff nod, they gestured for us to enter.

They didn't have to tell us twice.

My head was already pounding something fierce as we climbed the medium flight of stairs into the immense building. It mixed the modern and industrial style that dominated the human cities on Mazeria. Ironically, just like the campus, it also included some elements of Syllen architecture with giant faces carved into some of the walls and large columns that had an organic shape vaguely reminiscent of a tree.

To my dismay, as soon as we passed the door, half a dozen guards further slowed our progress into the venue with heavy security checks, including scans, patting down people, and even peering into their purses or bags. By the time we crossed the long corridor into the main hall, I acknowledged that coming here had been a huge mistake. Vicious needles pricked the back of my eyes, while my brain seemed determined to push its way out of my skull.

Multiple holocards sat on a large table near the entrance of the diamond-shaped room. They served as information packets for the attendees. I grabbed one and shoved it into the pouch hanging diagonally across my chest to carry personal items then turned to look at my mate. She didn't need me to speak to know the deal. From the moment we began our descent, her concerned emotions for me had increased exponentially.

"Okay, this had been a bad idea," I said, the pain I felt seeping into my voice despite my best effort.

"Go home, Kayog. I can stay and record the conference and bring it to you," Linsea offered.

"Recording is not allowed," I argued.

She gave me a look that screamed 'Do I look like I care?' before caressing my cheek.

"First, they need to catch me. And second, if they do and give me a hard time, I'll just pretend I didn't know better. By then, I will still have streamed most of it for you," she said with a mulish expression.

Under different circumstances, I would have laughed and probably even kissed her. But my stomach was starting to churn with pain-induced nausea. I didn't know what expression my mate saw on my face, but this time, she almost looked scared for me.

"Maybe it's best I just escort you back," Linsea said, slipping her arm around mine as if for support.

I smiled and patted her hand holding my upper arm. "No, my love. You can stay. Anyway, I'm just going to race back home and either pass out in bed or meditate. I'll be super grateful for whatever information you can gather here."

"Are you sure?" she insisted, her eyes flicking between mine.

"Yes, my mate. I'm sure."

I leaned forward and kissed her. She reciprocated and watched me take a step back with much reluctance. As she headed towards the conference room, I turned around and back-tracked towards the entrance. People arriving from the opposite direction slowed me down a little, which only had me feeling almost as if I was suffocating.

To my dismay, barely a few meters from my salvation, a couple of guards blocked my path.

"Wrong way, sir!" the guard said in a stern voice. "Please don't disrupt the circulation flow and head into the hall."

"I'm trying to leave," I explained.

The man shook his head and pointed towards the main hall with an inflexible expression. "The exit is that way, at the other end. The entrance is already crowded enough, and we have our hands too full with ensuring everyone's security not to deal with incoming people from behind us. Please move forward."

My fist burned with the urge to punch him in the throat. I needed to get out of this wretched place, and he was denying me the fastest way out. Of course, I understood his logic. Any other time, I would have thanked him and maybe even apologized for bothering him to begin with before following his instructions. Today, although I complied, I did so while muttering a series of highly inappropriate expletives.

I could have forced my way through, and in fact seriously considered it. But despite the chaos tearing my head to shreds, I clearly perceived that he wouldn't back down and that any attempts on my part would be met with extreme prejudice.

As if in a malicious attempt to prevent me from making a swift escape, the crowd appeared to close in on me. Random clusters of people would stop directly in my path to greet each other or launch into random conversations. Others would try to cut in front of me, further slowing my progress.

While the people present caused a significant part of my discomfort, it was the anger outside from both the protestors and the guards growing increasingly overwhelmed that were truly wrecking my brain. The sustained, shrill sound of their anger felt like a serrated blade drilling into my head.

I'd been so fucking stupid. I knew better, but my almost blissful week with my mate had made me reckless, convincing me that I could have somewhat of a normal life. How could I have been such a fool?

I peered outside through one of the large windows with protective metal bars cleverly designed to make them look like French windows. The unrest in front of the building was reaching critical levels. Some of the protestors had begun pushing and shoving the security guards, likely to force their way in. While I had faith that the guards would be able to control the situation, I couldn't help but wonder if I should have insisted Linsea leave with me. Judging by the emotions emanating from the people outside, things would likely continue to escalate until they got downright ugly.

But I cast that thought aside. The building possessed a few safe rooms that would be impossible to breach should things truly get out of hand. Anyway, I didn't doubt that the guards would keep the guests safe inside, not to mention the backup help they had on standby.

My stomach roiled again from pain-induced nausea. Pushing my way through the guest in my path, I finally reached the guard post towards the exit on the eastern side of the building. To my shock, as soon as one of the guards saw me approach, he stepped in front of me.

"I'm sorry, sir. You can't go there," the man said in an apologetic tone.

"I'm trying to leave," I growled, fighting the urge to throw him across the room and out of my way.

Visibly displeased by my tone, his face hardened, and he lifted his chin defiantly. "For your own protection, you may not leave now. Protestors are trying to break in. We cannot be held responsible if you get attacked. Therefore, you need to wait."

The feral rage that had slowly been building inside me in tandem with the agony shredding my mind to pieces cranked up another notch.

"I FUCKING NEED TO LEAVE NOW!" I yelled, my claws extruding, and my fingers twitching with the burning need to tear up his face.

This time, he placed his hand on his blaster, a menacing expression descending over his features. Two of his four colleagues standing watch by the door took a few steps towards us, ready to intervene if things got out of hand.

"Last warning, Temern," the guard warned. "Back off until things have cooled down. Do not force us to—"

He never finished his sentence. A massive explosion rocked the building. In my last moment of lucidity, I vaguely realized the explosion had come from right outside the exit door. I didn't know what kind of device had gone off. But by the way a few of the windows shattered, it had been something serious. Had the guard allowed me out when I wanted to, I probably would have been grievously hit by the blast.

Linsea's face flashed before my eyes as fear for my female swelled within me. But even that faded in the split second both these thoughts crossed my mind after the explosion. The most debilitating pain I had ever felt sliced through my brain and down my spine. My knees nearly buckled as I dry heaved, my stomach twisting atrociously. All around me, people were screaming, bumping against each other in their panic to seek refuge from the unidentified source of the threat.

Their terror was like so many blades repeatedly stabbing me and then having acid poured inside the wounds. I retched again, as I stumbled forward, slapping my hands against the wall, moments before I would have collapsed. My brain felt on the verge of exploding while a demonic hand was tearing my spine right out of my body.

I needed them to stop, to be quiet for just one second, one blessed second before they killed me. But they didn't stop. Instead, feeding from each other, the crowd only grew even more terrified, especially as some people started to fall, some getting trampled by those who were still standing and frantically trying to run for cover.

Something snapped in my head.

"STOP!" I shouted with such force that my vocal cords hurt.

But nothing could even remotely compare to the agony in my head. At the same time I pointlessly shouted that word, I attempted to push the debilitating noise out of my head with all my might. I couldn't explain how, but it felt like a massive blast detonated all around me.

And then, things went quiet.

No, not quiet. The noise still assaulted me, but it had significantly reduced, as if half of the people bombarding me with their wretched emotions had suddenly vanished. Leaning against the wall, my innards still horribly twisting, I blindly tried to make my way back towards the main entrance. After only a couple of steps, I nearly fell when my foot bumped into something soft. On instinct, I sank my claws into the wall for purchase and yanked myself back into a straight position.

Blinking, my head pounding, I tried to make sense of what my blurred vision was trying to show me. This couldn't be right. And yet, it couldn't be denied. Dozens of bodies lay at my feet. Everyone around me, all the way to the end of the corridor, was passed out on the ground. I couldn't say whether they were dead. One seemed to be breathing, but I couldn't swear to it. Anyway, even if I had wanted to help, I was in no condition to do so. The excruciating pain crushing my skull also had me on the verge of collapsing.

As I clumsily navigated my way around the fallen, the semi-reprieve all these people passing out had given me was quickly fading. More panicked voices and fearful shouts ahead assailed me like a rabid flock of screeching banshees. I doubled over and dry heaved again. Every muscle in my body screamed as if they were being pummeled by spiked clubs.

A warm liquid began to trickle from both my ears. A part of me knew what it was and understood that it indicated that my body was nearing critical failure. I didn't know if I would make it out in time. I could only focus on putting one foot in front of the other while I still had strength left.

To my horror, as I reached the main hall, I could vaguely see the silhouettes of people crouching on the balcony, looking for cover, while others were attempting to crawl towards one of the rooms likely to hide. The people on the opposite side of the hall from me were conscious and terrified. My brain couldn't comprehend why they were on the floor, most of them kneeling with their hands up.

But that also didn't matter to me. The thick liquid pouring out of my eyes was almost blinding me. Just as I was opening my mouth to yell at the people kneeling to get the fuck out of my way, two masked males burst into the main hall from the entrance.

"What the fuck is going on here?! What happened?" one of the men shouted as he glanced at all the unconscious people behind me. "Why are your eyes bleeding?"

"Quiet," I whispered, the sound of my own voice painful to my ears.

"What the fuck?!" the man exclaimed, raising his blaster towards me. "Get down on the floor, you freak. Don't take another step!"

"*Quiet!*" I repeated, this time louder as a murderous rage swelled within me.

"I fucking asked you to—!"

"QUIET!" I yelled, interrupting him.

With a will of their own, my hands rose before me. My palms tingled, and intense heat radiated around them before a blinding light went off. Both men looked as if they'd been hit by a ram, and they flew back, crashing brutally against the wall before sliding down to the floor, unconscious.

As one, the people on the other side of the room started screeching and scrambling to get away. It felt like a thousand hammers bashing my skull all at once. Something broke inside me as I tried to push them away. The air shifted around me, as if a powerful vacuum had sucked the oxygen out of the room.

Everyone went quiet. But I no longer cared. The floor rushed towards me. I never felt the moment I made contact with it as blessed oblivion claimed me first.

CHAPTER 12
LINSEA

I stirred awake to the sound of sirens, pained whimpers, and panicked voices. Shocked, I realized that I was lying on the floor in the aisle between the seats of the conference room. My head hurt a bit, like after a mild hangover. However, seeing everyone else around me also on the floor and groggily attempting to get back on their feet had a shiver of dread running down my spine.

A single glance at the room displayed no structural damage that an earthquake or something along those lines could have caused. That would have explained why everyone had fallen, some of us banging our heads which would have justified my headache and the fact that I had been unconscious. But clearly, something else had happened.

And then I remembered the sound of an explosion. The building had been attacked.

"Kayog!" I whispered, my voice filled with fear.

I raised my left forearm in front of me and tapped a few instructions on my bracer as I attempted to rush out of the room. To my dismay, Kayog didn't answer my call. I tried to reach his com again while elbowing my way out, only for it to ring without answer. Feeling faint with worry, I attempted to track his com.

My blood turned to ice when it indicated that he was only a few meters away.

He should have been long gone, and halfway to his house by now. How was he still here? Why was he not answering? My fertile imagination started conjuring up all kinds of horrible scenarios especially in the wake of the two explosions. However, a more horrifying tableau awaited me when I finally emerged into the main hall.

"KAYOG!" I shouted, terrified.

I ran to him, my chest constricted, and my stomach twisting with fear at finding him lying on the ground. He was crushing his right wing as he'd fallen on it at a bad angle. But the blood running down his face from his eyes and ears destroyed me. Involuntary spasms shook his body as he took shallow, whistling breaths.

"MEDIC!" I shouted while running my bracer over his head.

It only possessed the standard basic scanning abilities that most personal bracers offered. But it was advanced enough to confirm critical swelling and cerebral hemorrhage.

"MEDIC!" I yelled again, fighting the tears pricking my eyes.

To my relief, two guards came running. A single look at my mate sufficed for them to understand he needed to be rushed immediately to the hospital. With the aid of a couple more guards clearing the way, they carried Kayog outside near the medical shuttle where the medics were running around, catering to the wounded in the crowd.

As we ran, I called my grandmother.

"Sweetie, how are—?"

"He's dying, Nana!" I shouted, interrupting her. "Kayog is dying. We're at Hemlock Conference Hall."

"Where the attack took place?!" she exclaimed.

"Yes. Kayog collapsed. There's blood coming out of his eyes and ears, and my scan confirms there is heavy cerebral bleeding. We need help!"

"Understood. I'm rounding up a team of doctors right away. Let me know where they take him, and I'll send them there," Nana Arika said in a determined voice.

"Thank you, Nana," I said, my heart aching with fear for my mate, while filling with gratitude for my grandmother.

Complete chaos reigned outside. If the guards had been over-whelmed before, now they were dealing with total mayhem. Despite the mess from the attack, some idiots were still trying to protest, instigate, or rile up the crowd already on edge. People could be seen desperately looking for a friend or loved one they got separated from when the attack began. Others were seeking help for their wounds or providing assistance wherever they could.

As soon as the medics noticed the guards approaching with Kayog, they dropped everything they were doing to take care of my mate. Anyone with eyes could see he was the main priority. The first responders began loading him into the medical shuttle. To my shock, as I approached, one of the medics raised her palm in an arresting gesture.

"I'm sorry, ma'am, but you can't come in," she said in an apologetic tone.

"What?!" I exclaimed, outraged.

"There's no room. We must keep it for the other patients. A lot of people got hurt in the panic," the woman explained.

"But I'm his mate!" I argued, trying to circle around her to get in.

"I'm sorry, ma'am. We can't let you in. We're taking him to Danmere Hospital. Feel free to meet us there," the medic said in a tone that brooked no argument.

When I tried to further challenge her stance, two guards intervened, pushing me away so that they could load two more patients before departing. It took every ounce of my willpower not to throw a hissy fit and demand they let me onboard. A part of me was ashamed of my behavior. Obviously, they had to prioritize the injured. But seeing Kayog in such a dreadful state was robbing me of any rational thinking.

I immediately took flight ahead of them and called my nan to inform her of his destination. To my relief, she confirmed that her medical team would go there right away.

To my dismay, despite the great speed I could achieve while flying, I couldn't keep up with the shuttle, which zipped right past me at the highest speed allowed for emergency vehicles. Still, that I could fly was in itself a tremendous blessing. Had I been a non-winged species, who knew how I would have managed to follow him.

My mind raced with too many thoughts to organize them in a rational fashion. The main part of me was focused on Kayog and how much damage he might have sustained from being blasted by so many extreme emotions. The other needed to understand what had happened. What could have possibly knocked out so many people—myself included—without causing noticeable structural damage? What kind of attack had been unleashed on us? And who would have done that?

Worse still, had I sustained some sort of injury that I was currently aggravating by flying as hard as I could before getting examined by a professional?

I yelped, and my heart nearly leapt out of my chest when my com suddenly went off. My pulse racing, I answered the call, seeing Isobel's name on the interface.

"Linsea, are you okay? I saw the attack all over the news, but I can't reach Kai!" Isobel said in a slightly panicked voice.

"It's bad, Isobel," I said, my voice shaky with worry and grief. "I'm on my way to Danmere Hospital. They're taking Kayog there. He collapsed and was bleeding from his eyes and ears."

"No!" Isobel breathed out, horrified. "I'm coming!"

"Thank you," I said with genuine gratitude. "I'll see you there."

We ended the call, and I pushed myself as hard as I could to reach my destination. It took me well over twelve minutes—a fucking eternity—before the hospital finally appeared before me. As I began my descent, I gazed upon the utter chaos that also reigned here. Countless shuttles were jockeying for right of way and attempting to find a parking spot. My chest instantly constricted for Isobel. She would have to land quite far as there was no way she would find space here.

This place was usually easily accessible. But tonight, friends and relatives were undoubtedly rushing here as well to find out about the state of their loved ones. The worst part was that many of the people creating this unnecessary traffic didn't even need to be here. As was too often the case, people acted first and thought after. They heard wounded people were brought here, so they came immediately before they got confirmation their loved ones featured among them. And yet, I couldn't fault them for it. In their place, had I not been able to reach my mate, I also would have assumed he was among the victims who got taken to the hospital. And you better believe I would have dashed here.

Once again, I thanked all the powers in the universe that I was a Temern. I effortlessly landed near the entrance and ran inside. Total mayhem greeted me. To my utter annoyance, it wasn't victims shouting and begging for attention, but the families arguing with the receptionists and nurses, accusing them of lying when they stated that their loved ones weren't listed in their system.

Realizing I wouldn't get much help here with so many others monopolizing the already overwhelmed staff, I made my way towards the urgent care located on the fourth floor. Here as well, everyone was running. Those I tried to ask for help ignored me or shook their heads absentmindedly in response to my question as to whether Kayog was here.

In despair, I finally grabbed a male nurse running past me to force him to stop and talk. He gave me an aggravated look.

"I'm sorry, but I need someone to answer me!" I said in an angry tone that even scared me. "My mate was rushed to this hospital bleeding from his eyes and ears."

"I don't know where he is, and I'm urgently needed in the operating block. Ask the receptionist down this hallway and to the left," he replied in a clipped tone before yanking his arm free and hastening away.

Despite my anger—not at the nurse but at the sense of help-lessness I felt—I jogged in the direction he indicated. Halfway through the wide corridor, black uniforms in a connecting hallway drew my attention. I stopped dead in my tracks when I recognized them as Enforcers.

They're here for Kayog.

I couldn't say why that thought struck me with such force, but everything in me screamed that it was true. Without hesitation, I raced after them. They turned into a different corridor. A hover stretcher cutting in front of me forced me to slow down. I cursed inwardly, fighting the urge to push them to go faster to clear the path. What if those Enforcers entered a room or an elevator before I could see them? What if...?

My blood turned to ice, and all those questions flew right out of my head when I finally reached the corner and glanced into the hallway. Ten meters ahead, two Temern doctors were standing outside a room, talking to the Enforcers. One had dusty blue feathers with black specks on his chest and black feathers around the edges of his wings. The other was dark green with a white chest and head. A quick empathic scan of the doctors confirmed my worst fears.

They were ready to kill.

I ran up to them, raising my psychic walls to prevent them

from reading me. The blue doctor noticed me as I was closing the distance with them. He instantly tensed, his expression hardening even as he narrowed his eyes at me. His emotions screamed suspicion and a defensive stance that would easily shift into combative.

He had set a course of action that he was determined to see through at all costs. But why? Why did my mate's condition trigger such violent urges from people dedicated to saving and protecting lives?

"I need to see Kayog," I said in an imperious tone.

"Visitors are not allowed here," the blue doctor said coolly.

The Enforcers turned to look at me, their faces unreadable, although their emotions expressed a mix of reservation and curiosity. For now, they weren't a threat. I just hated that I didn't know these specific ones.

"I'm not a visitor," I said in a haughty tone. "I'm his mate. What's his status?"

The Temerns recoiled and exchanged a troubled look before glancing back at me with a frown.

"I asked a question," I growled when they remained quiet, their wheels spinning as they pondered the answer they would give... if any.

"He doesn't have a mate," the green doctor replied with something akin to disdain that made me want to punch him in the face.

"We're not married yet," I conceded with an annoyed gesture, "but we will be soon."

"I'm sorry, but there are no such indications in his file," the blue doctor said with a victorious glimmer in his black eyes, even as he lifted his chin defiantly. "His records also do not list any significant other or next of kin."

"Kayog has no one else but me to make sure he receives the proper care for his specific needs," I insisted, forcing myself to speak in a firm but reasonable tone.

"We have already discussed what needs to be done about Mr. Voln," the green doctor said in a way that clearly indicated that their decision was not open to discussion, and that I needed to get out of the way. "He is a very special case that must be handled at once before… an unfortunate escalation occurs."

"I'm not letting you kill him!" I snarled, pointing an accusatory finger at him while taking a menacing step forward.

The Enforcers visibly stiffened at my statement then jerked their heads towards the doctors to stare at them with a mix of shock and suspicion. That involuntary response from them gave me hope. They had not been sent here to execute Kayog or to bear witness to his murder.

So why are they here?

"What an outrageous statement! We're healers!" the green doctor exclaimed.

"Do not take me for an idiot," I hissed. "I'm a fucking Temern. I know what you 'healers' do to Edals."

This time, they both flinched, their back stiffening as they stared at me in shock. The blue doctor recovered first. Shedding all pretense, his face hardened, and an almost cruel glint sparked in his obsidian eyes.

"I will not ask how you are aware of Edals. But that means you know that he is a danger to everyone here," he said in a harsh voice. "At the last count, more than 426 people have been admitted in the past hour because of him."

It was my turn to recoil as I gaped at them in confusion and outrage.

"What the fuck are you talking about? What happened over there is not his fault. Explosive devices went off and—"

"I'm going to ask you to leave right now. You are further endangering everyone in this hospital with your interference," the green doctor said menacingly.

A cold shiver ran down my spine. Something had shifted after my last comment. When I first mentioned Kayog being an

Edal, their emotions had turned cautious and wary like when you realized you were in the presence of a potentially bigger predator than you were. But something I said convinced them that I knew far less than they first assumed, or that I was in fact not a threat to whatever they wanted to do. What did I miss? Surely they couldn't imply that Kayog set off those bombs?

"I will not leave!" I snapped.

"Is there a problem here?" the female Enforcer asked, her eyes flicking between the doctors and me.

"Officer, please remove this female," the blue Temern demanded in a commanding tone.

"They will kill him!" I exclaimed in a pleading tone.

The woman frowned and blinked twice rapidly as she processed what was going on. Her emotions indicated that a seed of suspicion lingered towards the doctors, but that she mostly felt I was being irrational. Thankfully, she was still reserving judgment and giving herself a bit more time to further assess the situation.

"They're doctors. They heal people," she said carefully in a gentle voice. "Considering the serious state in which he was brought here, surely you want them to take care of him."

"I'm his mate," I insisted stubbornly. "I'm also a Temern, so I can read their emotions. However over the top you might think this is, I promise you that they wish to do him harm. As his mate, I request a different doctor be assigned to him."

"He's not married," the green doctor snapped.

Ignoring him, I locked eyes with the Enforcer. "I am Linsea Kenna, granddaughter of Arika Sorek, Senior Legal Counselor of the UPO, daughter of Karis Kenna, UPO Head Negotiator, and of Randel Kenna, Lead Criminal Lawyer for the Enforcers, Ulthor Division. Arika Sorek already dispatched a special team of doctors to take care of Kayog. They should be here any minute now."

"They do not have jurisdiction here," the green doctor hissed, although a sliver of fear had now entered his voice.

"Like fuck they don't!" I snarled. "You stay away from him, or I will have your license and bring down this entire damn hospital. I just finished an internship with Ambassador Olmek on hostage negotiation and hostage takeovers. I know exactly what levers can be used to crush an organization and even an entire government. I have the type of connections that will destroy you, your whole fucking bloodline, and this entire place. So don't test me!"

"You just heard her threaten us, didn't you?!" the blue Temern said to the Enforcers, outraged.

I turned to the female Enforcer, her male counterpart tensing up, ready to jump into action if things escalated further.

"Call my grandmother," I said to her. "Call Arika Sorek for confirmation of my statements."

She narrowed her eyes at me. "Why don't *you* call her?"

I smiled in a way that said 'challenge accepted.' It was clever of her and clearly a test. If she truly was my grandmother, then I should have her direct line.

"Gladly," I replied. "And while I do that, please get Colin Wilson here. He knows me, and he's also very interested in my mate."

Without waiting for her answer, I used the com on my bracer and put it on speaker as soon as it began to ring. My nan answered almost immediately.

"Linsea, have they arrived?" my grandmother asked in lieu of greeting.

"No, not yet. But there are two Temern doctors here who want to kill Kayog," I replied, my eyes shooting daggers at them.

"We never said—" the blue doctor started to argue before my grandmother interrupted him.

"You are to stay away from Mr. Voln," she said with that icy cold tone that would have even the most vicious warrior cower in fear. "He's under the protection of the UPO. Confirmation has been sent to the hospital's directors. Verify with them. But stand down immediately."

"How do we know that you're even who she claims you are?" the green doctor challenged.

"A fair question," the female Enforcer stated. "I am Agent Tana Murphy."

"Tana Murphy, Team Lead of the Alpha Bravo Squad, freshly assigned to Mazeria after your service on Xoccoris," my grandmother said. "We talked in my office about the precarious situation of a new recruit whose potential you believed in."

"Counselor Sorek, thank you for confirming your identity," Agent Murphy said, her tone immediately deferent. "What are the UPO's orders?"

"Mr. Voln must be protected at all costs. These Temern doctors are *not* to approach him under any circumstances. Our specialists will arrive shortly to care for him," she replied with an authority that had my heart swelling with pride and gratitude.

"Acknowledged," Agent Murphy replied.

"Linsea, let me know once they've arrived," my nan said.

"Will do. Thank you," I said warmly.

As soon as we ended the conversation, I made to enter the room, but the wretched green doctor stood in my path, his anger almost palpable.

"You still may not enter," he hissed. "Not only are visitors not allowed in this wing, but only family can get special permission under specific conditions. There's no proof that you are his mate."

"She *is* his mate," a feminine voice said behind us.

Startled, we all spun around to the blessed sight of Isobel marching towards us.

"I am a certified Priestess with the Galactic Clerical College, here on Mazeria to complete my PhD," Isobel said with poise and assurance. "Linsea and Kayog are not married, but they are betrothed. I am Kayog's spiritual advisor. He has personally confirmed to me that Linsea is his soulmate, and that he intends to marry her this year. She also confirmed her affections for him directly to me. Furthermore, they have publicly been seen as a couple."

"That doesn't mean that they are—"

"Careful, Doctor, about accusing a Priestess of lying," Isobel said sternly to the green doctor. "You know there are serious consequences to that kind of slander. Additionally, you're a Temern. You can feel that I am speaking honestly."

He clacked his beak in a way that expressed deep frustration but also defeat.

"Now if you're done wasting my time, I will see my mate," I said, pushing past the doctors to enter the room.

They attempted to stop Isobel, but I grabbed her arm and dragged her in behind me. As soon as the door closed, I rushed to Kayog's side. Anger bubbled inside me at seeing him in this state, his skin burning, his body shaking with tremors, and his breath shallow. At least, the blood had been wiped off his face, although I could still see a few specs clinging to some of his feathers on the side of his cheeks.

"Thank you for helping out there," I said absentmindedly to Isobel while glancing at the monitor he was connected to.

"No, Linsea. Thank *you* for protecting him," she said in a soothing voice as she approached the bed on the opposite side from me.

"It's really bad," I said in a pained voice, anger and frustration bubbling deep within that the medical team had not arrived yet.

Isobel nodded. "It's total mayhem out there. With everyone freaking out, both here and in the surrounding area, all those emotions must be wrecking him."

My innards twisted with worry. "He's unconscious right now, but I'm not sure if it's still affecting him or if his current reactions are due to swelling or bleeding. He needs to be put in an isolation room or in stasis. Can you see if that can be arranged until the doctors get here?"

"Of course, right away," Isobel said before hurrying out of the room.

As soon as the door closed behind her, I irrationally felt abandoned. A wave of helplessness crashed over me as I looked at Kayog. I hated seeing him so broken when he was so strong. I hated the vile beings who had instigated so much chaos and violence as to make Kayog spiral. But above all, I hated myself for not accompanying him out of the hall the minute he said he was starting to feel overwhelmed. If only I had listened to my gut before we even landed and forced him to turn around, he wouldn't be hurt and potentially dying.

My heart leapt when Kayog suddenly whimpered. His face was constricted, and his body began to shake again. Whatever sedative they had given him had worn off.

"Kayog?" I said, leaning over him, and my hand caressing his head.

His eyes snapped open, and he immediately started screaming, startling me. Before I could speak a word, the Temern doctors burst into the room, followed by the Enforcers.

"GET OUT!" I shouted at the doctors.

Flapping my wings, I flew to the other side of the bed to block them from approaching.

"Ms. Kenna," Agent Murphy said in a reasonable tone, "Mr. Voln clearly needs help."

"He needs to be put in stasis. But not by these two. Get us someone else, now!"

"You do not understand what you're doing!" the blue doctor exclaimed. "He needs to be put down now before he kills us all!"

This time, the Enforcers gaped at the doctor with shock and horror that he finally confessed his evil intent.

"Get out of my way, you stupid female!" the doctor shouted, charging towards me.

He never got to me as the Enforcers tackled him. They each held onto one of his arms as he attempted to free himself, shouting a slew of swear words. Seizing the opportunity created by this chaos, the green doctor rushed towards Kayog, his murderous intentions so potent they were almost palpable. Without thinking, I yanked the blaster from the male Enforcer, who hadn't secured it again after loosening the safety latch earlier.

He gasped and attempted to take it back from me, but I flapped my wings again, flying backward to the opposite side of the bed.

"Stay the fuck away from him!" I yelled, the blaster trained on the doctor.

He stopped dead in his tracks, a couple of feet away from the bed.

"Back away, or I'll blow your fucking head off!" I shouted.

"Ms. Kenna! Give me that weapon!" Agent Murphy said, her voice tense as she extended a hand towards me and slowly advanced.

"Get them both out of here and send in a nurse to put him in stasis, now!" I snarled.

My heart dropped when the blue doctor yanked his arm free of the male Enforcer, who was still holding him. Hand raised, some sort of syringe held in his fist, he lunged for Kayog. I didn't hesitate and shot him in the chest. Shouts erupted all around, and a violent spasm shook Kayog. His screams grew louder. My heart broke as I realized my efforts to protect him were creating even more emotional chaos that had to be destroying him.

A couple of humans—a man and a woman—burst into the room, alerted by the ruckus, only to freeze at the sight of the scene before them. The woman rushed to the blue doctor on the floor.

"Take her out!" the green doctor yelled at the Enforcers while pointing an angry finger at me. "She's insane."

I opened my mouth to answer, but Kayog interrupted me.

"Kill me... Lin... Linsea. Kill me," he pleaded.

"NO! Kayog, no!" I exclaimed, my voice broken with tears as I turned my attention back to him.

"Free me. I... I can't. Make it stop. Please. Kill me."

"No! My love, no. You have to hang on. For me, for us. I will fix it."

"Please..."

Movement at the edge of my vision had me jerking my head back up. The green Temern had taken the syringe from his fallen companion and was approaching the bed.

"Put that down and get away from him!" I shouted, pointing the blaster at him.

"You heard him!" the green doctor said. "He requested it! You have no authority—"

He dodged just as I was firing at him, throwing himself sideways and crashing against a rolling tray, which thankfully was empty.

"YOU, PUT HIM IN FUCKING STASIS NOW!" I yelled at the human male standing near the door.

Judging by his uniform, he was either a nurse or a doctor, but undoubtedly a medical professional.

Although visibly frightened, he approached hastily, his eyes flicking between me, my blaster, and Kayog screaming in agony. Shaking, the man started tapping instructions on the medical device next to the bed. The blue doctor began to stir as the stun from my blaster shot started wearing off.

However, it was the genuine terror emanating from the green doctor that threw me off. He was terrified of Kayog and truly believed that if we didn't kill him immediately, something terrible would happen.

"My dove…" Kayog said, his voice broken.

Tears welled in my eyes when I glanced down at him. Beyond the atrocious pain destroying him, it was the look of betrayal he cast my way that wrecked me.

"Kill me."

"I can't. I'm not losing you. You fought too long, too hard to give up now. Please, hang on for me. I swear we will fix you."

My blood turned to ice when his eyes and hands began to glow. It was a white light, but it looked red around his eyes as blood began to trickle from them again.

"We're all going to die," the green doctor whispered in a terrified voice as he started backing away.

The glow intensified, and in that instant, I realized that whatever was happening with Kayog was what they'd been trying to prevent from the start… what they believed would kill us all.

And then Kayog went limp, the glow instantly fading from his eyes and hands.

"It's done," the human said in a trembling voice, before backing away from the bed.

Something broke inside of me. I hugged Kayog's unconscious form and wept.

CHAPTER 13
LINSEA

I didn't resist when someone pulled the blaster from my hand. There would be serious consequences to my actions. On top of stealing the weapon from an Enforcer, I had shot someone in front of multiple witnesses. The fact that I had known the weapon to be set at a non-lethal charge didn't make my crime any less serious. At least, I wouldn't be charged with attempted murder...

...or so I hoped.

But even that held little importance to me. My heart was breaking in too many pieces while guilt tore me apart. Kayog's voice begging me to set him free played in a loop in my mind. Despite my inability to feel his emotions, the blatant agony in his voice, in his body, in his eyes as he pleaded for mercy would haunt me for the rest of my life. I wanted to believe that it wasn't my selfish need to keep him that had driven me to refuse to grant him his request. Claiming it didn't play a part in it would be an obvious lie. But he had fought so hard and for so long, giving up now when the best doctors in the galaxy would look for a solution made no sense.

But what if they can't fix him? What if I've only prolonged his torture?

Tears rolled freely down my face as I held on to his limp body, stasis cheating me out of the comfort of listening to his heartbeat.

Too lost in my dark thoughts and sorrow, I blocked out the animated voices intensely debating around me. It wasn't until a hand shook my shoulder that I finally lifted my head to refocus on my surroundings.

The male nurse who had put my mate in stasis was standing next to me, a portable scanner in his hand as he gave me an inquisitive look.

"What?" I asked, confused as to what he wanted.

"I need you to sit for a moment so that I can scan you," he said in a soothing voice. "I understand that you were among the people at the Convention Center when the blast occurred. We need to make sure you are not... affected."

The way he hesitated before speaking that last word, and judging by the emotions emanating from him, he believed that what he perceived as my psychotic behavior might have been caused by some side effect of the blast that rocked the center.

I wanted to argue, but kept my mouth shut and complied. As he ran the device mainly around my head, I glanced at the two Temern doctors still engaged in an intense conversation with the Enforcers. Having fully recovered from the stun, the blue doctor appeared even angrier than his companion. Moments later, the door opened on the blessed sight of two doctors who I recognized as working for the UPO. I'd never directly interacted with them, but I had seen them on a few occasions while visiting my Nana.

Despite my unease at one of them being a Temern, the absence of aggression towards my mate emanating from him reassured me that he would be safe... at least for now.

"You have some slight cerebral swelling from the blast, but

you otherwise seem unscathed," the male nurse said, reclaiming my attention. "I can give you some painkillers if your head hurts, or—"

"No, thank you. I'm good," I said absentmindedly, wanting to focus on what the doctors were doing.

My stomach dropped upon seeing Colin also entering the room, his expression stern, if not icy cold. Gone was the semi-friend who I usually enjoyed pleasant conversations with. This man was the Director of the Enforcers on a mission. While he wasn't broadcasting threatening emotions as far as Kayog was concerned, they no longer held the warmth and keen interest he'd expressed before. This time, he was looking at a potential threat to be assessed and then dealt with accordingly.

Why the fuck are they all so afraid of him?!

"You are fools to keep that damn thing alive," the blue doctor hissed. "But he's your problem now. Just take that fucking abomination out of this hospital before he kills everyone."

"What is your damn problem?!" I exclaimed, disbelieving.

"My problem is—"

"Leaving," Colin interrupted, his voice as cold as the stare he leveled on the doctor. "As you can see, our people are preparing him for transfer. We'll be gone in the next few minutes."

"Can't be soon enough," he retorted, anger and contempt filling his voice.

The UPO doctors transferred Kayog onto a hover stretcher, shifting him to their own stasis device before giving Colin a stiff nod.

"See? Off we go," he said to the doctor in a voice heavy with sarcasm.

Agent Murphy and her colleague led the way out of the room, followed by the UPO doctors flanking Kayog's hover stretcher—one in the front, the other in the back. I hurried after them, only to have Colin grab my upper arm, stopping me.

"Not so fast," he said in a harsh tone. "You're coming with me."

My heart sank, although I had expected this. As resisting would only make matters worse, I nodded with resignation, even as I gazed at him with pleading eyes.

"Alright," I said in a conciliatory tone. "But please let me at least escort him to the shuttle."

My chest constricted further when he shook his head, his expression making it clear this wasn't open to discussion.

"Your priestess friend can see him off on your behalf," he said in an imperious tone, gesturing at Isobel with his chin.

Only then did I realize that she was standing by the entrance, as the stretcher glided in front of her. Having apparently heard the Enforcers Director's words, she gave me a reassuring smile before following Kayog and his escort.

I clacked my beak with annoyance, defeated.

"This way," Colin said, gesturing for me to follow him as he also exited the room, leaving the angry Temern doctors behind.

I complied quietly, only to find two more Enforcers waiting in the corridor. Without a word, they followed us as Colin led the way to a section of the hospital I'd never visited.

"You stirred quite the shitshow here, Linsea," he said, his voice still devoid of any warmth although it was no longer as harsh.

"I didn't have a choice. They wanted to kill him," I said in a self-evident manner.

"Did it ever cross your mind that they might have very valid reasons for this?" he asked in a neutral tone.

I recoiled, and my steps faltered. It wasn't only to shock at his words, but above all the emotions radiating from him. He also believed that killing Kayog might have been the wiser choice—a solution he was still considering.

"Why are you all so afraid of him?" I asked, flabbergasted. "Where are they taking him?"

"Relax, Linsea. Kayog is fine. For now, no harm will come to him. Arika would have our heads otherwise. But you and I need to talk."

"I'm listening," I said, my back stiff with apprehension at what would follow.

He shook his head. "Not here. The walls have ears."

To my shock, I realized he had taken me to the first responders and law enforcement parking area.

"A shuttle?" I asked, worry seeping into my voice. "Why are we getting on a shuttle? A disruptor or scrambler in any private room here should suffice, no?"

"No, neither would suffice," he said in a factual manner without slowing down. "Relax, Linsea. I'm not taking you off-world. We're just going to the Enforcers' offices for privacy."

"Is it really that bad?" I asked with a shudder. "I mean, if it's about the doctor, I will gladly pay damages for shooting him. But I knew it was set to stun. He was never in any real danger."

Colin scoffed. "Those doctors are the least of your concern."

"What do you mean?" I asked, despite knowing what his answer would be.

"Your man is a serious problem. Kayog is a walking bomb."

"What does that even mean?" I insisted.

"Just one minute," he said as we entered the parking lot and made a beeline for a medium-sized, black shuttle bearing the logo of the Enforcers in large gold and silver letters.

My mind raced as I tried to guess as to where this conversation was headed. I didn't doubt Kayog had been honest with me about all his abilities. So what else was I missing that had everyone in such a panic?

We entered the large shuttle, and Colin made a beeline for the boardroom. With each step, my pulse sped up a bit more. The conversation to come would undoubtedly flip my world upside down. I didn't know if I was ready for it. I just wanted to be with Kayog, seeing what was happening, and caring for him.

I settled down at the small table big enough for six. The room was mostly barren except for a large vidscreen, a 3D holographic projector, and a console with a drink and food replicator. As this transport ship was designed for short and mid-range flights, this space could be used as either a boardroom or mess hall. Colin retrieved two bottles of water from the small cooling unit I had not noticed under the counter, extended one to me, then settled at the table across from me.

"Arika and your parents are pulling some major strings right now," Colin said, taking me aback.

"About what?" I asked.

"About Kayog's fate."

"You mean whether or not to murder him?" I asked in a clipped tone.

He waved a dismissive hand.

"Killing your man was taken off the table the moment he released a psionic blast over a one-hundred-meter radius, knocking out four hundred and twenty-six people."

"That wasn't him!" I exclaimed, outraged. "Kayog was rendered unconscious by his condition. I found him lying on the ground, blood leaking out of his ears, eyes, and nose."

Colin shook his head with a sad expression. "No Linsea. It was him."

He moved his hand over the middle of the table to call up the embedded interface. On it, he typed a couple of instructions which turned on the vidscreen. Seconds later I stared in complete shock as he played the feed from the Conference Center's surveillance cameras. A soft gasp escaped me when it clearly displayed a blurred wave emanating from Kayog as he leaned against the wall near the back exit of the center. Immediately, every single person visible on screen collapsed, unconscious.

Tears pricked my eyes, and I pressed a palm to my chest as I watched him stumble half drunkenly towards the entrance. Seeing the targeted kinetic attack against the masked men, followed by the second, even more powerful blast that knocked out everyone else—myself included—right before he passed out left me speechless.

I stared numbly at the screen, long after it had gone dark, too stunned to speak or even form any coherent thought.

"Did you know he could do that?" Colin asked, his tone curious but devoid of any accusatory edge.

I shook my head. "No, absolutely not. I mean, I saw his eyes and his hands glow the day of that incident on the campus, but…"

My voice trailed off as my brain struggled to make sense of any of this.

"This makes me wonder what else he's hiding from you," Colin mused aloud.

I bristled at that comment. "Despite how this may seem right now, I'm convinced Kayog isn't hiding anything from me. I don't think he even knows he can do that or understands what abilities he possesses."

Colin gave me a dubious look. "Really?"

I nodded firmly. "Didn't you look at his face in that video? Judging by the way he was walking, Kayog was dazed, bloodied, and in obvious excruciating pain. After I heavily insisted, he gave me a glimpse of what it's like to feel emotions the way he does. I nearly passed out from the pain and the chaos. And that was what he deemed a low and bearable level for him while in the partial shelter of his bunker house."

Colin frowned and pursed his lips as he weighed my words. In that instant, I realized that what I would say during this 'conversation' could seriously impact Kayog's fate. He was trying to assess how much of a threat my mate was, and therefore how he was to be handled.

"The level of panic in the convention center after that explosion went off would have been pure agony for him. What I saw on this video was a male who had gone into survival mode. This chaos was literally killing him. His instincts kicked in to protect himself before he suffered irreparable damage. As far as I know, he's never been exposed to a situation as bad as this."

To my utter relief, Colin nodded slowly. "Yes, the priestess Isobel said as much. But he still struck four hundred and twenty-six people, some of them high-ranking foreign officials. They want a culprit to answer for this."

My stomach twisted with fear. But I clamped down on it. Now was the time to call upon my experience and the negotiation training I had benefited from.

"How severe were their injuries?" I challenged.

He slightly recoiled and gave me a confused look. "What does that have to do with anything? That's not the point."

"Yes, it is!" I exclaimed. "How serious were their injuries?"

He shrugged, still baffled but indulged me. "They will fully recover."

"So it's not that serious," I said triumphantly.

Colin gave me an outraged look. "People were still hurt!"

"Kayog stopped a terrorist attack and potentially prevented multiple deaths and grievous injuries," I argued. "I doubt that the masked people who set off that explosion were carrying Tasers as weapons. They were there to cause serious harm. You can easily spin a tale that will protect Kayog."

He narrowed his eyes at me, his expression hardening slightly. "Are you asking me to falsely blame the attackers for everyone getting knocked unconscious?"

I rolled my eyes and shook my head. "They set off two explosions, not a psychic blast. Whatever they used, the forensic team will not be able to justify how the guests were affected by them. However, no one expected this type of attack there. With enough digging, I'm certain the investigators will discover that the explosions triggered a chain reaction with something in the Convention Center. The Enforcers' science department should have no problem coming up with an explanation as to how certain chemicals in the bombs reacted in an unusual fashion with some of the foreign materials used to build the center."

"You forget the surveillance videos," Colin said mockingly.

I shrugged. "Unfortunately, they were severely damaged by the explosion and the unexpected blasts they triggered."

"What about all the witnesses?"

I waved a disdainful hand. "The flashing lights they saw in front of Kayog was just a manifestation of the anomaly—an early warning of the true blast that would follow. My poor mate sadly happened to be standing in the exact area that the blast went off, which both explains why it seemed to emanate from him and why he was the only person bleeding that way."

He snorted and shook his head at me. "Well, well, Linsea. Who would have guessed such a ruthless female lurked beneath that sweet and polished exterior?"

I lifted my chin defiantly. "As you humans say, Hell hath no fury like a woman scorned. No one is hurting my mate. This only happened because everyone failed him. *I* will not."

"Things are not that simple, Linsea," Colin said, tension seeping back into his voice. "Your grandmother doesn't know everything about Edals. It is kept secret for a reason to avoid panicking the population or other worlds. The doctors wanted to take him out to save the lives of everyone else in that hospital. Those two psionic blasts only caused concussions and some cerebral bruising to the people present. I want to believe that, even in his 'dazed' state as you claimed, Kayog *chose* not to harm anyone. But other Edals who used that ability killed hundreds of people."

I recoiled. "How is that possible? I thought every previous Edal died within hours or days after their birth."

Colin nodded. "They died from a brain aneurysm right after they killed or grievously harmed hundreds of people. You see, the handful of Edals who made it to their birth reacted so violently to the onslaught of emotions from everyone around them that they tried to eliminate the cause. They also emitted a psionic blast, except theirs was lethal. Psionic disruptors do not work on them. The minute their eyes begin to glow is when they are about to launch their attack. That's why those doctors were desperate to eliminate Kayog. He quite literally could have wiped out every patient, every medical staff, and every visitor in that hospital with a single thought."

I shuddered and hugged myself. The fear emanating from those two Temern doctors had been undeniable. I had also seen his glowing eyes before, at the campus, in the Convention Center's camera feed, and in the hospital right before the nurse put him in stasis.

Could he have truly been on the verge of killing us all?

"I hear what you're saying," I said carefully. "However, he unleashed his attack twice at the Convention Center and didn't kill anyone. He merely knocked us out to silence our emotions."

"And that's the only reason he's still alive as we speak," Colin said in a grim fashion. "You're being extremely naive right now if you think we can simply patch him up and send him on his way so that you both can have your happily ever after. Assuming we're able to fix him, what do you think is going to happen to him?"

"Why do I feel I'm not going to like your answer?" I asked, tension filling my voice.

"Because you definitely aren't," he conceded in an apologetic tone. "Kayog is not only unique, but he is an anomaly with terrifying powers. As we speak, our doctors and scientists are foaming at the mouth at the prospect of studying him."

"He's not a lab rat!" I snapped, straightening in my chair.

"Isn't he?" Colin challenged, raising an inquisitive eyebrow. "In order to try to find a solution to his condition, every professional will have to poke and prod at him to understand what he is, why he is unable to shelter his mind from others, the extent of his powers, and how to rein them in.

Honestly, granting him his wish to die might have been a mercy."

"I will not allow it," I hissed. "You are not turning him into a lab rat or some freakish experiment."

"What are you going to do about it?" Colin asked, a hint of mockery in his voice.

"You seem to forget that I know how the system works. I can create the worst public relations nightmare for both the UPO and the Enforcers," I replied in a frosty tone.

"We can stop you," he retorted with a shrug.

"Can you?" I challenged.

"Of course," he replied as if it was self-evident.

It was my turn to look at him with a taunting expression. "But after how much damage? You know once I get the ball rolling, it will wreck many things that will be nearly impossible to repair. Neither of us wants to go that route, do we?"

"Of course not," he said in a less friendly tone.

"Then don't force my hand," I said sternly. "The UPO and the Enforcers have many enemies who would be delighted to help me go on a rampage."

"Are you threatening us?" Colin asked, narrowing his eyes at me.

"I don't do threats, only promises. You know I don't want any of this. All I ask is that you protect my mate from the highly questionable plans that some people will entertain where he is concerned," I said in a reasonable tone.

I highly respected Colin, and making an enemy out of him would be a huge mistake. But in order for me not to be eaten alive in this 'negotiation', I had to demonstrate that I wouldn't be a pushover.

"We don't know what he is or how dangerous he can get," he replied, his voice heavy with frustration.

"Then find out, and then cure him," I retorted in a factual manner.

"And risk losing those incredible powers of his?" he argued.

I waved a dismissive hand. "What use are they if they break his mind? I may not be a doctor, but you don't need to be a genius to understand that repeated brain hemorrhage will leave permanent scars."

"And then what?" Colin demanded. "What happens once we've cured him?"

"Kayog is blessed with genius-level intelligence. He's a natural protector, possesses extremely high morals, has proven exceptional athletic abilities, and he's insanely charismatic. My mate could be a huge asset in a variety of roles within either the Enforcers or the UPO," I said with a bit too much eagerness.

With his powers, whether they disappeared after a cure or not, neither organization would ever want to let him loose, as his abilities could return. And assuming he never lost them, he would be much too dangerous a weapon roaming free in the wild without supervision. Worse still, enemies could seek to enlist him to turn him against us. Colin didn't have to go into details for me to understand my mate would never truly be free. But there were ways where he could achieve something close enough to it and live under his own terms within the organization.

And I intended to use every tool in my arsenal to make sure of it.

Colin shook his head. "I already approached him about joining us. He flat out refused. And judging by his tone, there would be no swaying him."

I scoffed. "Of course, he refused. With his current condition, it would have been completely impossible for him. Cure him and then ask again. I bet you will be pleasantly surprised by his answer."

He narrowed his eyes at me, a speculative glimmer sparking in his eyes. "Are you pledging that he will?"

I gave him a 'Don't be stupid' look. "You know I cannot

make such a commitment on his behalf. But make him an offer he can't refuse, and he will accept."

"That's a huge 'if' that you're expecting me to go to battle for," Colin argued.

I leaned forward, my gaze intense as I tried to convince him.

"No Edal has ever lived past a few hours or days," I countered. "You have a full-grown adult one, capable of speech and reason. How many others like him have died pointlessly because they couldn't express the cause and source of their distress? You have a golden opportunity to learn about people like him while searching for a cure. Temerns are important members of the UPO. The organization *owes* us to help find a cure."

He snorted. "Your own people want him dead."

I huffed. "Out of ignorance. They only pursue an old tradition born of fear. Science has evolved since those early cases. There is no reason why we couldn't look into it again now with a more open mind. By the way, isn't one of the core purposes of the UPO to put an end to these types of tragedies and slaughters based on primitive beliefs?"

He gave me a strange look, the corner of his lips discreetly quirking with a hint of amusement. "Temerns aren't primitive."

"In this, they *are* acting like a primitive species, thinking Edals are demons simply because they don't understand what's happening with them or how to fix the issues," I said with a shrug. "Didn't humans use to lobotomize people who suffered from mental health issues because they didn't know how to help them? This is no different."

"I will grant you that their policies regarding Edals date back many generations and need to be revisited," Colin said calmly.

"They do," I concurred firmly. "So talk to your scientists and spin a tale for the psionic blast at the Convention Center. I have wealth, and my family will provide any support needed to help research a cure. The UPO and the Enforcers stand only to gain by protecting Kayog. I have no doubt he will become a fantastic asset."

Colin leaned back against his chair, an undefinable smile stretching his lips as he gave me an assessing look.

"I like you, Linsea Kenna. You're cocky, ruthless, and undaunted with things that matter to you. By the way, nice disarm on my guard. Unfortunately for him, he's not going to enjoy the disciplinary measures coming his way."

I flinched, my heart going out to the poor agent. "Please, don't be too harsh with him. With my credentials and my grandmother's endorsement, he had no reason to expect I would pull a stunt like that. Don't forget that I also have self-defense and combat training, as is required for negotiators and aspiring ambassadors."

"True though this may be, he still allowed himself to be disarmed by not properly securing his weapon after he had initially unlatched it," Colin said in a tone that brooked no argument. "As no one died due to his negligence, he won't be dismissed, but he won't make that mistake again. Now, when are you joining the Enforcers?"

I snorted. "Never."

"Is that so?" he asked, seeming genuinely surprised.

"I'm joining the UPO to protect people like my mate from you guys making dumb choices. So don't make my hiring awkward by forcing me to first publicly shame you all," I said with a haughty tone.

He burst out laughing, and I smiled in return, pleased that my effort to dampen the tension that had been building worked.

"I cannot promise you anything, Linsea," he said carefully.

"I didn't ask for a promise, only that you make it happen."

He smiled. "I'll do what I can. And you see to it that he joins us."

～

Colin making it happen turned to days, then weeks, and then too many months. That day at the Convention Center, something happened that completely realigned Kayog's brain. The only blessing in this entire mess was the fact that I had taken a thorough scan of his brain prior to the incident. It allowed the doctors and scientists to see what had shifted after that episode.

It opened a floodgate of possibilities with countless experts in various fields joining together to study what was hailed as one of the greatest discoveries in the past couple of centuries. With our advanced technologies, stumbling on a new unknown species was nearly impossible. Despite being a Temern, Kayog was a whole new breed that fascinated the scientific community.

As they were failing to find a method to prevent him from being assaulted by other people's emotions, they couldn't awaken him to test their various theories and potential remedies. Instead, they recreated his brain virtually, down to the most minute detail. That alone required nearly three months with the best engineers, neurologists, and psionic specialists to build it. The simulator had an insane range, perfectly capturing and translating emotions on as vast a radius as my mate had been able to.

To their dismay, they never managed to get the virtual brain to recreate the psionic blast.

In the weeks that followed, every constraining system they attempted to apply to that virtual brain to block other people's emotions failed miserably. Finally, they realized that a different approach was required. Kayog lacked some of the neuronal pathways that normal Temerns possessed, which enabled us to block nearby people so their emotions wouldn't overwhelm us. Therefore, the scientists decided to stop looking for an external device that could permanently regulate the influx of signals he received. Instead, they devised a training tool to reroute the neural pathways in his brain.

Organic simulations confirmed the creation of new neuronal pathways and a reshaping of the pineal gland. Once confident that their method was safe, they used it on Kayog, while maintaining him in a semi-comatose state. Soon, he started forming the new neuronal connections he sorely needed.

After seven months, two weeks, and four days following the incident, they finally woke him up.

CHAPTER 14
KAYOG

My skin tingled, and my body felt in a semi state of weightlessness as I stirred from what felt like the deepest slumber I'd ever experienced. My muscles were numb and weak, as if they'd lost all strength from an extended period of disuse. A blinding light stabbed my eyes when I attempted to open them. I blinked repeatedly as I adjusted to the intense brightness around me.

However, something was terribly off. It took me a moment to realize what was affecting me so deeply until it struck me.

Total and complete silence.

Silence?!

Shocked, I straightened abruptly from the comfortable mattress of the bed I'd been lying in. A wave of dizziness almost had me collapsing back down. But the sight of a Temern and a human standing at the foot of my bed terrified me.

"Stay away!" I exclaimed, tossing the blanket off my legs so it wouldn't impede any effort to escape should that be required.

"Kayog, it's okay! You're safe," a most beloved voice said.

I jerked my head to the right to see my beautiful Linsea,

standing a few feet away from my bed, her face filled with joy, tenderness, and something else I couldn't define.

"They're your doctors appointed by my grandmother," she continued in a reassuring tone while closing the distance between us. "They've been healing you."

"Healing me?" I echoed, reaching out for her to make sure she wasn't an illusion.

She nodded and took my hand. It was like lightning striking me while simultaneously feeling wrapped in a warm blanket.

"Yes, my love. They've been working on a solution to stop the noise," she explained.

My throat constricted as the blessed silence continued. It was divine, an impossible dream that I still couldn't believe had finally occurred. Peace... so much peace.

"Is that why it's quiet?" I asked with a slight tremor in my voice.

"Yes," she replied with a smile. "There will be no more chaos in your head."

"So quiet," I repeated, tears pricking my eyes. "So incredibly quiet... Thank you. Thank you!"

I pulled her into my embrace and buried my face in her chest before weeping in the most pathetic fashion. I only meant to express my gratitude and affection, but something broke inside me. After a lifetime of misery, this newfound peace over-whelmed me. Every tear that fell out carried with it part of the pain, chaos, and despair that had made every moment of every day of my existence a living nightmare.

Linsea cradled me in her arms, and her pristine wings wrapped around me as I shed every tear in my body. Her beauti-ful, warm voice washed over me as she hummed a soothing song. I couldn't tell how long I wept. It took me forever to gather myself, but I'd never experienced such peace before. The whole time, the blessed silence continued to swirl around us, only enhancing the wonderful melody my mate sang for me.

But something even more perfect was missing.

"I can't feel you," I whispered, my head still resting on her chest. "I can't hear your song."

"You will, my love," Linsea said in a reassuring tone.

Although embarrassed to have made such a spectacle of myself, I lifted my head to look at her. To my relief, her face showed no disdain or disappointment that I should have so pathetically fallen apart in front of her and witnesses. As much as I loved this new peace, I'd lost a primary sense upon which I'd heavily relied my entire life. Not knowing what emotions animated the people around me was not only destabilizing, but it also made me feel vulnerable.

"The doctors can explain everything to you," she said, while gently wiping the lingering moisture on my cheeks with her thumbs.

"Hello, Kayog. I am Dr. Arafin Luleth, and this is my colleague, Dr. Ellen Schumer. But please call me Arafin," the Temern said in a friendly tone.

"And call me Ellen," the human doctor said in a just as welcoming fashion.

"Hello," I replied, my voice reserved as I eyed Arafin with a suspicion and distrust I couldn't quell.

Linsea gently rubbed the back of my shoulder in a soothing fashion. It did help a little.

"We spearheaded the efforts to find a cure to your condition," Arafin continued with enthusiasm. "But before I go into the details of what we've done and the path forward until your full recovery, we would like to run some quick tests to see how you're faring and make sure you're okay."

I quelled my instinctive urge to tell him to piss off and gave him a stiff nod instead.

"Very well," I said.

My heart skipped a beat, and a wave of panic surged within me when Linsea dropped her hand from my shoulder and stepped back. My hand all but lunged for hers, grabbing it before she could move further away.

"Stay!" I exclaimed, the worry I felt audible in my voice.

"Of course, my love. I'm not going anywhere," she said with a smile.

Once again, I felt utterly pathetic to be this needy. My entire world had just been turned upside down. I was confused, lost, and utterly overwhelmed. The last memories flashing through my mind were of an excruciating pain the likes of which I'd never experienced before and a desperate need to escape. It felt like only five minutes had passed since that incident. But clearly, far more time had elapsed.

A billion questions pressed themselves on my tongue, but I instinctively knew that they would be answered in due time. Despite my curiosity, my mate's presence reassured me enough to allow me to wait and not push the issue.

Both doctors did quick work of taking my blood pressure, running a scan similar to the ring Linsea used on me in my house —although this one was clearly an even more advanced model— and performing other tests, including drawing some blood with a stylus. Ellen tackled that last task. My gut told me it had been a deliberate choice that she should use a needle on me rather than Arafin. Despite his non-threatening demeanor around me, I couldn't help systematically tensing every time he approached or touched me.

Usually, I displayed a better control of my physical responses to others. But my current inability to read their emotions made me incredibly wary and defensive. My fight or flight instincts were going into overdrive.

"All done," Arafin said in that same cheerful way doctors often used with frightened children.

Once more, I felt mortified to be showing myself so skittish and weak.

"Everything looks good, aside from your blood pressure," the

Temern doctor said in a slightly reproving tone as if gently chastising a misbehaving child. "Your heart rate is a little too high, which means you need to relax. As your mate mentioned earlier, you are safe here. I understand why you would have reservations in my presence. So we're going to take care of that. In a few minutes, I will restore your empathic powers. Then you will see that I am no threat to you."

My cheeks burned with embarrassment. He hadn't done anything to earn my blatant suspicion. That my mate vouched for him further underlined the fact that my reaction was in fact rude. He gave me a reassuring smile and then pointed at my forehead.

"In case you had not noticed, you are wearing a special circlet," Arafin explained. "It works as a dampener specifically designed for your unique situation. It's currently what silences our emotions for you."

My hand flew to my forehead. I felt nothing until my fingers glided towards my temple, at which point I felt the very thin metallic device that circled around the back of my head to end at my other temple.

How the fuck did I not feel that sooner?

Now that I was aware of its presence, I could clearly feel it. Although it wasn't hugging my head tightly, it still blew my mind that I had been oblivious to it, even when my face was pressed against my female, and she was gently caressing my head.

"Will I always have to wear this," I asked, my fingers still tracing the discreet device.

To my utter relief, he shook his head firmly.

"This is only a crutch for you to use while we train you on how to block external signals on your own," Arafin replied. He picked up a very small device from the medical tray near my bed and showed it to me. "This is the controller for your circlet. Simply glide your thumb downward to reduce its dampening effect and glide it upward to reinforce it. I'm going to gradually lower it. Tell me when you start perceiving our emotions."

"Very well," I replied, unable to hide the excitement—not to say the hunger—in my voice.

I felt like an addict in desperate need for a hit. It boggled my mind how disabled I felt without my ability to feel others. But above all, I burned with the need to hear my mate's song again. To be right next to her and not feel her was akin to having a part of me torn out.

My back stiffened, and a soft gasp escaped me when a tingling at the back of my head gave way to the familiar sensations of others in my head.

"You can feel it?" Ellen asked, her voice and gaze intense.

"Yes," I said with a nod.

"Is it painful or uncomfortable?" Arafin asked, a hint of concern audible in his voice.

"No," I said without hesitation. "It's just noisy, especially now after experiencing what true silence feels like."

I opened my mouth to say something else, but words failed me. How did you apologize to someone for laying the worst suspicions at their feet not because of any of their actions, but simply because of their species and profession? Even in the chaotic noise of all their emotions mingling together, the total absence of any malice or evil intent from Arafin shamed me.

"Despite the noise, can you tell which emotion belongs to whom?" Arafin asked.

"Yes. I clearly perceive your emotions," I said sheepishly. "Thank you."

Although he was maybe only ten or fifteen years older than I was, the Temern gave me an almost paternal smile.

"Good. I'm glad that's settled. Now, I would like you to focus on your mate's emotions and to block Ellen and me."

I blinked, my eyes flicking in turn towards Linsea, Ellen, and Arafin.

"I… I don't know how," I said hesitantly.

"As part of the cure we devised for you, we helped your brain develop new neuronal connections that every other Temern naturally possesses and strengthens over time. They should allow you to isolate the emotions you want to perceive while blocking others. I'm going to send a weak signal to those specific neurons to stimulate them and help you see which part of your brain you need to activate."

"Okay," I said, my excitement cranking up another notch.

Since he lowered the dampening effect, the enthralling song of Linsea's soul had been washing over me in the most delightful caress. Sadly, its beauty was drowning in the—admittedly rather pleasant—emotions of the two doctors. But the thought of finally basking in the perfection of my female's melody without any other interference had me dying with anticipation.

I shivered violently as what felt like a tiny electrical spark went off deep inside my brain.

"Are you alright, Kayog?" Arafin asked in a worried voice. "Was it too strong?"

I shook my head reassuringly. "No, not too strong. It just took me by surprise. But yes, I see which part you stimulated."

"Perfect," Ellen said with enthusiasm. "Try to reproduce this on your own and exclude everyone but Linsea."

I nodded and attempted to replicate the spark I had felt. To my shock, it only took a couple of seconds. However, instead of isolating my mate, complete silence resonated loudly as I ended up blocking everyone.

It took about a dozen tries before I finally succeeded. Tears welled in my eyes when her mesmerizing song soared in its divine purity all by itself, untainted, unchallenged, undisturbed by other unwanted noise.

"You're so beautiful, my dove," I whispered, my throat constricted.

"It worked?" Arafin asked with a thrill in his voice.

I wanted to tell him to piss off and not distract me from reveling in my mate's mesmerizing song. But I quelled the ungrateful thought and forced myself to focus on the task at hand. The sooner I learned how to master this wondrous gift, the sooner I could finally be alone with my soulmate and grant her my full attention.

"Yes. I only hear her right now," I confirmed.

"Excellent. Now repeat the same thing but focus solely on me while blocking the other two, and then do the same with Arafin once you've succeeded with me," Ellen said.

I complied. To my dismay, it took a few attempts to be able to isolate them. Although I had a better understanding now of how to achieve it, it would take some practice for it to come more naturally and to succeed on the first try.

We repeated the process a second time with me focusing on each of them in turn, and then Arafin further lowered the dampening effect until it reached a level where I could no longer isolate anyone. He brought the level back up until it was comfortable again and where I could block others with minimal difficulty.

"We're going to leave the circlet at this setting for now," Ellen said.

"For now?" I echoed.

She nodded. "It's like a muscle to be trained. The more you practice, and the more control you will gain over those neuronal pathways, on top of likely creating new and better ones. If all goes to plan—and so far, it seems to be—soon, you will no longer need the circlet at all."

My happy grin quickly faded upon seeing Arafin's serious expression.

"However, you will need to stay here for a few weeks—and maybe even months—to properly train your abilities while we continue to run tests and make sure there are no negative side effects."

As distraught as the thought of having to potentially spend a few months in what resembled a high-tech medical facility, I accepted that comment with a level of serenity I never thought possible. They had given me a whole new lease on life. I was no longer a broken abomination, but a person who would finally be able to lead a normal life.

"Understood," I replied.

After a few more questions and comments, the doctors left the room, leaving me at long last alone with my dove.

I immediately drew Linsea against me, closing my wings around her even as I let her mesmerizing song wrap around me. It was odd how delicate and fragile she felt in my arms, and yet she was the rock that kept me from drifting into the ocean of madness that had threatened to engulf me.

We remained in each other's embrace for an undefined amount of time before I reluctantly released her. She rubbed her beak against mine, and my heart swelled to bursting with love for this female who had brought light and hope in the endless pit of despair and darkness that my life had been.

"How long was I out?" I asked while caressing the soft feathers of her cheek.

"A little over seven months," Linsea said in a commiserating tone.

I stiffened and gaped at her in complete shock. "Seven months?!" I exclaimed. "What the fuck happened?"

My mate nudged me to sit at the edge of the bed before cuddling against me. She then recounted all that had transpired since the explosion went off in the Convention Center to my awakening here in the Enforcers' advanced medical research facilities.

I ran a hand over my head, blown away and distraught by all that I missed, the heavy burden Linsea carried to keep me safe, and the insane new reality that my life had become.

"So what happened to your classes?" I asked.

"It wasn't easy, and I called in a lot of favors, but I managed to graduate. I took a page out of your own book and convinced them to allow me to attend most of them remotely so that I could stay by your side."

"Thank you, my dove," I said with sincere gratitude, my heart melting with affection for her. "Any legal fallout from what went down?"

She waved a dismissive hand. "We handled it. The Enforcers' PR department made sure that your name wasn't associated in any way with what went down in the center. You have nothing to worry about."

"Maybe not from the justice system, but what about from the UPO and the Enforcers? Am I a prisoner here?" I asked cautiously.

Although she immediately shook her head, I didn't miss the sliver of hesitation and worry that she attempted to bury.

"You're not a prisoner, but Colin will want to talk to you," Linsea said, choosing her words carefully. "When you do, please listen to what he has to say with an open mind."

My stomach knotted with apprehension, a sense of unease washing over me.

"He's going to try to recruit me, isn't he?" I asked, although it was more of a statement.

"There's no question that he will. But he already approached you about that long before this incident," Linsea replied in a noncommittal fashion.

My eyes flicked between hers as I studied her features to get an even better sense of what she was thinking beyond the reserved and cautious emotions emanating from her.

"You want me to accept his request?" I asked, tension stiffening my back.

To both my surprise and relief, my mate held my gaze unwaveringly as she responded with a sincerity that erased any doubt I might still have about her true wishes on the matter.

"I want you to do what you feel is right for you, Kayog. Whatever your decision, I will support you all the way."

"But?" I insisted.

"But you're extremely unique," she said in an almost apologetic tone. "You're insanely powerful—or at least you were when you collapsed in the center. Until they perform further tests, we don't know for sure what kind of power and abilities you possess."

"So they think I'm a security risk," I said grimly with sudden understanding.

"They have to consider the possibility that you might be," she corrected softly.

"Right, I can see that," I conceded begrudgingly.

She smiled and gently caressed my face. "If it's any consolation, Colin and I had extensive discussions about this. He really wants you to join them so he will make an offer that will likely be appealing."

Although Linsea said that she would support whatever decision I made—and while I didn't doubt that she meant it—my mate clearly hoped I would accept. If only because she saved my life, I likely would. But there would be time to dwell on this later.

I glanced around the room in complete awe, still struggling to believe this was my new reality.

"This is so unbelievably quiet," I whispered wistfully before looking back at my female with adoration. "Thank you for saving me, for not letting me give up when I was at my lowest."

To my shock, Linsea's beak quivered, and a powerful emotion mixed with intense relief flashed over her face.

"What is it, my dove?" I asked, confused by her reaction.

"I was so scared you would hate me for forcing you to stay when you begged me to grant you peace," she said in a shaky voice. "I just couldn't let you go. It was selfish of me, but so long as there was hope that you could be healed, I couldn't give up."

"And I'm glad you didn't," I said forcefully. "Do not apologize or feel guilty for what you did. It was my pain speaking at that moment. I just wanted it to end. But had our roles been reversed, I also would have fought with everything I had to keep you. Thank you for fighting for me when I no longer had the strength to do so."

Tears welled in her eyes while another wave of relief, gratitude, and deep affection surged within her. Linsea wrapped her arms around my neck, and we exchanged a deep and tender kiss. Maker! I was falling madly in love with this female.

With much reluctance, we stopped before passion would run away with us. While I doubted they were spying on us, our intimacy wasn't something for prying eyes to witness or stumble in on. My mate snuggled against me and rubbed her face on the crook of my neck. Fuck, how I loved when she did that!

"For what it's worth, Isobel helped a lot as well," Linsea said wistfully.

My chest immediately warmed for my human friend as my mate recounted how she intervened, using her priestess status to help Linsea in her effort to protect me. Isobel vouching for me with Colin, the Enforcers, and the UPO as a whole further appeased some of their concerns. In fact, her words weighed more than Linsea's, to the extent that she had known me for years. As my spiritual advisor and meditation mentor, she was able to provide an extensive track record of all the ways in which I showed restraint and no propensity to violence.

"She truly is the sister of my heart," I said affectionately. "Where is she now?"

"Isobel has taken a temporary assignment in a refugee shelter nearby so that she could be here for you. She's an amazing woman. You were blessed the day she entered your life," Linsea said warmly.

"I was indeed. Just like when *you* entered my life," I said with adoration. "But what of you?"

She scrunched her face. "I'm working for the UPO. Although that had always been my goal, I'll be happy when I can change positions."

"Oh?" I asked, worried. "Things aren't working out how you hoped?"

She shook her head. "It's not that," Linsea said in a reassuring tone. "I settled for a desk job so that I could stay close to you, right here in the research center. For now, I provide advice on various conflicts."

"And you don't like it?" I asked carefully.

"I don't mind it," she replied with a shrug. "In truth, it's an excellent learning experience. But I would prefer to be the one negotiating rather than just reading about the conflicts and providing talking points and potential solutions. Working with text isn't the same as direct interaction with people. Written words can be so easily misinterpreted..."

I nodded with sympathy. "Believe me, my mate. I know exactly what you mean."

"I bet you do," she said with a smile. "But for now, we need to feed you. You've been fed intravenously for far too long. And then, I'm sorry to say that a highly unpleasant amount of tests awaits you with Arafin and Ellen, your two doctors."

My shoulders slumped. Naturally, it made sense. In fact, I would have expected them to drag me directly into it. So this short reprieve with my dove meant a lot. It also struck me as their way of saying that—as inevitable as it would be for me to be somewhat treated as a lab rat—they would make it as comfortable an experience as possible. I hated that it was necessary, but the incommensurable gift of peace they had given me warranted any test they wanted to subject me to.

Lunch went by too fast. At least, Linsea was able to give me an update about everyone. Mares and Tala both graduated and were each participating in a different internship. To my delight, Mares had taken on the mantle of protecting the Syllens and joined a team dedicated to presenting a detailed plan for the slow phasing out of off-worlder presence and touristic installations in their ancestral lands. It didn't guarantee that their plan would be adopted, but he wisely involved the Edocit government in the whole process. Their obvious kinship with this primitive species had his people fervent about keeping them safe. Tala took on a similar internship to the one my mate had just completed before joining us at the university.

As for the band, they initially wanted to wait for me to come back, but Linsea made it clear that it would be unlikely. The Enforcers spun quite the tale as to why I never returned to school, claiming I sustained grievous cerebral injury following the explosion. And although I would make a complete recovery, it would take many months followed by even more time in physiotherapy and readaptation.

In the end, they took on a new lead singer and ended up signing with a label. As much as I rejoiced for them, it stung my ego a little that they replaced me so quickly. Granted, it took them over four months with countless rejections among the hundreds of applicants. However, learning that they shot down any requests from Temerns did something funny to me. According to Linsea, Ben declared that Echoes of Madness only had one Temern, and it was me. No one else would ever hold that title.

Did that stroke my ego? Absolutely.

At the same time, it struck me as a wise decision. Having another Temern lead singer would only have him constantly compared to me. By choosing someone from another species, they could make the role their own, bring in their own flavor and style without people having unrealistic expectations purely based on race.

Once our meal completed, I subjected myself to a never-ending string of tests. It sucked even more that Linsea couldn't stay with me through it all. Anyway, she had work to do. But my dismay hit a whole new level once they informed me that I would spend the night in observation in my medical room. Obviously, I hadn't expected to be allowed to return home. However, I foolishly thought I could stay with Linsea in the apartment they had temporarily assigned to her while she worked the advisor role for the UPO.

I shamelessly tried to convince them to let her stay the night with me, but the reason for their refusal quickly became apparent. By the time they were done setting me up, I had lost count of the number of wires, magnetic monitoring patches, sensors, and other devices attached to me in one form or another. It was a good thing I'd never been the toss and turn type or they would have had to strap me to the bed to avoid all this shit flying off the minute I attempted to move.

The second day started off with a few more tests before thankfully switching to a far more interesting one. Arafin led me to a lower floor of the building and introduced me to a Raithean male named Yinric.

Like all the members of his species, he didn't possess legs but a set of eight tentacles, only four of which boasted suction cups. His torso was muscular and well-defined, with two arms and five fingers like me. Where soft down feathers covered my torso, from a distance, his chest might have passed off for that of a human with dark-gray skin. But on closer inspection, one could see that his skin was a bit more akin to that of a sea mammal like a dolphin, and discreet scales were scattered along his shoulders, arms, and sides.

He extended a hand for me to shake in a traditional human greeting. Although I reciprocated, that took me aback. Neither his species nor mine normally shook hands. I could only speculate that frequent interactions with humans had turned this into an instinctive response when meeting strangers.

He smiled warmly, the tips of the shorter and narrower tentacles that graced his head almost like hair slightly curled in a way that expressed excitement. It should bother me that the prospect of running tests on me triggered this thrilled reaction. But there was something so innocent and enthusiastic about him that made his responses somewhat contagious.

"I leave you in Yinric's capable hands," Arafin said, the amusement in his voice hinting that he, too, had perceived the Raithean's eagerness. "Once you're done, please go see Ellen to make sure all is well. Do not let him overexert himself," Arafin added in a stern voice while eyeing his colleague.

By the sheepish expression Yinric gave him, I realized the warning was actually meant for the Raithean, not me. I suspected him to be the type to easily get carried away by a project of passion.

As the Temern doctor exited the immense room, Yinric waved for me to follow him. He walked to what resembled a crescent moon-shaped reception desk. A quick glance at it indicated that it was in fact some sort of elaborate control board. I suspected it could activate various apparatus throughout the space.

About five meters ahead of us, a large table with enough seats for eight sat in front of a theater-sized screen that spread over nearly half of the back wall. Currently, it displayed an idle animation of a luminous beam with shimmering pastel colors crawling lazily over the screen.

"My role is to help assess and train both your physical and kinetic abilities," Yinric said with a thrill in his voice as he stopped next to the control panel in the central area. "First, we're going to run you through some basic warmups and then cardio and strength exercises. The scans and tests your doctors performed indicate that you haven't suffered any atrophy while in stasis. However, you used to be a top athlete, and we want to be sure to bring you back at least to the same level you were before the incident and hopefully make you even better."

I gladly complied. My eyes widened when the Raithean tapped a button on the control console, and the floor parted in four different locations on the left side of the room, as did a couple sections of the wall behind it. The best training equipment available anywhere in the galaxy rose from the floor.

With a will of their own, my feet carried me closer, only to have Yinric stop me. He ran me through a specific series of exercises, which proved to be more like tests than an actual proper warm up and training session. Having me running on the treadmill almost qualified as such, but the wretched male stopped me right before I could get my second wind.

"You will get a real workout tomorrow or the day after next," the Raithean said with a chuckle when I glared at him. "Today, we're just making sure everything works as intended. And so far, it seems to be the case, which is excellent news!"

He pointed at a large rectangular room enclosed by a glass wall. It was completely empty and ate up more than a third of the right side of the room.

"The second half of today's training will take place in this holodeck," he continued. "These glass walls are reinforced and strong enough to sustain the pressure of outer space. I'm confident they will be able to withstand whatever you throw at them."

I couldn't help a frown that he should have made that last statement seriously instead of as a joke. Just how powerful did he believe me to be that this would have been a consideration?

"The main thing we want to assess is the extent of your kinetic powers," Yinric said while typing a few instructions on the control board.

A series of virtual targets appeared along the walls inside the glass room at different heights. Some of them were extremely small, requiring substantial precision to hit them while much larger ones would be nearly impossible to miss. The giant screen on the back wall also came to life, the swirling animation giving way to a series of charts and tables currently empty of data.

"Please hold still for a moment while I place these on you," the Raithean said.

He picked up a handful of wireless electrodes, which he strategically placed on my chest, temples, forearms, and lower legs. To my surprise, he added three more to my back: one on my nape, and the other two alongside my spine, between my wings. Various numbers instantly populated the tables on the giant screen while the charts came to life, indicating my pulse and other vital signs.

Yinric glided towards the holodeck, gesturing for me to follow. The swaying motion of his hips was hypnotic.

I vaguely wondered why he hadn't twisted six of his tentacles into makeshift legs as was his people's wont. As suction cups also allowed Raitheans to taste, they usually avoided gliding over the ground. After all, no one wanted to lick the floor. Granted, they could shut down the tasting ability, but some granules or residue always managed to find their way in.

"First, I will ask you to enter the room and try to summon the kinetic pulse you used to knock back the masked men in the convention center," Yinric said while waiving me in as soon as the doors parted before us.

I stiffened. "Errr... I'm afraid I don't know how. Honestly, I didn't even know I possessed that power until Linsea told me what happened."

He pursed his lips and slowly nodded. "Do you remember what you felt that day, and more specifically at that precise moment?"

"The only thing I felt was pain and anger. It was like a dagger stabbing at the center of my brain," I replied, my innards twisting at the memory of that horrendous experience.

"Try to focus on the seat of that pain. It could be the section that activates your power. Then try to channel it towards one of the targets in the room. Starting with a bigger one might be easier," Yinric said with enthusiasm. "But wait until I've exited the room."

I gaped at him while he swiftly slithered out. Did he think I had some sort of switch that I could just flick on and off to zap my surroundings with kinetic energy? The door closed behind him, and I just stood there, feeling lost and a little useless. He stopped on the other side of the glass wall and made a slightly impatient gesture telling me to get going.

Heaving a sigh, I tried to follow his instructions. Focusing on the seat of that pain was much easier said than done. Sure, I could try to zero in on it, but it still didn't give me anything to work with. I didn't feel any type of spark or dormant energy that I could attempt to enhance and project outward. The seconds stretched into minutes with nothing happening. Each passing moment increased my frustration and his impatience in equal measure. I couldn't even be annoyed with him as his outward demeanor was perfectly calm, composed, and even encouragingly supportive. But you couldn't fool a Temern's empathic perceptions.

"I'm sorry," I said at last, starting to feel aggravated and incompetent. "I don't know what to do as I'm not feeling anything in the area that had caused me pain. Maybe I lost that ability after the severe brain hemorrhage I sustained that day."

Yinric shook his head firmly in denial. I couldn't say whether genuine conviction that my powers remained prompted that response, or if he simply refused to accept that possibility.

"I'm certain you still have your powers. Considering you didn't even know you possessed them, it's not surprising that you are struggling to invoke them consciously," the Raithean replied in a soothing tone. "We just need to keep trying, and I have no doubt it will come."

To my dismay, he demanded that I keep trying. After ten, twenty, and then thirty minutes of this nonsense, I was seriously starting to get irritated. I didn't mind training to better myself at something challenging, but this was just a complete waste of time. How the fuck was I to ever make this happen when I didn't even know how I was supposed to do it?

I emitted an angry growl and opened my mouth to tell Yinric that I was done with this, and that we needed to move on to something else. However, his victorious shout resonating through the speakers of the holodeck silenced me.

"There!" he exclaimed, pointing at something on the giant vidscreen. "Whatever you did, do that again!"

I blinked, baffled as my gaze flicked between him and the monitor. A visible spike indicated that I had indeed triggered or invoked some sort of power surge. A part of me wanted to be excited, but I genuinely had no clue how I did this.

"I don't know what I did," I said in an apologetic tone.

Instead of being annoyed with me, Yinric raised his index finger in a manner that indicated for me to wait a moment.

"Hang on. Let me try something," he said excitedly.

The Raithean swiftly slithered towards the central control board and started typing some instructions on the interface.

Seconds later, the most unpleasant zapping sensation went off in my head.

"Stop it!" I hissed. "Don't do that again!"

But Yinric was too excited to worry about my displeasure. "There it is! You see that?" he asked, pointing at the spike on the graph of my brain waves on the giant monitor. "I'm sorry if it hurt you, but this is indeed the spot. Even your eyes are glowing. I'm guessing that this is a defense mechanism that triggers when you feel threatened."

I wanted to glare at him some more, but his excitement was once again contagious. It annoyed me that I couldn't see my own eyes glowing right now. I peered at my hands, but they still looked normal.

"Now that you see where it's located, try to work on stimulating it. Don't push too hard," he added quickly in a cautious fashion. "We can wait until tomorrow or over the upcoming days to actually have you use the full force of your powers. For the time being, we can just focus on getting you comfortable with summoning or activating your ability at will."

I understood his logic, but the curious side of me wanted to go all out as quickly as possible. However, considering I'd spent the past seven months—closer to eight—in partial stasis while they patched my brain, being cautious seemed like a wise approach.

For the next half hour, I followed Yinric's instructions. Although slow at first, I quickly became comfortable stimulating the part of my brain that controlled my kinetic powers. By the time the Raithean called a break, I was able to make my hands glow at will. While I still couldn't see my own reflection, I could now feel the very subtle tingling at the back of my eyes which indicated that they were glowing. The same sensation tickled my palms as my power was activated.

"That will be all for today," Yinric said, taking me by surprise. "You can go back to your doctors so that they can give you another checkup before you can call it a day."

"Already?" I asked, disappointed.

He gave me a knowing smile as he nodded. "Yes. As much as I share your impatience, I don't want to risk bruising you. Relax for the night and return to me well-rested so that we can crank things up at our next session."

"Right," I grumbled.

He chuckled. "So long as Arafin gives you the all clear, expect me to push you hard tomorrow."

"I look forward to it," I deadpanned before heading out of the room.

As I made my way back to the medical section of the facility, I couldn't help but wonder about the significant freedom they were affording me. Considering how much of a threat they seemed to think I could be, I would have expected to be constantly watched over—not to say spied on—and escorted wherever I went. Granted, they had security cameras everywhere and a variety of safety measures throughout the facility that could easily lock me in a contained area should the need arise. But I believed they were intentionally giving me more leeway to both prove myself trustworthy and show that joining them wouldn't be the prison I feared.

Seeing Ellen waiting for me in the medical room I currently called home surprised me. Arafin had clearly been the main doctor in charge of my care. For her part, Ellen appeared more focused on my blood work and endocrine system. She was reading something on the monitor next to my bed, an air of intense concentration on her face.

She jerked her head up to look at me when I stepped inside the room.

"There he is," she said in a friendly tone once recovered from her surprise. "How are you feeling?"

"Great," I said in all sincerity. "Although also a little cheated that he cut everything short. I wanted to push my training a bit further today."

"Patience is a virtue," Ellen said in a slightly chastising tone. "Your therapist was wise in cutting things short. Based on the data he forwarded to us, there is some bruising occurring inside your brain. Therefore, we're setting your circlet back to maximum intensity to reduce the strain and let you heal."

She gave me a sympathetic smile when I loudly groaned the minute the circlet fully blocked my empathic abilities as well as my kinetic powers. However valid the reasons to do so, it systematically made me feel disabled and robbed of an essential part of myself.

"A lot of this is new to you," Ellen said softly. "So we need to be very careful as you train and gain better control of your new abilities. It's important that you do not push yourself too much. You must rest tonight. No training at all, even your ability to block others. Do not reduce the circlet's dampening effect, no matter how much you might itch to do so. The better you follow our instructions, the sooner you will be rid of this temporary crutch. Do *not* strain yourself."

I nodded with a slightly pouty expression. "Yeah, your mate pretty much said the same thing."

To my shock, Ellen recoiled and looked at me as if I had said something absurd.

"My mate?!" she repeated.

"Yes, Yinric," I replied with confidence.

"Who?" she asked, confused.

"Yinric Myar, my kinetic trainer," I replied, now also feeling confused.

She shook her head. "Sorry, but I've never even met him. He is new here. And Arafin normally is the one who interacts with specialists in the other disciplines involved in this project."

"Oh wow!" I whispered, more to myself than for her.

She tilted her head to the side and gave me a slightly baffled inquisitive look. "Why did you assume we were mated?"

"Because you're soulmates," I replied in a factual manner.

She recoiled again, a million conflicting emotions coursing through her. Although I could no longer feel them, they were on full display on her expressive face. The professional in her was wondering if my brain was somehow addled. But her personal side seemed both intrigued and shocked by what she perceived as being completely impossible.

"He can't be. Isn't he a Raithean?" she countered.

I gave her a stern look. "How is that relevant? Someone's species does not define whether they can be your soulmate. And in this instance, there's no question that your souls are in perfect harmony."

Despite her embarrassment at thus being called out for her

silly comment, Ellen was too shocked to respond. She gaped at me for a moment, her wheels spinning.

"So your powers allow you to know when people are soulmates?" she asked carefully at last.

I nodded. "They do."

She shifted on her feet, a mix of excitement and denial plastered all over her face.

"Did you tell him that you thought we were soulmates?" the doctor asked, a hint of nervousness seeping into her voice.

I realized then that she feared a potential rejection by that male and therefore wanted to keep her expectations very low in case I was wrong. While her doubt made sense, it still stung my pride.

"No, I have not. The topic didn't come up. I just assumed you were bonded since you are both soulmates *and* working on the same project," I replied with a shrug.

Ellen ran nervous fingers through her long, dark-brown hair. "I don't know what to say."

I gave her an amused look. "To me? Nothing really. But you should go see Yinric. Maybe you can invite him for a coffee under the guise of discussing my case. Then the rest will fall into place."

The look on her face was hilarious. It took every ounce of my willpower not to burst out laughing. However, her underlying curiosity about the Raithean was what I latched onto. I loved that, despite her misgivings about the accuracy of my statement, she was actually open about looking into its veracity. Her blossoming excitement was contagious. I could grow addicted to stirring such responses in others.

After all, there was no greater feeling in the world than to be surrounded by soulmates reunited.

"Well, if I can go now, I would like to spend a bit of time with my own mate before curfew," I said teasingly.

That seemed to snap Ellen out of her wandering thoughts. She blushed prettily before nodding.

"I just need to draw another blood sample and download the data from your circlet, then I will call your mate so that she can escort you to her quarters."

My heart leapt. "Her quarters?!" I repeated.

It was her turn to give me an amused smile. "You're stable enough to be able to return to a more normal environment. No one likes being cooped up in the medical bay. So long as you continue to follow the medical instructions we provided, things should run smoothly."

Although she spoke those words in a friendly and casual manner, the underlying meaning was clear. Cooperate or lose your privileges.

Her words didn't fall on deaf ears.

CHAPTER 15
KAYOG

My eyes flicked this way and that as my mate escorted me through the long hallway connecting the research center to the residential building reserved for the staff and families that worked there. The main hall offered a grocery store, a bar, a restaurant, and a high-tech gym. At least thirty people were moving about, minding their own business. But my mind remained stuck on the fact that their presence didn't threaten or destabilize me.

Since my awakening yesterday, I'd never been in the presence of more than three or four people at any given time. That the circlet continued to fully shield me from the assault of so many random minds in my vicinity was nothing short of a miracle. For the first time ever, I could actually take the time to analyze people's demeanor and actions when out in the real world. Before, I would devote most of my time just looking for the safest place to hang out as well as pinpointing the fastest escape routes.

A whole new reality was now within reach. As much as I decried the circlet cheating me out of reading their emotions, it gave me a fresh challenge that I gladly tackled, which was to learn to interpret people's emotions based on their body language.

Too soon, we reached the elevators. By the tender—although slightly amused smile Linsea cast my way as we walked—she had guessed the reason I'd been strolling so slowly was to make it last, and she kindly adjusted her steps to mine.

We hopped into the lift, which took us to the fifth floor, the first five of them being reserved for temporary guests. We walked past multiple large doors to various dwellings as we headed to the very last one at the end of the corridor to the right of the elevators. My eyes widened as we stepped into a stunning apartment with a breathtaking view of the natural landscape of the planet. A crystalline river ran horizontally to the living area. Beyond its shores, a lush forest sprawled as far as the eye could see, framed by the majestic outline of the mountains far on the horizon.

I couldn't tell if the comfortable light-gray furniture had been handpicked by my mate or if it was already included in the temporary accommodations. Considering she had been here for months, she might have adapted the place more to her liking. Undeniable personal touches could be seen in the form of paintings by famous Temern artists as well as sculptures from species she had visited as part of her negotiation training internship.

The off-white walls, dark wood floors, and massive windows made the place feel luminous and spacious. Like in my own house, Linsea kept the decor to just the right level of sparseness to accommodate all your needs and comfort without becoming encumbered or noisy. Everything boasted shades of white, cream, and pale grey. But colorful accents with throw pillows, paintings, and other decorative items gave it the right balance.

She gave me a quick tour of the place. It only had one bedroom, the second closed room being used as an office. The open-floor concept of the combined kitchen and dining area clearly indicated that this was not meant as housing for a family, but more for a couple or a traveling single individual.

"Are you thirsty or hungry?" Linsea asked when we returned to the living area.

I shook my head. "They've been feeding me as if they feared I would die of starvation."

She snorted and placed her hands on my sides. I drew her closer into my embrace.

"I can see that," Linsea said, leaning against me. "You need to rebuild some muscle mass from being in stasis for so long. Considering how intensely they want you to train over the next few days—if not weeks—you will need to fuel that scrumptious body of yours. Speaking of which, how are you feeling?"

"I'm fine. Training with Yinric was both great and aggravating," I said with a long-suffering sigh before giving her a quick rundown of my day.

"Maker! Did you really match Ellen and Yinric?!" she exclaimed, when I revealed that last conversation to her.

I puffed out my chest smugly. "Yep, I most certainly did!"

"Wow! Now I can't wait to see how that relationship evolves," Linsea said wistfully.

"It will evolve to its natural conclusion, which is them falling madly in love with each other," I said with a confidence bordering on arrogance. "But speaking of that just further twists the knife in me being denied what I crave the most."

She raised an inquisitive eyebrow. "And what is that?"

"Hearing the song of your soul. Feeling you," I said with a dejected expression. "I'm forbidden from using any of my psychic or kinetic powers under any circumstances until tomorrow."

"Good!" Linsea exclaimed with an almost evil glimmer in her blue eyes.

I recoiled. "Good?! How is that good?"

"Because it means I finally get to give you a taste of your own medicine."

I blinked, utterly baffled. "What do you mean?"

"Ever since we've met, you've had unfettered access to my emotions while yours were hermetically sealed behind an impenetrable wall."

"It was to protect you!" I exclaimed, outraged.

"True though that may be, you still denied me what is rightfully mine. Now, I intend to indulge!" she said in a voice full of promises.

Before I could come up with a smart quip, Linsea's hands on my sides glided up to my chest in a gentle caress… then gave me a shove.

I yelped in surprise, throwing a hand behind me to stop my fall, only to land on the soft cushion of the couch behind me. Her palms on my shoulders kept me sitting down when I straightened. Whatever question or comment I'd intended to speak died on my tongue when my female leaned in front of me.

She rubbed her beak against mine before gently pecking it in a way that demanded access. I immediately complied, my stomach fluttering as our tongues mingled. Despite having a more dominant disposition, I allowed her to take the lead. As I reveled in her sweet taste and the possessiveness with which she kissed me, I fought the urge to take over.

I was hers to do with as she pleased.

To my dismay, she pulled away from me just when I was further leaning into the kiss. With a vocal command, she activated the music player, and a slow, instrumental song resonated through the room. With another vocal command, Linsea dimmed the light, setting the perfect mood.

Blood rushed to my groin, and I straightened even more on the couch to better enjoy the show taking place before my greedy eyes. Linsea moved gracefully, swaying her hips left and right, the long feathers of her flowy tail accentuating the motion as it trailed behind her like a cascading waterfall.

She spun around in a slow rotation, her hands roaming over her body in a sensuous fashion that heated my blood in no time. Turning her back to me, Linsea bent forward and shook her behind so that the tip of her tail brushed teasingly against my face. I wanted to lunge forward, pin her to the ground, and ram myself home before fucking her senseless.

The thrice damned circlet left my emotions wide open for my mate to plunder. Linsea chuckled smugly, reveling in her power over me. Wanting to up the ante, the wretched female bent even lower, lifting her tail, and spreading her legs wider. My cock jerked angrily, demanding to be freed from the confines of my protection pouch when Linsea opened her flap, exposing her slit in all its splendor for me to drool over.

Head down, my mate glanced at me from between her legs with a taunting expression. She licked her beak in a lascivious manner before teasing her slit with one finger, dipping it in and out a couple of times. She abruptly straightened, her tail feathers swiping across my cheek with an impertinence that warranted a proper spanking. But Linsea turned around to face me while licking the finger she had just touched herself with in a way that almost had me growling in frustration.

My female chuckled again as she strutted towards me with the grace of a predator closing in on prey paralyzed by fear. Except it was lust pinning me in place.

A fire lit in the pit of my stomach as she caressed my body with growing boldness. When I tried to reciprocate, she swatted my hand hard enough to give it a good sting. I burned with the need to protest, flip us around, and show her who was in charge. But I squashed it again.

My whole life, I battled to acquire some sort of control over my life when it constantly seemed to spiral. It had become an almost intrinsic part of me to always be the one at the helm of what I actually had a say in. But this was different.

Although I doubted Linsea was testing me and my ability to submit, I suspected at a visceral level that she needed to know that I trusted her enough to abandon myself to her. And I did. There was nothing I wouldn't do for this female.

A sound halfway between a purr and a coo vibrated through my chest as Linsea partially extruded her claws and carefully raked them between the down feathers of my neck, chest, and sides. A violent shiver coursed through me each time her thorough exploration triggered a strong reaction—whether physical or emotional—that revealed one of my sensitive spots. Just like I had done during our first time together, she was studying my emotional responses to her touch to narrow down my erogenous areas and what I enjoyed her doing to me.

Like her, I loved having the crook of my neck gently pecked, especially close to my nape. For some inexplicable reason, it always resonated directly in my cock. Her claws on my pelvis—right below my navel—also fanned the flame of my arousal. But the one thing I never expected to be a massive turn on was Linsea carefully scratching the inside of my palm with her beak as she traced the lines within before sucking on my index finger.

A bolt of lust exploded between my thighs. Linsea's smug chuckle as her tongue swirled around my finger both pissed me off and aroused me. It was the provocative way in which she tilted her head to lock eyes with me as she continued to suck on my finger. Her right hand covering my crotch made her underlying meaning clear. Maker, I could almost feel her mouth on my cock.

Her claws gently teased the seam of my crotch, coaxing me to extrude. For a split second, I considered resisting, both to provoke her and to see how she would 'punish' me for misbehaving. That latter thought almost made me deny her. But I had silently pledged to submit to her will—this time—and therefore complied.

The hiss of relief that escaped me took me by surprise. I hadn't realized just how strained my cock had become, stuck in its confines while growing increasingly hard. However, my female greedily wrapping her hand around my length had the hiss shift into a strangled moan.

Linsea slowly licked my finger from bottom to top in perfect sync with her hand stroking me. My abdominal muscles contracted, and a dull throbbing pulsated in my cock. My breath hitched when she extended her tongue to its fullest length just shy of nine inches and proceeded to lick the inside of my palm.

My cock jerked in response and, to my utter shame, a bead of precum seeped out. A triumphant smile stretched my mate's beak. Moving at lightning speed, she abandoned my hand to lick my head and then swallowed my length.

I cried out, my back arching as my wings twitched with the instinctive need to spread wide. Linsea squeezed the base of my cock almost painfully, as she began to bob over me. I could feel the head hit the back of her throat with each downward motion. I would have marveled at the fact that it didn't seem to trigger her gag reflex, but intense waves of pleasure robbed me of any rational thought.

She adjusted the angle of her head so that every time my cock would hit the back of her throat, each of my *ganacs* would come into contact with it. These small, natural bumps on my glans vaguely resembled subcutaneous implants. Aside from enhancing our female's pleasure during penetration, they were also highly erogenous for us males. Each impact on them felt like electric sparks of bliss setting off around the head of my cock, spreading down its length, and sending fiery tendrils running throughout my pelvic area.

The soft warmth of her tongue wrapping and swirling around the head with each stroking motion was driving me insane with pleasure. When she closed her beak, carefully scraping it against the spiraling ridges of my shaft, I nearly came undone.

I shouted, and my hips involuntarily bucked, nearly choking her. My loins were ablaze, and I felt faint with the need to give in to ecstasy. But I refused to find my release before my mate, especially not after so many months apart.

Just as I was about to yank her off me, Linsea gave my cock a final lick before rising to her feet from her kneeling position in front of me. She climbed in my lap, her seam parting to reveal her glistening slit. The delectable scent of her musk had my entire body seizing with need. It took my foggy brain a moment to understand what had prompted Linsea's almost pained moan seconds before she impaled herself on my cock.

I cried out again at the exquisite burn and searing heat of her sheath tightly engulfing me. By the expression on her face and the tremor of her body, my mate was feeling overwhelmed by both her pleasure and my own. I remembered all too well how insane it had been to have the bliss her touch procured me multiplied a thousandfold by the one she felt.

A savage series of grunts tumbled out of me as my female immediately set a feverish pace as she rode my cock with wild abandon. My fear that I would fail to pleasure her without my ability to feel her emotion completely vanished. Even with the circlet still blocking me, the voluptuous sounds emanating from my woman, her gorgeous face dissolved in a pure air of bliss, and the frenzied way with which she touched me and responded to my own attentions made it clear she more than approved of my ministrations.

Having memorized each of her sensitive spots from our previous couplings, I stimulated every single one of them, making her moan and whisper my name with the needy possessiveness I craved.

An inferno raged inside of me, burning me from the inside out. Linsea's inner walls clamping down on my cock threatened to send me toppling over the edge. Needing even more, I slipped my hands under her rump, effortlessly lifting her slightly before pounding into her from beneath. She hung on to my shoulders, head thrown back as an endless stream of moans tumbled out of her. She looked like a goddess with her massive, pristine white wings spread behind her, gently flapping with each thrust. Her long, fluffy tail also caressed my legs with each motion.

My mate's legs began to shake, and her claws dug into my shoulders as her breathing grew louder and more labored. Sensing her imminent climax, I drew her closer to me and reclaimed her mouth. With my left hand still propping her up above me, I slipped my right hand around her back to claw at the down feathers at the base of her wings.

I swallowed her shout of ecstasy as she fell apart in my arms. After a couple more thrusts into her, I gave in to my own climax. My spine seized, and my wings spread wide as I roared my release. My seed shot out into my mate in an endless flow of the purest bliss. As much as I hated not being able to perceive her own pleasure, I still reveled in the wondrous sensation of my Linsea's feverish body, still trembling in the throes of passion in my arms.

She collapsed against me, heart pounding, her face buried in my neck. I tightened my embrace, my heart filling with love for my mate. I wrapped my wings around her as she snuggled deeper into me. Hearing my mate coo with content put a smile on my face.

I fleetingly thought how this experience gave me a newfound respect for humans and other non-empathic species. Being able to feel our partner's emotions was really a form of cheating. We didn't have to focus as much on them or their responses to our actions because it was directly spoon fed to us.

"Stop fretting so much, silly male," Linsea said in a still slightly groggy voice. "You did great."

Maker, it would take me a while to get used to having my emotions fully exposed to others.

"Of course, I did," I replied smugly. "I'm Kayog Voln."

She burst out laughing and lifted her head to look at me as if I was a hopeless case.

"To be fair, I had a leg up from our previous times together. But I can't wait to feel you again," I said sheepishly.

"And you will soon," she said, rubbing her beak against mine.

"Soon," I concurred. "For now, though, I guess I'll just have to keep practicing interpreting your needs and emotions the non-empathic way. Let's see how I fare when I'm the one in charge."

She giggled prettily as I rose to my feet, my cock still buried deep inside her. Linsea wrapped her legs around my waist as I carried her to the bedroom, our tongues mingling...

The following week was an endless series of increasingly more intense training sessions. Most of my time was now spent with Yinric, with the usual quick fifteen-minute medical checkup by either Arafin or Ellen. To my delight, I was now able to use the circlet at less than half its dampening effect. In fact, I could function without it at all, but only over short periods of time before the strain wore me out. Still, it wouldn't be much longer before I stopped needing that crutch at all.

Arafin injected me with a series of nanobots that accelerated the healing process whenever I suffered bruising from overextending myself. They also hastened the formation of new neural pathways, which in turn gave me greater control over my powers.

The fact that they blocked my empathic abilities during the day continued to bother me. Although they claimed it was to limit bruising and reserve my psychic energy for my kinetic training, I strongly suspected that it was more a matter of them keeping me oblivious to whatever they were thinking or feeling in my presence. I didn't doubt for a minute that I was constantly being observed and evaluated by far more eyes than I could see.

I refused to let it bother me. I'd studied enough politics and how big organizations such as the UPO and the Enforcers operated to understand the need for them to thoroughly investigate what kind of a threat—or asset—I could be. My focus remained on gaining full control over my body and abilities, for which they provided the type of support I never could have dreamt of before. I would handle whatever followed next in due time.

For now, I was having a blast with the new simulation Yinric shifted me to. On the second day with him, I managed to summon my targeted kinetic power, which we labeled a kinetic pulse. Feeling that blast of energy building in my forearm, gathering in my palm, and then shooting out with remarkable strength was beyond exhilarating. It nearly gave me a hard on.

His excitement rivaled mine as he pushed me to use it on the various targets inside the holodeck. While clumsy at first, with a less-than-impressive precision, I quickly improved over the following couple of days. Besides my aiming accuracy, I also became more proficient at controlling the strength of the shot and projecting it over greater distances. It would take me a while to properly assess the required strength based on the varying proximity of my targets. But the highly competitive side of me reveled in the challenge.

Despite having extensive combat training—which helped me with focus and discipline over the years—I'd never been much into weapon-based sports or activities. But this was something else altogether. My weapon wasn't a blaster or sword, it was my very own body and the energy contained within.

Over the past three days, Yinric started running simulations where I battled virtual enemies. It was an immersive virtual scenario akin to a shooting gallery where villains of every type would jump at me from behind covers. Initially, only a small number of them would burst into the street to threaten me with a variety of blunt or long-range weapons. Then their numbers increased, the type of weapons they used grew more lethal and with greater range, and then they started coming from different areas. No longer did they come out of building doors or from behind predictable covers along the street. Now, some of them would fly down or emerge from the ground with very little to no warning.

The variety of species—from people to monsters—also increased the difficulty. I couldn't strike them with the same kinetic intensity as the blast would be lethal for certain species but barely even slow down or stun another. To my dismay, it took me a while to get a better understanding of how to scale it, especially on the fly as the species of my attackers would alternate quickly, giving me little reaction time.

The trail of corpses I left behind would have been staggering —not to say devastating—had they not been virtual. Still, the adrenaline rush I got from it whipped my blood into a frenzy. It was the ultimate video game packed with action which also helped me develop unbelievable skills.

I wasn't foolish enough not to know why Yinric was gradually adjusting the training so that the simulations shifted more and more towards rescue missions. Even now, as I flew around the holodeck, my eyes flicked this way and that, dodging incoming blaster fire while trying to take down a group of snipers hiding in buildings. On the street below, a getaway car was speeding off with a high-ranking official held hostage.

I soared a few meters vertically, positioning myself at a height that had every sniper located no more than three meters above or below me. I summoned my kinetic blast power—not the targeted pulse, but the area of effect. A powerful tingling at the back of my head indicated the building energy. I let it intensify until it reached the level I deemed appropriate to achieve my goal. I pushed it outward, willing it to spread within a specific radius around me but no more than a certain height above and below me. The vertical constraint was the hardest but necessary part as I didn't want to hit people on the ground, especially the driver of the getaway car. An accident could kill the kidnapped victim, which would defeat the entire purpose of the operation.

The air around me blurred as the kinetic blast erupted from me. Half a second later, the snipers appeared disabled. As much as I hated not having access to my empathic powers, I loved to see how well I could perform at identifying enemies without that additional tool. Even though the enemies were virtual, holographic simulations could send specific signals to empathic species like mine to fake the emotions of the characters or creatures within the scenario.

I dove towards the car, moving ahead of it before spinning around. Flying backwards, I fired a series of kinetic pulses to slow it down. To my dismay, the driver attempted a sharp turn and lost control. The car flipped to the side and would have rolled over multiple times had I not swiftly stopped it with many pulses.

I flew down to the wreckage and yanked the front door open, only to be met with a blaster aimed at my face. I barely managed to throw myself to the side to avoid a lethal shot—although in this simulator, I would have simply sustained an unpleasant zap. Anger surged within me, and the weirdest sensation went off in the very center of my head. It was different from the tingling I normally experienced when using my kinetic blasts of pulses. But something happened. When I positioned myself back in front of the open door, ready to hit the driver with a kinetic pulse, I found him slumped over, conscious, but twitching as if he'd been brutally tased.

Although confused, I glanced at the backseat where the kidnapped victim was smiling at me gratefully. But before I could help him out of the vehicle, his face took on a horrified expression as he stared at something over my shoulder. I jerked my head around to see a swarm of monsters—both landbound and airborne—making a wall as they raced towards us from the other end of the street.

"I will straighten the car. Keep cover inside," I ordered before using a kinetic pulse to tip the car back onto its wheels.

Flying towards the throngs, I summoned a powerful wave of kinetic energy before blasting it at them. Many of the smaller creatures immediately collapsed, but the rest single-mindedly continued their advance, trampling over the fallen with complete disregard.

Despite knowing that this was only a simulation, I didn't feel the normal fear one should experience in a similar situation. The only emotions coursing through me were the thrill of the hunt and an incredible sense of power.

It was intoxicating.

I bombarded them with kinetic blasts while dodging long-range attacks from the creatures that could throw darts and even some sort of lightning bolts. As I loved flying, the aerial acrobatics required to avoid getting hit only made the experience even more exhilarating. On a few occasions, that odd ability manifested itself again, some strange heat in the center of my brain that sought a target. It took me a moment to realize which of my enemies got struck by it. But I recognized the spasms that shook them as if they'd been zapped.

When I finally cleared out the onslaught, I almost felt cheated. My blood was pumping full of adrenaline, and I wanted to obliterate more abominations. The simulation ended, the city setting I had been fighting in fading and turning back into the clear glass walls enclosing the holodeck.

A clapping sound startled me, snapping me out of my blood thirsty trance. Jerking my head around, I saw Colin standing next to Yinric. My heart leapt in my chest. I had been expecting a visit from him from the moment I awakened, eight days ago. I could speculate as to why he had waited this long to finally pay me a visit. The part of me that was relieved that this would hopefully be settled at last couldn't silence the other part that feared that the comfortable routine I had established with my mate might be upended.

I bowed in gratitude at their applause as I gracefully landed. Both males stopped clapping, and Yinric enthusiastically gestured for me to come out of the holodeck. I complied, forcing myself to plaster a neutral but friendly expression on my face while reining in my emotions.

"We meet again," I said nonchalantly. "I wondered how much longer before it happened."

He smirked, indicating he understood my underlying disapproval that he should have kept me in limbo for so long.

"Believe me, I wanted nothing more than to come see you sooner. However, it felt a lot more sensible to allow you some time to heal and get your bearings," he said with an empathy that didn't fool me, even with my powers to read his emotions still being blocked.

There was no question in my mind the delay wasn't so much for the reasons he gave but rather for him to get a better sense of just how powerful I could be.

"That makes sense," I replied politely.

"As Yinric has a date with a charming woman, I've decided to kidnap you for the rest of the day," Colin said, casting a teasing look at the Raithean.

"A date?!" I repeated, my eyes widening in surprise.

I couldn't help but chuckle when Yinric's charcoal scales took on an even darker shade, betraying his embarrassment.

"I'm going out with Ellen," he mumbled shyly.

"That's excellent!" I exclaimed in an approving tone.

Not wanting to pry or meddle in other people's business, I had not prodded either Ellen or him since the first time I informed Ellen that she and Yinric were soulmates. It pleased me beyond words that they would pursue what would inevitably result in their happily ever after. I couldn't wait to be in their presence at the same time to bask in the perfect harmony of their souls.

"She's very charming," Yinric said, still sounding a little timid, in sharp contrast with his usually more assertive and overly enthusiastic demeanor. "Thank you for helping initiate that connection."

"My pleasure. Everyone deserves to find the other half of themselves," I said with a gentle smile before turning my attention back to Colin. "Would it be okay for me to shower first?"

"Of course!" Colin replied. "Take your time. Anyway, I have a couple of things to discuss with Yinric."

For a reason I couldn't explain, that instantly made me uneasy. My reaction made no sense to the extent that there was no question Colin was apprised of absolutely everything that happened with me during my training and medical exams. So any additional detail he might get from the Raithean couldn't be more harmful than any data he already possessed. Still, I couldn't help the wariness weighing on my shoulders.

I showered quickly then hurried back out to the training room only to find Colin standing on his own by the Control Board, my latest simulation replaying on the giant screen that filled the back wall.

"Impressive work," Colin said, as I closed the distance between us, his eyes still glued to the screen.

"Thank you," I said in a neutral voice as I stopped near him.

"You seem to be enjoying yourself," he continued before giving me a sideways glance.

I shrugged. "I do. I always loved competitive sports. This almost feels like playing Lazgar, but with combat. The only thing missing is a high score for me to try to beat."

He snorted, an approving glimmer shining in his eyes.

"Come, let's have a seat," he said, stopping the simulation replay before heading to the worktable in front of the screen.

Just as we were taking our seats, a server walked into the room with a hover tray laden with snacks and drinks. I repressed a smile upon seeing the grain crackers I had gotten Linsea addicted to.

"Hungry?" he asked, sounding like the perfect host.

I shook my head with a smile. "No, but I wouldn't mind a drink."

"By all means!" he said, gesturing at the bottles of flavored water.

I grabbed one, intending to only take a couple of sips but ended up gulping down the entire thing. Feeling a little mortified, I gave him a sheepish smile while putting the lid back on the empty bottle.

"Thanks," I mumbled.

"Have a second one!" he said, pushing another of the five bottles towards me.

"Don't mind if I do," I said, greedily accepting the offering.

This time, I showed a bit more restraint and only drank a third of it.

"Sorry," I said while putting the bottle down.

He made a dismissive gesture. "Don't be! It's normal to be dehydrated after such an amazing performance."

I gave him a look that made it clear he wasn't fooling me. "So you're here to recruit me again?"

"Of course," Colin replied in a self-evident tone.

I narrowed my eyes at him. "What if I say no?"

"Then we have a problem," he said in a factual manner.

My brow shot up at the blunt and nonchalant way in which he made that statement.

"Is that so?" I asked, genuinely intrigued to see where this was headed.

Not for the first time, I hated being unable to read his

emotions. I almost reached for my circlet to reduce the dampening effect. However, I had already made my peace with the fact that not only would I play by their rules, but that I would also accept joining the Enforcers so long as their requests weren't immoral to me. Beyond the fact that I wanted a peaceful life by my mate's side, I honestly owed them for this new lease on life they had given me.

"You're far too powerful, Kayog," Colin said in a reasonable tone. "The things you're able to do exceed anything I've ever seen before. And you're still not done."

I stiffened at that. "What do you mean?"

"Most species reach full maturity by the age of twenty-five, whether physically, mentally, or psychically. You went into overdrive when you got to that age. Even now, you are continuing to grow. God only knows when you will reach your peak."

"You can't be certain of that," I countered, my voice hesitant.

He nodded firmly. "I most certainly can. Your doctors have confirmed it. We don't know just how strong you will get and what new skills you may develop. That makes you unpredictable."

"And therefore dangerous?" I challenged.

"Potentially," he concurred. "That means we can't let you loose. Today again, there was an unusual spike during your simulation. It tapped into another part of your brain that had been mostly dormant before. Yinric will analyze the data where the computer indicated that you used a new ability against some of the targets."

Although I attempted to keep a neutral expression, something on my face or body language gave away the fact that he had accurately assessed what had happened during the simulation. I didn't know what new power I used or even how to deliberately replicate it. How many more new abilities would I indeed discover?

"As a member of the Enforcers or the UPO, you can receive

all the support you need while we also get to keep an eye on you. If you evolve outside, we would be required to expend far too many resources to make sure you do not become a threat, whether willingly or through coercion by hostile forces," Colin explained, his tone soft and reasonable.

"Then wouldn't it be simpler for you to just kill me?" I asked with a hint of dare in my voice.

He scoffed. "Nobody wants to do that, and as far as I'm concerned, it's not even an option worth considering. So we need to find a solution that will keep both you and everyone else safe. You also do not want to be alone if your brain continues to develop in unexpected ways. No one but the extensive resources of the Enforcers and of the UPO could have accomplished what we have for you."

"So now you consider me indebted?" I asked, narrowing my eyes at him.

To my pleasant surprise, he immediately shook his head. "Not at all. It was our choice to expend so many resources to fix you. You never agreed to anything in exchange for our assistance, and your mate made it clear that she would never make any promises or engagements on your behalf without your consent. We did it because we saw great potential in you, long-term benefits for other members of your species born with your condition, and because Linsea is one hell of a negotiator, especially when it involves the male she loves."

I lowered my eyes, moved to the core by his words. I had a fairly low opinion of mega organizations like the ones he was working for. But the sincerity in his voice as he stated his position on the matter resonated loudly. However, it was his statement about my dove's involvement that turned me upside down. I didn't doubt she had gone to every extreme to protect me. And I still didn't understand how I had deserved such a perfect female.

"I don't know you, Kayog Voln, only what I read in your

files—and you better believe I read the fuck out of them," Colin said in a serious tone. "You have a stellar record, and the medical team working with you are major fans of yours. It is not an easy feat to accomplish, especially where Arafin is concerned. I like Linsea and want to keep her happy. But my duty comes first. If you had been a threat, we would have already dealt with you a long time ago. Instead, everyone in this facility is desperate to make sure you will be fine and that no harm will come to you. So we must find a solution while honoring our galactic duty."

My eyes flicked between his as I studied his features. Once again, his words deeply touched me. I had indeed developed a more than cordial relationship with my doctors and trainers. The few times I'd been able to read their emotions revealed a genuine desire from them to see me thrive. The rest of the time, every single one of their actions and words reinforced my opinion that they were all good people with my best interests at heart.

"You can deactivate the circlet and read me so you know that I'm speaking the truth," Colin offered.

I shook my head. "It's not necessary, I know you are."

A subtle smile stretched his lips before he tilted his head to the side while giving me an assessing look.

"You're smart, charismatic, one of the most impressive fighters I've seen—"

"Stop," I interrupted him in an imperious tone. "I have no interest in becoming a soldier. I don't want to be an assassin, a spy, part of an infiltration team, or any of that other stuff."

"But you're formidable enough to excel in all of those fields," Colin argued, even though his tone was more factual than attempting to be convincing. "Your tests in the holodeck speak for themselves. Not to mention the fact that you clearly enjoy battle."

"In a competitive setting, yes," I conceded. "But I'm not a killer nor a predator. I like to win, to be the best, and excel at anything I do. I have no desire to cause harm. If you look carefully at my tests, you will see that I never used lethal force on my opponents, not even the nightmarish monsters you threw at me."

Colin pursed his lips and slowly nodded. By the look in his eyes, he was fully aware of my non-lethal approach throughout my training. Right this instant, I kicked myself for not taking him up on his offer to disable my circlet so that I could have a better understanding of how he was feeling about it. Did he think me weak? Did he wonder if it was a ploy to make myself look less dangerous than I truly was? Did he assume it was a limitation on my powers that kept me from inflicting greater damage?

"Do you know what kept me alive through the chaos that had been ruining my life?" I suddenly asked.

He shook his head, his eyes gleaming with keen interest.

"Joy," I said calmly. "Positive emotions soothed the pain I was in. This was one of the main reasons I joined the band. Have you ever been to a concert or sports event?"

He nodded in a self-evident manner.

"People attend them because the energy is electric. You want to be surrounded by that collective enthusiasm. It's contagious and makes the experience far greater than when you watch it alone in your home. It is almost like a hive mind that has everyone vibrating to the same tune for the duration of the event. But hatred, anger, and fear are extremely harmful to me. They're slimy and stab at my brain. I hate how those emotions feel, not to mention the pain they inflict me."

"Right," Colin said pensively. "Arafin explained that you perceive other people's emotions both as physical and sensory manifestations."

"I do. Therefore, I would never consent to performing a job that subjects me to these emotions or drives me to inflict them onto others. I want to protect people and bring them joy. The most wondrous feelings are hope, happiness, love, and above all being in the presence of soulmates."

236

To my surprise, Colin smirked with a knowing expression. "I knew you would say something like that."

"Oh?" I said, my curiosity piqued.

"Although your psychiatric evaluations state that you have very strong hunter and predator instincts, you're dominantly a protector and nurturer," Colin said with a slightly dejected expression. "It's a pity, really. You could have been one of our best squad leaders. But your offensive side will only kick in if you feel threatened, and especially if you see someone vulnerable in danger. You wouldn't thrive in the types of roles I would have wanted for you. That leaves us with the question of what shall we do with you?"

A fair question I had been pondering myself from the moment Linsea warned me the Enforcer's director would attempt to recruit me again.

"Maybe I should become an alien matchmaker," I said teasingly.

To my shock, Colin didn't smile or laugh at my lame joke but gave me an assessing look instead.

"It was a joke," I said in a self-evident tone when he appeared to be weighing the merit of that statement.

He tilted his head to the side and gave me an odd look. "Was it?"

"Of course!" I exclaimed forcefully. "I was just repeating a random comment a friend made a while back to lighten the mood. And anyway, what the fuck would the Enforcers or the UPO want with a matchmaker?"

"You're passionate about primitive species, are you not?" Colin asked, ignoring my question.

"Absolutely," I replied in an imperious tone. "They must be defended at all costs against greedy conglomerates and questionable people seeking to profit from more vulnerable species. Every world should have the right to evolve at their own pace and according to their own terms."

"Exactly," he said with a satisfied expression. "And you could help make that happen by matching them."

My brain froze, and I stared at him in complete confusion. What the fuck did that even mean? How did pairing a couple in any way help achieve the protection of primitive species?

He gave me an indulgent smile. "Throughout history, marriage has been used to build strong alliances between peoples. Primitive species are generally closed off and inaccessible to the commonfolk. You could help open those doors."

My face hardened. "Are you asking me to help infiltrate them?"

He snorted and shook his head. "No, I want you to help us form bonds with them. The best way to learn about someone's culture is by living with them. A temporary visit for a couple of days doesn't show you the real picture. Through their mates, we can learn a lot about them as well as provide both guidance and protection."

I narrowed my eyes at him. "What you're saying still sounds a lot like infiltration."

He smiled. "There's a fine line between infiltration, assimilation, and collaboration. Someone like you, with the power to know when two people are soulmates, will help create the kind of pairings that will ensure the protection of primitive people. I mean your soulmate will always want what's best for you, right?"

I nodded, although still far from convinced. "True though that may be, do you know what are the odds of me ever finding a primitive alien's other half? There are billions of people throughout the galaxy. I might as well try to count how many drops of water are in the ocean."

Colin's smile broadened. "What does it matter? You still get to meet those aliens, talk to them, and learn about their cultures. You always wanted to meet primitive species. What more perfect deal could you ask for?"

My heart leapt. He was making an excellent point. Even now, my mind buzzed with all the species I wished I could have interacted with directly or gotten to spend a few weeks in their midst. Despite the excitement bubbling inside me, I forced myself to rein in my enthusiasm. There were far too many holes in this plan. I hated failure. I didn't mind hard work, but embarking on a project that was doomed before it even began didn't feature anywhere on my to do list.

"Fair," I replied carefully. "But what if I fail to yield any positive results? What if I never match anyone or only once in a very rare while?"

He shrugged. "I don't worry about that. The result will slowly but surely come. You only need extensive exposure to as many people as possible. What you need to understand is that people will flock to you. Throughout the universe, love is one of the biggest businesses in any society. The industries that continuously thrive are those connected to helping people find a life partner. Do you know how many matchmaking agencies exist in the known galaxy?"

"Tons of them!" I exclaimed. "Which is exactly my point! When people think of finding a mate, they don't think Enforcers or UPO!"

Colin chuckled. "Which is why you will not be officially employed by either. You will simply have the UPO as an affiliate and major sponsor. People are tired of throwing their money at agencies that fail them and wasting their time dating partners that were pretty much guaranteed to be incompatible right from the start. With you, the perfect match is guaranteed. They will fight each other for your services."

"Assuming I even manage to find their soulmate!" I repeated, baffled that he seemed to fail to see my point.

He gave me an indulgent smile. "You worry too much. People buy lottery tickets knowing that their chances of winning are slim to none. But that chance exists. And the reward is more than worth the gamble. You can offer them the ultimate prize for free."

I perked up, that last comment catching my attention.

"The UPO will pay your wages as well as cover all your operating costs. Matchmaking is merely your cover with the added bonus of allowing you to do all the things you love most, which is to protect primitive species, bring joy to others, and surround yourself with soulmates. It's a win-win all around."

"You've really thought about this," I said, stunned.

Initially, I thought my joke about becoming a matchmaker had planted that seed in his mind. But it was now clear to me that he had already been studying this as a possibility.

He gave me a mysterious look. "I never act on a whim," he replied as if he had read the thought fleeting through my mind. "I've been weighing the pros and cons of that approach since you paired Yinric and Ellen."

I recoiled. "What?"

"Ellen *never* would have considered a Raithean as a potential mate, and neither would have Yinric even glanced at a human with a romantic mindset. It wasn't because of any negative perception of the other species. It simply wasn't something they thought about. Both assumed they would eventually end up with someone of their own race."

"Until I meddled in their affairs," I said with amusement.

"Until you offered them their happily ever after on a silver platter," Colin countered with an almost triumphant glimmer in his eyes. "As much as it surprised them, they didn't question it because they trust you. Kayog, you do not seem to realize just how charismatic and likable you are. You make people feel safe. The way you look at people and talk to them give them the impression that they hold your entire attention, like they are the center of your universe during the brief time they interact with you."

I shifted uneasily in my chair, unsure how to handle these compliments.

"Like I said, don't fret so much about quotas. Even if you only secure one or two matches a year, each one will reinforce your status and credibility," Colin said forcefully. "In the meantime, you get to visit all those protected worlds, talk to their people, understand their plights, and document the ways that we could help them."

I narrowed my eyes at him, looking for any sign of deception.

"Ways we could *help* them or *exploit* them?" I challenged.

The strangest expression flitted over his ruggedly handsome features.

"Are you asking *me*, Colin Wilson, this question? Or are you asking the representative of both the Enforcers and the UPO?"

Something in the way he spoke those words struck me hard. In that instant, I realized he was dropping the mask and laying everything on the table.

"Both," I said in a serious tone.

"Like any major organization, the UPO and the Enforcers will always want anything that can benefit their members, increase their influence, or give them something they can leverage later. These organizations are not saints, but beneath all the politics and power grabs, their mission remains something I am proud to associate with. So yes, they would love to receive any juicy tidbits that can serve their purposes," Colin said in a factual manner.

"Fair enough," I said, appreciating his candor. "And what about you?"

"I'm building a team of people who, like me, want to serve the true purpose of these two organizations. You've met our doctors and trainers here. Even with your empathic abilities blocked, you can see what professional, dedicated, and good people they are. You and your mate are exactly the type of personalities we're looking to add to our ranks. You're both highly qualified in your respective fields, truly devoted to protecting the people our organizations were created for, and possess remarkable moral values. We don't care about politics here. We care about doing what's right for the most vulnerable."

The passionate way in which he spoke once more screamed of sincerity. I also couldn't argue with his description of the team I got the pleasure to interact with here. If the rest of the staff under his supervision matched this one, then I could definitely see myself wanting to be a part of it.

"The Prime Directive is being trampled at every turn," Colin continued with a frown. "Many of these primitive species either get taken in by those who violated the rules or develop resentment towards off-worlders in general. You could help reset the balance. In many ways, you would act as an informal ambassador and help establish more positive relations with those species. With you bringing happiness to their people, with the endorsement of the UPO, you can help us be seen as friends as they grow into their own powers. It's a long-term game. And who better than you to provide recommendations as to how we can assist or raise red flags about current threats or existing rules that need to be revisited?"

To say he had me seriously excited would be the ultimate understatement. But still, I had countless reservations. Of all the ways this conversation could have gone, never in a million years would I have expected this one.

"You have given me some serious food for thought. But a matchmaker?" I said, my hesitation clearly audible in my voice.

He chuckled and eyed me with a smugness that pissed me off. In his mind, he had already won me over. Knowing that he was probably right made it even more annoying.

"Take the next two days to think about it, and then draft a plan for your matchmaking agency," Colin said in a commanding tone.

"Two days?" I repeated, confused by what seemed like a random timeline.

"Yes. My firstborn son is due tomorrow. My wife will skin me alive if I'm not there—not that I would want to miss the birth of my little Tedrick for anything in the world. Talk it out with your mate and come back to me with a plan detailing everything you want. Go as wild as you deem necessary. With these things, you're always better off asking for too much to get what you want than not asking for enough and screwing yourself over."

I gaped at him as he rose to his feet, gave me an almost taunting nod, then casually strolled out of the room.

CHAPTER 16
LINSEA

Sitting on the couch, my legs folded to the side, I couldn't stop laughing at my poor mate's dismayed expression. Caught up in my own work, I'd returned home a little later than usual to find him pacing back and forth in the living room, his emotions all over the place.

"Seriously, Lin, a matchmaker?" he repeated for the hundredth time. "In the next couple of years, you will become a big shot ambassador for the UPO. And me? Can you imagine talking with some of the most influential people in the galaxy and then introducing them to your matchmaker husband?"

"Hey! Don't be elitist!" I said with a frown.

He stopped pacing and turned to look at me with a slightly offended expression. "I'm not being elitist. But what about your image? You know how people in these upper circles get when they deem someone inferior."

"First off, I'm not elitist either. And judgy people can fuck right off," I said in a tone that brooked no argument. "It doesn't matter what career you end up doing. Mean-spirited people will always find something to bully others over. During my internship, I've seen how nasty some people got purely out of malice.

The real question is whether this is something you would like to do."

"Pairing soulmates while getting to hang out with countless primitive species under strict Prime Directive guidelines? Fuck yes, I would love that! But the odds of me ever making successful matches are next to nil," he said, his broad shoulders slouching.

"The odds may be slim but not impossible," I countered gently before extending a hand towards him.

He approached the couch and took my hand, allowing me to tug him closer. Kayog settled down next to me, and I snuggled against him. Maker, I would never tire of the wondrous feel of his body against mine, the possessiveness with which he wrapped his arm around me, and especially the incredible emotions that always emanated from him towards me. Kayog literally adored me. I never imagined anyone could be this happy just being in my presence and passively make me feel worshipped like he did.

"No matter how many or few of them you manage to make, every pairing is a blessing. In the end, it is just a really fun cover for your real goal, which is to help define the Prime Directive guidelines and intergalactic policies regarding primitive species," I said in a soothing tone.

He made the most adorable pouty expression that had me chuckling again and rubbing my temple against his.

"But I like excelling at everything I do," he said in a slightly whiny voice. "Being content with only making a few matches isn't up to my standards."

"You silly male. Stop fretting so much. There's no doubt in my mind that, against all odds, you will excel at this, too."

He grunted in an indistinct fashion, still pouting and unconvinced. Kayog was unbearably cute.

"You know," I said, sobering. "Colin is taking a huge leap of faith in you. The UPO is extremely picky when it comes to who gets to interact with primitive species. They did an incredibly thorough background check on you over the seven months that you were in stasis. Arafin has nothing but endless praises for you, which played a considerable part in tipping the scale."

"Colin said as much," Kayog mused aloud with a slight frown. "But it feels like too big of a leap of faith. After all, my emotions while getting examined only reveal a limited amount of information about who I truly am as a person."

I hesitated, which immediately piqued his curiosity.

"What is it?"

"Arafin didn't only assess you during your exams. The reason they enabled your circlet during the day was so that he and other Temern professionals could evaluate you in various circumstances. Your emotions during the battle simulations were of major interest. You reveled in the power you now wield, but never once showed malicious or psychopathic tendencies."

The shock and wave of betrayal that surged within him struck me hard.

"They were spying on my emotions this whole time, and you knew?!" he exclaimed, outraged.

"Yes," I replied calmly and slightly lifted my chin in defiance. "But it wasn't in an official capacity. I suspected what was happening the moment you told me they blocked your empathic abilities during the day. A bit of investigating confirmed it."

Although Kayog didn't pull away from me, the way his body stiffened against mine and how his arm around me loosened seriously stung. Our empathic powers could be both a blessing and a curse.

"Why didn't you tell me?" he asked.

"Because there was no need to," I said with conviction. "In fact, warning you would have played against you. The Enforcers were testing your reactions. The giant screen in the room is a two-way mirror that allows others to observe your training and behavior. Arafin attended some of the simulations to confirm that you were indeed a protector. This is a standard procedure for anyone being considered for a high-ranking position."

"But that still doesn't explain why you didn't tell me," he insisted.

"Because you had to succeed on your own merit," I said in a self-evident manner. "I already knew you would pass with flying colors. However, telling you might have tainted your reactions. Once you knew you were being observed, there was a high chance you might alter your normal reactions to meet what you believed they wanted to see. And they would also feel that you weren't being your candid self. Now they got to see the true you, unrehearsed. And as expected, they loved you."

He scrunched his face as he weighed my words, tension thankfully bleeding out of him.

"Fine," he grumbled before giving me an uncertain look. "You really think I should do this?"

"Yes," I replied with conviction and without hesitation. "You honestly excel at everything you do, and I have no doubt you will exceed all expectations here as well. More importantly, you get to live your dream of interacting with primitive species, help people find happiness, and above all do it under your own terms. What more could you wish for."

This time, I felt him let go of his last bit of resistance. A part of me believed that most of his reluctance didn't stem from his arguments about fearing not to get enough matches. Kayog was an overachiever who loved a challenge. There was a reason he had taken on canoe racing when possessing wings added an incredible level of extra difficulty. And still he managed to be among the top-ranking athletes in that discipline. He would rock his role as a matchmaker. It was fear of not living up to what he stupidly believed to be the right standard for being the partner of someone with my political ambitions.

For all his cockiness, my mate seriously lacked self-confidence at times. I would remind him every day just how perfect and amazing he was to me.

"So now you need to work on your plan for your dream matchmaking agency," I mused aloud. "That means the rules to apply, the rules to follow once people have been paired, which resources the UPO must provide you to operate your business, from transportation, to housing, and marketing."

"Ugh," Kayog said, with a crestfallen expression. "That's going to be a lot."

I shrugged and gave him a taunting smile. "That's fine. You have time. And you have me. I will happily review the rules you come up with and even help you brainstorm if you want."

"That would be fantastic," my mate said, beaming at me. "We're really doing this?"

"We absolutely are," I said with an excited grin.

Kayog snorted, and his eyes took on a faraway expression as he reminisced about something before refocusing on me.

"Mares will laugh his ass off when he hears this," Kayog said.

I burst out laughing. "He most certainly will, and with good reason."

CHAPTER 17
KAYOG

The next two days turned into four weeks of intense work. My master's degrees in xenobiology and primitive species helped tremendously while trying to define the rules of the agency. The number of edge cases and scenarios to account for was staggering. My mate even recruited her Nana Arika to assist me with some of the legal elements to take into consideration.

Despite all our interactions being limited to vidcalls, I truly liked Arika. I could see my mate in her, the efficient, no-nonsense female could be terrifying if needed but otherwise the sweetest, most loving and supportive person you could ever hope for.

After that first conversation with Colin, all movement restrictions that had been set on me were lifted. No area was off limits, I could freely come and go outside of the facility, and they no longer forced me to use the circlet, except on the few occasions where bruising became apparent. My mate had not exaggerated by saying he was taking a massive leap of faith in me. And that made me want to prove he'd been right to trust me even more.

Therefore, in between training and working on the project, I got to spend the most wonderful time with my Linsea. She gladly took me to all the places I dreamt about but never dared venture to as the result would have been catastrophic. The local fair undoubtedly proved to be one of my favorite places. Between the crazy rides, skill games, street entertainers, and the diverse crowd itself, I got to enjoy the most wondrous sensory overload without pain.

At times, I feared my mate would grow annoyed or feel neglected as I took in everything and everyone around me. I was like an addict gorging himself after an extended period of withdrawal. I would read the emotions of every person in my vicinity, bask in their collective thrill, or simply observe their behavior in a very busy public setting. My entire life, I'd been forced to move swiftly through such spaces to get to safety, never having the time or possibility to really appreciate the world around me and those who occupied it.

But she never showed any impatience or distress over it. In fact, my Linsea would be the one leading me to even more populated areas or places where thrill seeking people could get their fill of adrenaline rush. When I questioned her about it, she merely said that it was wonderful experiencing the world through my fresh eyes. She had started taking so many things for granted. Through me, she was rediscovering the beauty of the world we lived in and all it had to offer.

It turned out that my mate also loved dancing and was quite proficient at it. Saying that we took the local clubs by storm would be quite an understatement. As a former stage artist, I might have had a bit of a tendency to show off. That, too, didn't bother my mate. In fact, her possessive pride whenever people expressed admiration for me tickled me in all the right places.

I loved belonging to this female in every way.

Every night, we would do something different, from movie theaters, restaurants, shopping malls, even casinos. For the first time, I truly experienced what it was like to be normal. No more searching for quick escapes or safe havens. No more keeping count of how many people were entering a given space for fear their emotions would overwhelm me.

At long last, I was finally starting to live.

To my great chagrin, three weeks after my discussion with Colin, Linsea had to leave on a mission. It would only last a week, but the mere thought of parting with her for even just one day felt like an eternity. Granted, it proved to be a good test for our respective future careers. That didn't make it any less difficult. But at least, we commed each other every day. Each time, my fingers twitched to reach through the vidscreen to touch her beautiful face. Worse still, being unable to hear the song of her soul turned out to be the most painful part of this separation. To my shock, more than once, I caught myself humming it. It couldn't replace the real thing, but it soothed me.

I might have made a bit of a spectacle of myself upon her return. First, I arrived much too early to wait for her shuttle to land in the research center's hangar. Second I paced and muttered impatiently to myself so much, the security guards playfully warned me that I would be fined for the repair costs of me wearing out the floor. They even offered me a bench and water—all of which I declined.

Yeah, I was pathetic, but I sorely missed my other half.

Once the shuttle entered the hangar, I nearly got myself crushed in my haste to run to it before it had finished landing. Thankfully, Linsea was the first to disembark. Otherwise, I might have barreled through the other passengers to get to her. She couldn't decide between the very justified need to chastise me, and the urge to just rejoice in our reunion and hug me.

I took that option away from her.

I kissed her like a starving male, then hugged her so tightly and for so long that some smartass asked if we needed a crowbar to get us unstuck. I glared at him while he strutted away with a smug expression, the other passengers chuckling as they also exited the hangar. My palm itched with the urge to release a strategically placed kinetic pulse on his ass. A harmless face planting should take him down a notch or two.

My mate's claws digging into the sensitive spot at the base of my wings wrested a weird sound halfway between a yelp and a moan as I jerked my head back towards her.

"Behave, you naughty boy," Linsea said sternly, despite the underlying amusement in her voice. "No harming innocent people for calling you out on your excessive enthusiasm."

"Behaving is the farthest thing from my mind right now," I growled in a voice filled with promises.

I hadn't meant anything by it—or at least nothing raunchy at the time I spoke those words. I merely meant that when it came to my mate, I didn't care how people felt about how I acted. For too long, I had been denied the basic pleasure of allowing myself to feel anything. Now, I fully intended to indulge as much as possible and just live to the fullest—other people's opinions be damned.

However, my dove's instant arousal sent blood rushing to my groin. And now, I definitely wanted to... *misbehave.*

"Is that so?" she asked in a sultry voice.

"Most definitely so," I replied in a deep whisper filled with promises.

Her arousal cranking up another notch whipped my blood into a frenzy. All thoughts of the romantic reunion I had planned faded away. It was her turn to yelp as I picked her up, chest against chest, and started flying towards the exit. She laughed, although the loveliest mix of embarrassment, lust, and amusement radiated from her as she wrapped her legs around my waist.

While the high ceilings allowed me to fly my female past the other passengers to the exit of the hangar, I was sadly forced to land to traipse the long corridors back to the elevators to the residential floors. That didn't stop me from still carrying my mate to the amusement of the random folks who saw us.

252

But I honestly didn't give a shit what anyone thought anymore.

I took Linsea straight to our bedroom and spent the next couple of hours showing her just how much I had missed her. Then again, she reciprocated in the naughtiest ways.

After a long shower—which involved some more wandering hands—we finally went back to the kitchen where I reheated the meal I had prepared for her. We ate in a relaxed atmosphere. As we had talked every day, there wasn't much left for her to update me about her trip. Therefore, she quickly dove into the topic I'd been feeling rather nervous about.

"Are you done with your plan for the agency?" she asked between two bites.

I shifted my wings and fiddled with the food on my plate as I gathered my thoughts.

"A lot of the administrative stuff like my office, information site, traveling, and assistant will mostly be handled by the UPO's logistics department. I've already discussed many of those aspects with them and Colin. It is the agency's operating guidelines that I mainly needed to finalize. And I'm rather pleased with what I came up with. Hang on."

I ran to the office—that we now shared—and retrieved my tablet. Linsea watched me approach with an excitement that moved me deeply. She didn't understand how much her support and faith in me gave me strength. With her by my side, nothing seemed too daunting or impossible. Despite that, I still felt a great deal of nervousness as I sat back down next to her. Pushing aside my plate, I positioned the tablet between us and activated the holographic display so that we could both stare at the screen comfortably.

"Here, I've outlined the main points of the plan," I explained. "Each of these points are described in more extensive detail further in the document, but this is the overview."

She nodded with an encouraging smile. I took a deep breath and then went for it.

"First, I want to focus on pairing human partners with the primitive aliens I will work with."

Right on cue, Linsea stiffened and stared at me with surprise.

"Why humans? What if two soulmates are of different species?" she asked.

I smiled. "I will not exclude other species. If I find a match that doesn't involve a human, I will obviously pair those people. But humans are the most adaptable species in the galaxy. They're compatible with the greater number of other races, or generally quite flexible in embracing new cultures, and can thrive in a variety of environments, given the right tools. It's easier for me to focus on one pool of candidates—at least at the beginning—and then eventually expand."

"Fair enough," Linsea conceded. "So long as others also get an opportunity, your logic makes sense."

I smiled again, relieved by her reaction. "The second point is that the couple must marry following the customs of both cultures to make it fully binding on all sides. The Galactic Hall of Records only requires one marriage certificate to deem a union valid. However, some species will not recognize a foreign contract, which would leave the partner without protection in that new world should things go awry."

"Very good point! I'm impressed!" my mate said proudly.

I gave her a sheepish expression. "Sadly, I cannot take full credit for this. While talking with Isobel, I mentioned that she could tag along to perform the wedding ceremonies for the occasional matches I make—since she also is fascinated by primitive species. She's the one who pointed out that there might be legal issues with some of them. And your grandmother confirmed as much."

"But you're still the one who came up with the final rule by taking into account the feedback of the wonderful people you surrounded yourself with. That makes you a competent project manager instead of a narcissistic fool who thinks he has all the answers. No one succeeds on their own when it comes to projects of this scale. It's good that you give credit to others where it's due, but do not sell yourself short either."

"Noted, my love," I said before rubbing my beak against hers.

Fuck, how I loved this female!

Before I even got to read the third point, Linsea's strong reaction revealed she'd already taken a peek at it and was flabbergasted, as I expected she and everyone else would be about that request.

"Sex on the first night?!" Linsea exclaimed, stunned.

I nodded and held her gaze unwaveringly. "Yes. I thought about it long and hard, and I have come to the strong conclusion that it's the best approach. It will bring the couple closer together a lot faster, and it will remove a tremendous amount of stress. Deciding when to move to the next step in a relationship is always quite a headache. You don't want to come across as too impatient, too easy, or too hard to get. By imposing it, we remove that barrier right away, and they can focus on falling in love rather than tiptoeing around the inevitable."

"I hear what you're saying," my mate said carefully. "However, everyone's situation is different. They may have trauma or other circumstances that could make that requirement a harmful experience for them."

To her surprise, I smiled in agreement.

"That's correct. But that rule will truly serve these couples, even those with special circumstances that would make it a bad idea to sleep together right away." My smile broadened at her confused expression. "This isn't an enforceable rule to the extent that we're not going to perform blood tests to make sure they copulated. We're also not going to set up cameras or spy on them during their wedding night. In truth, I expect at least ten to twenty percent of the couples not to follow that rule."

"Then why instate it to begin with?" Linsea asked, baffled.

"Because it will force that uncomfortable conversation and get it out of the way immediately. In turn, it will help form trust between them as well as show the respect they will bear each other. These people will be soulmates. Whatever the circumstances that will lead them to be paired, they will naturally want to protect their partner. And if that means waiting a little longer until they're ready for it, it will have been discussed and agreed upon."

"That's an interesting way of looking at it," my mate said, nodding slowly. "I could see myself being stressed about how to broach the topic if I was in such a situation. It would make for an extremely tense first few days as we danced around it. That said, I'm still curious to see how that will work out. But I can get behind the concept."

I smiled and caressed her cheek. She leaned into my touch, which had me melting from the inside out. She was so damn perfect. Tearing my gaze away from her beauty, I glanced back at the holographic display projected from my tablet.

"The next point will be for the UPO to grant me a discretionary budget for all the paired couples," I continued. "Relocation to primitive planets could be fairly expensive. I don't want this to be an obstacle. Granted, I have added a few provisions so that people don't just abuse it, but as true soulmates, I'm not too worried about candidates attempting to use this as a means to get a free trip to an exotic location."

"Another good point. They will probably try to rein you in as far as the amounts they will agree to. But so long as there are reasonable justifications, it shouldn't be too much of a problem."

"Relocation is the last thing they will complain about. It's the startup gifts I want included that will probably make them balk," I said in a mischievous tone.

"Startup gift? I'm intrigued."

"In all likelihood, the human partner will be the one moving to the primitive alien's planet. The other way around would not benefit the UPO, whose goal is to create stronger bonds with those species, which can only occur if we have a physical presence on their homeworld. But they're primitive, which means they will likely lack certain things that are essential to the welfare of a human. For example, medical care, appropriate basic equipment to help them survive in potentially harsher environments, and other such things."

"Another excellent point. However, why do I feel there's more to it that you're not stating?" she asked, with a suspicious glimmer in her beautiful blue eyes.

I chuckled, impressed by her intuition.

"Because there is. I do not want to box myself in so narrowly that I won't have any wiggle room. Based on my studies on primitive species and of the countless violations to the Prime Directive, I can picture scenarios where a wedding gift— although I'm labeling them dowries—could indirectly help mend some of the harm caused to that species. There are many ways that you can help someone by toeing the line without actually crossing it."

"You know, maybe you should be the one becoming an ambassador," Linsea said, only half teasing.

"Technically, that's what Colin said I would be, but doing so undercover," I replied with a grin. "Actually, the next point would be to add a trial period. It's not only to reassure each partner, especially the one relocating, that they won't be stuck in a loveless or abusive marriage, assuming I had made a mistake. Obviously, I won't. But people always love knowing there's a way out if needed."

"Obviously, you won't," she repeated mockingly, while shaking her head at me as if I was a hopeless case.

"That's right," I replied smugly. "That said, the trial period will also grant me additional time to see if that dowry needs to be increased or modified to address the specific needs of that couple or species."

"Wow, you really are thinking of this almost more in terms of assisting the primitive species," Linsea said, surprised.

"This project is giving me the power to do everything I thought I never could. I won't be able to rewrite history or prevent wars. But I will be able to mitigate the damage, prevent some of it from ever occurring, or mend what has been done," I said in a serious tone.

"I cannot wait to see what you will do with this agency. I knew you would be amazing, but I'm starting to think you will blow everyone away with what you will actually accomplish," Linsea said with awe.

"Hopefully, your prediction will prove accurate. The one thing I fear the UPO will push back against is the fact that I want to keep these benefits exclusively to pairings involving a primitive species. If I match a couple where they both belong to an advanced species, relocation and everything else should be at their own expense."

"Hmm, why is that? If the UPO is funding this, why deprive some couples from those benefits?"

"Because I want to save as many resources as possible for the PMA to provide incentives and benefits to people willing to mate with primitive aliens. Members of advanced species will have the means to get together or have access to programs for low-income people to help them achieve their goals. I also do not want the PMA to turn into a matchmaking agency for the elite. People coming to me will know from the start that they will be paired with someone from a developing planet."

"I agree. But you said PMA twice. Is that the name of your agency?"

My face heated, and I nodded with a sheepish expression. "Yes. After much reflection, I decided to call it the Prime Mating

Agency. It's a bit on the nose, but I will be pairing people with mates under the Prime Directive."

"I think it sounds great," Linsea said with genuine enthusiasm. "You're going to have a crazy number of people knocking down your door."

"I both hope and dread it," I said with a nervous laugh. "At first, I will have people apply online, but with the understanding that a meeting in person is required so that I can hear the song of their souls."

"Hmmm, I agree with the online application for people to reserve their spot. But I think it should be done with more of a fair approach. You announce that you will be at a specific place, on a set date, between a defined time range. People can reserve a slot to meet you."

"That would work eventually. But I don't expect to have enough people at the beginning to support that," I said in an indulgent tone.

Linsea laughed and shook her head at me as if I was clueless. "Sweetie, you have no idea what kind of marketing machine the UPO and the Enforcers are going to unleash on your behalf. You cannot begin to imagine how invested they are in your success. The most efficient way that I can think of for you will be to go by region. Just like with a music tour, you announce which region you'll be touring and the dates, and people will reserve their seats to see you."

"But then what will that mean for you and me?" I asked, my chest constricting at the thought of extended periods of time apart from her.

"We'll just have to coordinate our missions so they can take place in the same general area. I will have less flexibility on that front as whatever conflict occurs will dictate where I have to go. But you will mostly be your own boss."

"Then I'll make sure I'll be *touring* the area you're in," I said, relieved. "That said, I need to make sure that the UPO and the Enforcers are not going to try to dictate the pairings I come up with. I will only match true soulmates."

My heart sank when Linsea slapped a neutral expression on her face. That she also tried to block part of her emotions cut me deep. Now that I no longer wore the circlet, the full extent of my empathic powers had returned, minus the chaos that used to drive me insane. No one could prevent me from reading their emotions if I so chose.

"Do not shut yourself down from me," I said, the hurt I felt audible in my voice.

The wave of guilt that surged within her slammed into me.

"I'm sorry," Linsea said with sincerity. "It wasn't intentional, just a professional reflex when dealing with delicate matters."

"Why is the fact that I don't want to make fake pairings a delicate matter?" I asked, my back stiff with tension.

"For political reasons, they could ask you to help facilitate—"

"I don't want to match people that are not meant for each other," I said forcefully, interrupting her. "Why would I condemn them to a potential life of misery? It would be a gross misuse of my gift."

She caressed my cheek in an appeasing fashion while giving me a sympathetic smile.

"I understand very well how you feel. However, your assistance in this matter could actually prevent the couple from that very life of misery. Arranged marriages between wealthy families, nobility, and political leaders have always existed and will continue to do so. You could help pinpoint the most compatible pair or nearest match from a very strict pool of candidates. They wouldn't be soulmates, but they would be the better option."

I frowned and studied her features as suspicion blossomed within me.

"That sounds rather specific," I challenged.

"Because it is," Linsea replied in an unrepentant fashion. "I have to leave again on a mission in three weeks. A very influential executive is looking to make an alliance with a rival firm by marrying off his daughter. We have strong reservations about that pairing. If you tagged along, you might be able to assess the threat."

That left me speechless. In that instant, I realized that things would never quite be the way I envisioned. My visceral wish to refuse to get involved was immediately squashed by my protective instinct rearing its head. I didn't even know the daughter in question, but I always had issues with the idea of using one's child as an asset or trade item, ignoring their own wishes and aspirations.

That I would get to travel with my mate and be by her side as she performed her magic was also too great an opportunity to pass up.

"Fine. I will assess the candidates, but I will not commit to any pairings. I will leave that mess to the rest of you," I mumbled.

Linsea chuckled and rose from her chair to settle in my lap.

"You know something, you're really sexy when you're grumpy," my mate said teasingly.

"I'm always sexy, period," I said in a haughty tone.

She snorted and rubbed her beak against mine. "Sexy, and all mine."

"All yours, now and always."

CHAPTER 18

KAYOG

Presenting my plan to Colin went shockingly smoothly. We were sitting in the training room, at the same worktable by the giant vidscreen as our first meeting following my awakening. He didn't give me any of the pushback I expected, although he thoroughly questioned certain parts of it, namely the dowries. However, he didn't question it in a challenging fashion but merely to get a proper understanding of my goals and motivations. To my surprise, he wholeheartedly approved my wish to exclude advanced species from enjoying the same types of benefits I would grant pairings involving at least one primitive alien.

"This is excellent," Colin said approvingly. "Your record and psychological profile stated you were a perfectionist. It pleases me to see how much you stepped up and took this seriously. Although the higher ups will balk at some of your requests, they are reasonable. You've also provided me with sufficient arguments to shut them up."

"Thank you," I said, unable to hide my growing excitement about this project.

"While we get everything rolling, I strongly encourage you to socialize as much as possible. You need to cultivate an erudite rockstar persona but focused on matchmaking. People need to see you as the god of matchmaking. The same way the crowds fanned themselves when you used to perform with Echoes of Madness, and how they quietly fangirled whenever they saw you walking past, we need the general population to react in a similar fashion when it comes to finding love."

"How exactly am I supposed to do that?" I asked hesitantly.

"Be cocky," Colin deadpanned. "Be arrogant and assertive about your certainty that your talent is never wrong, but not in an obnoxious fashion. You have a pleasant sense of humor, let it shine through. Our marketing team will take care of the rest. We just need you out and about, being your charming self. Those who get to benefit from your services should feel like they were blessed with entry to an exclusive club."

"I don't want to be exclusive," I argued with a frown.

"You won't be," Colin replied with an indulgent smile. "People simply must feel like it's the case. But realize that you will be swamped with far more requests than you could possibly imagine. I know you don't believe it. And I like that humble side of you. Never lose it but still be cocky."

I chuckled. "That's not contradictory at all."

"Not in the least," he said teasingly before taking on a serious expression again. "Your mate has a series of important events she will participate in over the upcoming weeks. We want you to accompany her and to establish as many contacts and rapport as you possibly can. Many of these people will be elitists. Do not let their holier-than-thou ways destabilize you. In comparison, half of them couldn't even claim a third of your pedigree. Show them why you can be a force to be reckoned with and a great ally to have on their side."

"And how exactly am I supposed to do that?" I asked, baffled.

"Although that's for you to figure out, I will say that you have extensive knowledge about many of the species you will encounter. Leverage it, especially in ways that could benefit them."

I shifted uneasily in my seat, beginning to feel a bit out of my depth. Despite not possessing any empathic abilities, Colin appeared to immediately guess what thoughts were coursing through my mind.

"Relax, Kayog. No one expects you to perform a miracle during your first outings. This truly is simply about forging relationships and getting your name out there. Do not fret. We will be here to support you every step of the way. If you have questions, ask. If you need more resources, ask. If you are uncertain what you may or may not do..."

"Let me guess... Ask," I said teasingly.

His gray eyes sparked with mischief. "Actually, I was going to say follow your gut and good judgment. And if you're still confused about it, then ask."

I burst out laughing. That human was seriously growing on me.

We continued going over more practical details, including my wages, expense account, schedule, and other annoying formalities. I then headed back to our apartment, my stomach fluttering with nerves.

Linsea's parents and grandmother arrived an hour ago—three hours earlier than expected. I intended on being there to greet them at the ship hangar but ended up stuck in the midst of a training session. As Colin was leaving on a mission in the morning, we couldn't postpone.

Saying I was a nervous wreck would be the understatement of the millennium. I felt them long before I reached the door. As I drew closer, I battled with the urge to shut down my emotions. I had no difficulty completely blocking them out. As much as that would make me feel a lot more comfortable, it would come across as me being deceitful, distrustful, and fairly rude.

Obviously, no one would expect one of us to leave ourselves

wide open for others to plunder our feelings. However, it was common courtesy—and a sign of both goodwill and the absence of ill intentions—to allow others access to our surface emotions. Considering they were well-aware that I could fully read them regardless of whatever psychic wall they might erect, closing myself off to them would be even more disrespectful.

I reminded myself that, although they didn't know me, Linsea's parents and grandmother leveraged all their influence and called in as many favors as possible to help protect me. Even though it hadn't been for me personally, their desire to make their daughter happy played a huge part in my standing here today. They wanted me to be the right male for her.

My hand shook slightly as I opened the front door. They hadn't been aware of my approach until that moment. A mix of relief and heightened nervousness washed over me when their relaxed emotions suddenly shifted to excitement, eager anticipation, and a surprising level of nervousness as well. It blew my mind to realize in that instant that they, too, were hoping to make a good first impression.

"There he is!" Linsea exclaimed as soon as I entered the apartment.

The pride and joy in her eyes wrecked me. I didn't understand how such a perfect female could care so deeply about me. She came to me and wrapped her arms around my waist before lifting her face towards mine to receive my kiss. A silly voice at the back of my head wanted to be self-conscious and pull away so that her parents wouldn't be offended by this display of affection. But I squashed it.

I loved my mate. Allowing my natural feelings towards her to shine through would be the best testament for her parents of my devotion to my little dove. As was our wont, we embraced each other, Linsea flattening her wings against her back so that I could close mine around both of us. I loved how she responded to that gesture. Every time I did that, she would broadcast loudly a sense of safety, well-being, and belonging. It made me feel like the greatest protector in the universe.

She cooed as she rubbed her face in the crook of my neck before giving it a little nip just the way I loved. Then, with much reluctance, she pulled away from me. I caressed her cheek with infinite tenderness before glancing at the three people standing at the end of the short corridor from the entrance to the living area.

My eyes were immediately drawn to her Nana Arika. She was magnificent and majestic. An aura of authority, confidence, and strength radiated from the older female. At a glance, she appeared to be in her late eighties. As our people had an average lifespan of one hundred and fifty years, she would still be deemed in her prime by most other species. She was the mirror opposite of my soulmate, with completely black feathers and white specs on her chest, but with the same striking blue eyes. She observed us with an approval that did funny things to me.

Her parents were looking at us with similar warmth. Her mother, Karis, had silver-gray feathers with black accents, and the prettiest green eyes. She was surprisingly petite compared to her daughter. For his part, my mate's father had greatly taken after his mother Arika, with all black feathers and matching blue eyes. However, he didn't have the white specs on his chest or wings.

"Kayog, please meet my parents. My mom Karis, and dad Randel. You have already met my Nana Arika during vidcalls," Linsea said in a voice filled with emotion as she gestured at each of them in turn. "Mom, Dad, Nana, please meet my Kayog."

The possessiveness and pride with which she introduced me seriously turned me upside down. By the way their approval cranked up another notch, they clearly perceived how her words were affecting me.

"Hello, Son," Karis said in a sweet voice, while approaching me. "My Linny has had nothing but utmost praise for you. Welcome to the family."

My throat constricted as she drew me into her arms to give me the sweetest maternal hug. Considering her petite stature, it felt odd taking the submissive role in that embrace, with me flattening my wings so that she could fold hers around me. It was brief but unforgettable. She stepped aside so that her husband could greet me. To my shock, he also drew me into a tight, winged hug. We were of comparable height, but he had the lither, more slender build of our people, whereas my obsession with sports and training had given me a more muscular frame.

He released me only to hold my shoulders with both hands, his blue eyes boring into mine. "Until you, I thought no one would ever find grace in her eyes. But for you, my baby was willing to take on the UPO itself and go to war with the Enforcers. You must truly be an amazing male."

"It is Linsea who is amazing," I said, relieved that my voice didn't shake. "She saved my life when I had given up and blessed me with a life I never thought possible. Linsea is my angel," I added, glancing at my mate who was standing next to me.

She melted against my side. Her father released my shoulders, and I placed a possessive arm around my female.

"Do not let that pretty face and sweet demeanor fool you, Son," Arika interjected in a teasing fashion as she approached me. "She's a dragon with the most lethal talons when she's crossed."

Karis snorted. "You would know a thing or two about that as she's inherited those traits from you."

"Fact!" Randel said with a chuckle, eyeing his mother with a mischievous expression while Linsea giggled.

Arika waved a dismissive hand. "I've passed on the best this family has to offer to my granddaughter. You can all thank me later."

Arika unceremoniously pushed Linsea away from me so that she could also give me a maternal hug.

"Welcome to the family, Kayog," she said, echoing her daughter-in-law's words. "And thank you for being so incredibly *badass*, as the humans like to say. The UPO is abuzz with talks about the kinetic demigod in my family."

"So are the Enforcers," Randel snickered. "People are staring at me in awe as if I had any merit in this thing."

"You did," I said, amused. "You helped keep me alive."

"Why, you are correct! Am I ever going to brag now!" Randel exclaimed with playful excitement.

We all laughed, then went into the living area to share drinks and conversation. Naturally, Linsea's family took great pleasure embarrassing her with funny anecdotes about her youth. But they also shared plenty of fascinating tales about their work within the UPO and the Enforcers, as well as giving me a treasure trove of advice for my future within the organization. Although they never pried, I reciprocated their candor with stories about my own youth, both pleasant and challenging.

By the time the evening drew to a close, I had now experienced what it felt like to truly belong to a family. Another incommensurable gift from my beloved...

CHAPTER 19
LINSEA

I was flying high as I watched my family wholeheartedly embrace Kayog. Despite expecting they would click, a sliver of apprehension had still lurked at the back of my mind at the possibility that things might go awry. I couldn't decide whether to be amused or roll my eyes as my mom kept fussing about how handsome and sweet he was. Even my nana was shaking her head at Mom.

Considering how picky I'd always been about potential partners, her enthusiasm made sense. For a while now, Mom feared that I would remain single forever. That always struck me as silly since I was still only twenty-six. But it didn't matter. I had found the love of my life.

Watching him engaged in an animated conversation with my father about some of the cases he had litigated on behalf of the enforcers had a warm and fuzzy feeling settling in my chest. Once you got my father going about the law, good luck ever getting him to stop. Granted, his stories about some of the Prime Directive violations he encountered were quite fascinating. Many times, he had to get creative to find workarounds for the Enforcers to intervene locally despite the strict regulations forbidding access to the planet. It was always touchy when, in order to catch trespassers, you had to break the very law you were trying to arrest them over.

I left my mom with my nan to chat while I walked over to my mate to see if he needed rescuing from my overly verbose father. I gently scratched the feathers on Kayog's nape, and he wrapped a possessive arm around me as I leaned against him.

"How are you two doing?" I asked. "I hope Dad isn't driving you crazy."

My father snorted and gave me a playfully outraged look.

"No, he wasn't," Kayog said, amused. "His stories are truly enthralling and quite educational."

"Uh oh! You've been ensnared in his trap. There might be no saving you," I said with an overly dramatic crestfallen expression.

My father huffed. "I'm not the one who should be entrapping him. The question is more when are you going to officially shackle him?"

My jaw dropped, and a deafening silence settled over the room.

"Dad!" I exclaimed. "That's not a proper question to ask!"

"Why not?" he countered, looking genuinely surprised. "Beyond the fact that Kayog can see when two people are soulmates—which he stated you are—anyone with eyes can see how perfect you are for each other."

I shifted uneasily and cast a nervous glance at Kayog. The only thing keeping me from panicking was the peaceful and amused emotions radiating from him.

"Be that as it may, he shouldn't be pressured into settling down with me," I mumbled.

Kayog tightened his hold around my waist before drawing me into his lap.

"That's one thing no one will ever have to pressure me into. You are my heart and my soul. I would marry you right this instant if you were ready. There can never be another one for me. However, the day we officially commit our lives to each other will be on whatever timeline is comfortable for *you*. Whether in a week, in a month, or in a decade from now makes no difference to me so long as you're in my life," he said gently.

With each of these words, I melted a bit more against him.

"There can never be another for me either," I said, wrapping my arms around his neck. "I'm ready when you are."

"Well then, the family is here," Mom chirped enthusiastically.

A part of me wanted to tell my parents to back off, but another was too busy basking in my mate's love. Kayog's hopeful expression did the strangest thing to me.

"Fair point," I said pensively. "However, Tala is constantly threatening to pluck me. If she finds out I got married without her present, she will go berserk on me."

My entire family burst out laughing, along with Kayog, who nodded with a mischievous glimmer in his eyes.

"Hey, that would spare you the long and unpleasant process of your next molting. But I doubt it would make an appropriate look for your upcoming mission," he said teasingly.

"Definitely not fashion-appropriate," I replied with an overly dramatic expression before sobering. "Tala and Mares aren't too far away. We could fly them over for a night."

Kayog nodded. "I would also love for Isobel to attend."

"Then let's make it happen," Nana Arika said in an imperious tone.

And just like that, we quickly made arrangements, and our friends were over the moon at the unexpected invitation. As Temern weddings were always a small and intimate affair, we only had to arrange transportation, accommodation, and a simple buffet for the small group of people in attendance. Normally, only the parents, grandparents, and siblings were present, although you occasionally included other very close relatives or dear friends. Still, the ceremony rarely involved more than eight or ten people, the couple included.

Traditionally, the wedding took place in the garden or backyard of the couple's marital home. As we were still temporarily living in the apartment attached to the UPO's research center, we only had a balcony. And the common courtyard didn't feel appropriate for the event.

Working her magic, Isobel secured permission for us to use the stunning garden in the religious sanctuary attached to the refugee shelter she volunteered in during the time Kayog had been kept in stasis. It put the fanciest botanical gardens to shame with exquisite floral arrangements in a pastel palette. As per our customs, we held the ceremony just at the beginning of nightfall. As many of the exotic flowers naturally glowed in the dark, it bathed the garden in a dreamy halo of soft colors. Strategically positioned glowstones marked the pathways and provided additional light via the various statues and sculptures they had been seamlessly embedded into.

Isobel led us to the open area in front of a massive, intricately sculpted fountain which protruded from the wall at the easternmost end of the garden. Around the edges of the oval basin that received the water from the fountain, religious symbols representing multiple faiths could be seen illuminated from within.

Kayog and I stood face to face, holding hands. Isobel presided over the ceremony, an honor normally reserved to the oldest matriarch in the couple's bloodline, which would have been either my oldest grandmother or his. As Kayog didn't know his family, it automatically defaulted to mine. With my maternal grandmother having passed away a few years back, it should have been Nana Arika. But she graciously passed on the honor to Isobel. In more ways than one, the priestess helped keep my mate alive all those years before I finally came into his life. She wasn't simply his best friend anymore, she was my sister, and a cherished member of our family.

My parents, Tala, Mares, and Nana Arika were standing in a circle around us. A wider space between Dad and Mom was left for Isobel to join them. Once the first part of the ceremony was completed, she would close the circle as they would all hold hands, my friends inserted in between a member of my family.

"We are gathered here to bear witness to the union of two souls, of two wonderful people who have overcome incredible challenges, and emerged from them stronger and more unified than ever. It is my tremendous honor to preside over the joining of my dearest brother and beloved sister."

We both glanced at Isobel, the same love I felt for the human priestess emanating from my mate. Contrary to many human religions, Temern couples didn't exchange vows or follow any complex rituals. Anything that needed to be said was communicated through our empathic abilities. That connection would be made even stronger—and in fact unbreakable—once we completed the bond.

Still, Kayog and I both chose to exchange a few words. She nodded at us to tell us to proceed.

"Kayog, you entered my life like a whirlwind. I wasn't looking for love or a partner. But the moment I laid eyes on you, I knew. I foolishly tried to resist, but some things cannot be denied. Fate brought us together. I chose you then, now, and always. For you, I will fight the gods themselves, if I must. No one has ever brought me greater happiness or made me so complete as you have. You make me laugh and rediscover the wonders of our worlds with fresh eyes. With you, I feel safe, respected, worshipped even. Every moment by your side is a blessing. I vow to love you until my last breath. Whatever the future holds for us, whether the storm or a clear blue sky, nothing can ever tear us apart. You are my heart and soul. And I am yours forever," I said, my voice constricted with emotion.

The adoration in his eyes and radiating from him wrecked me. His hands around mine tightened.

"In my darkest hour, you shed a divine light that guided me to the type of peace, joy, and happiness I never even imagined possible. You fought for me, protected me, and loved me when I was beyond broken. You gave me a new lease on life, a wonderful family to belong to, and a future that I cannot wait to explore with you, regardless of its highs and lows. I vow to be your partner, your best friend, and most loyal supporter. I promise to cherish and honor you, to love you unconditionally whatever challenges arise, and to be your safe haven, just as you are mine. My heart, my body, my soul, everything that I am is and will always be yours. I love you, Linsea."

Tears pricked my eyes. My eyelids fluttered in an attempt to stem them back. Our gazes locked, I let him draw me against his firm body. We released each other's hands so that he could hold my waist. Just as I was placing my palms on his muscular chest, a mischievous glimmer sparked in his beautiful silver eyes.

"And I promise to always let you have the last grain cracker, even if I badly want it," Kayog deadpanned.

I gasped, stunned before bursting out laughing with the rest of my family. Isobel snorted, then chuckled while shaking her head at my mate. I should have wanted to kick his behind, but I just wanted to hug and kiss him. Maker, he was so perfect.

And now, I wanted a grain cracker...

I gave his chest a playful tap, and he tightened his hold around me, his face radiating love and amusement. He rubbed his cheek against mine, and I felt myself melt from the inside out. Kayog loosened his hold and faced me, his beak aligned with mine.

My stomach fluttered with excitement and anticipation at what would follow. Isobel held a horac between our beaks. It was a special fruit, with the same size and bumpy exterior as a lychee, but with the soft skin of a peach. Its interior resembled a white star apple, aside from the creamy white nectar in the center that glowed. The horac possessed psychotropic properties. In our case, it further opened our third eye, allowing a couple to form a permanent psychic bond. With it, Kayog and I would be able to perceive each other's emotions at an even deeper level, sometimes anticipating the other's needs as they arose.

We held the horac between our beaks and waited for Isobel to step back and complete the circle. Only then did Kayog and I bite into the fruit, both swallowing one half of it. A tingling sensation quickly overshadowed the delicious sweetness of the fruit. It began on my tongue, sliding to my throat, and then spreading throughout my body. Kayog and I pressed our foreheads against each other's and closed our eyes as the horac filled us.

The melodious voices of my family rose around us. A violent shiver coursed through me in response to the specific frequency and tones aimed at stimulating our third eye. Seconds later, my family clapped their wings to emit a soft rattling sound—not quite a drumming. The rapid movement of their wings and of their specialized primary feathers further enhanced the effect of the horac.

Kayog and I opened our psychic selves wide as we focused on each other. Moments later, a bright light exploded before my mind's eye. The world vanished around us. Nothing existed but my mate, in and around me. I felt infused with his presence, his love for me, and all that he was as if we had become a single being. We literally entered a trance, no beginning, no end, just one soul reunited at last.

And then I heard it.

It was a haunting melody. Faint at first, it resonated inside me, swelling into a mesmerizing crescendo. I wanted to wrap myself in it, drown in it, and forever bask in the enthralling song. I had never experienced such a thing before—or heard of this happening to any other Temern couple. I realized then that it was the song of our souls playing in perfect harmony.

Now I understood why he loved it so much.

Something settled inside me as our bond locked into place. The tingling gradually faded along with our dazed trance as reality crept back in. But the languid sense of well-being lingered as I slowly opened my eyes. I locked gazes with my soulmate, and tears once more threatened to surge forward. No one should be able to love the way he did. And he loved *me*... Linsea.

His wings wrapped around me, sheltering us from prying eyes as he deepened the kiss. The singing and wing clapping stopped, followed by the cheers from our friends and family.

We broke the kiss with much reluctance and enjoyed each other's embrace one final time before turning to our guests. I was giggling like a silly teenager as everyone hugged and congratulated us one after the other. We then enjoyed the snacks and drinks laid out on a table left of the fountain, with a stunning statue of the Syllen Goddess Etreya looking down on us with a benevolent expression.

"Mares and I will be bonding as well in two weeks, after I complete my current mission," Tala said in a conspiratorial tone before taking another sip of wine. "And then we will marry one month later once I've had my *veris* to do the whole vine intertwining thing."

Although she said it as if to imply it was weird, her excitement and anticipation shone bright. She was as madly in love with her mate as I was with mine.

"Congratulations!" I exclaimed. "It was time for him to make an honest woman out of you."

As expected, she huffed at that human saying. "It will take far more than that to make me an honest anything. Mischief and troublemaking are my middle names. And also part of my irresistible charm."

"No lies detected," I said with a chuckle.

"I will have to find a way to one up you, though. This setting is stunning, and the ceremony was lovely," Tala said pensively.

I snorted. "You will have no issue achieving that. Edocit marriages are beautiful with all the intertwined vines and circle of life. It must be wonderful to not only marry the love of your life but also the very land that welcomes you," I said wistfully.

Her face softened, and she took on an air of wonder and vulnerability that she rarely displayed.

"I can't wait. I've met his mother tree and visited the land many times. I look forward to being one with them. But this day is all about your happiness. And right now, I believe it is time for you to go be naughty."

"Tala!" I exclaimed, my cheeks burning with embarrassment, which had her laughing in the most unrepented fashion.

"I only speak the truth. It is naughty time for the both of you," she said, wiggling her eyebrows in a raunchy fashion.

To my dismay, her words immediately had me aroused. And our bond instantly alerted Kayog to my needs. He jerked his head in our direction, and our eyes meeting felt like a physical blow. My talons curled, and my stomach fluttered.

He smiled and extended a hand towards me.

"Have fun," Tala whispered as I walked to my mate.

I took his hand, and our friends and family gave us a final parting hug, words unnecessary.

Hand in hand, Kayog and I took flight. He lifted gracefully, his maroon feathers caressed by the soft glow of the moonlight.

We soared through the sky, twirling and spiraling in an unrehearsed aerial ballet. We danced to the melody of our souls and the rhythm of our hearts beating in perfect harmony. I always wondered what my nuptial flight would feel like. Never could I have imagined being so completely in sync with anyone.

Lost in my mate, I didn't realize how far he had taken us away from prying eyes. Below us, a lush forest gave way to a large body of water. The moonlight on its surface made it glimmer like an ocean of precious gems. But Kayog drawing me close against his body wiped out any thoughts of our surroundings.

I instinctively adjusted the flapping of my wings to his as he claimed my mouth in a passionate kiss. His hands roamed over me with growing urgency, caressing and exploring with a possessiveness that had me throbbing with need. He pulled away from me to rub his face the length of my body. I flapped my wings just enough to hover in place. His hand probing the closed seam between my thighs prompted me to part it open. My mate sank in two fingers inside my slit, wresting a strangled cry from me.

It destabilized me for a split second, but I quickly readjusted my movements to remain semi-stationary. The nuptial flight could prove challenging, but also helped cement the fresh bond, forcing us to really become attuned to each other. And the thrill and hint of danger that came with it was the biggest turn on.

A bolt of lust exploded in the pit of my stomach when Kayog let himself drop enough so that he was facing my pelvic area. I yelped when he lifted my right leg over his shoulder, while still fingering me with the other hand. It was a risky move, as my foot could have knocked on his wing. His mouth replaced his fingers, making me cry out as he deftly settled my other leg over his right shoulder. I held onto his head, an inferno raging inside me as his tongue delved greedily into my core.

Kayog maintained us airborne with slow, controlled, and powerful flaps of his wings. I barely used mine, except to adjust our vertical position as he continued to devour me. Pleasure built quickly, enhanced by the emotions flowing freely through our connection. His arousal might as well be mine. I could also feel the burning need in his loins to lower me onto his cock and fuck me senseless.

I couldn't say if that thought or his response to how my own musings affected me, but it sent me over the edge. I cried out and threw my head back as my climax crashed into me. The sudden movement sent me toppling over. It should have scared me, but the smug and victorious emotions emanating from Kayog kept me riding high.

He caught me with a swift swoop and pulled me close as the wind whistled past us. The world spun around us as he resumed his aerial dance, heart against heart, the flowy feathers of his tail caressing my legs with each tumble.

Just as I was regaining my bearings, I felt him extrude. He didn't have to speak or nudge me in any way for me to wrap my legs around his waist. We locked eyes, and a silent communication passed between us. Holding on to his shoulder with my left arm, I slipped my free hand between us and gave his cock a couple of strokes. Maker, his pleasure blasted into me with such strength I nearly came undone again. I loved how his silver eyes darkened with lust, their intensity sending a delicious shiver down my spine.

I aligned his cock with my opening and lowered myself onto it even as he thrust upward. Fuck! He felt even thicker than usual, despite how wet and relaxed he had gotten me. Kayog swallowed my moans in a voracious kiss as he began to pump into me. Each stroke drove me insane with bliss. The swirly ridges of his shaft always procured me with the most delightful sensations. But it was his *ganacs*—the wicked bumps on the head of his cock that did a number on me.

They were designed to stimulate the erogenous nerve endings in a Temern females inner walls. However, they were also extremely sensitive for males. And right now, each time they rubbed against me, they sent electric sparks of ecstasy through Kayog, and straight back to me through our bond. The sensory overload had me screaming in no time as another brutal orgasm swept me away.

The world below vanished as we physically became one, soaring through the starry ocean of the night sky. My entire body was shaking, burning from within as waves upon waves of pleasure crashed over me. I felt on the verge of combusting, the wind whipping past us preventing me from bursting into flames.

Through his own bliss, Kayog relentlessly pounded into me, wresting one orgasm after the other from me until I felt on the verge of breaking. More than once, Kayog nearly joined his voice to mine, but with a near godly level of self-control, he managed to pull back from the edge to continue wrecking me.

And at last, after he claimed the fifth or sixth climax from me —I had lost count—Kayog surrendered to his own release. His pleasure struck me with such violence, a bright light blinded me, and my brain froze. Time stood still. For a moment, I wondered if I'd been knocked right out of my body, until my skin began to tingle. His seed erupted in me, bathing my battered insides as he continued to pump in and out of me until he was fully spent.

He reclaimed my mouth, our tongues mingling in a shared breath as sparks of ecstasy went off each of my nerve endings. It was sweet and tender, stripped of the almost rabid passion that had burnt so brightly between us. It was a promise, a pledge, a seal to the unbreakable bond between us. Wrapped in a cocoon of love and devotion, linked bodies and souls, we glided toward the horizon, towards a future of endless possibilities.

CHAPTER 20
KAYOG

I entered the large gathering hall where the Galactic Trade Symposium was taking place. Important people, high-ranking politicians, business owners, traders, lobbyists, and every other type of people involved in any form of commerce milled about this room, and the adjoining art gallery. As part of the event, visual artists from the attending planets had been invited to display their best pieces in this exclusive art exhibition.

No word could describe just how much I felt out of my depth here. It wasn't that I didn't have the knowledge and competence to converse with these people. I simply struggled to justify my presence and how it would benefit anyone. Sure, I understood that Colin wanted me to establish a rapport with as many people as possible who had any type of sway over the governments and ruling bodies of various species. But as a matchmaker, how did you even strike that initial conversation?

If not for my beautiful wife by my side—fuck how I loved calling her that—I probably would have made a beeline for one of the tables laden with fancy amuse-bouche and prefilled glasses of various wines. I wasn't hungry or thirsty. In fact, I usually avoided eating at those events as they always offered foods from different worlds. Unless you knew exactly who had prepared them and how, it was wise not to get too bold unless you were willing to spend the rest of the evening feeling like your stomach was trying to carve its way out of your belly. But eating and drinking would give me something to do—or rather an excuse to avoid talking to people.

Sensing my unease, Linsea squeezed my hand in a reassuring fashion. The wave of love she channeled through our bond appeased me in a way that couldn't be described. I squeezed her hand back, gratitude filling my heart. It annoyed me that I should be so needy and insecure when I should instead do my best to make her shine and help people realize what a fabulous ambassador she would soon become.

Instead of going to interact with the people she knew or was expected to make contact with, Linsea led me to the gallery. I understood perfectly that she had done it to give me an opportunity to relax further before jumping into socializing. Maker, how I loved this female. Being used to the public, I didn't doubt my ability to quickly adapt. But I still welcomed this extra reprieve, which also allowed me to do a surface scan of the attendees' emotions. It was an incommensurable tool that helped me adjust the way I would approach each individual based on the energy they projected.

For all that, I genuinely enjoyed the diversity of pieces on display. Some were a lot harder to relate to as they were so far out the mainstream definition of art that one didn't really know how to respond to it. Others could only be fully appreciated if one possessed specific abilities inherent to their species that allowed the viewer to perceive other dimensions of the art which made it complete. In some cases, a special visual aid was made available next to the display so that people could compensate for their anatomical limitations.

"A beautiful piece isn't it?" a male voice suddenly said

behind us as we were admiring a magnificent sculpture of a winged horse being hugged by a human female.

We turned around to see Taylor Darby and his brother Lucas. He was the head of a powerful conglomerate that 'invested' in many off-world companies, usually among less advanced species. Although legal, Taylor's practices could be deemed morally gray. He often purchased or acquired controlling interests in struggling businesses, optimizing them to increase profit —which usually meant massive layoffs, automation, and severe straying from the cultural authenticity of the products being produced. In the end, it rarely benefited the local population.

Still, without his investments, many of those firms would have completely shut down, which would have been even more harmful to those communities. But that didn't make him a saint or an altruistic man.

"Quite beautiful," Linsea said. "I love fantastic creatures. And human mythology certainly has an amazing array of them."

"We do. And it always surprised me that, after visiting hundreds of other worlds, we have never found a flying mount that fully matches our Pegasus," he said pensively. "But apologies for being rude and not introducing myself."

"Taylor and Lucas Darby," my mate said pre-emptively with a charming smile. "It would be scandalous for me not to know who you are."

"You flatter us and put us to shame..." he added sheepishly.

Despite his apologetic stance, the calculating glimmer in his black eyes fully matched the cold emotions emanating from him. He was a predator assessing nearby potential prey. Without our empathic abilities, we would likely have fallen for his charming demeanor. Tall, slender, elegantly dressed in a black suit and white shirt with a dark blue tie, he was the embodiment of the polished businessman. His ruggedly handsome face framed by neatly trimmed dark brown hair would have many women fanning themselves in his presence.

His younger brother—with whom he shared the same mother but had different fathers—exuded the same type of shark energy. His green eyes brimmed with intelligence. Whatever my feelings about them, these men radiated an unshakable loyalty to each other, which was quite commendable.

"There's no shame to be had for not knowing me," Linsea said in a friendly manner. "My name is Linsea Voln, and I am a recent hire of the UPO. My presence here is specifically to establish new connections and get a sense of some of the challenges that are not as broadly covered but that plague our members. Therefore, expect to see me often in the future."

"Linsea? I've heard many praises about a Temern named Linsea. But I believe she was named Linsea Kenna," Taylor said with surprise, although I suspected he already knew the answer.

"We are one in the same. This is my wonderful husband, Kayog Voln. As humans say, we tied the knot barely two weeks ago."

"A pleasure to meet you," Taylor said with enthusiasm before extending a hand towards me.

It still baffled me that humans instinctively continued to do that, especially since it made certain species uncomfortable. In some cultures, you never touched someone else unless they were a blood relative, your mate, or a criminal either to be taken to jail or executed. Nevertheless, as it didn't conflict with my own culture, I gladly shook his hand before doing the same with his brother.

"So what do you do, if I may be so bold?" Taylor asked me. "Are you a negotiator or ambassador like your mate?"

Once again, I got a strong feeling that he knew exactly who and what I was. It suddenly dawned on me that he hadn't accidentally strolled over here and struck that conversation over some human art he was proud of. This man had a huge team to perform thorough background checks on the companies he might be tempted to acquire as well as the people who ran them. I didn't doubt that he had performed a similar investigation about many if not all of the attendees ahead of this event. Information was the greatest tool and leverage in business.

"Not at all," I said enthusiastically while stomping on my fears of embarrassing Linsea, which were trying to rear their ugly heads again. "I'm a matchmaker for primitive aliens."

The way he faked his surprise erased any doubt I might still have had about this whole conversation being staged. His emotions reeked of mockery laced with a hint of disdain.

"A matchmaker?! Well that was unexpected. But for primitive aliens?" Taylor said looking confused, his brother nodding in a way that implied he too was baffled by that part. "Why would anyone fall back on primitive aliens? Are people truly so desperate for love that they would settle that way?"

It took every ounce of my willpower to keep a neutral expression on my face as he spewed his disrespectful drivel. A part of me believed he was deliberately trying to get a rise out of me or simply embarrass me as any good bully would.

"People do not *fall back* or *settle* on primitive aliens," Linsea said in a calm but slightly chastising tone. "The technological advances of one's species do not define their value as an individual. Love doesn't care about whether you have achieved warp speed or not."

"Fair enough," Taylor conceded.

"But why focus on primitive aliens?" Lucas asked, this time with genuine curiosity, although his disdain for a group he considered inferior still radiated from him and his brother.

"Because I understand them and their needs better than anyone else out there," I said in a nonchalant but confident fashion.

Right on cue, both brothers raised their eyebrows at me in a dubious fashion.

"Is that so?" Taylor asked. "What do you base that assertion on?"

"I have a master's degree in xenobiology, a second one in galactic history with a focus on primitive species, and I'm currently writing my third master's thesis on the Prime Directive," I said in a factual manner. "So yes, very few people could claim to have a better understanding of those communities. There are already a billion matchmaking agencies out there. But none of them cater to this group, in large part because they don't know how to."

"What Kayog didn't add is the fact that his matches are 100% accurate, unlike the complete gamble that other agencies offer. He has a unique talent that the competition would die for," Linsea said proudly.

To hear her standing up for me like this did the funniest thing to me. Obviously, I expected no less from her. But it was the emotions emanating from her as she did so that truly boosted my confidence. If such a wonderful female could be so proud of me just the way I was, why the fuck was I undermining myself with stupid doubts?

Taylor opened his mouth to say something else—I assumed to challenge my accuracy—but a Stornian male interrupted him with a greeting.

"Well, well, look who we have here!" the Stornian male exclaimed with the fakest air of surprise. "Taylor and Lucas Darby! We meet again!"

Typical of his species, the Stornian was an imposing male. His charcoal skin, broad shoulders and the spikes covering his bald head would be deemed very intimidating by most people. A smattering of dark scales covered his body, some of them much longer and slightly protruding. The latter were the same type of horns that adorned his head. When in danger, the darker 'scales' would stand up as vicious spikes that would inflict grievous injuries on any enemy attempting to touch him.

Despite his pointy ears that were usually associated with elves, people often mistakenly assumed his species to possess draconic ties, especially when you considered his long, lizard-like tail. But the lightning-shaped darker patterns on certain areas of his skin told a different story. Humans often compared Stornians to stone elementals or golems.

A young female companion quietly accompanied him. She seemed to be barely a few days over twenty. While petite compared to him—as was the wont of the Stornian females—they shared undeniable features that marked her either as his daughter or much younger sibling. I definitely leaned towards the former.

"Kateros Granger," Taylor said in a polite voice, just the right level of welcoming without being deemed warm. "I didn't expect to see you here."

I flinched inwardly at the less-than-subtle dig. Although the newcomer didn't seem to realize it, Darby had implied his business wasn't high-ranking enough to justify his presence at this symposium. Kateros came here on a mission, and it seemed to heavily involve the two brothers.

"Please, meet our new friends, Linsea and Kayog Voln," Taylor said, waving in turn at my mate and me.

I repressed a smile when the Stornian barely spared us a glance.

"Kateros Granger. Pleased to meet you," the Stornian replied, granting each of us an almost dismissive nod before refocusing on Taylor.

"I wouldn't miss this event for anything in the world. But have you met my beautiful daughter, Shaya?" Kateros asked, placing his hand on the small of her back to bring her forward.

A wave of anger instantly swelled within me. Thanks to my studies, I knew well how common arranged marriages occurred within certain species. In this instance, Kateros wasn't even trying to be subtle about wanting to trade his daughter in exchange for a beneficial business arrangement. The sad part was that to him, it was normal, and not at all highly offensive and disrespectful to his child. Moreover, I could feel genuine affection from him towards her.

If he indeed secured a marriage proposal from one of the brothers, he would be deemed to have performed spectacularly well for his daughter. To Stornians, marriage was not about love but about securing the welfare and future of the bloodline. It was about strengthening one's status.

The resignation emanating from Shaya was heartbreaking. She would comply with whatever agreement her father secured because it was her duty as his child. At least, these unions were not misogynistic in any way. Sons and daughters were equally traded in whatever deal the parent deemed beneficial.

"I had that pleasure a few years back," Taylor conceded, his gaze roaming over the young female in an appreciative fashion. "You were but a child back then. But you have blossomed into quite a beautiful woman."

"You flatter me," Shaya replied with the perfect level of demure and polite.

Although it annoyed me to perceive the covetous emotions emanating from both Taylor and his brother, I at least felt relieved that neither of them had looked at her in a way that was lurid or disrespectful. There was nothing wrong with a male being aroused by an attractive female, and Shaya qualified as such. But both men were nearly twice her age with clearly no interest in settling down with her. Why would they when some of the wealthiest and best-connected females in the galaxy gladly threw themselves at them? I could only hope that their interest in bedding her would remain that—the natural sexual attraction between compatible adults, and not something they would act on. However, it was something else that retained my attention.

Her song was familiar to me.

"She is my pride and joy," Kateros said, puffing out his broad chest. "Shaya is my greatest treasure, my company being a pale second."

"And what company would that be?" my mate asked.

"Granger Mining Corporation, the biggest provider of azonite and other rare metals of Khelesar, our homeworld," Kateros boasted, before casting a less-than-subtle glance at Taylor to assess his reaction to his claim.

"Ah yes! Azonite is a pillar of the Stornian economy," Linsea said.

She was furiously reflecting about something related to this. Right this instant, I wished I could read her mind.

"Absolutely. It's a metal highly sought after throughout the galaxy. Our order book is overflowing," Kateros replied, this time facing Taylor directly. "Frankly, we've reached a point where supplying the demand will be near impossible unless we expand."

I sensed the very moment Taylor switched from having a casual conversation into business mode. And it clearly wasn't going to bode well for the Stornian.

"Yes, azonite is a fantastic metal. It's a pity that extracting it creates such massive hazardous waste," Taylor said in a polite tone that also loudly broadcast the fact that he wasn't interested. "If not for that, I'm sure investors would be beating down your doors to help you with this endeavor."

The light of hope instantly faded in Kateros's eyes, even as he tried to hang on with a last plea.

"The waste is obviously a problem that we have been diligently working on. But with the right investors, we would be able to turn things around swiftly, with huge profits guaranteed for everyone involved," the Stornian replied eagerly.

"It would take years if not decades to recoup that initial investment," Taylor countered in a slightly cooler tone. "Other, smaller mining firms have already optimized their equipment and methodologies so that they fall within the prescribed guidelines. The UPO is seriously cracking down on environmental violations. No one wants to get on their bad side over it."

"As my father said, we have been diligently working to improve our infrastructure, facilities, and methodologies so that we remain in compliance with the ordinance," Shaya intervened with an assurance that took me aback.

Initially, she had struck me as being submissive and reserved. But I could now see the strength and fire that lurked beneath that demure facade. It made sense, considering what was now obvious to me.

"Are you involved in your father's company?" I asked, wanting to confirm my suspicions.

She nodded. "I am in fact part of the science and research team and lead the environmental task force. We have significantly reduced the toxic waste produced by our operations, and we continue towards making even more improvements."

"You seem quite young to be in such a role," Taylor interjected in a slightly patronizing tone that made me want to smack him.

"I guess some of us are prodigies," she retorted with a hint of sarcasm that had her father clearly wanting to facepalm while I itched to applaud.

I loved nothing more than seeing an obnoxious prick get put back in his place. Her poor father continued to hope that he could somehow pull off an arranged marriage between them to help save his business. But even without my empathic abilities, I could see that these two would never be a match. She had a spine, he wanted a doormat.

Anyway, she belonged to another.

"Some people most certainly are," I said with an approving smile. "But if I may be so bold, may I ask if you are mated? Your species tends to marry fairly young."

"My daughter is completely unattached!" Kateros exclaimed, sounding almost outraged at the implication that she might not be free. "But she is indeed at the perfect age to find a mate, as per our people's customs," he added, glancing back at Taylor.

I felt second-hand embarrassment at the near desperation with which he tried to make the impossible happen.

"I'm *very* happy to hear it!" I said with a slightly excessive enthusiasm that I knew would draw all attention to me.

"Why is that?" Shaya asked, taken aback.

"Because I happen to know your soulmate," I said smugly.

As one, everyone gaped at me, my beautiful mate included. You'd think a bomb had just gone off in our midst.

"What?!" Shaya asked at last, recovering first.

"I know your soulmate," I repeated with assurance. "I went to university with him."

"He's a Temern?!" she exclaimed.

I shook my head. "No. He's a Daigan."

As one, Taylor and Lucas snorted, and they stared at me with a disbelieving look. Their disdain for my profession—which had temporarily faded while discussing with Kateros—came back with a vengeance. Except, this time, they now believed me to be a charlatan.

That was fine. In a few minutes, they'd be eating their hearts out.

"A Satyr?!" Lucas repeated, flabbergasted.

I gave him an indulgent smile. "Based on human folklore, it would be a fair comparison as they share many similarities with them. His name is Straef Dharam. He's a fantastic young male. Charismatic, ambitious, innovative, and extremely smart. Straef is also a prodigy. He got his degree three years earlier than the average person in his discipline. He's also given me a serious lesson in humility by systematically defeating me at Five Kings."

"I love Five Kings!" Shaya exclaimed, perking up. "No one can beat me at this game."

I chuckled. "Are you sure? Straef remains undefeated. I believe you may have found your match... in more ways than one."

"Absolutely not. *He* has found his match. I'll gladly teach him how it's done," she said, lifting her chin with the most adorable air of defiance.

"Assuming you ever meet him," her father countered in a stern voice before glaring at me. "You shouldn't put such wild thoughts in her mind. A Daigan and a Stornian together makes absolutely no sense."

"Actually, it makes all the sense in the world," I said smugly. "Your species are very much compatible."

He recoiled and stared at me as if my brain wasn't functioning properly.

"Whatever would make you think such an insane thing?" he asked, the look in both brothers' eyes echoing his sentiment.

"You weren't there when I informed our friends here of the fact that I have a masters in xenobiology. And I assure you that your species are totally compatible. And now, you just made me realize that this pairing is the greatest thing that could happen to you, your business, your people, and Straef."

"My business?" Kateros echoed, this time, curiosity dampening some of the aggression in his voice. "How would a union with a Daigan benefit my business in any way? As far as I know, their people do not deal in metals and minerals. They mainly trade in wood products, farming, and animal breeding."

"Correct, but like I mentioned, Straef is a visionary and always pushing the boundaries of innovation," I said enthusiastically. "Last year, he graduated with a thesis on an insect native to his world and that can be bred under very precise conditions to extend their otherwise very short lifespan. It turns out that the lumoth can safely eat radioactive and toxic waste and turn them into energy."

"What?! I've never heard of such a thing," Kateros exclaimed, unsure whether to be excited by that prospect or angry at the possibility that I was playing him for a fool.

"Because he's in the final stages of developing sustainable breeding farms as well as the conversion technology to turn it into a massive industry. He owns the patent to his discoveries. And his goal is to use these creatures on a large scale to sanitize disaster zones. A discussion between you two could solve or massively reduce the problems you're currently facing."

"That... that would definitely be food for thought," Kateros said before exchanging a look with his daughter.

She, too, was bubbling with excitement. Although Shaya didn't seem particularly keen on meeting Straef on a romantic level, she was very eager to discuss ways to save her family business, and definitely to face off against a worthy opponent in a game of Five Kings. She had no reason to think I could effectively know when two people were soulmates. But that would only be the added bonus.

However, it was the thrilled emotions emanating from my mate that reclaimed my attention.

"I wasn't aware of these lumoths," Linsea said pensively. "But if you do enter into such a collaboration, the UPO has many support programs catering to any effort towards environmental protection and especially toxic waste reduction."

"Really?" Kateros said, perking up even as the two brothers tensed. "Such as what?"

"There is potential financial support if the project is deemed beneficial and sustainable," Linsea said. "But there are also other forms of assistance that can be offered, such as logistics, some equipment, and even the services of highly qualified experts for a short period of time at absolutely no cost to you. The UPO is devoted to environmental protection for both developing and member planets. As it sounds like this project is entering the early stages of deployment, anyone participating in the trial run could benefit from greater support than usual. I highly recommend that you look into it. And feel free to reach out to me for guidance or assistance during the process."

"I'm definitely interested in investigating the matter,"

Kateros said eagerly. "I guess I will get to talk to your Daigan once he begins his courtship of my daughter."

I repressed the urge to laugh, further compounded by the dismay from the two brothers. Once this project took off the ground, Kateros and Straef stood to make insane profits. Having partnered with Kateros first would have granted the brothers access to the wealth that might flow from this.

"I will promptly make the introductions," I said with a smile. "Do not fret, my dear Shaya. Once you meet him, you will thank me. When it comes to matching soulmates, I'm never wrong."

"We'll find out soon enough," she replied politely, although with a sliver of hope.

"We will look into this Straef and his innovative venture as well," Taylor interjected. "If this information is accurate, then maybe we should revisit potential collaborations."

"Maybe," Kateros replied politely.

But I already knew that once he got the confirmation that all my statements were true, Kateros would no longer want anything to do with Taylor. You didn't do business with people like him unless you were desperate.

This moment marked a radical shift in my understanding of my role and the impact I could have. Granted, such beneficial matches would likely be few and far between. But every single one would be a massive victory. And if only for the pride and joy emanating from my mate right this instant, it would all be worthwhile.

CHAPTER 21
LINSEA

I was flying high, living my best life with the most amazing male. Three months after the symposium, I couldn't stop poking fun at him for how silly he had been in his belief that people would snub him. Sure, the occasional idiots like Taylor and his brother approached him with a haughty demeanor. But many members of the less advanced species—without actually falling into the primitive category—were greatly pleased to see a service catering to other groups than just the *elite*.

More importantly, they were blown away by his personality. My husband was smart, knowledgeable, insightful, charismatic, and genuinely passionate about improving other people's lives, especially those deemed weird or freaky. You couldn't fake that.

Colin had been extremely clever by requesting all this early socializing for Kayog. His reputation grew quickly, in no small part due to that extremely lucky pairing between the Daigan and Stornian. The amazing information he shared regarding the lumoths benefited my own career.

I became the main negotiator between the UPO and Straef regarding all the ways his research could be further funded. Needless to say that Kateros was over the moon when he received the grant I helped them secure for the trial run of the program. Countless other people came knocking at both our doors hoping for the same type of windfall. Obviously, we didn't have any magic trick to dish out such beneficial outcomes to the masses. It still opened many doors for us.

Simultaneously, Colin had not been playing by saying our public relations and marketing department would go all out for the official launch of the Prime Mating Agency. They had the coolest and wildest ads playing in a loop with a countdown to the registration site opening.

And the day it did, the site crashed within ten minutes from too many simultaneous signup requests. It shouldn't have been surprising to the extent that the clever ads from the UPO essentially guaranteed that any match would be a perfect one. That resonated with those desperate for love.

Due to the insane numbers of candidates, Kayog went straight to a fair format. Candidates within a given region were chosen lottery style from the pool of applicants to come to the three-day fair in their sector. Each candidate only got a ten-minute one-on-one meeting with my mate. An assistant recorded those meetings and entered all the information thus gathered in a database.

But Kayog didn't need it.

Although he didn't possess the traditional eidetic memory, my mate never forgot a person's name or face. They were literally carved into his memory. Despite the limited time afforded for each meeting, people absolutely loved him. Kayog had a way of making you feel like no one but you mattered whenever you were together. His entire focus was on you. He made you feel understood, respected, and like he truly cared about helping you find happiness.

And he absolutely did.

Although he was no longer part of a band, I often felt like I was married to a rock star always on the road while touring. To the candidates, that's exactly what he was. And that became even truer once he started making matches.

At first, it was a trickle. Each time, he would message me as soon as the candidate left his office and would pretty much lose his mind. He would jump all over the place, doing a happy dance that had me in stitches. He was so excited. To him, every match was like winning the lottery.

In no time, the number of pairings almost became a tsunami. He traveled so much and met so many people that it became easier with the massive database organically stored in his wondrous mind. He only deplored the cases that would sit idle on the shelf of his brain as he failed to find their partner. It messed with him receiving messages after a few months from candidates he had met and who were distraught that he kept finding mates for others but not for them.

Some of them truly broke his heart, but others were downright infuriating. Entitled messages demanding he get off his ass and find them their partners happened a few times too many. The worst were those who became flat out nasty, calling him names and insulting him for 'not doing his job.' And then, there were the idiots spreading rumors that he was lying about those pairing being true soulmates. The candidates were just brainwashed into believing they were actually in love with their match but that it was all an illusion, a hoax that would eventually come crashing down and leave them devastated.

I wanted to tear them a new one, but Kayog always calmed me down, truly amused by their nonsense. He wisely reminded me that there was no point arguing with fools, in that time would prove him right.

A few of those 'fools' turned out to be *rival* matchmaking agencies, pissed off that many of their candidates would just flock to the PMA. A few even tried to sue my mate over unfair practices over the fact that his services were free. The incentives from the UPO in the form of free relocation and dowries further constituted unfair advantages in their eyes. Those lawsuits were dead on arrival as they were founded on the false premise that they were competitors. Kayog catered to a very specific group that those agencies always snubbed. It wasn't his fault that their other candidates came to him instead.

Anyway, my husband was far too proud and honest for that kind of shady behavior. I found out that Kayog was constantly cataloging the soul of every person he encountered, even those who were married. He was almost obsessive in his need to hear people's songs. To my shock, he confided that he had defined a personal chart based on those melodies. Apparently, the rhythm, tonality, amplitude, and complexity of a person's song revealed specific common traits about them.

For example, he could already narrow down certain things about people only with that, which in turn help him identify the species or type of candidate that might be a good match. It still boggled my mind how he could recognize two people from the insane pool of potential partners. But he made it work.

Above all, he got to live his dream of visiting and interacting directly with countless primitive species under different levels of restrictions of the Prime Directive. He was taking very seriously writing amendments and reforms to the guidelines specific to different planets. What I loved most about him was the fact that he didn't simply push for his personal ideas and opinions on the matter. He used his incredible empathic abilities to discreetly assess the local population's feelings about his 'innocent' comments regarding specific issues faced by that species.

Each time the laws were modified to reflect his suggestions were a massive victory.

However, all of this made coordinating our respective missions harder. We parted often, though thankfully for fairly short periods. But our steamy reunions more than compensated for it.

We had just gone out to celebrate his 250th official pairing when I suddenly felt faint. Before we even reached our table, I got hit by three dizzy spells back-to-back. Not wanting to take chances, Kayog insisted that we go to the doctor immediately. I wasn't too thrilled about it as it was a forty-five-minute flight back to the research center where we still lived. But my mate's genuine worry swayed me.

I simply thought low blood sugar from not having eaten a proper meal all day had been the cause. The verdict I should have seen coming instead actually took me by surprise.

We were pregnant.

My excited squeal—not to say screech—instantly died in my throat when Kayog remained stoic. A wave of worry surged within me when I perceived nothing but great tension emanating from him. Why such a cold and reserved reaction? We had spoken about having children, and my mate always expressed his desire to have lots and lots of them. I shifted my attention to Arafin. Discovering that he had blocked his emotions from us— something he had never done before—had my blood turning to ice.

Of all people, Arafin knew that he couldn't hide his emotions from Kayog. So either he had done so subconsciously, or he was deliberately trying to hide something from *me*. I opened my mouth to ask what the fuck was going on, but Kayog spoke first.

"There's something wrong, right?" Kayog asked, his voice as devoid of emotion as his face.

I held my breath, fear wanting to take root in the pit of my stomach as the doctor lowered his eyes for a moment, an air of sorrow and guilt fleeting over his features before he collected himself.

"Currently, we cannot see any anomaly with the fetus," Arafin said carefully. "However, Linsea's blood tests confirmed something we dreaded."

"Something you dreaded?!" I exclaimed, torn between fear

and outrage that he might have kept some vital information hidden from me. "What's going on?"

He glanced at me with an apologetic look before turning back to Kayog.

"To be frank, we thought you would be sterile. Your hormonal discrepancies affect many of your organs, which in turn grants you those incredible powers," the doctor said instead of answering my questions.

"Clearly, I'm not sterile," Kayog retorted in a clipped tone. "So what gives?"

"Based on the blood samples taken from Linsea, your child is provoking the same hormonal imbalance in her, but to a lesser degree," he explained.

As one, Kayog and I recoiled with complete shock.

"Linsea is becoming an Edal?" he exclaimed, reaching for my hand, fear soaring inside of him. "Is she going to suffer like I did?"

Arafin lifted his palm in an appeasing fashion while shaking his head. "No, she's not," he said before turning to me. "Your pineal gland is normal, so you cannot become an Edal."

"Then is our baby one?" I asked, my hand tightening in my husband's grip for comfort.

The doctor hesitated. "Yes and no."

"What the fuck is that supposed to mean?" Kayog snapped. "If it is, surely you can use all the testing and research you've done on me to protect it?"

"The baby is not an actual Edal, although I believe it was initially going to be," Arafin replied, choosing his words carefully. "In all the cases where this kind of hormonal anomaly occurred during a pregnancy, the baby was not viable."

His words struck me like a boulder to the chest. My mate shut down his emotions, closing himself off to me. But he didn't do it quickly enough for me not to perceive the sharp pain that lacerated his heart at this horrible news. The selfish part of me that needed his support wanted to tell him not to shut me out. But the still rational part of me understood that he was doing this to protect me, not to exclude me.

"It's going to die?" Kayog asked, pain audible in his voice despite his effort to keep it neutral.

"Normally, with cases like these, the fetus either dies early in the pregnancy or will go to term but die within twenty-four hours," the doctor said in a gentle tone. "The longest recorded survival period was four days."

"But what does the baby die from? And like Kayog said, can't the research you performed on him help protect our child?" I asked, clinging to hope.

"It is not a case of a traditional Edal," Arafin said with sorrow. "With this specific condition, the abnormal hormones prevent the baby's organs from fully forming. The fetus relies on its mother to survive. After birth—assuming they make it all the way there—they quickly collapse as they no longer have the necessary support."

"And you're saying that this is the case with our baby?" I asked, my throat constricted.

"It's too early to tell. Your current hormonal discrepancies are simply the warning signs of what has a high probability of happening," the doctor said cautiously. "But you both must mentally prepare for this outcome. If the fetus survives all the way past the three-month period, then it pretty much guarantees that you will go to term. You are now only at seven weeks."

"Are you saying that we should terminate our pregnancy?" I asked, anger at the unfairness of it all seeping into my voice.

"Only you two can make that decision," Arafin said swiftly.

"How is that even a decision to be made? You're saying that our baby is almost guaranteed to be born without the essential organs to sustain life. Why would we want to bring them into the world just so that they can suffer for the short period of time they will be here until they die?" Kayog snarled.

"Oh no!" Arafin countered. "The baby will not suffer. The good news in this tragedy—if I can use that term—is that these babies do not feel pain. They are born with CIP—Congenital Insensitivity to Pain or Congenital Analgesia."

"How does that work exactly?" I asked, my mind reeling.

"Basically, the nervous system doesn't send pain signals to the brain. Therefore, no matter how injured they may be, people with that condition don't feel any discomfort. So it would be a painless experience for the child until they sustain enough catastrophic failures to pass away."

I hugged myself, tears pricking my eyes as my brain struggled to come to terms with this news. To have been so high with joy at finding out we were pregnant only to crash and burn seconds later like this was beyond devastating.

"Take your time to decide what you want to do," Arafin said in a soothing voice. "There's no rush right now. You are both Temerns. You can perceive what the baby feels. So you will know for certain that it is not feeling any pain. And keep in mind that we're not sure yet whether your child will develop that condition. It's just the hormonal results that forces us to contemplate the very real possibility of a less pleasant outcome."

"Why didn't you warn us?" Kayog asked angrily. "Clearly, you knew that probability existed from the start. Did you do this so that you could run more fucking experiments on the Edal freak?"

My instinctive wish to calm him down and gently chastise him for such a cruel accusation faded almost instantly. As much as I liked Arafin, Kayog's question was sadly a fair one to ask. That they might have allowed us to become pregnant only as part of some twisted experiment would utterly destroy me.

"No, absolutely not!" Arafin exclaimed, with a genuine outrage that acted like a potent balm on my wounded heart. "We didn't warn you because we had no certainty that this could happen. Ellen and I had extensive debates about this. In the end, we decided that you had gone through enough already without us creating more stress and anxiety for you based on pure speculations. Again, we truly thought you were sterile. And if a pregnancy did occur, then we would address any complication should they arise. If it was the wrong decision, then please accept my most sincere apologies. We were trying to protect you and did what we thought was right."

Once again, the honesty that radiated from him further silenced the anger I wanted to direct at him. Had our roles been reversed, I also would have struggled to decide how to handle this situation. It didn't make any of this easier.

"Fine," Kayog said, his voice still cold although his stance no longer held the same level of aggression towards the doctor. "But what does that mean for Linsea? What risk does this pregnancy put her in?"

My heart melted for my mate that he quickly shifted his focus on my welfare.

"None whatsoever," Arafin said firmly.

That took me aback. Judging by Kayog's expression, he was also stunned by that unequivocal answer.

"Really?" I asked, my tone dubious.

The doctor nodded with conviction. "Absolutely. In previous cases, the mother has never sustained any negative side effects."

"But what of the abnormal hormones?" Kayog argued.

"Their levels are much too low to have an impact on Linsea," Arafin explained. "Her pineal gland is also normal. So there are absolutely no risks to her, only to the fetus."

My mate nodded slowly, and a heavy silence settled over the room as we digested his words. Then, in perfect sync, Kayog and I locked eyes and a wordless communication passed between us.

"Thank you for this information," Kayog said in a controlled voice to the doctor. "My mate and I will go reflect on the matter and keep you posted."

"Of course. Take all the time you need," Arafin said.

My husband helped me up and led me out of the doctor's office, his arm protectively wrapped around my shoulders.

As soon as we entered our apartment, and Kayog closed the door behind us, I turned around to face him.

"Do not close yourself off to me," I said in a pleading tone.

He flinched, and that look of despair I hadn't seen since our early days on the campus flitted over his face before being quickly hidden.

"You don't need to feel my pain and shame on top of your own grief," he said in a dejected tone.

I stiffened and stared at him in disbelief. "Why shame?" I demanded. "You did nothing wrong!"

Kayog huffed and marched past me into the living area to stand in front of the giant floor to ceiling window overlooking the breathtaking landscape outside.

"Everything about me is wrong," he hissed with self-loathing. "I can't even be a proper mate to you."

"What the fuck kind of nonsense is this?!" I exclaimed before hastening to his side. I grabbed his upper arm and forced him to turn around to look at me. "You being a good mate does not equal being a sperm donor! There are tons of people out there who cannot have kids or have multiple failed pregnancies. That doesn't make them lesser people. That doesn't make them bad partners. You are not lesser or a failure."

He tried to turn away from me, but I tightened my grip on his arm and grabbed the second one to force him to stay in front of me.

"Kayog, look at me," I commanded. "As much as I wish we had known from the start the potential risk of a pregnancy, right now I only want to focus on the fact that our baby is fine. Who knows what the future holds? Maybe everything will work out just fine."

"But what if it doesn't?" he challenged, the pain in his voice and in his eyes tearing me apart.

"Then that will be Fate's will," I said in a factual manner.

His shoulders slouched, and he stared at the floor with a lost expression that clawed at my heart.

"Do you want me to abort?" I asked in a soft voice.

He jerked his head up to look at me, his gaze intense even as he tried to hide the shock my words stirred within him.

"Is that what you want?" he asked, his voice tense.

"I asked you a question first," I countered in a gently reproving tone.

"It's not *my* decision to make, my love," Kayog said in a voice full of sorrow. "I'm not trying to shirk any responsibility in this. But it is *your* body."

"Carrying *our* child," I countered. "You have a say in this."

"It still remains *your* body, and it should therefore be *your* choice," he insisted. "The connection you will share isn't something that I will. You will bear it all and experience something that I cannot even begin to imagine. Therefore, I cannot impose any of this on you."

I nodded slowly. "But if it was your decision to make, what would it be? And please give me an honest answer, Kayog. We've always been truthful with each other, and that should never change, especially in times of crisis. Please open to me as I am open to you," I begged.

He hesitated, visibly torn by conflicting emotions, although sadness dominated on his features.

"If his assertion that this pregnancy will not cause you any harm is accurate, and if the baby will truly not feel any pain, then yes, I would want to keep it," Kayog said at last, the sorrow he felt audible in his voice. "But this should only be if *you* really *want* this, and not because you feel obligated in any way."

He took my face between both hands, the love in his eyes dominating the deep chagrin he couldn't hide. My husband locked gazes with me, and a sense of peace settled over me.

"I truly mean it, my love. Whatever your decision, I will

stand by you and will not harbor any resentment. My heart is broken, which is the only reason why I'm closing myself off. It's not out of any ill will or twisted sense of shame. I just don't want to add to your burden."

"Don't, Kayog," I said in a soft voice. "We're soulmates, together through the good and bad. Like you, I want to keep our baby so long as it doesn't feel any pain. We don't know that it won't make it. But whatever Fate decides, we will face it side by side. We fought to save you and achieved the impossible. We will fight to save our baby as well."

A powerful emotion crossed his handsome face. He drew me into his embrace, and I melted against him.

"I love you, Linsea," he whispered in a choked voice. "I love you with everything that I am, now and always."

As he closed his wings around me, he opened wide the walls that had kept me out. The depth of his sorrow struck me hard. But I didn't push it away. I allowed it in but focused on the other emotions that needed to be nurtured. Lurking beneath the pain, infinite love, hope, and gratitude attempted to pierce through. I latched onto them and fueled them with my own.

CHAPTER 22
KAYOG

The following four months turned into a brutal emotional roller coaster. For the first few weeks, shame, guilt, and anger at the unfairness of it all ate at me. Why was I always broken? Why was there always something wrong with me that kept me from having the simple life everyone else got? Had I not suffered enough? Except now, my shortcomings were also causing pain and distress to the two people who absolutely didn't deserve it: my beautiful mate and my innocent child.

And yet, the darkness swallowing me gradually faded thanks to those same wonderful two people. Seeing Linsea glow, her belly growing, and being surrounded by the joy and infinite love radiating from our baby's blossoming mind defied description.

It was pure bliss.

Our little one—who turned out to be a female—loved hearing me sing and whenever I would tickle her mom. Daily, her song grew stronger and even more haunting. It increasingly harmonized with ours, which gave me goosebumps. I hadn't seen my little princess yet, but I already adored her. Linsea would constantly bemoan what a hopeless girl dad I was going to be. And she was right. I would spoil the fuck out of my little angel.

Medical appointments became the bane of my existence. Every time Linsea had to undergo a scan, I braced for the devastating news that something had gone wrong. But as the weeks and then months went by, hope steadily grew in my heart. Our baby was going to be fine. She was going to make it.

And then, halfway through the fifth month, our entire world came crashing down.

The first signs of fetal abnormalities began showing up on the scans. In the following weeks, they became more and more notable until the verdict we dreaded came down: our baby would not be viable.

No words could describe the devastation we felt. For a while there, we truly convinced ourselves that things would workout. If the scientists had managed to save me, surely they could save our angel as well, right?

The question as to whether we would terminate the pregnancy was never addressed. For us, that was not even an option. It wasn't selfish reasons, but the fact that Arafin had been right in his predictions. Our daughter was not feeling any pain. In fact, she was the one cheering us up when we cried.

Our little Thea—as we decided to name her—radiated endless love. The charts demonstrated that she possessed almost the same powerful empathic abilities as I did, except she had formed the proper neural pathways not to be assaulted by other people's feelings. Even in this early stage of development, she could perceive and respond to surrounding emotions in a deliberate fashion. Whenever she perceived sadness from us, she would blast us with a wave of love until we started smiling. And then her own emotions would shift to the brightest, purest love.

This gave us the strength to cast away our sorrow. We redoubled the affection we projected her way, determined to savor every moment that life would grant us with her. During that time, we pretty much stopped any work-related activities. Thea became the center of our universe.

Just a week shy of the eighth month—a standard gestation period for our species—our daughter came into this world through natural birth. In my entire life, I had never seen anything as mesmerizing as our baby. Thea was the perfect mix of her mother's white feathers and my maroon color. She had a beige skin, which took on a slightly darker tinge with a hint of red in her down feathers and wings. Where I had a golden chest and head, Thea had her mother's white feathers with dark specks on her chest. But she gazed upon us with my silver eyes.

She was breathtaking.

A single look at her face and at the beautiful smile she gave us wiped away all sorrow. The doctors moved swiftly, providing her with an implant that would release the right level of nutrients to maintain her during her short stay among us. By their estimation, she would have two, maybe three days at best. But thankfully, they would be painless for her. And we made certain to make them the happiest we could.

As she loved when we sang, I composed a song specifically for her, just as I had done for her mother. Except this one thanked her for blessing us with her presence, however brief it would be. This time, I wrote the lyrics in Khelese—the Temern mother tongue—instead of Universal. She obviously couldn't speak just yet, but that didn't stop her from trying to mimic the main line of the chorus. It didn't even qualify as baby speak, more the cutest cooing that was still recognizable enough for us to understand she was echoing our words.

Linsea and I would harmonize, and little Thea would jump in at the chorus to say *coo lee coo*. It was beyond adorable. Naturally, she had no idea what those words meant. But they would translate as 'I will always love you.'

Arafin allowed us to bring her home so that she would not spend her short life in a medical facility. We set up cameras to record every moment of our precious time with her. As Thea couldn't use her wings, I would hold her up, zipping around the room while moving her up and down to create the illusion she was flying. Linsea would jump in, either playfully giving us chase, or pretending to run away only to let herself be caught.

The sound of Thea's laughter filled the space, casting away the looming darkness. Every time it reared its head again, our angel would simply say *coo lee coo* for us to instantly melt for her. She would immediately grin in response, having achieved her goal of cheering us up.

Nevertheless, watching her fade away a bit more with every hour was heartbreaking. We didn't sleep during the sixty-eight hours of her passage in this world. A part of us believed that she understood that she would be leaving us soon. I also believed that she was trying to tell us that it was okay, and to not be sad because she wasn't... because we made her happy.

During the last hour of her life, Linsea and I sang her song to her. Every time we would stop, she would say *coo lee coo* and touch our beaks multiple times to tell us to sing it again. As soon as we would, she would smile and wiggle her tiny talons and hands as if to mark the beat.

After we concluded singing it one ultimate time, Thea grabbed her mother's beak with both hands, drawing Linsea's face closer so that she could rub her own beak against it in a gentle kiss. She then turned to me and repeated the gesture. In that instant, I realized she was saying goodbye.

"We'll meet again, my little angel," I said, my heart breaking. "In this world or the next, I promise that we shall meet again. And I'll take care of you the way I couldn't this time. Your mother and I love you, always. *Coo lee coo* my baby."

"*Coo lee coo*, my little angel," Linsea echoed, in a shaky voice.

"*oo lee oo*," Thea whispered, her tiny beak stretched into a smile.

As the light faded from her silver eyes, her eyelids fluttered before shutting. Then her gorgeous face went slack. I picked up

Thea's fragile body and cradled her in my arms before drawing Linsea into my embrace.

I couldn't say how long we held our baby while tears freely rolled down our cheeks. Despite my burning urge to shut myself down, I allowed Linsea to feel me without restriction. Yes, there was a great deal of sorrow, but also a tremendous amount of love. Perceiving the same emotions from my mate actually gave me comfort through this difficult moment. And granting her the same seemed to also appease her.

We washed our daughter and placed her in the delicate stasis chamber that the doctors had provided us with. She looked so peaceful, as if she was merely sleeping. I rested my palm over the glass lid, my heart heavy as I glanced at my mate.

"I'm sorry," I said at last.

"For what?" Linsea asked, with a bit of a challenge in her voice. "And don't you dare spew more of that nonsense about failing as a mate or father. Thanks to you, I got to experience pregnancy with a wonderful partner. Although very brief, I also got to experience motherhood to the sweetest angel."

"But I couldn't save her," I said in a choked voice.

"*No one* could. Fate had other plans for our baby. Do not focus on our loss but on the gift that was bestowed upon us," Linsea said forcefully. "I heard her song, Kayog! Through you, through our bond, I heard the song of our daughter. Nothing can ever compare to that. The love she brought into our life will stay forever with me, with you, with us. Knowing what I know now, given the choice whether to do this again, I would say yes without hesitation. I cannot bear the thought that Thea might have never been in our lives."

Those words struck me hard but also changed my entire view of the situation. It didn't take away the pain, but it helped me cope in a way I didn't think I could have before. Yes, I couldn't imagine a world where I never would have met my baby.

Thea would forever be with me, in my heart.

Over the next few days, we had many conversations about our future, and about trying again to start a family. In the end, we agreed that I would have a vasectomy. We also decided not to pursue adoption for the time being—although I strongly suspected that we would never do it. It wasn't that we didn't love the idea of becoming parents, but we didn't want to replace Thea. An adopted child deserved to be fully loved without reservations or hesitation. In our current headspace, we feared we might resent the innocent child we adopted for not sharing with us the same perfect connection we had with our baby.

You didn't gamble with someone else's life, least of all a young one seeking a forever home and a place to belong.

Sadly, I went through a somewhat dark phase where I didn't immediately resume matchmaking but instead took on the type of missions for the Enforcers that I always said I didn't want to perform. Although it disturbed Linsea, she understood and supported me within reason, while reminding me not to lose myself over grief. But performing rescue missions, especially ones where hostages were taken, or mass shooting scenarios where countless lives were on the line seriously helped me work through my guilt.

Although I knew better, I couldn't help feeling like I failed my child by not finding a cure. These tangible actions allowing me to save numerous lives soothed my sense of inadequacy. People got to live because of specific things I did.

With time—and a hefty dose of therapy—I finally found my way back to the light. In a way, every woman I matched became a daughter to me. Often, I would picture that these women were in fact my Thea facing a similar plight. It drove me to try even harder to do right by them and grant them the happiness they deserved.

The months gave way to years. And three decades later, Linsea and I were living the dream careers we aspired to back in university. As the number of my successful matches increased, so did my influence. With my mate becoming one of the most respected ambassadors for the UPO, we were a force to be reckoned with.

My Linsea turned out to be a genius in pointing me to various programs that I could leverage to help the couples I matched. In other cases, she was the mastermind pulling the strings in the shadows to launch programs that didn't exist but that completely turned around the challenging circumstances of certain species.

One such amazing success had been helping make the Daughters of Meterion program come true. Despite my previous meddling in other pairings, the UPO initially tried to give me a hard time over some of the dowries I wanted to send.

By then, Colin had moved on to even higher spheres of the Enforcers. Thankfully, his son Tedrick took over his previous role—which slightly evolved over the years. It had been strange going from being his Uncle Kai to now having him in a senior position over me—although that was unofficial as I technically wasn't a member of either the UPO or the Enforcers.

Still, Tedrick filled me with pride. Contrary to the vitriol spewed by jealous people, he hadn't inherited his role. He worked his ass off and earned every accolade and promotions he received. He shared the same vision for the two organizations as his father did. But he'd been even more die-hard in building his core team of trusted collaborators and agents.

I'd just found a match for Susan, a delightful young woman raised on Meterion—a farming colony—and doomed to a life of hardship simply because she was a third daughter and therefore deemed a burden. She'd been quite troubled to be paired with an Andturian named Olix—a lizardman species that had fallen on hard times.

When I presented the dowry list for Susan, the UPO started

balking. I was on my way to Xecania, the Andturian homeworld when I received a vidcom request from Tedrick. I was already chuckling even as I accepted the call.

"Kayog, up to mischief again?" Tedrick asked in a falsely severe tone, in lieu of greeting.

"When am I not?" I deadpanned.

He snorted, and his handsome face—so similar to his father's—softened. He ran a hand over his short black hair and leveled his gray eyes on me.

"The UPO is breathing down my neck over your latest requests," Tedrick said in a more serious tone. "I know you like to push the limits for the sake of your clients, but you know what major risks are involved whenever you introduce new plants or animals in a foreign ecosystem. That's a lot of seeds you want shipped to Xecania. Those seeds produce plants that are not local to that environment."

"Of course, and as you undoubtedly guessed, I didn't do so lightly," I said in a reassuring tone. "Our science department went over all the seeds I proposed to make sure none of them would be a threat to that planet."

"I suspected as much. So thank you for confirming it. However, I'm having a much harder time justifying you including reezia berry seeds in the order," Tedrick said. "This is not a fruit either humans or Andturians normally consume."

"No," I conceded. "Nor is it for them."

He stiffened and immediately narrowed his eyes at me. "Then why would you include it?"

"Because the Bozengi refugees would be keenly interested in them," I said with a shrug.

"We cannot meddle in the local population's affairs. You know that," Tedrick said, his voice hardening.

"Nor am I," I retorted with the most dishonest innocent face. "I'm providing a variety of safe seeds for a gifted farmer to grow on that world. It is up to Susan whether she does it or not. But if she's wise, she could use them in a way that could significantly help her new people. The decision will be entirely hers and the Andturians to make. Therefore, no rule has been broken."

"You're playing a dangerous game, Kayog," he said, looking troubled.

"Xecania has the potential of becoming the food pantry of the galaxy while giving back to its people control of their own planet. The Andturians are on the verge of starvation while sitting on some of the most fertile agricultural lands in the entire sector. I'm merely giving them the tools to set them on that path and fight back the conglomerates trying to appropriate their lands, if they so choose. Isn't that what we're here for?"

"It is, but we cannot be perceived as interfering or influencing the locals for our own purposes."

"And we're not," I quipped in a singsong voice. "Like I said, I'm merely adding a different seed to the rest of the lot. What Susan does with it is entirely up to her and her people. All rules are respected."

"Fine!" Tedrick grumbled. "I'll figure out a way to get them off my back about it. But please try not to make my life unnecessarily difficult."

"Where would be the fun in that?!"

He muttered something under his breath, which had me bursting out laughing.

Susan not only understood the hinted assignment, but the clever woman took it to another level I couldn't have dreamt of. In the end, she helped her new people thwart the nefarious plans of the greedy conglomerate that sought to crush them, provided that primitive species with the means to achieve financial independence, and even offered other third daughters of Meterion new prospects and opportunities for a better life.

It was Susan's idea that gave birth to the Daughters of Meterion program, which my Linsea heavily helped set in motion.

Being able to use my matchmaking ability to literally save

the lives of amazing women in dire situations, especially due to unfair accusations, were some of the other highlights of my career. Serena and her Ordosian mate Szaro certainly came to mind. Granted, she had broken the rules by trespassing on their sacred lands, but it had been for a good cause—saving a mother and her child from being devoured by bloodthirsty monsters. That successful union enabled us to strengthen the fragile bonds with this Naga-like species normally extremely reluctant to open up to foreigners.

And how could I forget about the mischievous Rihanna? The petite smuggler had been framed by her former business partner to take the fall for a crime she hadn't committed. If not for my intervention, she would have been sent to Molvi, the deadliest prison planet in the galaxy. Her most unlikely pairing with the Yurus Great Chieftain Zatruk—an Orc-Minotaur like species—completely changed the fates of the three main species sharing that planet. It brought hope, prosperity, and peace to the Yurus who had previously been on the verge of self-destruction.

But from a selfish point of view—and more broadly for the benefit of the Enforcers and the UPO—I couldn't have been more grateful for having a hand in matching Kaida and Cedros. In truth, they found each other on their own during a mission, but I just helped convince Kaida to give it a shot. As a top agent of the Enforcers, Kaida wasn't unknown to me. That day, she'd gone inside a research center as part of Tedrick's team to investigate a mysterious portal that had opened inside their power core, and from whence a giant shadow dragon had emerged to battle fiendish shadowy creatures.

That dragon happened to be Cedros, the sweetest Shadow Lord who desperately needed the hugs of his Ejaya—the only female in the universe that could stop him from succumbing to the madness that otherwise plagued beings like him. And that Ejaya had been none other than Kaida.

Who would have thought that this pairing would give us a

steady supply of shadow stones? They allowed us to open portals to any preassigned destination, anywhere across the galaxy. This meant no more week-long space travels to various worlds. Within seconds, I could be in and out, and back to my mate. Obviously, we couldn't abuse such a great tool, not only because shadow stones were rare, but also because, should they fall in the wrong hands, untold damage could ensue, especially if used to launch a surprise attack on an unsuspecting world.

However, never in a million years would I have thought that a pairing I performed could lead to a great wave of injustice. When I received an urgent message from Torgal regarding a young woman named Malaya about to be sent to Molvi, a wave of anger surged within me. I had no qualms with true criminals being incarcerated there. But Torgal—the Temern lawyer representing her case—stated unequivocally that she was innocent, and that the judge overseeing her case was in fact corrupt.

It should have been an impossibility as his people, the Obosians, were known to be rabidly obsessed about enforcing the law and abiding by the rules. There was a reason they operated Molvi. As per Malaya's request, the lawyer hoped I could arrange a marriage for her like I did with Rihanna. Sadly, the rules had changed in retaliation to my saving Rihanna through a pairing. That same corrupt Judge Wuras had presided over her case and felt personally slighted that I would have spared the young woman from the horrible abuse and death that would have awaited her on Molvi.

Therefore, he helped pass new laws that prevented convicts from dodging their sentences by being matched. Should I find their soulmate, that person would have to join the inmate on the prison planet for the duration of their sentence, or live separately until they were freed.

The only hope to save Malaya was to find a Hell Lord, guard, or employee on Molvi that I could match her with. It was a relatively weak workaround, but it would meet the core requirement

that the condemned serve their time on Molvi. It didn't actually
spell out that they had to be in one of the detention quadrants.
But for this, I needed to meet her to get an idea of her song
before scouting the planet for a potential partner.

Therefore, Linsea and I went to the holding cells where she
was being held while waiting for her transfer to the prison planet.
Normally, my mate didn't get involved directly with the initial
interview for a pairing. But this situation was different. We were
dealing with a rogue Obosian judge. The Enforcers and the UPO
wanted to get involved to put an end to this. But the political and
legal fallout could have catastrophic repercussions. This entire
mess needed to be handled very carefully. Linsea would manage
the diplomatic and legal aspects while I attempted to work my
magic.

As much as I hated the prospect of breaking my perfect
streak of only matching true soulmates, saving the life of an
innocent young woman was far more important for me. Had she
been my daughter, I would have wanted someone in a position of
power to intervene on her behalf.

Two Obosian guards led us through the long corridor where
countless cells lined the sidewalls. Every single person in there
was definitely guilty. Some of them oozed with pure malice that
sent a cold shiver down my spine. If not for my blessed ability to
block others, I would be writhing on the floor right now in sheer
agony. At the end of the hallway, we went down to the bowels of
the detention center, which housed the solitary confinement cells.

My anger cranked up another notch. Based on Torgal's feedback about the young woman, and my own examination of her
file, nothing warranted such isolation. For a split second, I
wondered if they had moved her here, away from prying eyes, so
that they could eliminate her. However, considering the large
number of security cameras covering this area, it would be
nearly impossible to get away with murder.

But all those wandering thoughts flew right out of my mind

as we approached the cell where Malaya was detained. A wave of fear slammed into me, which was to be expected under the current circumstances. But it was something else that nearly had my knees buckling.

"Impossible," I breathed out, completely shocked.

CHAPTER 23
LINSEA

The powerful emotion that blasted through my bond with Kayog nearly made me lose my footing. I cast a confused look at him, wondering what could have prompted such a strong reaction from him. It went beyond mere shock. He had perceived something devastating. To my dismay, moments after he whispered his disbelief, my mate slammed down his psychic walls, shutting me out. That further stunned me. I couldn't remember the last time he had done that.

Kayog normally only ever closed himself off to me out of his need to protect me. But what could I possibly need to be protected against? If not for the two incredibly stuck up Obosian guards escorting us to Malaya's cell, I would have questioned him. But now wasn't the time. Although still visibly shaken, my mate grabbed my hand and gave it a gentle reassuring squeeze. As disturbed as I still felt, this soothed me. At the appropriate time, he would tell me everything.

I could feel the fear emanating from a nearby room. My protective instincts immediately flared with the need to appease them. There was something about that aura that felt familiar. I couldn't quite explain it as I knew for a fact that I had never met the young woman.

The obnoxious guard opened the door to a narrow, rectangular space that had to be no more than three meters wide by five meters long. Malaya was sitting on the flat surface with a thin cushion that they dared to label as a bed. A toilet and tiny sink completed the dreary space the poor woman had been locked in for the past few days while awaiting transfer.

Malaya emitted a choked sound upon seeing us. The hope and joy that immediately stirred within her upon recognizing us struck me with incredible violence. It left me confused and dizzy. Once more, the burning sense that I knew her gnawed at me.

I stole a glance at my husband. His face completely hid whatever emotions swirled within him. To anyone else, he would appear to be his usual relaxed, warm, and friendly self. But the way he held his wings betrayed an insane amount of tension. If not for being married to him for the past thirty-seven years, I might have been fooled.

"You have visitors," the guard told Malaya in a clipped tone that had me itching to peck his eyes out.

I wasn't the violent type, but seeing an innocent person being mistreated pissed me off to no end. The second guard placed a couple of stools across from the bed where Malaya was sitting. Kayog thanked him politely then, with his usual infinite tenderness, my mate gestured for me to sit first before taking the second stool. Both Obosians walked out of the room and closed the door behind them. The light on the lock turned red.

"Oh, my God!" Malaya exclaimed with a shaky voice. "I could hug you both right now. I thought you'd forgotten about me."

"No, my dear. We had not forgotten you," I said while removing a small sphere from the pouch hanging on the discreet belt around my waist.

Once I activated it, the sphere hovered a meter over our

heads, and a beam of light surrounded us, forming a cone of silence.

"A scrambler?" Malaya asked, stunned.

"To make sure no one is eavesdropping," I said, my voice hardening. "You've made a powerful enemy who is highly displeased to see us getting involved."

"But you *are* getting involved," Malaya repeated, her voice thick with hope. "Your presence here means good news, right? You found a workaround?"

I hesitated before answering. "Not exactly. As Torgal informed you, there's no way around you going to Molvi. Our only hope is to pair you with someone on that planet."

She recoiled and stared in turn at me then at Kayog in horror.

"Paired with a prisoner?! How the hell is that going to help me?"

"Not a prisoner," Kayog corrected in a gentle, almost paternal tone that took me aback. "The goal is to match you with an Obosian or one of the employees on Molvi. But ideally, it would be with an Obosian."

As expected, Malaya rebelled at that prospect. After all, they were trying to send her to a certain death, even knowing that she was innocent. But once we explained how a union with a Hell Lord could give her the necessary means to prove her innocence, she reluctantly warmed up to the idea.

"Okay. I see your point. Does that mean you already have someone in mind?" Malaya asked, feeling both hopeful and dejected.

I glanced at Kayog, who shook his head.

"I have spoken with a few potential candidates to assess their willingness to consider such an unusual pairing," Kayog said carefully. "I have not found your soulmate, although I'm getting a bit of a hunch. My presence here was merely to assess your personality to have a better sense of who could make a successful pairing for you."

Malaya waved a dismissive hand. "He doesn't have to be a soulmate match. After six months, we can just divorce, and I'll be free."

As one, Kayog and I shook our heads.

"You got a life sentence," I reminded her in a gentle but firm tone. "The only thing that can overturn your sentence and give you back your freedom is Wuras's demise."

"This also means that it is imperative that you find a way to please whoever you are paired with," Kayog cautioned her.

"What does that mean?" she asked, worry seeping back into her voice.

Once again, the powerful need to protect and comfort her surged within me with a violence that left me reeling. Why was she stirring such strong responses from me? Malaya wasn't the first person in desperate need of help that I had assisted. None had ever affected me so deeply.

"It means that your mate is the only one who can terminate your union after the six-month trial, if he is displeased with you," Kayog explained. "Should that happen, you will be sent to one of the prison Sectors below to serve the rest of your sentence. Therefore, my priority is to find your soulmate. But failing that, I want someone who you can have a good life with for the long term."

She stared at us in shock. Obviously, this wasn't what she'd hoped to hear from us. But Malaya needed to understand the reality of her precarious situation and be ready for the tough battle ahead.

"You think I will fail in my efforts to find proof," Malaya whispered, crestfallen.

Kayog shook his head with far more confidence than I felt. "We think taking down Wuras will be hard and will take a long time. Chances are, it will take longer than those six months. For this reason, I'd rather you spend this long time with someone who makes you happy and who won't divorce you as soon as the trial period has ended."

"We just need you to continue to have faith," I added in a reassuring tone. "We're fighting for you. On the day of your transfer, we promise it will be for you to meet your chosen mate."

As we rose to leave the room, I barely stopped myself from drawing her into a comforting embrace. Beyond the fact that it was an odd behavior from me, it would also have the Obosian guards coming down on us in a fury. There were strict guidelines where our interactions with prisoners were concerned. And absolutely no touching featured high on that list. They were already showing us an extremely high level of courtesy by leaving us alone in the room with Malaya.

My chest constricted, I watched as Kayog knocked on the door for the guards to let us out. The speed with which they opened hinted that they felt we'd overstayed our welcome. As we made our way out of the detention center connected to the Obosian courthouse, I kept stealing glances at my husband. He was still blocking me out. Despite that, I had felt the tension bubbling inside him during the entire interview, although he did a fantastic job of hiding it.

He walked at a brisk pace back to our shuttle. To my shock, as soon as we boarded and the doors closed behind us, Kayog abruptly dropped his mask of stoicism. He leaned against the wall as if he feared collapsing without that support. His wings sagged, and his face took on an expression that I couldn't define. Shock, distress, sorrow, but oddly also joy battled for dominance on his features.

"Kayog! Are you okay? What's going on?" I exclaimed, rushing to his side and caressing his back in a soothing motion.

By the way he looked at me, his silver eyes welling with tears, I nearly went into a full panic. But then his words broke my brain.

"It's her," Kayog said in a shaky voice. "It's her. Our baby... It's Thea."

"What?!" I exclaimed, yanking my hand away from him as if his contact burned me, and I took a step back. "That's impossible."

"IT'S HER!" he exclaimed forcefully, before running a shaky hand over the down feathers on top of his head. "I could never forget that song. Malaya is our baby reborn. Fate is giving us a second chance to save our little girl the way we couldn't the first time."

My mind reeled. I opened my mouth to argue that this made no sense, but Kayog dropping his walls had my knees buckling. His emotions crashed over me like a tsunami. With lightning speed, he caught me by my upper arms and drew me to him. If not for that, I would have collapsed.

Although my brain kept telling me this was impossible, the emotions emanating out of Kayog shouted loudly that he believed his claims beyond any doubt. In our thirty-eight years together, my mate had never been wrong when it came to recognizing a soul. Why would he start now? Had he made such an outrageous statement within days, weeks, or months following our baby's passing, I would have attributed this to a trauma response or coping mechanism. But Thea left us thirty-seven years ago.

I froze when struck by a sudden thought. Malaya was thirty-six years old. She was born to a Filipino couple on the first anniversary of Thea's death. Although I had noticed that fact while reviewing her file, I hadn't thought much of it back then. But now...

Temerns believed in reincarnation. However, the chances of us encountering a reborn acquaintance or loved one were slim to none. And yet, as I replayed the meeting in my mind, I couldn't help but acknowledge that my reactions to Malaya defied logic... or rather they had seemed illogical within the original context. I had badly ached to hug and comfort her. The guards' rudeness towards her had whipped my protective instincts into a frenzy. The need to save her had exceeded anything I ever experienced in other cases before.

My soul knew hers.

I burst out crying. And Kayog hugged me in an almost bruising hold, while also giving in to the overwhelming emotions engulfing us. These weren't tears of sorrow, but an indescribable mix of joy, relief, hope, and gratitude.

Fate was giving us a second chance. And this time, we were much better equipped to rise to the occasion. That corrupt Judge Wuras was going down, and our baby was walking free.

We headed straight for Molvi so that Kayog could meet as many other potential partners as possible. We hated that our daughter would likely end up with someone who wasn't her soulmate, but it was a necessary sacrifice to keep her safe until all charges could be dropped and her sentence overturned.

On our journey there, we called Tedrick to give him an update on the situation. By the speed with which he answered our com request, he had likely put everything else on hold specifically so that he would be available to speak with us. This case was huge with potentially devastating consequences.

"How did it go?" Tedrick asked as soon as the connection was established.

By the look of the background, he was sitting in his office, leaning against the high backrest of his black leather chair.

"As Torgal stated, she's innocent," Kayog said, his voice tense and determined. "We must use any means necessary to save her and bring down that corrupt judge."

Tedrick narrowed his eyes at my mate. Even without being able to perceive his emotions through the screen, I knew him well enough to understand that Kayog's strong reaction was raising red flags for Tedrick.

"As you know well, there's nothing we can do about her

sentence," Tedrick stated in a careful tone. "Obviously, we hope you can do something through matchmaking to keep her safe a while longer. But our hands are tied. We can only hope to gather enough evidence, especially with her help as an investigative journalist. This is the Obosian justice system we're going up against. It will be nearly impossible."

"I don't give a fuck!" Kayog hissed, making Tedrick recoil. "If I have to burn that entire planet down and break her out, I will."

He blinked and stared at my mate with a flabbergasted expression. "Kai, what's wrong? You know we can't do this. The repercussions..."

"Fuck the repercussions! I'm not letting my daughter die in this foul place!" Kayog shouted. "She's innocent. I don't care what needs to be done to prove it, but we will. And if you can't help, I will handle it. You know I can."

I placed an appeasing hand on his forearm. That seemed to startle him out of the rage brewing deep within. He gave me a sideways glance, and then his shoulders slouched as he realized he was letting his emotions get the best of him. On screen, Tedrick's expression had shifted from shock to a hint of pity, before settling on something more neutral and professional.

In that instant, I realized he believed Kayog was having a mental breakdown.

"He's not crazy," I said in a calm but factual tone.

Tedrick flinched. It had been subtle but unmistakable. I locked eyes with him, my chin lifting in defiance as I held his gaze unwaveringly.

"It is fair for you to make that assumption under the circumstances. But my mate is correct. Malaya is our daughter reborn. For thirty-seven years, Kayog has loyally served both the Enforcers and the UPO. Not once has he been wrong about the song of a person's soul. Do you really think he could possibly be mistaken about the one from our own child?" I asked in a stern tone.

Tedrick frowned, an air of uncertainty settling over his features as he weighed my words.

"I was there in the room. While I cannot hear souls the way Kayog does, everything in me claimed her and wanted to protect her. There's no question in my mind that she's our child," I continued calmly. "But whether you or anyone else believes it is completely irrelevant. Just be aware that we will stop at absolutely nothing to save her. That said, we have a huge problem on our hands with that judge. There's something much bigger and foul happening here. It must be addressed before the domino effect leads to a much more catastrophic outcome."

The wave of gratitude that emanated from Kayog glided over me like a warm summer breeze. He took my hand in his and gently caressed it with his thumb. I peered at him and smiled, only for him to smile back at me with an infinite love.

After thirty-eight years and counting, I just kept falling more and more in love with this male.

"There's no question that something foul is happening," Tedrick said carefully, reclaiming our attention. "But like I said, our hands are tied. All the evidence is insanely incriminating against Malaya. I do not doubt her innocence, but we need proof or at least some sort of lead. We have none of that."

"Give us Maeve," Kayog said forcefully. "She's the Enforcer's best hacker. With her current 'free agent' status, she will be able to dig into even more restricted places without bringing unwanted attention to your organization or the UPO. Make it happen, Tedrick. I've never made demands or threats. And this isn't a threat either. I'm just giving you the fair warning that if nothing can be done on the legal front, then I will take matters into my own hands."

"Do not act recklessly, Kayog," Tedrick warned. "We're on

the same team. Do what you can on your end to buy us as much time as possible. We'll do what we can on our side."

"Thank you. That's all I ask," Kayog said, some of the tension bleeding out of his shoulders.

"Yes, thank you," I echoed.

Tedrick gave us a sad smile. He still didn't believe that Malaya could be our reincarnated daughter. However, he had known us long enough to realize that we weren't prone to flights of fancy. Therefore, he acknowledged the real possibility that our claims might be true.

We ended the communication and completed the long journey to Molvi. Our respective assistants did a fantastic job of scheduling a slew of meetings with the various Hell Lords managing the prison planet. The Obosian nobles who acted as wardens there had been named as such by humans due to their appearance reminiscent of demons found in Earth mythology.

They were tall, with massive horns, silver-white hair, leathery bat wings, and a long tail. Unlike the demons of human lore, the Obosians had a dark-gray skin, luminous silver-white or blueish eyes surrounded by black sclera, and a smattering of dark scales on their foreheads, arms, and legs. With Molvi being the most savage and unforgiving prison in the galaxy, it perfectly fitted the human description of Hell, thus making the wardens Hell Lords.

The problem was how rabid Obosians were about upholding the law. In their eyes, criminals were the foulest type of individuals. Therefore, the majority of potential candidates we met immediately shut down even considering a union with a convicted murderer. Implying that one of their judges could have wrongly convicted an innocent person was akin to blasphemy. We expected resistance, but not this fierce and this unforgiving. Without a mate to keep Malaya out of the actual holding area for the prisoners, our daughter would never survive long enough for true justice to run its course.

It wasn't until we met with Lord Amreth that hope finally returned. Despite being as stuck up when it came to upholding the law, Amreth was a truly outstanding male with a kind heart and a sharp mind. He witnessed events that led him to believe that there was indeed corruption taking place, however unbelievable it seemed. Therefore, should we not find Malaya's soulmate among the other candidates we would meet with, Amreth agreed to take her as a mate to keep her safe until the investigation was concluded.

I nearly wept with relief. The same gratitude radiated loudly from Kayog. With a much lighter heart, we went on to two more meetings, feeling totally unfazed by the expected rejection from these potential partners now that we had a fallback plan secured.

And then we met Lord Kronos.

Where the other potential partners had simply expressed curiosity as to what brought us to them, Kronos radiated aggravation from the moment we landed. I previously met Kronos after he had been rescued by Maeve and Helio—another couple my mate had paired. He had been held prisoner by a foul Nazhral female called Saydi, who had been abducting young Edocits to harvest the down leaves from their hair, which was the most potent—but safest—recreational drug in the galaxy.

He was standing, back and wings stiff, looking at us with eyes narrowed with suspicion as we disembarked. The landing pad was located on an elevated plateau overlooking one of the many stunning terraces of his mansion.

"If you're here to ask me to release a prisoner for one of your matchmakings, the answer is no," Kronos said preemptively in an imperative tone in lieu of greeting. "Whoever you want to pair with one of my wards will have to come and settle on Molvi with their match."

"That's exactly the goal!" Kayog said with the excess enthusiasm that always destabilized grumpy candidates like this one.

I repressed a smirk as we closed the distance with the

impressive male. My mate could be quite the irreverent jerk when he wanted. He particularly excelled at putting people back in their place with a smile and a kind word, which made it sting even more.

Despite our very respectable heights, Kronos towered over us. Human women—and females from many other species—systematically fanned themselves in the presence of Obosians. They were indeed gorgeous species. Just like Amreth, Kronos was extremely easy on the eye, and his many piercings—deemed trophies and signs of status for his people—only added to his dangerous charm.

"And hello, Lord Aramon," my mate said in an overly sweet voice. "As you've apparently guessed, I am Kayog Voln—though I would prefer you simply call me Kayog. And this is my lovely wife, Linsea Voln, who I understand you've met before."

He scrunched his face with embarrassment to have thus been called out over his rudeness in not properly greeting us upon our arrival.

"I have indeed. Welcome to Molvi, Linsea, Kayog," he said begrudgingly, nodding at each of us in turn, before staring at Kayog. "You may call me Kronos."

My interactions with him at the time of his rescue had been cordial. But Obosians tended to be a little distant. Some perceived their attitude as being haughty. However, my frequent interactions with them in my line of work had made me realize that it was merely their tradition of holding oneself in proper form and decorum that gave the misleading impression that they were snobs and thought themselves superior to others.

"Excellent!" Kayog said with the same enthusiasm that was clearly getting under Kronos's skin. "We have much to discuss. Serious matters."

"Then let's go to my office. This way," Kronos said in a grumpy tone.

I wanted to cut this short. That male was as gorgeous as he

was obnoxious. And frankly, I was getting fed up with making the same pointless sales pitch to self-righteous fools too stupid to realize they were in fact the ones unworthy of my daughter.

However, something shifted in Kayog's attitude as the Hell Lord led us into the office of his spectacular mansion. Shock, excitement, and triumph swelled within him.

No fucking way?!

I cast a worried look at my mate only to have him give me a subtle nod with as wide a smile as his beak allowed. My mind reeled at this most improbable outcome. A part of me wanted to rejoice at the thought that we had found our daughter's soulmate. Lord Kronos belonged to one of the wealthiest and most influential noble houses of Vargos—the Obosian homeworld. They would have the resources and determination to fight tooth and nail to have a member of their family cleared of any wrongdoing. However, that same elite status would make them even less likely to consider any kind of association with a convicted criminal.

A tough battle lay ahead.

My gaze roamed over the magnificent property as we headed for the giant floor to ceiling patio doors that led to the entrance of the mansion. Every Hell Lord built their personal residence at the top of the mountain bordering the far edges of their Sectors. They were sprawling dwellings with multi-level balconies, natural waterfalls, and breathtaking views of the landscape of the planet. Countless deadly traps disguised as exotic plants or rivers kept their home safe from any intruders should the inmates beat foolish enough to try to escape.

We followed him into his office, as elegantly decorated as the rest of his mansion. I could totally picture my baby living in such a place: peaceful, classy, and elegant.

"Have a seat," Kronos said, gesturing at a comfortable set of couches in the seating area next to the patio door onto one of the many terraces of his domain.

"Thank you," I said with a grateful smile.

Kayog and I settled on the large couch across from the chair he headed towards. To both our delight, the back support was set at a convenient enough height to accommodate our wings. It was one of the benefits of visiting other winged species.

After politely declining his offer of refreshments, we immediately dove into the reason for our visit.

"We're here on a mission to stop major criminal activities and protect innocents who have been seriously wronged," I said.

I smiled when he instantly perked up at those words. When it came to upholding the law, Obosian were ridiculously predictable.

"You have my attention," Kronos said.

"What we are about to share with you will be shocking. Please hear us out with an open mind," I said, bracing for what would follow. "A very important member of your society, Judge Wuras, has become corrupt and needs to be stopped."

Kronos jumped to his feet, his *lumiak* surging from his fingertips and the electrical tendrils crawling around his hands as he glared at us in outrage. Warriors of his species could invoke this energy at will. At a lower level, it could zap someone into obedience like a Taser. But at maximum strength, it could literally reduce you to cinders.

"You dare?!" Kronos exclaimed.

"Peace, Kronos," Kayog said in a soothing voice, his palm raised in an appeasing gesture.

"You can see souls. Do you see any deception in ours?" I asked in a similar tone, before gesturing at his chair. "Please, sit."

Teeth clenched, he doused his *lumiak* and reluctantly resumed his seat.

The next half hour turned into the most infuriating experience in my life. The stupidly stubborn male systematically rejected the thought that one such as he could be paired with a convict. No matter how many times we explained that Malaya had been framed, he couldn't accept that one of their top, highly respected judges could possibly be corrupt.

More than once, I had to stop Kayog from drop-kicking him. But I also wanted to peck the fuck out of his pretty eyes, tear off his piercings, and shove them up his rear end to keep company to the self-righteous stick he had stuffed in there.

How can that judgmental moron possibly be my daughter's soulmate?

"Fine. If you cannot be bothered to save the life of your soulmate or assist in righting the terrible wrongs committed against innocents, another will show more courage," Kayog said at last in an icy tone that even had me stiffening.

"Excuse me?" Kronos said, in just as cold a voice.

"You may be fine with letting an innocent be thrown in with the foulest criminals in the galaxy, but we're not going to let Malaya die. Thankfully, Lord Amreth will take her," Kayog said in a disdainful tone.

Kronos recoiled and stared at my mate with a flabbergasted expression.

"Amreth?! Amreth has consented to such a union?"

"We approached him and a few others we knew could potentially be more... flexible before meeting with Malaya," I said, invoking every ounce of my willpower to remain diplomatic. "We wanted to be certain that we could provide her with a few options. But once we met her, my husband got a hunch that she was yours. So naturally, we came to you first after that discussion."

It wasn't quite accurate, but close enough.

"But since you cannot be bothered—" Kayog added.

"Do not test me, Temern," Kronos growled.

"I'm not testing you, Obosian," Kayog replied in just as stern a tone. "We do not have time for you to sort out your inner conflicts. In two days, Malaya will be sent to Dakon's playground. You know perfectly well that she will not survive there a week. So if *you* won't, *I* will save her."

This time, Kronos flinched upon hearing the Sector she would be sent to. Dakon only accepted the foulest miscreants. Life expectancy of his prisoners rarely exceeded a few days, or a few weeks. Sending Malaya there was a death sentence.

"What's the point of giving her to Amreth if they're not soulmates?" Kronos challenged. "I thought you only performed perfect matches."

"So far, I have. But if breaking my perfect streak is the price to save this sweet woman, then I'll gladly pay it," Kayog said, lifting his beak defiantly. "Malaya and Amreth may not be soulmates, but their personalities are well-aligned and compatible. They will have a happy enough life together. Compared to the others, he is the best alternative match."

"Tharmok take you and your threats," Kronos snarled.

At that moment, I realized we had won. He just needed an extra nudge to get him over the finish line.

"They're not threats, Lord Kronos," I said in a gentle voice while reaching for Kayog's hand and giving it a gentle squeeze. "This is our only other option to save Malaya. Would it help if I told you that all Prime Mating Agency unions come with a six-month trial period?"

That caught his interest. After a few more back and forths, he finally caved in, scrunching his face as if he'd bitten into something foul.

"Fine. She has six months to prove you right. But may the gods protect her if she proves false," he grumbled.

"She won't," Kayog said with triumphant confidence.

"We shall see," Kronos replied.

∼

I felt dizzy walking through endless rows of wedding dresses with Tala pulling me in every direction. As a Temern, I had never worn clothes, so shopping for them wasn't particularly familiar to me. The number of choices, styles, sizes, and level of demure or spiciness overwhelmed me. And yet, I was determined to see my daughter have as perfect a wedding as possible under the circumstances.

As we had to rush the entire process before she would be sent to Dakon's Sector, her family wouldn't be able to attend. In truth, Kronos could still back out of this agreement if he perceived her soul to be deceitful on the day she arrived.

It crushed me that I wouldn't be able to attend the ceremony. An urgent mission had popped up, forcing me to go handle it. But if I couldn't be there, I would do everything else a mother would want to provide for her child's special day. As she would arrive on Molvi wearing nothing more than her prisoner jumpsuit, I refused to let her exchange vows in such an abhorrent outfit.

After literally going nuts trying to find my bearings in the sea of options, it suddenly dawned on me that I should narrow my search down to something that would be meaningful to Malaya. Her file revealed that she was of Filipino descent, and that she had undergone quite a bit of training in their traditional dances. That led me to assume she might want a traditional dress for her culture.

Tala all but dragged me to the right section. As she shared a similar height and body type as my daughter, she gladly volunteered as a model. Although Tala had a darker complexion than my daughter, it still gave me a good idea of what the dresses would look like against Malaya's light brown skin.

My jaw dropped when Tala stepped out of the changing room in a stunning, modern take on a baro't saya gown. The baro't—which was the top of the dress—boasted a gorgeous floral lace embroidered on the most luxurious piña fabric. It formed a rather sexy bustier that didn't cover her belly button. The same flowery dentelle adorned the edges of the oversized butterfly shoulders of the baro't.

The full-length skirt—the saya—was adorned with the same lacework in strategic places, and an insane slit ran up to the middle of the thigh. It was scandalously sexy and unbelievably flattering. I could picture how breathtaking Malaya would be wearing it.

Tala struck a few poses in a flaunting and flirtatious fashion that had me chuckling.

"The look on your face reflects what I'm feeling inside. That's the one," Tala said with conviction.

I clicked my beak with hesitation. It was indeed a breath-taking dress. "Is it too suggestive with the exposed belly?" I asked warily.

"Pfft! Are you kidding? In case you hadn't noticed, Malaya's body is almost as hot as mine, *and* she has a belly piercing!" Tala exclaimed as if it should have been self-evident.

I burst out laughing at the playful boast as she wiggled her hips in a way reminiscent of belly dancers.

"That Obosian mate of hers will drool his horned little head off when he sees it. You know how crazy they are about piercings. Our girl needs to flaunt the heck out of it."

"Right," I said, scrunching my face. "That piercing can only further underline the fact that they are perfectly aligned, even in this. Still, a mom doesn't necessarily want to hear about how males drool over her daughter."

Tala snorted. "Girl, have you forgotten that your soon to be son-in-law is a freaking incubus? What do you think he's going to do to her? You know their tongues extend up to a foot, right?"

"Maker! Tala!" I exclaimed, slapping my hands over my ears. "I do not need to hear this."

My friend laughed, her eyes brimming with an unrepentant glimmer.

"It's only fair. You think I didn't also freak out when my own two kids got old enough to start getting frisky?" She glanced down at herself and ran both hands down the laced fabric of her skirt. "Poor Kayog is going to lose his shit when he sees her at the wedding. Dads can be such jealous fools."

I chuckled. "He might. But then again, he might simply be relieved. Either way, I will take him being the jealous-possessive dad over committing murder because Kronos is being a stubborn idiot."

"Amen to that!"

With the dress secured, we spent the next couple of hours finding the perfect shoes, jewelry, and all the sexy underwear, lingerie, and nightgowns Malaya could possibly need to seduce her stuck up soulmate. There was no way I was shipping the dreadful stuff I had found in her drawers when I went to gather a few suitcases of basic necessities for her. Tala had called them 'granny panties' and I couldn't have agreed more.

My daughter would marry and live in style.

CHAPTER 24
KAYOG

S tanding on the landing pad next to Kronos and Isobel as the shuttle carrying Malaya approached, I summoned every ounce of my willpower not to beat the wretched male into a pulp. Not for the first time since meeting the pompous ass, I wished I had been wrong about him being my daughter's soulmate.

Even now as the shuttle completed its approach, contempt and disgust radiated loudly from him. As breaking one's word was an incredible source of dishonor, that Hell Lord felt compelled to go through with this while resenting every minute of it. However, it was clear that he expected her to fail as he scrutinized her aura.

Obosians had the power to read auras and see them even through the most powerful cloaking shield. This made them the best wardens as no inmate—or any other living being for that matter—could use any power or technology to escape.

Well, no living being but me...

The final power that had first manifested itself during my early training in the research center fully developed over the following couple of years. At low intensity, it behaved as a psychic disruptor that prevented the targets I aimed at from using their psionic abilities. At medium intensity, I could disrupt some-one's mind enough that their brain would be stuck in a loop, not seeing or hearing what was happening around them. It was like time temporarily stood still for them. At high intensity, I could knock them unconscious. And at maximum power, I could fry their brains.

Thankfully, I'd never needed to use the latter, other than in simulations. But I had used all the other levels on covert missions for the Enforcers, especially during the dark times that followed Thea's passing.

And right now, I wished I could use the full spectrum of my powers on that fool. Instead, I focused on blocking him from sensing my true emotions. Obosians could perceive aggression. The last thing I needed was to make matters worse by making him feel threatened or believe I might attack him.

A flurry of emotions crashed over me when my angel disem-barked the shuttle. Despite my anger at seeing her shackled and in a convict suit, I basked in the perfection of her soul's song. Since leaving her in the solitary cell, I kept wondering if maybe I had indeed imagined that she was my baby. Maybe I was having a psychotic episode and hearing things because I'd never gotten over her loss. But as the guard removed her shackles, something settled in my heart. This truly was my daughter.

And then my dumbass future son-in-law had to ruin the moment with his foul emotions.

"My dear Malaya, here you are at last!" I exclaimed in a warm and enthusiastic tone, as soon as the guard was done and gestured for her to approach. "I hope you had a safe trip."

"The trip to Molvi was uneventful. But the one from the spaceport to here was extremely comfortable, and the view was breathtaking," Malaya said before casting a grateful smile at Kronos, no doubt as a thank you for the fancy shuttle he'd sent to fetch her.

That asswipe didn't respond or otherwise react, content to

stare at her with a frosty demeanor. Maker, how I wanted to blast his ass with the most vicious kinetic pulse I could muster.

"I'm glad to hear it," I said, still ignoring Kronos's rather rude behavior. "Malaya, please meet Priestess Isobel Biondi, who will officiate your union today."

I always tried to get my best friend to tag along and officiate my arranged marriages whenever her schedule permitted it. This time, however, Linsea had insisted Isobel be there to keep me from losing my temper and doing irreparable damage to Kronos and Malaya's chances of surviving this entire ordeal.

The two women exchanged a polite smile. Then I turned to the dumbass.

"And this is Kronos Aramon, your betrothed. Kronos, meet Malaya Velasco, your bride."

"Hello, Kronos," Malaya said in a friendly fashion, although her nervousness seeped through. "It is an honor to meet you."

When Kronos didn't reciprocate, content to examine her from head to toe with a haughty expression, I nearly lost my shit. The same anger shone brightly within Malaya. But the stoicism she outwardly displayed put me to shame. If she could show such self-control while in a dire situation, I should be able to do better.

Not wanting to allow things to further go downhill, I shifted the topic by turning to pick up the large, ornate box, which had been sitting on a small hovercart behind me. My wings had hidden it from Malaya.

"My beloved Linsea sends you her regards, as well as this little wedding present," I said, showing her the fancy box. "Under the circumstances, she figured you would like something a bit more fitting to wear for the ceremony."

The joy and gratitude that blasted out of her turned me upside down. What I wouldn't have given for Linsea to bask in it as well.

And then fuck-face ruined the moment again.

"Whatever for?" Kronos grumbled, his voice laced with outrage.

I gave him a stern look. "Surely, you cannot want your bride dressed in a convict's uniform for your wedding?"

Kronos shrugged, an air of pure annoyance settling on his features. "What does it matter? This is merely a five-minute formality to make the agreement binding. There is no need for dresses or any other such nonsense."

The sharp tongue-lashing I was about to serve him died on my tongue when Malaya interjected.

"It's okay," Malaya said with a stiff smile. "He's right. While I'm deeply touched by the gesture, a dress isn't important under the circumstances. I don't mind getting married like this."

To our collective shock, Kronos took a menacing step towards Malaya, fangs bared, and his icy-blue eyes glowing. Startled, Malaya took a step back and pressed a palm to her chest. If not for his emotions loudly broadcasting that he had no intention of harming her, I would have stepped in.

"You've been here less than five minutes and already you lie?" he hissed.

"It's not a lie. It's called being diplomatic and considerate," she snapped back. "You've made it abundantly clear that my presence here inconveniences you. I'm trying to lessen the burden I'm imposing on you and sided with your argument so that you wouldn't be the bad guy in this situation."

"You assume that I care whether people deem me the 'bad guy' or that I can't handle contradictions," he replied, his voice just as stern.

"I'm not assuming anything. I'm merely trying to be nice," Malaya said, refusing to be cowed.

"I don't need you to be nice. I need you to be *honest*. Can you be honest, little human?" Kronos asked in a condescending tone.

"No woman wants to get married dressed like a criminal,

especially when she's innocent and has been framed," Malaya said in a controlled voice. "Kayog doesn't need to tell me that you are reluctant to have me as a wife. The coldness of your 'welcome' has made your feelings abundantly clear. But whether you want me or not doesn't change the fact that marrying you is my only chance to survive this mess and hopefully get justice. So if that means I have to bend over backward to make my presence tolerable to you, I will do it. And that includes casting aside my childhood dream of marrying in the traditional gown of my people."

My heart swelled with pride at my baby for standing up for herself. Kronos studied her features for a few seconds before smirking again.

"Well, that wasn't so hard, was it?" he asked in a taunting voice.

"Actually yes, it was," Malaya snarled, angry tears welling in her eyes. "It was extremely hard, and it's fucking humiliating. I may not be a saint, but I'm not a goddamn criminal. Yet here I am, having to choose between getting slaughtered by actual criminals inside Dakon's Sector, or marrying a man who clearly has nothing but contempt for me. And I have no choice but to take the abuse with a fucking smile if I want to live. All this because a corrupt Obosian judge is empowered to pursue his life of crime with all impunity. Is that an honest enough answer for you?"

And that was when the shift I thought would never happen finally occurred.

Kronos recoiled and stared at Malaya with a stunned expression throughout her diatribe. He studied her face, and then his gaze slightly went out of focus as he peered at her soul. The shock coursing through him felt like an earthquake. His genuine belief that she was just a despicable criminal trying to dodge accountability came crashing down. His entire world view of his own people being incapable of crimes went up in flames.

In those few seconds, the Hell Lord went through the first four stages of grief, before looking at me with a flabbergasted expression. You'd think he was hoping I would reassure him by saying he saw wrong, that she was in fact the criminal he needed her to be.

But being my charming and diplomatic self, I lifted my chin with the most obnoxiously smug expression I could muster. It was nearly orgasmic watching Kronos scrunch his face while choking on the foulest piece of humble pie in the universe.

For all that, a deep sense of peace and relief washed over me when he gestured for the guard—who had still been waiting inside the shuttle—to leave. Malaya radiated the same relief upon realizing that Kronos had thus confirmed he would keep her instead of shipping her to Dakon's Sector.

The Hell Lord took the box from me and gestured for Malaya to follow him.

"This way, then," Kronos said in a grumpy tone.

She gaped at his receding back before casting a confused look at me. An incommensurable amount of paternal pride swelled within me. I could see so much of Linsea's strength in her. A billion words burned my tongue, but I swallowed them back. Instead, I clapped in a silent applause and jerked my head towards Kronos to tell her to get going. That snapped Malaya out of her shocked daze, and she hastened after him.

Isobel gently caressed the side of my shoulder in a comforting gesture once they both disappeared inside the house. I smiled at her and gave her hand a gentle squeeze of gratitude. In the minutes that followed, I felt the gradual shift in Kronos as he slowly came to terms with the fact that Malaya truly was his mate and an innocent victim who deserved his protection.

Wanting the perfect spot to hold the special ceremony Isobel had helped me prepare for my daughter, we walked down the ramp to the main terrace and chose a spot by the stunning pool that ran the length of the immense balcony, which overlooked the lush forest of Kronos's Sector.

The sudden surge of lust emanating from him shortly before they both came out of the house struck me hard. The possessive and protective dad in me wanted to smack him for it. But the rational matchmaker in me understood that this was great. With any other couple, I always smiled when that first spark of attraction ignited between them. Seeing her walk towards us, looking breathtaking in the dress chosen by her mother, explained everything.

Emotion choked me at the wave of joy Malaya projected the moment Isobel retrieved the Veil and the Cord used as part of a traditional Filipino wedding. I couldn't officially stand here as the father of the bride, but I proudly played the role of Ninong instead—the godfather of the couple's wedding.

Throughout the ceremony, Kronos softened a bit more for Malaya as he infused himself with her emotions and the beauty of her soul. By the time we were done, he had fully made his peace with it and accepted her as his wife. Despite my lingering annoyance that he resisted so long before seeing the light, the beautiful harmony of their souls filled my heart with joy. He would take care of my baby and protect her.

"You have gone through some truly difficult and frightening times. But those hardships had a purpose, and it was to bring you here to this male," I said. "There is absolutely no question in my mind that you two are soulmates. He's a good male. And together, you will accomplish great things and save many innocents."

"Thank you. Thank you for everything," Malaya said, her voice full of emotion.

To my shock, Malaya threw herself into my arms. My surprise gave way to a tsunami of love that nearly had me come undone. How I had ached to hug my baby again. I returned her embrace, my wings wrapping around her before rubbing the side of my beak on her temple. I wanted to hold her forever, sing for her, and tell her how much her daddy loved her. But I forced myself to let go before I betrayed the secret I could never share with her without sounding insane.

As we went through the last formalities, hope filled my heart. Although a difficult road still lay ahead, this time, we would prevail.

~

Naturally, things didn't go as smoothly or easily as they should have. Discovering that Malaya nearly died only a few days after her wedding almost sent me on a murderous rampage. Of all the things I could have feared, an assassination attempt never popped up on the list.

Being forced to sit on the sideline while my baby's life fell apart was driving me insane. With the deadline quickly approaching for her and Kronos to come up with proof of Judge Wuras's foul play and no leads to follow, I began planning to break her out of Molvi before it was too late.

And then the breakthrough we had started losing hope would ever occur was handed to us from the most improbable source. It was all there, the culprits, the business, and enough evidence to put away the entire crew involved in this massive network of corruption led by Judge Wuras's father. Except, we couldn't access the key elements that would make sure they couldn't get away with it.

I angrily paced my living room while Linsea frowned at the vidscreen where Maeve and Tedrick had joined our vidcall from various locations.

"I'm sorry, Kayog," Maeve said with a deflated expression. "The data we need is right there, but I cannot access their servers without being discovered. The only way to tap into it requires a scrambling device placed directly on one of their physical servers or computers. Their security protocols are way too high to remotely hack into them."

"Do you know where those servers are located?" I asked, stopping mid-stride to stare at her on the giant screen.

"They're in a highly secure location. No one can break in. It would have to be an inside job, and we don't have any double agents there—at least as far as I know," Maeve said carefully.

"Understood. But do you know their exact location?" I insisted, slightly irritated.

"Yes, but—"

"Then send me the coordinates and the device you need installed. I'll take care of it," I said, interrupting her.

She blinked and stared at me as if I'd gone off the deep end.

"Kayog..." Tedrick said in a reasonable tone.

"Don't Kayog me," I replied sternly. "You knew my position from the start about what I would do if we failed to keep Malaya safe. That evidence is within reach. I can make it happen, and you know it."

"Kayog, you can't infiltrate Komoro's headquarters," Maeve said, unnerved. "No cloaking device can fool their systems."

"Do not worry about that, Maeve. My husband can get in and out without being discovered. We just need to know where those servers are located and what steps he must follow to place your device," Linsea said in a gentle but firm tone.

My heart soared for my mate. It had been years since I last took part in an infiltration mission. Back then, it helped me cope with the loss of our daughter. That trying to save her now led me back to that path seemed fitting, even if only for one last time.

Maeve glanced at Tedrick on the vidscreen. He was pursing his lips, eyes cast down as he assessed the situation. While he knew of my psionic disruption abilities, very few other people were aware of it. Although Maeve belonged to the high-ranking inner circle Tedrick had been building, she wasn't apprised of the full spectrum of my powers. Completing this mission would require it.

I had no qualms with it. Not only did I trust her with my life, but I also had the honor of pairing her with her Edocit mate, Helio.

"Even if we wanted to let you handle it, your presence will raise suspicions," Tedrick argued.

"Not if he conveniently happens to be accompanying his ambassador wife on one of her business trips," Linsea countered. "We've been sitting on the Damira project for a while. One of their main investors has his offices in that building. It wouldn't be the first time Kayog tagged along during one of his down-times between candidate interview fairs. No one will question him being there."

"Fair," Tedrick conceded. "But the UPO has no interest in participating in that project."

Linsea shrugged. "Not every negotiation results in an agreement. I often have follow-up meetings to see if potential partners have changed their positions in a way that is more amenable to us."

Tedrick snorted. "Did I tell you that I like how ruthless you can be behind that sweet and gentle exterior?"

"One does not exclude the other," I said, glancing affectionately at my mate. "She's exactly everything she needs to be whenever it's needed. That's why my Linsea is the best ambassador you have."

She puffed out her chest and winked at me.

"Why do I somehow feel like I just stepped into the secrets of the gods?" Maeve asked, her eyes flicking between each one of us.

"Because you have," I said with a mysterious smile.

Two days later, we walked into the secured headquarters of Komoro, the main company Wuras used as front for his shady businesses. No one questioned our presence. In fact, quite a few actually decided to strike conversations with me, either hoping I could give their love life a nudge, or to tell me about an acquaintance that could use my services.

Saying that I was restless would have been quite an understatement. After many back and forths, I finally decided to complete my task right before dinner, when the staff would be less likely to be roaming corridors as they enjoyed their limited break. Being caught wandering through the secured sections of the facility late at night would be harder to justify.

Invoking my empathic abilities, I spread my senses far and wide, cataloging every person whose consciousness I could touch within the building. To think, before Linsea entered my life and completely turned it around, this would have been impossible to do with such calculated precision. Simply standing here would have had me writhing on the floor in agony. Instead, I casually walked towards the staff elevator, targeting every person that would likely cross my path with a medium, steady stream of psionic disruption.

I entered the elevator and placed the snitch Maeve sent to me on the control panel. While she could provide instructions through my earpiece, and I could speak to her, we agreed to keep communications to a minimum to avoid the signal getting picked up.

As soon as I activated the snitch, a red light on it blinked until it turned blue. The cabin immediately started moving to the lowest floor where the security control room was located. Before the doors opened, I reassessed the people that I could detect nearby on that floor and stopped my disruption on those who were no longer likely to run into me.

Thankfully, I could only sense three people, one of them with their brain waves dimmed in a way that indicated a solid wall separated us. Not wanting to take chances, I send a small dose to them with just enough psionic waves that they would enter a state where they were daydreaming or appearing to be. Once I released them, they would just resume whatever they had been up to prior to that disruption.

I removed the snitch from the control panel seconds before stepping out of the elevator. I breathed a sigh of relief when the door opened on an empty hallway. The two people I was picking up were walking in a connecting corridor to my right. Lucky for me, my destination lay straight ahead. I strolled casually through the pristine white corridor with only a handful of doors scattered down its length, aside from another connecting hallway halfway down. Two cameras on the ceiling made certain no one could come and go without being detected.

That the alarm hadn't gone off confirmed that Maeve had tapped into their feed through the snitch. That woman was truly a wizard when it came to technology. I didn't know how long she could fool them, but I planned on being gone in the next five minutes.

Although I expected it, my stomach dropped when I closed in on the third door on the left side of the main hallway where the security control room was located. Three people were inside, two of them fairly close to the door, the third farther back. There would be no way for me to enter without walking in their path.

As if she read the thoughts crossing my mind, Maeve spoke into my earpiece.

"Two guards, three meters in, facing the door. A third guard in the backroom located at nine o'clock. No line of sight. Servers at three o'clock."

She didn't need to go into further details, keeping to the strict minimum to limit the length of our communications.

I blasted the two guards with a strong enough disruptive wave that they would literally freeze, and I swiftly entered the room. Despite knowing the guards were sitting at their desk, only three meters away from the door, finding them staring blindly at each other, their eyes empty, still freaked me out. There was something uncanny about breathing people frozen into wax statues.

Ignoring the knot twisting my insides, I made a beeline towards the tall racks of machinery with blinking lights which lined the sidewall. I crouched behind one of the massive servers and released the two human guards from my thrall. Although it would have been safer for me to keep them in this frozen state while I finished my task, the longer the disruption, and the greater the chance they would realize something abnormal had happened. I also didn't want to risk the third guard wandering into the room and finding their colleagues in that state.

The two guards resumed chatting as if nothing occurred. As I plugged the scrambling device into one of the appropriate slots of one of the servers, I absentmindedly listened to them for any signs that they might be onto me. But one of the males was discussing a financial investment he'd been considering venturing into.

Heart pounding, I watched the five solid red lights on the device. The first one blinked, indicating that it was starting to work. After fifteen seconds—that felt like twenty years—that first light turned a solid blue, and the second red one started blinking.

My heart skipped a beat when the third male exited the back-room and approached the desk where his two colleagues were chatting away.

"I'm going to grab a drink," one of the voices said—which I presumed belonged to the newcomer. "You guys want something?"

They both declined, and the man started walking away before one of the other two suddenly changed his mind and requested a candy bar. The third guard acquiesced with a grunt and walked out of the room.

I peered back at the device, my heart soaring upon seeing four solid blue lights with the final red light blinking. Seconds later, it switched to blue, then all five lights blinked before turning green and then shutting off.

"All done," Maeve said in my earpiece with a triumphant tone. *"You can remove the device. Hang tight. There's a group of six people hanging by the elevator on the main floor. If they don't move quickly, I will create a diversion."*

As I unplugged the scrambler, I fought the urge to tell Maeve a diversion wasn't necessary. Despite being informed of my powers, she didn't fully understand their extent. But maybe she was seeing something through the cameras that I couldn't. Anyway, arguing wasn't an option with the two guards sitting inside the room. I wanted to limit the use of my disruption to only when it was necessary.

"Go!" Maeve suddenly said.

She didn't have to repeat. I froze the two guards and hurried out of the room, before immediately releasing them. I forced myself to cross the hallway back to the elevator at a brisk enough pace without being too quick it would raise suspicion. It wasn't the people that worried me, but the motion detectors that could trigger an alarm if they picked up abnormal activity, such as people running in the secured areas.

As soon as I stepped inside the cabin, I made to place the snitch onto the control panel, but the door instantly closed, and the cabin flew up to the lobby. At first, I feared someone on a different floor had called the elevator, but I couldn't feel anyone close enough to have done so. I realized then that Maeve had worked so damn quickly, she no longer needed the snitch to control the elevators.

I stepped out of the cabin to find the place deserted. As I approached the end of the hallway leading to the staff quarters, I noticed a group of people congregating around a refreshment table. Making sure not to draw attention to myself as I entered the main hall, I took on the typical curious bystander expression as I stretched my neck to see what was happening. Water was pooling at the foot of the table while the maintenance staff was frantically cleaning the mess.

By the way a couple of them were scratching their heads, they were baffled as to what had caused the issue. And then I spotted the burnt spot against the wall where an electric surge apparently occurred, frying the electrical outlet and the cool beverage distributor.

I didn't have to ask whose handiwork caused it.

"There you are!" Linsea exclaimed, behind me.

I turned around to see her strutting towards me with her usual graceful gait. A human I didn't know was accompanying her.

"Here I am," I said warmly, broadcasting loudly the successful outcome of our mission through our bond.

Her smile broadened, and she hooked her arm around mine, resting her other hand on my upper arm. To the random observer, the gentle squeeze she gave it would only be an affectionate gesture from a female to her husband. But this was my mate congratulating me for a job well done.

I smiled back.

EPILOGUE
LINSEA

Two days after our little meddling escapade, the entire Wuras empire came crashing down. Watching the footage that Maeve and Tedrick generously shared with us of the massive raids against the judges' front companies, vineyard, and homes was beyond orgasmic. Having my daughter fully exonerated, the threat over her husband's family lifted, and the exemplary sentence passed down onto the corrupt judge and his father was the icing on the proverbial cake.

In the weeks and months that followed, I was blessed to have semi-frequent interactions with Malaya. Obviously, she knew nothing of our bond. However, since she had become an official investigative journalist for both the Enforcers and the Obosian Conclave, we got to collaborate on quite a few occasions. Granted, I could have worked with other journalists to cover some of the projects and missions assigned to me. But why deprive myself of such precious moments?

To her, Kayog and I were the heroes who helped save her from certain death by pairing her with the love of her life. As much as I had wanted to hold Kronos by the horns to repeatedly smash his obnoxious face onto a wall, now I just wanted to hug him.

He had done a complete turnaround where Malaya was concerned. The love—not to say adoration—he lavished on her always melted me from the inside out. My baby was happy, truly happy. And today, she was celebrating the christening of their firstborn child.

When she asked Kayog and I to be little Odessa's godparents, I wept like an idiot. I had missed my daughter's wedding, but I would be part of the life of my grandchild in a way I never imagined I could.

Standing here in their stunning mansion on Molvi, I gazed affectionately at the people who had become friends and even family over the past three decades. I had watched Tedrick grow from a little boy to an honorable man, just like his father, Colin. Even now, they were having an animated conversation with Isobel, Amreth, and his lovely wife Ciara. Who would have thought a random encounter during that medical symposium would have allowed my mate to reunite these two beautiful souls and save an entire species from extinction?

Water splashed everywhere as Kaida's three children chased each other in the giant pool, the future little Shadow Lords and Lady flapping their beautiful golden wings to rise a few meters over the pool before diving back down. Their father, Cedros, had deeply moved Kayog when he first heard of his condition. Like my mate, Cedros had spent most of his life in isolation as the presence of others made him ill until his Ejaya—Kaida—entered his life. And now, he also got to enjoy a normal life, socializing with friends and family. So seeing him and his wife chatting with my mate warmed my heart.

I snorted when I spotted Helio and Maeve chastising their son for using his *veris*—the vines that could extend from their feet, arms, and hair—to bind Nero. The shadow dweller companion of

Kaida's children was in no way helpless. In fact, he was a force to be reckoned with and acted as a fearless protector for the young Derakeens. His body was a shadowy sphere with two massive eyes and a terrifying set of teeth filling his oversized mouth. All around him, his shadowy tentacles waved as if rocked by a magical breeze.

I burst out laughing when the little fiend wrapped his tentacles protectively around Maeve's son and made sad eyes hinting that she shouldn't chastise him. Clearly, Nero had been on board with the whole thing.

After putting my empty glass down on one of the refreshment tables by the pool, I headed towards one of the seating areas where Malaya's biological parents and Kronos's parents were fussing over little Odessa. Kronos and Malaya were proudly watching their daughter being doted on. Saying that I didn't feel a great deal of jealousy not to be an official grandparent as well would be a lie. And yet, I couldn't resent her parents.

Over the last couple of years, we had grown quite close. To them, Kayog and I were just a gift from God who helped save their daughter and led her to a happy life. But just as I was closing the distance with them, Malaya took the baby back from her stepfather and started walking away. Her steps faltered when our eyes met. She seemed to hesitate then gestured with her head for me to approach. Curious, I complied.

"My little one seems to be hungry. Do you mind tagging along?" Malaya asked.

"Not at all!" I replied with enthusiasm.

Although she smiled, the strangest mix of relief and worry radiated from her. As we resumed walking towards the tall patio doors leading into the living area of the house, Malaya glanced over her shoulder at Kronos. He nodded and gave her what I could only interpret as an encouraging smile. My stomach immediately knotted. The ceremony hadn't taken place yet. Was she going to tell us that Kayog and I would no longer be the godparents?

Don't be silly…

Filipinos often had multiple godparents for a single child. So it wouldn't make sense for her to remove us. Did she worry we might be offended if another couple was added?

Offended, no. But maybe a little hurt.

At the same time, Malaya and Ciara—Amreth's wife—had grown quite close. It would make sense for Malaya to add this couple as a second set of godparents for her baby.

It was stupid, but I wanted to be able to claim something about her as solely mine. We entered the house and followed the hallway to the left of the living area which led to the bedrooms. They had turned one of the guest rooms into a massive nursery that could easily accommodate half a dozen cribs. They still mostly kept Odessa in their master bedroom but would use this one for the changing table, feeding, and various toys to play with.

Malaya placed Odessa on top of the table. The adorable little girl immediately started wiggling her tiny hands and feet. She was her mother's spitting image, but with her father's gray complexion, a delicate version of his bat wings, and four baby horns protruding from her head. Contrary to most Obosians, Odessa hadn't inherited their silver white hair but had the darkest mane instead.

"Can I help with anything?" I offered.

"Would you mind grabbing a towel over there?" Malaya asked, pointing at a shelf to my right. "Knowing her, she'll likely overindulge and then regurgitate half of it on my shoulder."

"Sure thing," I said, amused as I promptly marched towards it.

I was reaching for a towel when a loud noise startled me. Glancing over my shoulder, I observed as Malaya frowned at her daughter with false severity before crouching to pick up the bottle of milk that had fallen off the table. It took me a moment to realize Malaya had brought it there and was reaching for the warmer before the bottle fell. To my shock, no sooner did she put the bottle back on the table than Odessa knocked it off with a decisive swipe of her tail.

I snorted as Malaya put her fists on her hips to look severely at her daughter. Unrepentant, Odessa giggled before giving her a wide, toothless grin.

"Now is not the time to be a diva, young lady! Least of all in front of esteemed guests!" she said.

Unfazed and unbothered, Odessa slowly waved her tail from side to side, as if daring her mother to try to give her the bottle again.

"Maybe she's not hungry?" I suggested carefully as I approached them.

"Oh no, she's definitely hungry. But she's picky. She wants to be breastfed," Malaya said, rolling her eyes.

Although I didn't perceive any real aggravation from her, I hesitated before commenting, not wanting to come across as pushy or judgmental.

"Is that something you don't do?" I asked.

Malaya smiled in a reassuring fashion. "Oh, I do it all the time. But she knows now that I don't do it when we have guests. Some species can get weird about it."

"Right," I said with sudden understanding. "If you want privacy—"

"Don't be silly!" she exclaimed, looking at me as if I'd had one drink too many. "I invited you to tag along, remember? And I doubt you would get all weirded out by something as natural as a mother feeding her child."

"Right again," I conceded, although still confused as to why she wouldn't do it then. "You worry someone might barge in?"

"No. I'm using this as an excuse to give my nipples a rest," she admitted sheepishly. "Odessa is a bottomless pit. And when she latches on, she means business."

I almost felt guilty for laughing, but her expression and emotions didn't actually convey any distress.

"Fine, you little diva," Malaya added while turning back to her daughter. "Breastfeeding it is, but only because today's your christening."

She leaned forward and nuzzled her daughter. Just as she was beginning to straighten, Odessa grabbed her mother's face with both hands and caressed her cheeks.

"*Oo lee oo*," the baby cooed.

I gasped, my blood turning to ice as I took an involuntary step back. Malaya jerked her head up to peer at me, the strangest emotions fleeting over her face. Under different circumstances, I would have wanted to analyze the conflicting feelings radiating from her, but I was in too deep a state of shock.

Surely I had misunderstood... right?

"What...? What did she say?" I asked, my voice shaking.

"She said *coo lee coo*," Malaya replied, her gaze intense.

My knees nearly buckled beneath me. I hastened to a plush chair near the table, which I assumed she used to feed her baby while enjoying the breathtaking view of the landscape of Molvi through the large window.

"Linsea, are you okay?" she asked, approaching me with an air of concern.

"Yes. I... I... Where did she learn that?" I asked, my eyes flicking between hers.

Malaya licked her lips nervously and seemed to wage an internal war as she chose her words carefully. Why would she hesitate before answering such a straightforward question?

A loud knock on the door spared her from doing so. The newcomer didn't wait for an invite, and the door immediately opened on a very worried Kayog. His eyes zeroed in on me.

"Is everything okay?" he asked, rushing to my side. "I felt your distress."

"Yes, I'm fine," I said while failing miserably at sounding reassuring.

"What happened?" he insisted, his gaze flicking between Malaya and me.

"Actually, it's a good thing that you're here so that I don't have to repeat the story twice," Malaya replied with a nervous chuckle.

Kayog and I exchanged a baffled look as she headed towards the door left opened by my mate's sudden entrance and carefully closed it before looking back at us with that same strange expression.

"I'm afraid my daughter's babbling triggered a strong response in Linsea," Malaya said, avoiding eye contact as she went back to the baby.

"What kind of babbling are we talking about?" Kayog asked, confused.

"A word from a song I often hum to her," she said, her eyes flicking towards me.

My blood turned to ice again, further confusing my husband while an impossible thought took root in my mind.

"You see, a few days into the fifth month of my pregnancy, I started having the strangest dream," Malaya said while putting a bottle inside the warmer, despite having previously stated she would breastfeed Odessa.

"Strange how?" Kayog asked, tension filling his voice.

"Strange in that I was a baby bird. I believe I was a bird of paradise, although the colors didn't match," she added with a nervous laugh. "My feathers were light brown, almost the same shade of my skin right now."

The shock that rippled through my mate struck me hard. In that instant, I would have given anything to be able to read his mind.

"And what were you doing?" he asked, his voice almost a whisper.

Malaya looked away, her eyes slightly going out of focus as she prodded her memory. "It's hard to say. I believe I was sick since I was always lying down."

"You *believe* you were sick? You're not certain?" he insisted.

"I don't recall any pain, which is why I can't say for certain that I was sick," she said with a shrug. "But every dream involved my parents singing to me. The first few times, I dismissed it as just being a weird fantasy. And then the dream kept coming back more detailed, more intense, more vivid. I can almost recall the feel of my parents' feathers when they held me."

"And then what happened?" I asked, my hand slipping into Kayog's for comfort.

"And then the dream changed. I realized that I wasn't a bird of paradise, but a Temern. And in that dream, the two of you were my parents."

A choked sound escaped me, and tears welled in my eyes as I held on to Kayog's hand with bruising force. Malaya blinked rapidly, visibly trying to fight back tears pricking her own eyes. She was battling powerful emotions as well, but I was too overwhelmed to properly interpret them. From Kayog, shock had given way to a mix of peace, joy, and wonder.

"You would make me pretend to fly around because I couldn't flap my own wings. You would play with me and sing to me. That song has been haunting me. It pops up in my head at random hours of the day, and every time, I remember responding once we got to the chorus. I didn't understand the lyrics. But I knew that every time I spoke the one word from the lyrics, it would make you happy. And your happiness filled me with the greatest joy."

"And what was that word?" Kayog asked, his voice trembling a little.

"It sounded like *coo lee coo*."

This time I started bawling. Malaya's lips quivered, and tears began trickling freely down her cheeks. She hugged herself while Kayog crouched next to my chair to wrap his arms and wings around me.

"What does it mean?" Malaya asked, in a shaky voice.

"It means 'I will always love you,'" I replied.

"It wasn't a dream, was it?" Malaya asked, although it sounded more like a statement.

"What do you think?" Kayog challenged in a soft voice.

"I think that I would give anything to hear my parents sing it again the way they sang it for me when I was a sick baby," she replied.

Without hesitation, Kayog sang, his voice deep, rich, powerful as it rose through the room. Malaya leaned against the changing table, crying loudly. Odessa glanced in turn between her mother and my mate with undisguised curiosity. As an Obosian, she could see auras and read emotions from them. Although confused by what was happening, she didn't perceive actual distress from her mother. Those weren't tears of sorrow.

Kayog leaned down, rubbed his temple against mine in an affectionate gesture, before freeing his hand from mine. He walked towards Malaya. Seeing him approach, she pushed away from the table and ran to him. She threw herself into his arms, and he hugged her tightly. Resting his cheek on top of her head, he continued singing, his wings closing around her. It took me a bit more time to regain my bearings enough to get back on my feet.

I walked to them, joining in the song, my voice harmonizing with his like when we would sing to little Thea. As soon as I closed the distance with them, Kayog opened his right wing to draw me in. Malaya immediately let go of Kayog with her left arm to wrap it around me.

And there went the waterworks again.

My poor mate ended up having to carry the song on his own while the two of us got his whole chest fully drenched. Except, as he began the second chorus, a high-pitched little voice joined in, although totally out of sync with him.

"*Oo lee oo!*" Odessa chirped after Kayog. "*Oo oo... Oo lee oo!*"

Between two sniffles, we all burst out laughing. With much reluctance, my mate released us both, only for me to draw Malaya into my embrace. For the first time, I got to fully hug her like my heart had ached to do since finding out she was my angel. She reciprocated, burying her face in my neck as I wing-hugged her.

KAYOG

My heart filling to bursting, I stared at the two most important females in my life intertwined in the maternal embrace I never thought would come. Malaya was glowing, her song soaring in perfect harmony with ours. No more secrets, no more pretending we were just good friends.

"Thank you for saving me," Malaya said as Linsea released her at last.

"We failed you once. We were not going to fail you twice," I said.

To my shock, she frowned, stepped away from Linsea, and came to stand in front of me. She reached for both my hands and held them in hers.

"You never failed me. I was sick with a congenital illness that couldn't be cured. You gave me the best life possible for the time I had back then. Your love and the happiness you gave me were so great that I had to come back to give this another go. Both times, the two of you gave me my best life. So thank you for finding me again, for fighting for me, and for loving me more than anyone deserves to be."

"We can never love you too much," I said, caressing her cheek.

She suddenly scrunched her face and gave me the oddest look. "By the way, thank you for putting your life on the line to retrieve the data that helped take down Wuras."

As one, Linsea and I recoiled.

"How do you know that?" Linsea asked.

She gave her a sheepish look. "I mentioned those weird recurring dreams to Tedrick. His reaction to it had been strange, but I didn't think much of it. Then last week, when he sent me more files for my reports to the Conclave, he *accidentally* included a couple of highly classified files concerning, among other things, an off-the-record, high-risk mission."

Linsea snorted.

"That little shit..." I whispered, my voice filled with affection and gratitude. "Who else knows?"

"Kronos, but no one else, aside from anyone *you* might have shared it with," Malaya replied.

"We will leave it up to you whether to share it with more people or not," Linsea said affectionately. "We do not wish to cause any distress to your biological parents or make things awkward for anyone. All that matters to us is that we can finally tell you that we love you."

A knock on the door interrupted us.

"Come in!" Malaya shouted.

I almost rushed to release her, but realized that since her bonding with Kronos, she could also see souls to a lesser extent. She would know that it was her husband at the door.

Kronos stepped inside, his silver-blue eyes scanning the room. He glanced tenderly at his wife before frowning at us with false severity.

"Your little family reunion is nice and all, but you need to tone the happiness down before my Nundars all suffer massive indigestion," Kronos grumbled playfully.

We all laughed. Nundars were highly intelligent beings who attached themselves to an Obosian household. They performed chores around the house and cooked and could even provide healing or protection when needed. It was in fact they who saved Malaya's life when she was attacked by a wild beast, keeping her safe until Kronos could intervene. They fed off the energy from positive emotions. And there was no question that the ones emanating from this room had to taste divine.

"You're one to speak about having indigestion," Malaya said mockingly at her husband.

"Malaya!" Kronos and Linsea exclaimed at the same time.

I cackled, looking at all three of their embarrassed faces. Obosians fed off emotions too, but usually during sex. That was one of the reasons humans compared them to Incubi—minus the leeching your lifeforce part.

Malaya scrunched her face and muttered something unintelligible.

"How about you go hang out with our guests? I will feed Odessa," Kronos offered.

"That's sweet of you," Malaya said, lifting her face to receive her husband's kiss.

He turned to the baby, who giggled excitedly at seeing her father. In that instant, I felt the same love between them than the one that had burned so brightly between my Thea and me. As if sensing the weight of my stare on him, Kronos peered at me, and a strange expression flitted over his face.

"Thank you for knocking sense into me when I was being an idiot," Kronos said.

"Thank you for sparing me from having to escalate things so you would see the light," I deadpanned.

He snorted and bowed his head in concession.

"Above all, thank you for making my baby happy," I said, this time my voice filled with sincere gratitude.

"Always," he replied, his voice solemn.

We walked out of the room to mingle again with the love of my life and my beloved child by my side. As my gaze roamed over the people in attendance—loyal friends who had become more like family to me, I realized I had achieved my impossible dream.

I glanced down at my beautiful mate to find her staring at me with infinite love.

"Thank you, for giving me the world," I whispered.

"Thank you for giving me the same," she said, caressing my cheek. "*Coo lee coo*, Kayog."

"*Coo lee coo*, my dove. In this life and every other, *coo lee coo*."

THE END.

KAYOG & LINSEA

MARES

DARWANDIR

NORDJARIMM

SYLLEN

YINRIC

HORAC

SHAYA

STRAEF

THEA

KRONOS

KRONOS & MALAYA

OLIX & SUSAN

SZARO & SERENA

ZATRUK & RIHANNA

HELIO & MAEVE

CEDROS, KAIDA, NERO & THE KIDS

AMRETH

AMRETH & CIARA

NUNDAR

ALSO BY REGINE ABEL

THE VEREDIAN CHRONICLES
Escaping Fate
Blind Fate
Raising Amalia
Twist of Fate
Hands of Fate
Defying Fate
Imperial Fate

BRAXIANS
Anton's Grace
Ravik's Mercy
Krygor's Hope
Keran's Dawn

XIAN WARRIORS
Doom
Legion
Raven
Bane
Chaos
Varnog
Reaper
Wrath
Xenon
Nevrik
Rogue
Doom: A Graphic Novel

PRIME MATING AGENCY
I Married A Lizardman

BLOOD MAIDENS OF KARTHIA

Claiming Thalia

EMPATHS OF LYRIA

An Alien For Christmas

OTHER

True As Steel

Alien Awakening

Heart of Stone

Oops! I Summoned a Liderc

ABOUT REGINE

USA Today bestselling author Regine Abel is a fantasy, paranormal and sci-fi junkie. Anything with a bit of magic, a touch of the unusual, and a lot of romance will have her jumping for joy. She loves creating hot alien warriors and no-nonsense, kick-ass heroines that evolve in fantastic new worlds while embarking on action-packed adventures filled with mystery and the twists you never saw coming.

Before devoting herself as a full-time writer, Regine had surrendered to her other passions: music and video games! After a decade working as a Sound Engineer in movie dubbing and live concerts, Regine became a professional Game Designer and Creative Director, a career that has led her from her home in Canada to the US and various countries in Europe and Asia.

Facebook
https://www.facebook.com/regine.abel.author/

Website
https://regineabel.com

Regine's Rebels Reader Group

https://www.facebook.com/groups/ReginesRebels/

Newsletter

http://smarturl.it/RA_Newsletter

Goodreads

http://smarturl.it/RA_Goodreads

Bookbub

https://www.bookbub.com/profile/regine-abel

Amazon

http://smarturl.it/AuthorAMS